The Royal Game

ANNE O'BRIEN

ONE PLACE. MANY STORIES

HQ
An imprint of HarperCollins*Publishers* Ltd
1 London Bridge Street
London SE1 9GF

www.harpercollins.co.uk

HarperCollins*Publishers*
1st Floor, Watermarque Building, Ringsend Road
Dublin 4, Ireland

This edition 2021

1

First published in Great Britain by
HQ, an imprint of HarperCollins*Publishers* Ltd 2021

ISBN:
HB: 9780008422844
TPB: 9780008422851

MIX
Paper from
responsible sources

FSC
www.fsc.org
FSC™ C007454

This book is produced from independently certified FSC™ paper
to ensure responsible forest management.

For more information visit: www.harpercollins.co.uk/green

Printed and bound in Great Britain by
CPI Group (UK) Ltd, Croydon, CR0 4YY

With all my love, as always, to George, who kept me sane through a year of tiers and lockdowns, during which (fortunately) he became equally engaged with the Paston people as I have been.

'Kepe Wysly Youre Wrytyngys.'

MARGARET MAUTBY PASTON

'The reason I write to you in haste is to have an answer from you in haste.'

MARGARET MAUTBY PASTON TO JOHN PASTON

Dramatis personae

The Pastons

Clement Paston, the peasant

Beatrice Goneld, Clement's wife

Justice William Paston, son of Clement and Beatrice

Agnes Barry, William's wife, an heiress

Children of William and Agnes:

  John Paston

  Edmund

  Elizabeth (Eliza)

  William

  Clement

Margaret Mautby Paston, wife of John Paston, an heiress

Children of John and Margaret Paston:

  Sir John (Elder) Paston

  John (Jonty) Paston

  Margery

  Edmund

  Anne

  Walter

  William (Willem)

Lady Anne Beaufort, daughter of Edmund Beaufort, 2nd Duke of
  Somerset; wife of William Paston

Richard Calle, the Paston bailiff

James Gloys, Paston family chaplain

John and Elizabeth Damme, friends and legal associates of the
    Pastons
Mistress Elizabeth Clere, Margaret Paston's cousin

The Poynings family
Sir Robert Poynings, husband of Elizabeth Paston
Edward Poynings, son of Sir Robert and Elizabeth
Eleanor Poynings, wife of Henry Percy, Earl of Northumberland;
    niece of Sir Robert
John Dane, the Poynings man of business

The Court
King Henry VI; House of Lancaster
Queen Margaret of Anjou, wife of Henry VI
King Edward IV; House of York
Queen Elizabeth (Woodville), wife of Edward IV
Anne Haute and the Haute family, cousins of Elizabeth Woodville
Sir Anthony Woodville, Lord Scales, brother of Queen Elizabeth
The de la Pole Dukes of Suffolk
The Mowbray Dukes of Norfolk
Sir John Fastolf, soldier, administrator and patron of the Paston
    family
Lady de la Pole who gave a home to Elizabeth Paston

Norfolk society: enemies and friends
Robert Toppes, Mayor of Norwich
John Hauteyn, a Carmelite friar with designs on Paston property
John Wyndham, a notorious Paston enemy
Lord Moleyns, an ambitious claimant of Paston land
William Yelverton, a Fastolf executor
Sir Thomas Howes, a Fastolf executor
William Worcester, Steward to Sir John Fastolf

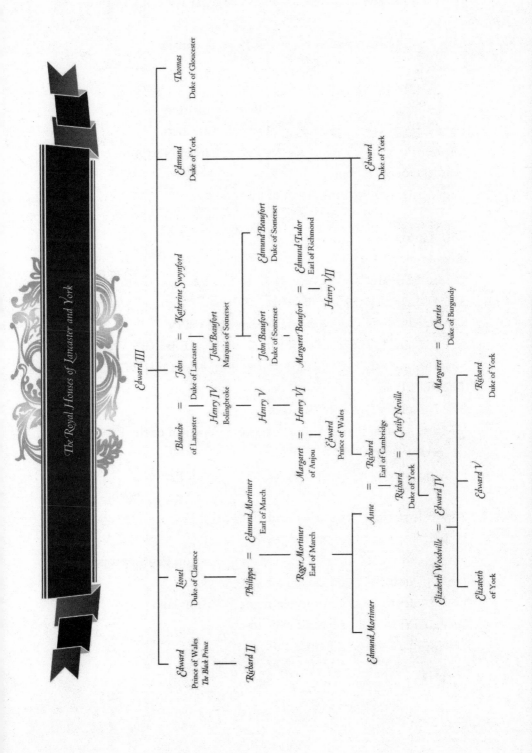

The Royal Houses of Lancaster and York

Edward III

Edward Prince of Wales *The Black Prince*
— Richard II

Lionel Duke of Clarence
— Philippa = Edmund Mortimer Earl of March
— Roger Mortimer Earl of March
— Anne = Richard Earl of Cambridge
— Edmund Mortimer

John = Katherine Swynford Duke of Lancaster
Blanche of Lancaster = John Duke of Lancaster
— Henry IV Bolingbroke
— Henry V
— Margaret = Henry VI of Anjou
— Edward Prince of Wales

John Beaufort Marquis of Somerset
— John Beaufort Duke of Somerset
— Margaret Beaufort = Edmund Tudor Earl of Richmond
— Henry VII

Edmund Beaufort Duke of Somerset

Edmund Duke of York
— Edward Duke of York
— Richard Duke of York = Cecily Neville
— Margaret = Charles Duke of Burgundy
— Elizabeth Woodville = Edward IV
— Elizabeth of York
— Edward V
— Richard Duke of York

Thomas Duke of Gloucester

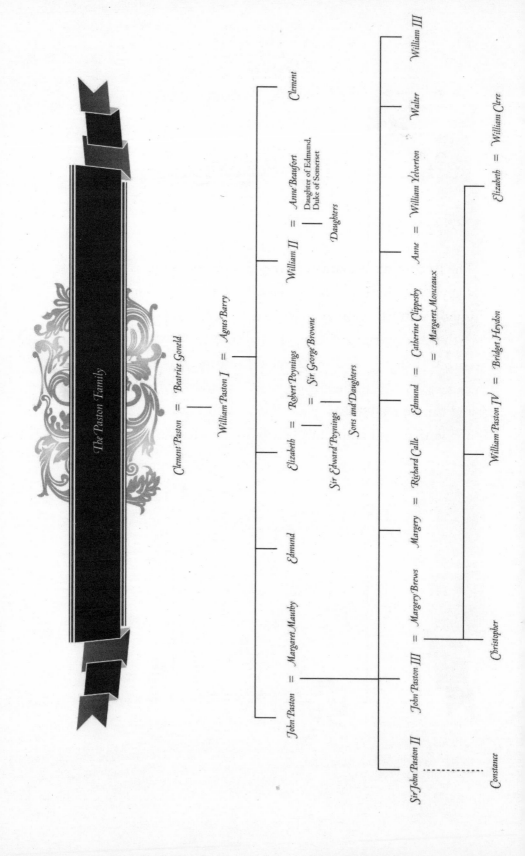

The Paston Family

Clement Paston = Beatrice Goneld

William Paston I = Agnes Barry

John Paston = Margaret Mauthy   Edmund   Elizabeth = Robert Poynings   William II = Anne Beaufort   Clement
       = Sir George Browne   Daughter of Edmund,
       Sir Edward Poynings   Duke of Somerset
       Sons and Daughters

Daughters

Sir John Paston II   John Paston III = Margery Brews   Margery = Richard Calle   Edmund = Catherine Clippesby   Anne = William Yelverton   Walter   William III
                                                 = Margaret Monceaux

Constance   Christopher   William Paston IV = Bridget Heydon   Elizabeth = William Clere

The Pastons

The Pastons were a family living in Norfolk in the Middle Ages. They wrote letters to each other, both the men and, even more importantly, the women, Margaret Paston being the most prolific of the letter-writers. How fortunate we are that so much of this correspondence, full of detail on family dispute, of love and tragedy, as well as the minutiae of everyday life, was kept intact and can be read today. They open a window for us into the life of a vibrant and ambitious family in the fifteenth century.

Chapter One

Margaret Mautby Paston

St Bride's, London: 21st November 1444

On the first day of February in the year 1444 the great spire of St Paul's Cathedral was struck by a bolt of lightning and burnt to the ground.

'Beware the wrath of God!' thundered our priest from the pulpit in the Church of St Peter Hungate in Norwich. 'Fall to your knees and repent.'

What cataclysm did this disaster foretell? It was much discussed in our household. Perhaps another dose of the pestilence to sweep through the realm, winnowing both rich and poor. Perhaps some diplomatic squabble to hinder the proposed marriage of our young King Henry VI to the illustrious lady Margaret of Anjou. No one gave any thought to the fact that it might be the death of Justice William Paston, man of many talents, both meritorious and dubious.

In November John Paston, the heir, and I, Margaret his wife, were summoned to London where Justice William lay sick in rented rooms close to the Inns of Court. John left me in a gloomy chamber smelling of damp and disuse and possibly mice, while he climbed the stairs to his father's room. Since he had left the door ajar, distantly I heard the rumble of his voice, and then his mother's in reply, sharp and reproachful. Mistress Agnes Paston was clearly in command in the sick-room. On John's return only a handful of minutes later, I knew from his face what news he would bring.

'He is dead,' John Paston announced. His voice registered irritation rather than shock. Certainly no grief. 'My father is dead. We arrived too late.'

'We travelled as fast as we could,' I said. 'There is no blame can be placed at your door, whatever Mistress Agnes says.'

It had taken us five days of hard riding to cover the miles between Norwich and London, and I felt every one of them in my bones. John, as weary and travel-stained as I, beating dust from his garments, would not be mollified.

'No, there is no blame. We nearly killed the horses to get here. I just wish he could have held on for one more hour. Or that my mother had sent for us sooner.'

'I grieve with you,' I replied, accepting that my husband was wont to blame anyone but himself even though on this occasion he was in the right. Nor would he speak his sorrow aloud, but I would. 'Your father will be greatly missed for upholding the law so rigorously.'

'There are even more who will not rejoice,' John replied. 'There will be few who will mourn with me.'

The house around us was still, that strange dry emptiness that death often brings in its train before the business of the day must take over. Ill health marked by pains and high fever had dogged

Justice William through the whole of that summer; death had finally claimed him in its grip, his eyes closed for the last time by Mistress Agnes's busy fingers.

John was regarding me in weary contemplation. I knew that I must look as dust-ridden and mud-splattered as he.

'Now that my father is dead, Margaret, it will not be an easy life for us,' he said as if I needed to be lectured on what must have been obvious to all. 'Or not until I have learned to apply the legal strategies so expensively acquired at Peterhouse, to drive off the vermin that stalk us. I have neither the experience nor the reputation of my father.'

He might be young in years but, as I had learned during my short marriage, John Paston was old enough to know his own mind in all things legal. He was also now much empowered as head of the Paston family.

'No, it will not be easy,' I agreed, my thoughts scrambling, one over the other, as the impending changes to my life struck home. Justice William might have been ailing in recent months but he had cast a long shadow.

'Success gives birth to enemies.' John's face was severe, all lines of humour and tolerance obliterated. Stepping across the room, I tightened my hands around his. John allowed himself to squeeze mine in return. 'I know that you will stand with me in all times of duress. The Pastons know how to wed strong women.' I felt his hands grip mine harder still so that my ring, symbol of that union, dug into my flesh. 'It will mean that we must often live apart. Can you accept that?'

What choice did I have? I already knew that John Paston was unlikely to indulge his wife by keeping her company when his estates were being usurped by some wily local landowner.

'Yes,' I said.

'You are a brave woman, Margaret.'

'I am. We will face these foes together.'

'And remember. Whatever the future holds, even when I forget to tell you, my love is yours for all time.'

Such an unexpected accolade startled me, but not for long.

'Do you not forget that you own my heart, as well as my considerable Mautby acres. I expect you to protect them just as well as your own.'

John laughed, kissed my whitened knuckles and then my lips.

'Before I die I will write the name Paston across the length and breadth of Norfolk,' he said.

Not that I doubted John's steadfastness in this task. Self-deprecation was not a trait he possessed. Within the four years of our marriage I had learned to respect his iron strength. Land was wealth. Land was influence. Land was power. Land was status. And to be fair, even when John abandoned me for a dispute over some distant manor, or rights to gather crops, or ownership of plough horses, my mind ran along similar pathways. I was an heiress before my marriage, and I too would fight for what was mine.

Our enemies would not be allowed to have victory over us.

Fleetingly, I considered John's inveterate ability to make enemies rather than friends, but it was not worth worrying about now. There were enough anxieties lurking in the shadows to keep me awake at night.

★

Success gives birth to enemies, John had said in anticipation of conflict with our neighbours who despised us for Justice William's

4

successful harvesting of valuable manors. When we met to hear the reading of the will, we had no presentiment of a declaration of war within the Paston family itself.

'I should have known,' John remarked when the dust had settled a little. 'Who understands better than a lawyer that a will can split a family down the middle with weapons drawn?'

We gathered in the chamber: Mistress Agnes, the grieving widow, together with John and I, with Master John Damme, the close family friend who would be one of the executors with my husband and Mistress Agnes. The rest of the Paston children were also present, standing in a neat line of age and thus of height: John's sister Elizabeth, next to his brothers Edmund and William. Finally there was Mistress Agnes's most recent child, Clement, irrelevant to such a gathering but present at his mother's request, his hand held tight by Elizabeth. My own children were not with me but left safe in our house in the village of Paston.

'I wish to know the content of my father's will,' John said after prayers had been said for the soul of the departed. 'We must waste no time. My father's enemies gather, like vultures, to pick off any manor that seems vulnerable.'

Mistress Agnes crossed to the window where a coffer stood; taking a key from the bunch at her belt she unlocked it, removed a document and handed it to Master Damme who read it aloud.

It was all clear enough and much as had been expected. Justice William had made provision for his widow and all five of his children, with the weight of the inheritance passing, of course, to John whose burden would be to keep it all intact.

To Agnes was apportioned the manor at Oxnead as her jointure, to provide her with an income as Justice William's widow, as well as assorted properties that had been her dower. It was a substantial share, reflecting her own status as an heiress when she had wed Justice William. To John came the bulk of the properties not willed elsewhere, as well as the manor of Gresham which Justice William had purchased and which had provided my own jointure. John would get Oxnead on Agnes's death. A cluster of small manors were named for Edmund, William and Clement, to maintain them and provide for their education until they reached their majority. Eliza would have two hundred pounds for her marriage provided that she wed in accordance with the advice of Mistress Agnes and Justice William's executors. Her future husband must be of equal age, sufficient status and sound lineage and must supply a jointure of land with an income of not less than forty pounds a year.

John nodded. Justice William had been fair and even-handed but with close concern to keep the bulk of the Paston property in the hands of his heir. It was not over-generous to John, but of course he had my properties too. With two small sons of our own, the inheritance was essential to us for the future if we wished to make a mark in the world.

'This is much as I had expected. There should be no difficulty in carrying out my father's wishes.' John strode up and down the chamber, assessing all he had heard, smiling at his brothers. It was only right that the young ones had money to complete their education. For myself, I was simply satisfied that I would retain Gresham as my own. All was as it should be.

John held out his hand for the will, intending to read through it again for the detail of all the Paston manors.

'These are not your father's wishes.'

Those fateful words, clear and unambiguous, were spoken by Mistress Agnes.

'What are not my father's wishes?' John, distracted, was already reading.

'He did not wish this distribution of his lands.'

Now John looked up. 'But it is written here, in his will.'

Mistress Agnes did not falter. 'Your father changed his mind. He decided that he had not done rightly by the younger children.'

I felt John tense as he came to a halt beside me, his fingers clenching to crease the edge of the document. Master Damme remained silent in the storm clouds that began to hover between mother and son. I placed my hand on John's arm to remind him to keep his temper at bay.

'Then why not write a new will?' he asked, gently enough.

'I accept that he should have done so. But when he felt death approaching, your father spoke to me about his concerns. It was then that he made an alteration in the distribution of his property.'

'To whom did he make this alteration?' John glanced towards Master Damme, who shook his head.

'To me,' Mistress Agnes replied.

'Where is it?'

'It is not written. He spoke it. He told me what he wanted.'

Once again John looked towards Master Damme for enlightenment. 'This is most irregular.'

'But not unknown.'

'But will it stand in law?' John demanded. And then, as the possible repercussions hit home: 'What did he want? What changes did he wish to make to the will?'

Mistress Agnes was as phlegmatic as if listing a recipe for braised venison with thyme and bay leaf. 'Your father wanted to give your brothers more security. He wanted the transfer of specifically named properties to William and Clement. To safeguard their futures, since they are still so young.'

'So these manors will be stripped from my inheritance?'

A question posed with deadly calm. We already knew the answer to that.

'Yes.'

'My brothers are to benefit at the expense of beggaring the heir.'

'You will not be beggared.'

'Not far off!'

Mistress Agnes had not finished. 'Your father also wanted to have Masses said in his name, thus he wished to leave a grant of land to the church.'

'I don't begrudge him the Masses. But for how many years?'

Even Mistress Agnes hesitated here.

'In perpetuity.'

'Before God! I must lose a manor that my father fought hard for, so that prayers might be said for his soul for ever. Which manors am I to lose, all in all?'

Mistress Agnes took a breath. 'East Beckham ...'

'We have only just fought and won a difficult battle to gain East Beckham ...!'

'East Beckham and Sporle should be given over to William and Clement. Swainsthorpe should be granted to the church for the promise of Masses.'

I could see John struggling in his choice of words, and failing.

'God's Blood! Did you persuade him to do this, mother?'

'I talked with him. It was his own decision.'

'I do not accept that.'

The tension in the room had been replaced with a bright

anger, but Mistress Agnes was not to be intimidated. 'It was your father's wish.'

'And to my disadvantage.'

A silence fell, broken only by the scuffing of Clement's shoes as he grew querulous so that I took him and lifted him into my arms. He had no idea of the wealth he had just been willed, and the conflict it would inevitably cause. His head rested against my shoulder and he fell asleep in the manner of all small children. John once more took to pacing the room.

'Does this stand legally?' he demanded of Master Damme.

'It may well do so. If you are willing to accept it.'

'Accept it?' The anger burst out in a flare, like the lightning that had destroyed St Paul's spire. 'But where is the legal evidence? There is no will in writing, only a cosy chat, allegedly, between my mother and her dying husband. No, I will not accept it.' He swung round to face Mistress Agnes again, snapping the document between them. 'Those manors that you say my father wished to assign to my brothers and the church will remain with me. How could he even consider this decision which will do nothing but weaken me? Am I not the Paston heir, left to fight for our position in Norfolk and Suffolk? I am to face numerous enemies, without my father's connections and reputation and experience in the legal field. Yet now you say he has robbed me of some of the most valuable lands of my inheritance. He has tied my hands behind my back in the coming battle. I do not believe for one moment that he would take such an ill-planned step. My father would consider it a foolishness.'

Mistress Agnes stiffened. 'Do you accuse me of lying?'

'I accuse you of being sparing with the truth. I accuse you of meddling in your own interests. If my father had wanted to redistribute the manors he would have had it written down, even if he were drawing his last breath. My father never trusted his wishes to mere words, whatever you say.' John shook the will once more. 'This is the will that will be put into effect. The written will. Not some travesty of a conversation between you and a dying man.'

Still she persisted. 'You would deny your father's last wishes. That is a shame on you, my son.'

'Shame? There is no shame on me! These are his last wishes.' Once again the document was shaken.

Mistress Agnes strode to the door, where she turned and looked back. 'I will not allow you to thwart your father. I will fight you in the courts, if necessary.'

Her brisk footsteps echoed on the boards, and then clipped on the tiles of the hall.

With a shrug and a twist of his mouth, Master Damme followed her, perhaps with an intent to placate. I motioned to Eliza to take the young ones out, handing sleeping Clement over, which left me alone with John. We regarded each other for a long moment.

'What are you going to do?' I asked when he made no attempt to break the silence. 'Can you stop your mother enforcing the legality of a spoken will?'

'I'll do my best! There is no evidence of my father's change of mind other than her own words.'

His gaze left me and moved to the coffer. Mistress Agnes had left it unlocked. I could sense John's anger waning. The legal brain was once more working.

'I can read your thoughts,' I said.

'So I should imagine. Come here.' And when he lifted the lid of the coffer, 'Hold these.'

Delving into the depths, he began to extract and pile into my waiting arms scrolls and folded documents. Some were new, some dusty, some with broken seals. Others were newly written, the signature of Justice William still clear.

'I'll have these deeds of Paston properties safely in my own possession. If I leave them with my mother, who knows what she will do with them? They might just conveniently disappear.'

'Are these all deeds?' I asked, trying but failing to read all but the barest words as one document followed the next. Some I dropped on the floor.

'I have no idea. I'll read them later. Do be careful with them, Meg. They may stand between us and penury if I have to fight every step through the courts.'

John gathered up those I had dropped, walked to the door and opened it, gesturing for me to follow.

'What will you do with them?'

'Lock them in my own coffer,' he growled.

'Your mother will not like it.'

'I do not like what my mother appears to be doing at my expense.' All I could see was trouble ahead if Mistress Agnes and the heir were in direct confrontation. 'The first thing is to get the award of probate. Then we shall see. But I tell you this, Meg. I'll not allow any action, by my mother or anyone else, that will weaken my position of head of this family.'

We carried the documents to our own chamber where John proceeded to pack them into saddlebags for our return journey to the house we were using at Paston. Then he poured a cup of ale and drank it off as if he were a man suffering from drought in a desert.

'Will you tell me something?' I asked.

'Of course.'

'Do you truly fear that the men who were hostile to your father are waiting to attack, now that he is dead?'

'Oh yes. They will leap on me, like a vixen after a lamb, and it is to our disadvantage that our estates are so widespread. I'll be as generous as I can be to my brothers. I'll even arrange a Mass for my father's soul. What I will not do is allow the family to be so weakened that it sinks back into the ranks of the peasantry from which it came. My father and my grandfather would condemn me for it.'

'But your mother …'

'My mother holds a substantial amount of Paston land. She is in no position to carp.'

My anxiety must have shown on my face. John's tone softened, as did the fire in his eye, and he came to put his arms around me.

'Don't fret over it. We will come about. You'll see.'

I would pray for a little breathing space before the attacks began. I feared that Mistress Agnes would nourish resentment and anger against her son for the rest of her life. She was not a woman who found forgiveness easy.

It did not bode well.

'But if my mother wishes to have Masses said in perpetuity for my father's soul,' John announced as a parting shot, 'she can pay for them herself.'

★

My husband John was twenty-three years old when his father died. I was of the same age, now a wife of some experience. I had just given birth to my second son.

Who was I before I was Mistress Margaret Paston? If I was an heiress in my own right, how was it that I came to wed John Paston, a man descended in so few years from a man who worked the land? A peasant, in effect.

I was Margaret Mautby, daughter and heiress of John Mautby of Mautby, a substantial manor in Norfolk. An only child of considerable value to a future husband. Because my father died when I was ten years, I had been living with my mother and stepfather at Geldeston in the south-east of Norfolk, where I had stepped within the avaricious gaze of the Pastons. My mother had carried no children to her new husband, so that on her death I would inherit her property too. Justice William, by chance or design, was a trustee for the Mautby estates. Who would know better than Justice William that I had the promise of a legacy worth a considerable sum to my name? Justice William had seen me as a juicy Norfolk plum, waiting to drop from the tree into his hand, the perfect bride for his eldest son and heir.

Did my mother value a Paston alliance? Could she have done better for me? It was not for me to know, as it was not for me to object to the proposed alliance. Later I suspected Justice William had used his persuasive tongue to paint his family prospects in glowing colours. Besides, Paston and Mautby lands marched side by side. No one would deny that the Pastons were a family destined for a reputation as lawyers and land-holders.

John and I first met in April of the year 1440, four years before Justice William's death, although legal arrangements had been under discussion for some time between my trustees. Not that

Justice William made that decision without first consulting his wife. I soon learned that if Mistress Agnes had rejected me, then the marriage would never have come about. It was arranged that I should visit Mistress Agnes at the manor of Oxnead, a handful of miles north of Norwich.

Escorted there by a servant, without my mother's company as Mistress Paston had requested, I rode into the courtyard at Oxnead, impressed with the buildings ranged on three sides and the absence of weeds and detritus from the stables. A dovecote caught my eye, its inhabitants squabbling with a flash of their white wings. It all spoke of good husbandry and management. When I was shown into a parlour, the impression was the same. The furniture, although sparse, was highly polished. The rushes on the floor were satisfyingly fresh and fragrant. I would not object to a husband who would one day own this property.

There, against the backdrop of the Paston wealth, stood Mistress Agnes, slight and angular, as dry and sere as a stalk of rye that all but rustled, the keys of the property clasped to a silver chain at her waist. She might be clad as drably as a mouse, her hair hidden in a plain coif, but the quality of the woollen cloth of her high-necked gown was as good as any that Norwich could provide.

I curtsied, eyes lowered in demure greeting. I was to be assessed as a bride. If I was not liked, I would be sent home, heiress or no. I knew that I looked my best.

Without a word, Mistress Agnes raised her chin and looked me over, as if I might be a prime ewe at market. I looked back.

'Mistress Mautby.' Her voice had a harsh timbre and little welcome; her eyes, hard as agates, were inclined to the censorious. 'I presume that your mother has told you of the reason for your visit.'

'Yes, Mistress Paston.' I kept my gaze steady. I knew my worth. Any local family would be fortunate to take me as a bride. 'I am aware that you are considering me as a wife for your son.'

She gave no reply to that. Instead: 'You look to me to be a sensible girl.' She ran an eye over my clothing, chosen with discrimination for this visit. As demure as my initial approach but not lacking in an embroidered girdle. Norwich had clothed me in its best weave too, of a soft spring green. 'I see a degree of time and money has been spent on your clothing, Mistress Mautby. There is no place for extravagance here.'

Would I be expected to dress as plainly as Mistress Agnes? There was no embroidery to see on her cuffs or at her neckline. It did not sit comfortably with my young ambitions.

'Have you learned well the skills of housewifery?' she asked.

'I have, mistress. My education at my mother's hands has been excellent.'

Her straight brows, also mouse-brown, rose.

'Could you run a house such as this? Better for me to know now than later, if you are not a capable girl.'

'I could.' I was not intimidated. 'My stepfather's house at Geldeston, where I am presently domiciled, is more exten-sive.' I was eighteen years old with a quiet confidence. 'I know well the tasks necessary. I can do them myself, but I would have need of a good and reliable Steward, of course.'

'The Steward in my household is appointed by me. He is perforce reliable. Any lack in household management will be your own.' Mistress Agnes's brows had now snapped together. 'We will not know if you will prove to be fertile. It will be a matter for prayer. We need Paston heirs for the future, Mistress Mautby.'

'Yes, Mistress Paston. I, too, would offer daily prayers to the Blessed Virgin.'

'Your parents had only one daughter,' she considered.

'Then I must set myself to do better, mistress.'

She continued to regard me, giving no intimation of her thoughts. Would I pass muster?

Mistress Agnes nodded briskly.

'I think it would be well for my son to meet with you.'

Thus I was dismissed and sent home. I presumed that I had been liked well enough to further the negotiation, and I would meet the heir. After the interview with his mother, I was unconvinced that I would find anything to like in him.

★

I first met John Paston at my mother's manor at Reedham, under the aegis of both my mother and his. I had made it my task to discover as much as I could about him. He was not unimpressive. Following legal studies at Trinity Hall, he had spent some months as Yeoman of the Royal Stables; thus he was a young man with an education and Court polish, although neither were obvious to my critical eye. His hair was dark and badly clipped into his neck, his figure sturdy, his face smooth and solemn, but not I thought without a promise of humour, probably when not in the company of his mother.

'Good day, Mistress Margaret.'

'Good day to you, Master John.'

He bowed, I curtsied.

When he smiled at me, I felt an instant urge to smile back. He led me into a little space with a window seat overlooking my mother's walled garden, where he encouraged me to sit. I glanced across at my mother who nodded. Mistress Agnes made no response. They were not quite beyond earshot so circumspection would be wise. John sat beside me, a suitable space between us.

'We are to be wed, it seems.'

'If your mother approves.'

'My father does.'

I slid a glance to his austere face. 'Of course he does. And we both know why.'

His solemn expression immediately lit with appreciation. 'My father always has an ear and eye to wealth and land for our family. But between the two of us, would it please you, Mistress Margaret?'

Would I like to be wed to this man? Could I live for the rest of my life with him? No romance. No throbbing of my heart. I had read a little of the romance of knights and ladies where the world was lost for love. But I liked him sufficiently and I liked the style of his living at Oxnead. Nor was that his only property. I could do much worse.

'I think it would please me well.'

And here was Mistress Agnes, as sharp-eared as a bat, standing beside us.

'It is settled. Surely there can be no complaints from either of you.'

But Master John Paston took my hand, addressing me. 'Since you are willing, I think you will be a most acceptable wife, Mistress Margaret.'

Whereas I had an eye to Mistress Agnes. I knew just how to respond to this.

'If you are half the man your father Justice William is, sir, you will be a most acceptable husband to me.'

Mistress Agnes's face relaxed into what might have been a smile if she had allowed it. John kissed my cheek. Mistress Agnes promised me a gown of a good blue colour. My mother offered a fine pelt with which to trim it. It was settled, as simply as that, because I was worth one hundred and fifty pounds a year in landed property, my manners were good and I was not too uncomely. Nor, I presumed, did Mistress Agnes see me as an obstreperous daughter-in-law.

On that very night I travelled with them from Reedham to Paston, the new bride to be wed to the heir.

★

I liked John from the very beginning, and he liked me. Sensible and pragmatic, it proved that neither of us was given to romantic extravagance, but neither of us would deny the warmth that had touched us both that day at Reedham. It seemed that we had, if nothing else, an affinity. I bore my first child in little more than two years after we exchanged vows, despite the fact that John returned to Cambridge to continue his studies at Peterhouse, before taking lodgings in London to become acquainted with the family business with his father.

John was not with us at Oxnead when I announced to Mistress Agnes that I was carrying a child, perhaps a future Paston heir. I cannot say that her expression softened, but she stepped forward and took me into a brief embrace. I think I trusted her less when she tried to appear friendly.

'We must tell my son.'

'I could wish your son was here with us.' I refused not to feel neglected.

'You must accept that his life will always be dictated by his affairs of business.'

'I could enjoy it more if it were occasionally dictated by my existence.'

There was no answer that Mistress Agnes could make as I stalked from the room. How could she, since she too had frequently been slighted by Justice William in the interests of Paston ambitions. I took myself to the Steward's room and commanded him to write to my dictation. The words flew from my lips.

★

To my very honourable husband,

It pleases me to inform you that I am carrying your child. I offer prayers to the Blessed Virgin that it will be a son.

As a token of your pleasure and respect I would remind you of a grey-wool gown that you had promised to buy for me. I have no gown to wear this winter but my black and the green that I find very heavy except in the coldest of weather. You may have noticed that women who carry a child are no longer slender and thus I am in need of a girdle that will meet in the middle.

I send you a ring to remember me by, with the image of St Margaret, the particular saint of value to pregnant women. Since you have given me a remembrance that keeps me awake both day and night, I trust you will wear the ring and think of me.

Perhaps you could tell me what name you would like for your son if you do not manage to come home before the birth.

Yours M P

★

It spurred John into a flying visit between Peterhouse and Oxnead. I carried a son, a noisy, restless child, and we called him John. We agreed it was a good name, and I forgave my husband his absence in wifely style.

★

I remained in Norfolk, sometimes living with my mother, more often with Mistress Agnes, where I learned to tolerate her tongue and place my own handprint on the Paston household. It was not always easy to remain courteous when I did not have my husband to give me his authority. I was not always victorious. When my little son John wanted to invite into the house a sharp-nosed terrier from a litter in the stables, Mistress Agnes put down her well-shod foot.

'Dogs belong outside. We will give no space to one in here with its fleas and scavenging.'

Son John had to be consoled with a sweet wafer, to his grand-mother's disgust. I admit to not fighting very hard for my son's desire for the creature. There was enough to do in the household without a small dog to chase after.

But as the winter nights crept on, full of darkness, after we had eaten supper and drunk our cup of ale, Agnes acquired a habit of sitting near the fire, talking of old times, wasting good candles and firewood. My mother would never have sanctioned it. I could stand neither the repeated reminiscences nor the wastage. Unable to tolerate yet another telling of Justice William's struggle with the law, I made a brisk movement towards the door.

'We will go to bed,' I announced. 'We will all go to bed. To sleep. Are we not weary after a day's work? We will rise and break our fast early and so make the most of the morning hours. To sit here in idle chatter is of no value to God nor man.'

After a week, I noticed that the candles were doused not long after my departure and new ones not lit. The fire had been banked down. A little battle but I had won and would win more.

Nor was it easy living apart from John, as I soon discovered. Three years after we were wed John fell ill of a severe fever, news reaching us at Oxnead from London, written in the precise hand of a physician. What could we do? Struck with terror for his health, Mistress Agnes and I wore out our knees in prayer. In extravagance born of true fear, Mistress Agnes promised a wax effigy to be offered at the shrine of the Blessed Virgin at Walsingham if John was spared.

'And I will go on a pilgrimage there, to give thanks,' I promised, 'whatever the cost.'

Meanwhile I wrote to John to encourage him to eat and drink well to offset the fever. Or that is to say that I ordered our Steward to write it for me. I could read but my writing was not good.

And keep your feet dry, for wet feet are sure to exacerbate your symptoms. And finally because it came into my mind: *I would rather that you were at home with me, far rather than the gift of a new gown, even though it were of scarlet.*

I could not bear the thought of becoming a widow so soon after becoming a wife, so soon after finding a deep affection for him. And to remind him when he had recovered from the fever, as I prayed that he would:

Our son John fares well, Blessed be God.

Mistress Agnes was not called upon to go on pilgrimage and neither was I. My advice and Mistress Agnes's offerings to the Blessed Virgin had their reward. John survived the fever and grew strong again. On his recovery, I was provided with evidence that he read my letters for I was in receipt of a package. It was a gown of rich scarlet. Mistress Agnes regarded it as a squandering of money. I loved it, close-fitting as it was. I would wear it as soon as the birth of our second child would allow it to be worn. I stroked the fine woollen cloth, enjoying the slide under my fingers.

'You are a good daughter to me.' Mistress Agnes allowed herself a moment of rare praise. 'Far better than Eliza.'

I already knew that my sister-in-law Eliza had her own problems with her mother. The fact that she referred to her more often than not as Mistress Agnes rather than mother spoke volumes, but Eliza did not easily confide. It was not for me to become involved.

*

Our second child, another son, was born in the spring of 1444, at Geldeston where I had gone to stay with my mother. There I gave birth with the requisite pain and inconvenience but without much difficulty, and welcomed my husband John after I was churched. He looked windblown and tousled but full of energy. I had not seen him for a good two months. We were pleased to be reunited in the privacy of a wood-panelled parlour where a fire warmed the air with the spice of pine-cones.

'What do you wish to call your son?' I asked, after he had bent over the cradle and inspected the child who watched him with a placidity missing in our first offspring.

There had been no such question about his first-born. This child seemed to be a matter to engage my husband's decision-making. Were there not enough family names which we would happily give to our son?

'It will all depend, dear Margaret, on whom we invite to be the boy's godfather.'

'Is there a problem?'

'There may be if we invite your powerful cousin Sir John Fastolf.'

I could see where the problem would lie. A godfather might expect the child to be similarly named, causing us a permanent complication for the future. Surely we would be foolish to land ourselves in this difficulty, when we could make other choices.

'Could you not consider calling him William for your brother? Or even Edmund. Would not either of them be happy to stand as godfather?'

Sometimes my husband could be persuaded by a sideward step rather than a head-on attack. Not on this occasion.

'No.' He was adamant. 'Sir John Fastolf will be his godfather. This child's name must be John.'

And it was done. Elder John and Young John. Not to mention my husband John. I set myself to some careful explaining in the future when addressing my family. Sometimes men could be distressingly intractable.

Paston: December 1444

It did not take our adversaries long to sharpen their talons. Barely had the body of Justice William been brought home to Norwich, to be laid to rest in the Lady Chapel of the Cathedral as he had requested, than the carrion-eaters were gathering on the fences and hedges of the Paston estates. Justice William's wealth and power were talked about wherever men gathered to drink ale. So was his lack of principle where his own interests came into

23

question. Justice William could be harsh and manipulative. Justice William had pulled himself up by his boot-lacings from his lowly beginning as son of a plain husbandman, trampling on anyone who stood in his way to become a student of law at one of the London Inns of Court; Steward to the Bishop of Norwich; Justice of the Court of Common Pleas. Could those Paston boot-lacings be sliced through, now that Justice William was dead?

The enemies emerged from the woodwork like pernicious beetles.

Although probate was awarded to John for the written will, and we kept all the manors in spite of Mistress Agnes's rantings, the disturbances began. Some would say in a minor fashion but it should have been our warning of worse to come.

It all began in Paston on a morning when I was considering how much I disliked living in this house. It was cold, its rooms poorly furnished, Mistress Agnes having taken all the better pieces to Oxnead, the paths and small courtyard prone to mud and deep puddles of brackish water so that I must invariably wear wooden pattens to protect my shoes between October and March. Nothing could protect me from the winter-whiff of decay. I caught John, swathed in a coat and hood and mounting his horse a mere hour after sunrise.

'Escaping from your mother?' I queried.

'It tempts me,' he grinned. 'It will please me well when she returns to Oxnead. I'll not give in and the sooner she accepts it the better.' The raw humour vanished as fast as it had come.

'Where are you going?' I asked.

'To have a few choice words with our rector, before his actions poison the whole village of Paston against us.' His eye rested on me, considering. I tilted my chin. 'Come with me,' he said. 'Our parson might respond to a gentle female voice. My mother sets him to vituperative defiance, and I fear he will not listen to me with more than common courtesy.'

I remained unmoving. 'Could you not have given me warning?'

John had the grace to look a trifle sheepish. 'I have only just thought of it.'

'I doubt I'll make much impression.'

'We can but try.'

Within a quarter of the hour, in cloak and hood, my hair quickly braided and contained by a plain linen coif, I was riding beside him. John pointed out the holes that had once contained markers beside the road, angling off to the right, markers that had been moved.

'It did not take him long,' John snarled.

'Between one Hail Mary and the next, I'd say.' We had discussed the affair over supper in recent days.

This would be the first personal challenge to John's authority outside a court. I wondered how he would deal with it, since it came from a man of God. We were admitted into the rectory, into the parlour where the priest had a cup of ale and a platter of bread and meat before him, his feet on a footstool before a low fire, a book in his hand, his finger keeping the page. There was no hint of holy poverty in the room. The man's collection of books was impressive. I thought the priest had a sullen air as he rose to his feet, although our visit cannot have been a surprise in the circumstances. John, unsmilingly, proffered a signed and sealed document that he took from the purse at his belt. He was all formality as he placed it on the table before the priest with a courteous little inclination of his head.

'I have here, sir, an agreement, made between you and my late father Justice William Paston, that the road in the village of Paston should be diverted from its proximity with my father's new manor house. I see that you have been busy, sir, in the short time since my father's death. You have reneged on the agreement and removed the markers that positioned where the new road would run.'

The cleric's reply came promptly, and not as John would like.

'I have, Master Paston. The change was not acceptable to the villagers.'

'And yet you agreed to it.' John pointed at the document that the priest had not touched. 'Is that not your signature? Is that not legally binding?'

We had known it would be a contentious issue, to allow the manor house more privacy at the expense of the convenience of the villagers, but the priest had agreed to the diversion of the road in exchange for a considerable donation to St Margaret's Church.

'It is indeed legal and binding, sir,' I added in John's support, pointing at the joint signatures and the seal when I caught a hint of a shrug of the priest's shoulders. 'Is it wise to break the law?'

'Will you take me before the law for so paltry an affair?' the priest asked. He ignored me, his regard fixed on John.

'Can we not come to some arrangement?' I suggested, trying for calm in the eye of the coming storm.

But John had had enough. 'My father would not blink at litigation. Neither will I.'

The priest's reply was inappropriately aggressive. 'Then you had better do it fast, Master Paston, before I have a drainage ditch dug across the path of your proposed new road. Drainage is always a problem on that low-lying land, as the villagers will testify. It will be to their advantage for me to dig a ditch.'

There it was. A challenge to the new heir to the Paston title and lands. John stiffened.

'I regret that there is so little Christian conscience in you, sir. You will be hearing from me.'

'I advise you to say no more, Master Paston. Building a wall across the old road has raised a tempest amongst the villagers that will not die down, short of you demolishing the structure. The wall has blocked the path of the processional around the church, which we make for some of our services, a ceremony that is much loved.'

'There was no difficulty with that wall when you first set your name to the agreement!'

'Well, there is now. The villagers are angry.'

Before John could say more, I drew him to the door and, with a curt bow on either side, we left. John grimaced as we mounted and turned our horses in the direction of the manor and the disputed road.

'Can we buy him off?' I asked.

'I doubt he will be willing.'

'But can we afford to take this through the courts?' As I knew from my own housekeeping, ready money had been tight in recent months, rents from my own manor of Gresham being slow to come in. Litigation could drain our strength like an ulcer. 'Is a road worth it?' I asked.

'It's not the road but the challenge to my authority.' John applied his heels to the horse's sides. I followed suit to keep up with him. 'My father is hardly in his coffin. But I'll not be beaten. I have something to show you when we get home.'

Since he seethed with anger all the way back, I rode in silence, knowing better than to try any soothing remedy. This challenge to his local power over something so trivial as a wall would set a dangerous precedent.

Once more at Paston, John marched ahead of me to the room he used for business dealings, unlocking the door which kept out any curious member of the household. Scrolls and documents littered the table but they did not interest my husband. Instead he made his way to a large travelling coffer that stood to the left of the fireplace. It was still covered with dust and was well locked with the addition of leather straps.

'It arrived yesterday,' he said. He flung off his cloak and hood, followed by hat and gloves which slid from the settle to the floor. 'You were supervising the cheese-making in the dairy with my mother.'

'So it was hidden from her.'

John slid a glance in my direction as I retrieved his garments and placed them out of the way. Crouching before the coffer, taking another key from his pouch, he released the complicated locks, unbuckled the straps, and flung back the lid so that it thumped against the wall. The dim light that the small windows allowed to enter the room flashed and glinted on the contents. I knelt beside him, astonished at what I could see in the shadows. Items of silver plate, gold chains and the hint of jewels. Hessian bags that chinked delicately when I poked at them.

'What is this?' I asked, lifting and weighing one of the bags in my palm.

'All the valuables my father placed with the monks at Norwich Priory over the years for safekeeping. I'll not let them fall into the hands of the Priory or my family. Or more specifically into the hands of my mother. We will need this.' He took the bag from me and shook it. 'One thousand pounds.'

I lifted an engraved silver cup. 'I can see me using this for my ale at dinner.' I tipped it with an elegant turn of my wrist.

'I can see me selling it to raise money to spend on the coming litigation,' he said.

'And this?' I lifted out a silver crucifix, all set with dark sapphires. 'Do you sell this too?'

'And that, too.'

'Oh John, how miserly of you.' I held it against my bosom where it glowed strangely against my gown of plain woollen cloth.

'How careful of me, more like. Our money will drain away in the courts like spring floods into a storm-drain. The priest and the road may be the least of my worries.'

I kissed his cheek, reluctantly placing the crucifix back into the coffer. 'How fortunate that your father saw fit to educate you in the law.'

'Indeed.'

A sound beyond the door caused me to rapidly close the lid. Mistress Agnes entered. I doubt she would have noticed if the jewels had been spread over the floor. A document was in her hand, one that she proffered with fury. She was followed by John's brother Edmund, younger by four years, tall and rangy but with a typical Paston's dark hair and forceful nose.

'Where have you been?' Mistress Agnes's questionable greeting. 'I have been looking for you, John. Why are you never here when I need you? I have just this moment received this. It is disgraceful!'

Relations might be strained between them, but she knew where to come for aid. John took it, allowing his eye to move down the single page, exhaling loudly as he did so.

'So it begins.'

'So it does,' Mistress Agnes almost hissed her disgust, her features tight with it. 'Justice William would never allow it. I trust that you will fight for my claim, John. Oxnead belongs to me. This man – this creature – has no claim. He is a priest. He has no right to lay claim to any land, and certainly not my property.'

'That's not the worst part of it,' Edmund added in his laconic fashion. 'The man has been here, demanding to see our mother. He was refused entry at the gate. When he seemed reluctant to go away, I accosted him.'

There was a twinkle in Edmund's eye.

'What did you say to him?' I asked.

'I said that if he wanted anything from us, he must declare it before the royal courts in Westminster Hall. Then I told him to be on his way.'

John clapped him on the back. 'Well done, brother. We'll make a lawyer of you yet.'

'I am already a lawyer, if you had but noticed. He said he would go to court.'

'And you said?'

'That we would refute all suggestions of illegality in our inheritance.'

The two brothers grinned at each other, while I took the document from John, smoothing it out. It was clear enough even though I had to struggle with some of the legal words. A man named John Hauteyn, a Carmelite friar, was claiming rightful possession of our manor of Oxnead. His family had owned it, he said, a hundred years ago, long before it fell into the hands of Justice William. He claimed the support of the powerful Duke of Suffolk in taking his land back again.

'Hauteyn! A man of bad reputation! He cannot inherit

property,' Mistress Agnes repeated, as if to say it again would make it true.

John's lips tightened as he retrieved the document. 'That may be so, but Hauteyn has obtained a dispensation from the Pope, to renounce his position in the Carmelite order, which makes him free to claim the property. Did the family once own it, as he claims? I have no idea.'

'He says that he will sue you through common law,' I said, recalling the pertinent statement.

'He cannot sue for something which is clearly mine.' Mistress Agnes was beyond reasoning.

'We have no choice, if he brings a case.' John tried to soothe, bending his dark gaze on his mother.

Agnes walked out, as angry at both her sons as she was with the unknown friar. Edmund followed at a safe distance.

'Who is this man? Do I know him?' I asked.

'He was the disreputable and malodorous priest we came across in Norwich market place last year, selling false relics to the gullible, no doubt for an exorbitant sum, until the Cathedral authorities shuffled him away.'

And I remembered. Phials of Virgin's tears and little packets of saints' bones, all counterfeit, held out in the man's filthy hands to anyone fool enough to part with coin for water and pigs' bones. A man without honour or integrity who would fleece the gullible townsfolk was now setting his sights on Paston property.

'Can Hauteyn do this?' I asked.

'He can if he has the Duke of Suffolk's favour. I think I will need more than a silver cup to get us out of this. What's more, I fear that Hauteyn will be a minor irritant, a somnolent wasp, when we should be worrying about a swarm of them.'

He drew me into his arms, his chin resting on my coifed head as he looked out of the window at the Paston acres that would cause us so much heartache.

'And now, my wife, it would be good policy for you to follow my mother and calm her down with a cup of ale – not a silver cup, mind – and some words of wisdom. She will listen to you rather than to me. And don't mention the contents of the coffer. She has no idea that I have it. Persuade her if you can to talk to no one about Hauteyn's claim.'

I patted his shoulder, knowing from experience that nothing I could say would make matters easier for John, and went to draw the poison from Agnes's thoughts if I could.

'I'm sorry to hear that the Duke of Suffolk would give his support to Hauteyn.'

John's final words followed me.

★

The Duke of Suffolk remained a thought to trouble me while I plied Mistress Agnes with a pottery cup of our better-quality beer and I discussed with her the less than vital question of what to do with the windfalls that littered the orchard. It was important for a family of our inferior rank to be in good company with the local magnates. William de la Pole, Duke of Suffolk, was one of the most powerful landowners in these eastern lands of England. What's more he had emerged as one of the sixth King Henry's chief ministers and Steward of the King's household, which meant enormous influence at Court, given Henry's frequent instability of mind. The Duke, with a loud voice in the King's Council, had little time to spend in his lands around Norwich, but enough to dabble in the interests of those men who served him.

I had seen him once in Norwich, a large man, full of self-importance, surrounded by his retinue in de la Pole livery. Clad in a be-furred damask houppelande that reached to mid-calf, his head graced with a large chaperon in black velvet, he dominated the space around him as he discussed business with the Mayor. He did not deign to notice any of lesser rank. He would give no time for a Paston. When a beggar risked approaching his horse, arms outstretched, requesting alms, the mighty Duke loosed his foot from his stirrup to kick the man from his path. There was no charity or compassion in him. I did not like him.

'Are we then a lost cause?' I asked John when we met in our own private chamber as we knelt together for prayer at the end of the day before climbing into the large curtained bed inherited from Justice William. 'Do we return to the rank of husbandmen as our lands are stripped away?'

'We are if we are dependent on Suffolk's goodwill,' he grumbled as he removed his hose which, inconsequentially, I noticed had worn into holes at the heel. 'The Duke has none for us. There are precious few for us to turn to.'

'What about the Duke of Norfolk?'

John Mowbray, the Duke of Norfolk, also owned widespread holdings in our part of the world. In his young days, Justice William had served as Steward in his household. Would the Duke, in recognition of past services be prepared to use his aristocratic powers on our behalf?

'No hope of help from there either. He might have vast estates hereabouts but he's just not powerful enough at Court or even in local politics. Suffolk holds everything in a stranglehold. Besides,

33

even the Duke of Norfolk can't be trusted if he decides a Paston manor is ripe for his taking. Norfolk is nothing but a disreputable thug.' Sitting up against his pillows, John glared at me, as if I were the problem. 'What I need is a man who has access to the King, who owes nothing to Suffolk or Norfolk. I need to look elsewhere, and to do that I need to return to London.'

I sighed a little. Had I not foreseen it? He would definitely need new hose. 'When do you leave us?'

'In two days.'

It was already planned in John's mind. There would be no arguing with him. But I tried, with a little female guile. 'And I must not fret? With you away in London, not knowing what will happen next?'

'We will do what is necessary. You were not born to be a husbandwoman, Mistress Margaret. Now come and kiss me and I might just allow you to keep the crucifix. Are you not my own dear sovereign lady?'

'You are very flattering.' John was not given to such high-flown compliments.

'I have been spending time at Court,' he explained, quite seriously.

I felt his smile against my hair as his arm slid around my waist: his words warmed my heart, Court flattery or no.

'The problem is,' he said as I fell towards sleep, my head on his shoulder, 'that so many of our estates have been purchased into the Paston family so recently. We cannot claim that we have owned them for even a dozen years.'

'No.'

'They would never challenge Justice William. They will challenge me.'

'Yes.'

I fell asleep with the dangers and difficulties alive in my mind, as well as the possibility of keeping a jewelled silver crucifix.

Ever practical, I sent a letter with John, a reminder to buy new hose, as well as to send home two caps for the boys and some black lace for me. His previous purchases for our sons had been too small and of poor quality, quick to wear around the brim. We might be under threat but we could do better than that.

Chapter Two

Margaret Mautby Paston

Norwich: autumn 1447

'Repeat that to me again, if you will.'

Whatever emotions might be awakening within me, I kept my tone level, merely one of enquiry. Mistress Agnes and I were residing in the Norwich house with the young children. John was in London, upholding Paston interests and working hard for Sir John Fastolf, a gentleman of some reputation, now in his elder years, who was intent on acquiring land with the fortune he had made in the French campaigns. John saw an opportunity to make an alliance with a man of the Court, a man who was my own cousin from my mother's side of the family. John lost no opportunity to work effectively in Sir John's interests from his house in Southwark.

'What did you say?' I repeated, hoping against hope that I had misheard, my hand stilled in my lap, pressing the linen I was stitching into my thighs.

The Steward of Mistress Agnes's household swallowed heavily, his throat working.

'It has come to my attention, mistress, that there is a claim being put forward against one of the Paston manors.'

'Which?'

'Gresham, mistress!'

For a moment I was speechless. His eyes could not quite meet mine. Mistress Agnes, who had followed him into the room, sensing disaster as a cat senses a rats' nest in the cellar, came to stand at my shoulder. As bleak as a crow in her widow's black, Mistress Agnes was as forthright as ever in her defence of Paston interests.

'Which is palpable nonsense!' she stated.

'Indeed it is not, mistress,' her Steward denied. 'There is much talk of it in the streets and around the market.'

'You have misheard it. My husband bought that manor of Gresham.'

She turned to go, dismissing the whole episode, but I saw the expression on the Steward's face.

'Who has made a claim? What is his name?'

The Steward swallowed again.

'Lord Moleyns, mistress.'

The Paston manor of Gresham was highly important to me. Not just that it was a valuable manor with a fine castle situated in the village, Gresham had been settled on me as my jointure at the time of my marriage. It was mine, as was the income from it, so to have unquestioned possession of it was for me of vital importance.

In the early days, when John and I were still growing to know each other, we lived mainly at Gresham, and I still returned when I could to ensure its careful maintenance. It was a fair place in my eyes, a considerable structure built of stone with crenellations and round towers to offer protection. If I ever feared for its safety it had a moat and a drawbridge, within which the accommodations were comfortable, built into a square block of rooms. The courtyard was paved and well-drained. I would be as fervent as my husband in fighting for it.

'And who might Lord Moleyns be?' I asked.

Not a local man, I thought, and one with no right to my manor. Justice William's purchase was legal and complete; Gresham had been Paston property for a good score of years. Why question it now, twenty years after the event? But it troubled me. People around here had long memories. Was this Lord Moleyns a man whom Justice William had antagonised?

'I know not, mistress.'

'Then you must find out for me. Does Master John know of this?'

'Probably not yet, mistress.'

'Then discover our clerk and write to him and tell him. And tell him he is needed in Norwich. I think you will find him at Sir John Fastolf's house on the Thames in Southwark.'

'Yes, mistress.'

'And don't speak of this to Mistress Agnes. She will forbid you to trouble her son. It is my instruction that you write that letter.'

'Yes, mistress. I will do it immediately.'

And meanwhile I would do my own investigating.

★

I talked with one of the priests from the Cathedral who proved well-informed about local affairs. His face settled into lugubrious lines as I walked with him in the quiet of the cloister.

'He is what you might call an adventurer, mistress, so I am led to believe,' the priest explained, not averse to a little gossip. Lord Moleyns was a common man from Wiltshire called Robert Hungerford who had taken the title from his wife. At the same time he had grasped whatever claim he might make against our manor of Gresham, which had belonged to the Moleyns family until a half-century ago. He was an arrogant, ambitious man who was not slow to use his new title.

'I should also tell you, Mistress Paston ...'

'Can it be worse?'

'It can. Lord Moleyns is one of the Duke of Suffolk's affinity.'

Any man with the Duke of Suffolk's friendship would be a power difficult to undermine. This was the second claim against us from men close to the Duke of Suffolk. First Hauteyn, now Lord Moleyns, who I suspected would prove to be a far more menacing individual than the friar.

The priest shook his tonsured head. 'Dangerous times, Mistress Paston. Dangerous times.'

I could not disagree. I thanked the priest, with a donation towards candles to be lit for the quiet repose of Justice William's soul.

I needed John here.

★

We spent Christmas in Norwich, with even John joining us, abandoning his work in London for a few days with his family. When not celebrating the birth of the Christ Child, we dissected the imminent threat against us.

'Moleyns can do nothing against our legal rights,' John

reassured me, in an expansive mood after a cup and more of wine. 'We have all the documents of ownership. I know exactly where to put my hands on them. Gresham was sold to my father by a Moleyns executor, in the name of the Moleyns heiress whom this man Hungerford wed. It is not within his power to take back a manor that was bought from his wife before he had ever considered marriage to her. Don't be anxious, Margaret. Gresham is ours and cannot be taken from us.' John thumped his fist on the table. 'A storm in a wine cup.' He ate a plum, then dropped the stone into the remains of his wine, watching the ripples. There was a light in his eye, as if he contemplated the coming battle through the courts with relish, foreseeing only victory.

'Besides, we have heard no more about it,' John added. 'Perhaps Moleyns has turned his attention to his lands in Wiltshire. And bad luck to him.'

It was a comforting thought. Without legal rights, what could Lord Moleyns do to harm us?

★

'It's gone! It's been taken, Master John.'

No sooner had we marked Twelfth Night with wassail and bean cake than John and I, when we were gathering together his documents for his imminent departure, early on the seventh day of January, were drawn to our courtyard by the clatter of horse's hooves in the frost. The message-bearer did not even dismount before announcing his news.

'Before our very eyes!'

The rider, sweating in spite of the January cold, slid from the steaming horse, almost falling to his knees at my feet. The words were gasped out as he tried to catch his breath. We had been lulled into a false security, but here was one of our men from Gresham, his cloak and hood still white with hoar frost. He must have been on the road before dawn.

'Stand up, man. Stand up. What's gone?' John took his arm and steadied him.

'Gresham, sir. Lord Moleyns has sent in his men. They've taken the castle. Our Steward and servants have been forced out. We were not prepared. We were not strong enough to stop them. Who would have thought that he would do this?'

John all but shook him.

'How many troops?'

'Enough to overrun us before we could even lay a hand to our weapons. They caught us out. We could not stop them.'

'Was there any bloodshed?' I asked.

'Only a punched nose or two.'

John was scowling. 'You have done all you could. Go in and find food and ale.'

We followed him, standing in the dark entrance hall as we closed the door on the outside world. Horror at what had occurred howled like a rabid dog in the shadows. My blood had frozen like the ice on the puddles, at how easily this had been accomplished.

'Moleyns!' John snarled, snatching off his cap. 'I should have expected it! Why did I think that he would be satisfied with a battle in the courts? While I was thinking about legal documents, he was sending a troop of armed men to do the deed!'

Which summed it up perfectly. It jolted my thoughts into action, or lack thereof.

'What do we do now?'

'You stay here. I go to Gresham.'

But John's anger was obliterating his good sense. However much I might wish to ride, fast and furious, for Gresham and demand the return of my property, I could see the outcome if I did.

'And what would be the point of that?' I asked. 'Will you stand outside the gate and demand admittance? Will you shout your demands? You will be laughed out of the manor. Moleyns will probably put an arrow in your gut and solve the problem once and for all.'

'So we do nothing?' John was beyond reason, fury giving off heat, his fingers white-knuckled where they kneaded the felt of his hat to the detriment of the brim. 'He thinks I am of weaker stuff than my father. I will show him that—'

I gripped his sleeves and shook him. 'No. Stop and think. The law is on our side.'

'The law! Moleyns did not even spit in the direction of the law when his men marched through my gates.'

'But we will spit in its direction. We must. We do not have the manpower to oust him. You know how secure Gresham can be if defended by a suitable force.'

By this time I had all but pushed John into the parlour and closed the door to prevent Mistress Agnes from bearing down upon us. She would add nothing to this debate, merely exacerbate it by blaming John for his lack of foresight.

'True,' he admitted at last. He frowned and downed the cup of ale I presented to him, wiping his mouth on his sleeve.

'What we need is a mediator,' he said. 'It will take time, but it's our best hope.'

'Who? To whom will Moleyns listen? Who will mediate for a Paston, taking on the Duke of Suffolk?'

John was staring into space over my head. Then he shook himself free of me and strode to the door, leaping up the stairs to our chamber. There I found him moments later, pen in hand, already writing.

'Who do we know?' I demanded.

John replied only when he had completed the letter.

'Waynflete, Bishop of Winchester. I have met him at Court. He is important, eloquent, bombastic, all we need in a patron. He might agree to act as arbiter, and I doubt Moleyns will reject his advice.'

'But does he have any influence?'

'I believe so. He is close to the King. I can do no better than one of the foremost prelates in England.'

The Duke of Suffolk loomed in the corner of the room, a malevolent toad. Would the worthy Bishop be a match for him? Would the King support the Bishop against the powerful Duke of Suffolk? I doubted it, but now was not the time to air my doubts.

'Then we will put all our trust in the Bishop. Meanwhile I will say a Hail Mary.'

John, it seemed, also had his misgivings.

'I think that you will need to say more than one!'

★

The weeks passed, becoming months. Our friendly Bishop of Winchester agreed to arbitrate and our unfriendly Lord Moleyns declared himself amenable.

Yet still there was no acceptable outcome.

Lord Moleyns's men remained in my manor at Gresham and collected the rent from my tenants there. Any formal hearings

43

were postponed again and again. Moleyns was an expert at coming up with excuses: he was too busy in Wiltshire, he had a sickness, he was engaged in a dispute over the ownership of cattle. But, yes, he would come to London and negotiate over Gresham when he could find the time. All empty words. John lost his temper with increasing frequency.

'He will argue that the Angel Gabriel himself stands in his way with a flaming sword! How can we defeat him at law if he will not appear in court? He says that the seals on our document of ownership of Gresham are not yet cold. Our seals are almost older than I! And I'll be damned if I give in!'

I all but wore out my knees with petitions to the Blessed Virgin.

Sixteen meetings took place between the lawyers from both sides. Sixteen times there was no result until our lawyers threw up their hands, unable to go any further. John's personal visit to Salisbury to beard the recalcitrant Moleyns in his den ended with no result.

'What is he like?' I asked when John returned, rumbling with frustration.

'Suave. Expensive. Just as you would expect, all clad in velvet and damask to impress his visitors. Even wearing a peacock feather pinned to his hat with a diamond larger than my thumb-nail. And underneath it lurked a knave with a slippery tongue. I would not believe a word he says. Oh, he was not hostile. He did not threaten me with physical violence. He even gave me a cup of ale for my troubles, but his mind was as hard as the surface of this table.' He rapped his knuckles against it. 'He'll not move on the case.'

What advice could I give? There was none. Gresham, it seemed, was lost to me for ever. In my mind's eye I could see my much prized hall where Moleyns's men now sat at ease: the furniture, an array of stools and coffers and a substantial aumbry to keep glasses and pewter platters secure, all made by a local craftsman, but skilfully decorated and well-polished with an aroma of rich beeswax. The tapestries stitched with care in greens and browns by some Paston wife before my time, warm with plants and flowers, as well as somnolent rabbits still to be hunted by an approaching hound. How heart-wrenching it would be if it was lost to us. Would they despoil it with the drunken ways of soldiers? I could not bear to think of it.

In the privacy of my chamber, as I prayed once again, I was not averse to shedding a tear. It seemed to be a hopeless case.

Norwich: May 1448

As if the Gresham invasion was not enough to worry us, as well as Hauteyn's noisy claims on Oxnead still not settled and thus a constant bother, there came others fast on their heels. It was a Friday that the very personal repercussions of Justice William's death were truly driven home for us. It started all innocently enough. Mistress Agnes and I, clad in seemly fashion, went to attend Mass in our parish church of St Peter Hungate in Norwich. A busy church and a devout congregation from the merchants and traders, and we, Mistress Agnes and Mistress Margaret Paston, had much to be grateful for. Early in this year, I had been blessed with the birth of a daughter whom we had named Margery for my mother.

'A fine child,' Mistress Agnes had stated. 'Think what a value she will be when you need an alliance with one of our important families. She will make a worthy bride, much sought after.'

'She is barely two weeks old,' I had replied, smoothing the

scant hair of the scrap of humanity that I held in my arms, before replacing her linen coif. She was strong and had a powerful wail when hungry. 'We will not be seeking a husband for her for a good few years.'

It pleased me to have a daughter. I held her close, marvelling at the perfect fingernails, the soft curve of her cheeks. Her hair was fairer than mine, her eyes blue, but whether it was John or I that she would resemble as she grew I had no idea.

'John should be seeking one. It cannot be too soon to look for wealthy families with appropriate sons.'

'It would be a far better use of his time for John to seek a husband for me.' The embittered words came from my sister-in-law Eliza who still resided at home with her mother. 'I am nineteen years old with no prospects.'

Mistress Agnes's expression became rigid with displeasure. 'I have the matter in hand, daughter.'

'Then when will I meet him? When will I be wed with a child of my own?'

Mistress Agnes rounded on her daughter as if she were an enemy at the gate. 'There is nothing for you to see here. Go down to the kitchen and fetch your sister a cup of ale. The best, mind. It will strengthen her.'

Eliza departed, shimmering with resentment.

'She speaks the truth,' I ventured, prepared to broach a difficult subject since I was firmly in Mistress Agnes's aura of approval.

'Maybe. The sooner I can find her a husband the better. She is a difficult girl to live with.' But then my mother-in-law turned her mind to the immediate. 'Have you thought of seeking a husband amongst Sir John Fastolf's family for this child?'

It was a consideration, and Sir John Fastolf might be amenable. But not yet.

Yes, we had much to be thankful for as I sank to my knees in the church on that Friday morning. Not least for John who was once more engaged in legal matters in London with that same Sir John Fastolf. He was paid well for his tasks and might buy me a gift to mark Margery's birth. I was in need of another new girdle now that my waist had returned to its customary measurement.

In my prayers I remembered John's name before the Blessed Virgin.

Barely had the host been raised, barely had we made the sign of the cross, than we heard a commotion outside in the road. So loud were the voices, and since the door of the church had been left open, we could recognise one of them without difficulty. James Gloys, the new chaplain in the Paston household. He might be a favourite of Mistress Agnes but I still had to be convinced. Master Gloys was a forceful character, a young man with a mind of his own and hot-headed when challenged, a trait that was not always clerical, although his beliefs were sound enough, as was his attention to his clerical duties. There were sounds of a scuffle, the rattle of stones being thrown, and then a melee of other voices. Mistress Agnes and I exchanged glances.

One voice rang out above the rest. It was powerful and coarse, imbued with authority and vulgar words. It was a voice well-known in Norwich.

'Wyndham!' I inclined my head to whisper in Mistress Agnes's ear as the priest began his exhortation to the sinners in his midst. Repentance was suddenly not uppermost in my mind. The congregation around us also stirred, intent on listening in to the distant altercation.

John Wyndham was a man who had little love for our family, from pride and covetousness, we presumed. He had grown rapidly rich from trade and buying up land, much like Justice William. We had already had a sharp dispute with him over the services of a shepherd on our manor at Soarham, a case still pending at the King's Bench.

'Wyndham,' Mistress Agnes muttered, 'would make a case against us out of a cask of sour ale.'

The voices were now raised to shouting level, and some blasphemy, although from whom I could not tell. I glanced again at Mistress Agnes, and she at me, the sanctity of the host forgotten. We could not ignore this. That we had no male servants with us was not a deterrent.

'Come with me,' I whispered.

Thus Mistress Agnes and I slipped out, missals tucked in sleeves, hurrying through the churchyard and into the road beyond, where interested spectators had already begun to gather in the vicinity of our Norwich house. There at our door was James Gloys himself, being pelted with stones as large as farthing loaves, by Wyndham and some of his associates, all to raucous cheering whenever one of the stones struck home. Not that Master Gloys, tall and slender and furious, was intimidated. By the time we arrived on our threshold Gloys and Wyndham were squaring up to each other, each drawing a dagger, out for blood. Master Gloys might have been a man of God but he had a temper. His language was distinctly un-clerical with words he had not learned in our household.

Mistress Agnes and I lifted our skirts from the dust and hastened as seemly as possible without running. If this ended in bloodshed, what of our standing in the town? The Pastons would quickly be tarred with the same ignominy if their chaplain, brawling in the street, lacked such control of himself and his words. Without thought for my own safety, using my elbows I pushed through the growing crowd and stepped between James Gloys and John Wyndham. I might glare at him in disfavour but Master Gloys was after all one of my own and in John's absence it was my duty to protect him. Meanwhile Agnes took him by the arm, holding out her hand for the knife. His garments were soiled with direct hits from the stones, a bruise growing on his cheek with a smear of blood, but his eyes gleamed with fury and he would not give up the weapon. His teeth bared in a snarl, indiscriminately at Mistress Agnes and John Wyndham.

'What is the meaning of this?' I demanded so that the whole crowd, looking from one to the other in anticipation of further scandal, might hear. 'You are so noisy in your squabble that you interrupt the Holy Mass. What is so important that you must come to blows on my doorstep?'

My heart quaked but I would show no fear.

Wyndham swung round to face me.

'Your minion refused to raise his hat to me!' he roared, still brandishing his knife. 'He is a knave who must be punished. Do you employ such churls in your household, Mistress Paston? Is it like employing like?'

Churl? How dare he! It was waving a red flag before a bull. Briefly I was relieved that John was not present, before taking up the challenge for myself. I did not get the chance. Master Gloys's face was screwed up in hot resentment.

'I will not be addressed as churl!' he spat back. 'I am no churl, and this man's family is no better. Did Wyndham not come from the soil and the cow-byre before he made money by cheating

49

all of you who have bought from him? I'll not raise my hat to such a one. Not even if he threatens me with a knife.'

Which was incendiary speech in this situation, and at our very gate, the crowd now nodding in agreement with the accusations or shouting in support of Wyndham.

'Go into the house, Master Gloys,' I ordered.

'I'll not retreat before this serf …'

'Go in now! I command it!'

Would he obey me? For a moment all hung in the balance, until at last his eye met mine and read my determination. With urgings from Mistress Agnes, still pulling on his sleeve, he stalked off into the house, leaving me to continue my confrontation with Wyndham, who was quite as low-born as Gloys had intimated. His hand still gripped his knife, and he brandished it so furiously that for a moment I feared that he would vent his wrath on me with a blow.

Would he dare to attack a Paston woman in the street? If so then our situation was even worse than we had feared. With that thought in my mind I knew that I could not afford to retreat, even though I was now alone in the unfriendly crowd.

I took a step towards him. I would call on these witnesses to stare down John Wyndham.

'You will not harm me, with so large an audience, Master Wyndham,' I said, as calmly as if it were a daily occurrence to step between two weapon-brandishing men. 'Have you no dignity? Have you courage only when you face a woman? Or do you need to order your minions to carry out your vile practices in your name?'

The crowd laughed, which brought Wyndham's anger down on my head.

'Whores!' he snarled, as Mistress Agnes reappeared to take her stand at my side. 'Knaves and churls. Thieves! The Pastons are not worthy of my notice. You and the old woman are whores, both of you. You will sell your souls and bodies for what you can get in coin and land.'

My belly churned with dismay. I had not alleviated the situation at all. He ranted on, while I closed my mind to the worst of the epithets. Yet I stood and faced it, until Wyndham, seeing no response in me, turned and strode off, his friends following.

'Whores! Churls!'

I heard the final crude words echo along the street. The crowd, with much comment and some pleasure at the entertainment, dispersed and I was free to enter my house.

That afternoon, after some discussion, and an acknowledgement that Master Gloys was not repentant to any degree, and neither was Master Wyndham, Mistress Agnes and I went to the Prior at the Cathedral to seek his help. It would not be good for us if we feared to step outside our house for risk of further attacks. The Prior might have sufficient influence to calm the situation. Suitably clad in sober gowns, we waited on the Prior in his austere room with its crucifix on the wall and a prie-dieu.

It was a brief conversation. The Prior had already heard of the altercation and agreed that it would be bad for the town if there were any repetition. He was not without compassion and would summon Wyndham. It was as much as we could hope for although I had little expectation of Wyndham's concurrence. We promised to have equally stern words with Master Gloys, which I did as soon as I arrived home.

'I will have no more public exchange of insults. If you

cannot control your tongue in the street, I will send you to London to my husband. You can work for him and he can keep you under surveillance. I doubt that he will be pleased. Do you wish that?'

'No, mistress.'

He was sullen, his narrow face defiant, but at least he was accepting.

'Then let this be the last we hear of it.'

'I am no churl!'

'Neither am I. Wyndham's accusations are baseless. Let it all be at rest.'

Silently, I had to admit that it was the one weak step in the ladder of our climb to influence. Clement Paston had been a man of low birth. Clement Paston had indeed been a churl.

★

Next morning, early, before the noises of a busy household awoke, I was made aware of shouting beneath my window, and groaned into my pillow. Master Gloys's voice again. Tugging a linen coif over my hair which I had no time to pin in place, I pushed open the window and looked down.

There he was, faced by some of Wyndham's adherents, although the man himself was not present. The Prior's intervention had failed miserably. Neither, it seemed, had I imposed my authority on my chaplain; my threats had fallen on stony ground. Swords were drawn by the Wyndham coterie. Suddenly it looked bad, even worse than the previous day.

What should I do now? To my regret, my courage failed me. Yet there, below me, Eliza was stepping out of the door. My heart leapt. What could she do? I might face Wyndham, but Eliza was not known for her strength under adversity.

'Go back inside,' I shouted down, leaning out.

She looked up.

'It's Master Gloys,' she said.

'I know. Go back inside now,' I repeated. I slammed the window and ran down the stairs.

By the time I reached the door, thrusting Eliza out of the way, Thomas, one of my mother's servants, was already in the midst of the fracas, come to support Master Gloys. When I heard a crow of anguish I realised that one of the swords had struck home.

This was not a time to consider lack of courage. Here was a need for Paston authority. I bustled out with two more of our servants at my heels, but by then Wyndham's men had taken themselves off, leaving an intractable priest and a bleeding Thomas, holding his hand against his chest. Even more unfortunate was the interest drawn once again from the Norwich populace who, on their way to market, had not been slow to come forward and enjoy the spectacle of a Paston servant bleeding in the street.

How many times would I have to put up with providing common entertainment?

'What was all that about?' I demanded, once we were all inside and the door shut.

Master Gloys refused to answer.

I sent for our clerk and dictated a letter to John in London, explaining the quarrel, deleting the worst of the insults, and ending with:

★

I am sending Master Gloys with this letter. It will be better if he is employed in your household in London. He is proving intractable over his unfortunate behaviour in Norwich.

I should warn you. Wyndham also plans to travel to London. I pray that you will have a heed for your own safety. Wyndham is so stirred up that he might attack you. He said in my own hearing that he would not repent if Master Gloys had died in the confrontation. He may not attack you himself, but he is not beyond paying some knave to do so.

I do not wish to hear of your being in danger. I would not have that for forty pounds in gold. Your mother is in agreement.

★

I thought for a moment. Was it not my duty to inform John of the language that was used against us in the street? I dictated again, changing my mind, hating the words that must come from my clerk's pen. Better coming from me than from the malicious tongues of his enemies.

★

You should know, my husband, that Wyndham called your mother and I whores. He called us knaves and churls. It was not pleasant. Your wife, M P

★

And since I was taking the time to send this to London, I would not waste it:

54

★

It would please me if you would buy some frieze for me to make your children's gowns. And for me a yard of black broadcloth for a hood. I cannot get good cloth here in Norwich.

★

The whole episode left me with a sour taste on my tongue. It was unnerving, that I must watch with care when I ventured out into the streets of Norwich or even further afield, where this private quarrel might be played out again and again to the disgust or secret pleasure of our neighbours. Wyndham's accusation of Paston low birth had come too close to the bone.

'The thing is,' said Mistress Agnes as we sat down to break our fast, later than usual, Thomas's hand now bandaged and Master Gloys sent off to London, 'that you and I, Margaret, are both better born than our husbands, and certainly of far higher status than either Gloys or Wyndham. My own father, as you know, was a knight, Sir Edmund Berry. As in all cases of marriage, Margaret, our present rank rests on that of the man to whom we are wedded. Justice William Paston was no gentleman, while his father Clement, truth be told, had no claim whatsoever to gentility. To call him a churl is not far from the truth, a fact that will always be a weapon to be used against you and your husband. We must fight to repair what has been damaged.'

We must indeed. For the moment all was quiet on the streets of Norwich but my anxiety for John in London grew with every hour that we were apart.

55

Chapter Three

Elizabeth Paston

Oxnead: spring 1448

I had come to a realisation quite early in my life that my mother despised me. It was not an occasional lack of tolerance in her formidable heart, nor a minor irritation with any deficiency of skill in me. It was not a flare of temper when her patience was compromised, such as might be experienced by any child in the years of growing to adulthood. It was clear to me that my mother disliked me with a growing intensity.

It was clear to all in the family, but no one spoke of it. Perhaps the younger ones did not notice. John was simply too busy and not so often at home.

It might be argued that my mother, Mistress Agnes Paston, lacked affection for all her children. In truth, after my father's death and the horror of his will, she had little good to say about her eldest son, my brother John. Her discourse was full of complaint when he refused to follow her demands. She had hopes for Edmund, thought well of William, while Clement, the baby of the family, she doted on. It had also to be said that my mother held a strong affection for her daughter-in-law, John's wife Margaret. I was the one who engaged her wrath. It grieved me immeasurably, even when I left my childhood behind.

It might be argued that a wilful child could expect to be shut in her chamber, or refused supper, or suffer a cane snapped across her knuckles. But I was not wilful. Nor were these the worst punishments meted out to me by my mother.

I was Elizabeth Paston, the only daughter of the late much-lamented Justice William Paston and his ever-present wife Agnes Berry Paston. Matters grew to a head in this year when I was nineteen years old and unwed, with a marital match not even under discussion.

What could be so difficult in discovering for me a suitable husband? Was my family not one of the most noteworthy in the town of Norwich? Was my brother not making a name for himself? We were not without land. We were not without income. My father had been a Justice of the Court of Common Pleas, giving him status as well as the opportunity to increase our family fortunes, by fair means and foul. He had wedded an heiress and arranged my brother John's marriage to another heiress. We had become in two generations a family to be respected.

Why then was I not yet wed? Would I not be a valuable bride, enticing a husband of wealth and influence to join ambitions with the Pastons?

I posed the question to my sister-in-law, Margaret Mautby Paston, seven years older than me. She had now been wed to my brother John for thirteen years. Margaret had been eighteen years old on that celebratory day. Now she had children of her own and was carrying another. I would never be a young bride.

It worried me that I would be past the age of bearing children unless something was done fast to relieve my misery.

'Why can they not find me a husband?' I demanded on one of Margaret's frequent visits to Oxnead where my mother and I and my youngest brother Clement were living. I had managed a moment of seclusion with her amongst the pungent aromas of lavender and rosemary in the stillroom, while my mother busied herself on some domestic crisis that involved raised voices in the kitchen. 'Am I so ill-favoured that no man will look at me with more than a passing glance? Surely there is one man in Norfolk who will offer for me and meet the high expectations of my mother. Am I so surpassingly ugly?'

It was not the first time that I had asked these questions in one form or another. I admired Margaret's strong will, her independence, her resilience. I admired her ability to ignore my mother's ill temper, or to turn it to her own use. Margaret was everything I was not. Her resistance in the dispute with Master Wyndham had to my mind been nothing short of admirable. When she challenged his appearance outside the church in Norfolk where he had threatened Master Gloys with a knife, I would have hidden behind the curtains of my bed. I was not a courageous woman.

I envied Margaret the close intimacy she had with my brother, the love that had grown between them, if that was what it was, even though they spent so many months apart. John was never vocal, but Margaret was not beyond sometimes sending him tender farewells in her letters amongst the household necessities. Yes, I envied her that.

When I asked my question, Margaret considered me solemnly, with all the dignity of an heiress in her own right, and now a wife secure of her position in the family. Her gaze fell from my face to my feet, taking in all between. Then back again.

'No,' she said. 'You are not ugly.'

'Don't be too enthusiastic, Meg,' I replied, low-voiced, not wishing to draw my mother back into the room. I had developed keen hearing for the brisk step of my mother's feet. 'Am I then passably comely?'

'Your face is handsome enough, your figure good and your mind well-informed,' she replied. 'A little tall perhaps for some men but that is no detriment. I know that you can read and write and manage a household. If your dowry was of a suitable extent, I can see no reason why you would not be a valuable asset to a man of substance.' She considered a moment. 'I know that you have a dowry. I was there at the reading of your father's will.'

So had I been. The dowry was not the problem.

'Unfortunately,' Margaret observed, 'as I recall, you will only receive your dowry if you wed with your mother's permission.'

I breathed out heavily. 'You could be more encouraging.'

'I am encouraging. I have listed your assets. Speak to your mother.'

Without thinking I replied: 'My mother detests me.'

Margaret frowned. Yet I could see her own suspicions writ plain on her face. The sour atmosphere in our household could not go unnoticed.

'You do not know what goes on between the walls in this house,' I said, my words coloured with an acrimony born of long experience. 'I have decided that it must be so. That she despises me. Or why else would she treat me so badly?'

Margaret continued to frown as she removed the dried lavender flowers from their stems. 'Then what better way to get you off her hands than with a marriage? I see no sense in keeping you tied to her side – if in truth she does dislike you – when a husband would solve the problem. What could be better for you, and for her, to marry you off and dispatch you to another household?'

'My mother is not always driven by a sense of what would be best for me. My future must not be allowed to undermine the rank of our family. If a man of suitable status does not offer for me, then I will not be allowed to take a husband who is less worthy.'

When Margaret still shook her head, not willing to believe my accusations, I held out my arm. She tilted her head in enquiry.

'Look at it!' I said.

Abandoning the flower-heads, Margaret pulled back the loose sleeve of my over-gown. She drew in her breath in a little hitch of surprise, her brows climbing.

'What do you see?' I asked. 'This is not the result of an affectionate maternal embrace.'

She took my hand, pushing my sleeve further towards my elbow. 'They are bruises.'

'Do I not know?' My cynicism spilled out. 'Do I show you my ribs as well? The discolouring there is not gained from any household tasks. I did not trip and fall in the buttery when counting barrels of ale.'

Margaret regarded me with horror. 'Agnes, I suppose?'

'Don't tell me you never suspected it. Do you not talk to your husband?'

'Infrequently,' she admitted. 'And when I do, it is about which neighbour is casting his glance over our manors this week. Or about Gresham.' Slowly she drew my sleeve down, hiding the bruises that were the shape of fingerprints. 'Yes, I had my suspicions,' she admitted. 'But I wasn't sure. How did your ribs become damaged?'

'A punch here. A clout with a bread pan there. Whatever she

has to hand. And if she does not find a platter or a jug, then she takes a stick to beat me.'

'Eliza!'

'Can you not stop her?' I asked, even though I knew that it was futile. 'I am in despair.'

'You could hit back ...'

I regarded her in disbelief. 'Do you truly advise me to strike my mother?'

'No. Of course not.'

'Then can you not help me? I cannot live like this. Please, Meg ...'

I heard the fear in my voice, the whine of despair, and despised myself for it. I should be stronger and face my mother, defy her, question her right to inflict such indignities on my person. I was no child.

For a brief moment Margaret put her arms lightly around my shoulders.

'I can do nothing,' she stated. 'For me to interfere could make things worse for you. You know how self-willed your mother is. She takes advice from no one. I must not antagonise her since I must stand as mediator between her and John.'

I pulled away, to push back the neat coif that contained my braided hair, revealing my brow near the hairline. 'This one is fading but it broke the skin. She used a platter which broke in the applying. I swear you can still see it.'

'Why?'

'Who knows. I irritate her. Simply by being here and drawing breath.'

'Surely there has been some offer for your hand in nineteen years.'

'Yes. I have been sought as a bride, but my husband must be of sufficient status and sound lineage, or he will not be acceptable to the Pastons. He must be able to supply a jointure of land for me with an income of not less than forty pounds per year.' I tried not to sneer, pushing my hair back beneath my coif. 'That was four years ago, when I was fifteen. I might even suspect my mother of secreting away the two hundred pounds of my dowry into her own coffers. Money is all-important to her.'

With gentle fingers Margaret pushed a strand of hair back beneath the linen. 'Does John know of this?' Gently, she touched the abrasion on my hairline.

'The beatings? Certainly. In a moment of pain and desolation I opened my heart to our cousin, Mistress Clere. I know that she implored my brother to pay attention to my physical plight. These beatings are not new.'

'And John did nothing?'

'John is self-interested. His mind is on other matters, as you are aware. He speaks his compassion, promises to rescue me. I know that you have asked him to address the case of a husband for me. But then he forgets about it when Sir John Fastolf calls him to negotiate for yet another estate, or when Gresham pushes every other thought from his mind. Sir John's patronage brings my brother prestige. I am worth nothing to him.'

'But you are of value. As a sister, a daughter, you will be the opening of a new door to further wealth through a good marriage. If you wed unsuitably you drag the Pastons down.' Margaret leaned to whisper, as if even the stems of lavender had ears and would gossip to Mistress Agnes. 'What about Master Stephen Scrope? Surely he could help you to escape from this misery.'

In the corridor we heard the flat slap of leather shoes, the unmistakable sound of my mother returning.

'We will not mention Stephen Scrope,' I whispered back. 'We will never mention Stephen Scrope again.'

Margaret squeezed my hand in pity, which made me feel no better.

Mistress Agnes entered, bustling in with two more baskets of drying herbs and a smile for Margaret.

'Why are you standing there with your hands empty?' she demanded of me. 'And your coif awry. You look no better than a kitchen slattern. If this work is not to your liking, I can find you something more energetic to do.'

I was dispatched to the dairy to help with the cheese-making. There was no smile for me.

★

To admit the truth of it, I had almost acquired a husband earlier that very year, in the person of Master Stephen Scrope, the subject of Margaret's whispered enquiry. He was of excellent family, the stepson of Sir John Fastolf. It was thus an alliance to be encouraged to the benefit of the Pastons. Even Sir John Fastolf, a man who always had an eye to furthering his family interests, was in agreement with such a betrothal. I would become Mistress Scrope with my own home and household. I would never be beaten again.

As I applied myself to the butter churn, enjoying the smooth movement of my arms and shoulders, the milk thickening under my ministrations, the memory returned to me with sharp clarity. My only meeting with this possible husband had been when

Master Scrope was invited to the Paston house in Norwich to meet his prospective bride. All I knew of him was that he was a widower with children from his first marriage. This would not be unacceptable to me. I would enjoy having a family before my own children. I would accept a widower. I would accept a family of stepchildren.

I was dressed for the occasion with appropriate solemnity and wealth, in woollen cloth of a rich russet. My hair was confined in a coif of gold mesh, borrowed for the occasion. My mother in a spirit of largesse lent me her crucifix on its beaded chain. Any imperfections on my skin from my mother's fingers were hidden beneath close-fitting sleeves, the cuffs embellished from a rabbit pelt. My spirits had leapt in anticipation of stepping out of this house, out of my mother's dominion, into a new home which would become my own preserve. And that of my new husband. I would be stepdaughter by marriage to Sir John Fastolf. The thought pleased me. But would Master Scrope like me?

'You might try to smile more,' Margaret had advised.

I waited in the parlour, sitting neatly with hands clasped on my lap, shivering with anxiety at the approach of horse's hooves outside. There were voices. Footsteps. The door opened.

Master Stephen Scrope entered the room, ushered in by Mistress Agnes.

Immediately, I stood.

'Elizabeth. Here is Master Scrope.' My mother's tone froze me into perfect behaviour. 'Master Scrope. Allow me to present to you my only daughter, Elizabeth.'

I curtsied. I rose to my not inconsiderable height, my expression marvellously bland. Was this the man destined to be my husband?

My hand was in his as he bowed. His fingers were rough against mine, his nails ill-kept, his lips dry against my skin. Thus my first impression, and that he was considerably shorter than I. None of which would be injurious to our union.

'Mistress Elizabeth. It pleases me to make your acquaintance.'

'Master Scrope. I am gratified.'

He led me to sit on the window seat; my mother poured cups of wine, handing one to each of us, while I surveyed him fully for the first time as he sat beside me, his shoulders hunched like a raptor in moult. He was a widower, which I knew, but not a youthful one. Master Scrope was elderly, more than fifty years, and far from robust. His hair, escaping from beneath the folds of his velvet chaperon, was thin and grey, his face lined on brow and deeply carved beside his mouth. His meagre body, clothed in a damask tunic which he probably wore to appear impressive, instead was swamped in its folds even though it only reached to mid-thigh. Nor was the rich crimson hue flattering to him. His legs were thin, the muscles of thigh and calf ill-formed. His voice contained no warmth. It was thin and not mellifluous.

How hard I had to work to conceal my horror.

'I trust you are in good health, Mistress Elizabeth,' he said.

It would be important to him, if he hoped for more children, I thought.

'My health is excellent,' I replied. I felt my throat dry. 'I trust that you too enjoy good health, sir.'

I knew that I must ask, as good manners prompted me, but it was not the most compassionate query. Master Scrope's advanced age and frailty were not the worst of it. It was the scars on his face that drew my eyes, testimony to a severe bout of smallpox. It was a disfigurement that repelled as well as elicited pity, for some of the scars still wept along the edge of his jaw. It was hard to look at him. I also thought it had left him in some pain. I found myself wondering if the rest of his body was similarly scarred. I wondered what it would be like to share a bed with him. I recalled his dry fingers scratching on mine and clenched my hand around the untasted cup that I still held on my lap.

He sniffed, and dabbed the edge of his nose on his cuff.

'As you see, mistress, I do not enjoy good health. I have suffered an illness for fourteen years that has left me severely weakened and in constant pain.'

'I am sorry, sir,' I replied. I could think of nothing else to say.

A discussion developed between Master Scrope and Mistress Agnes in which I had no part. My mother fired the questions, much in the fashion of a woodpecker seeking beetles within the bark of a tree trunk. What was the extent of Master Scrope's income? Was any of it inherited from his late wife? Would any of it be willed to his children? Did Master Scrope have any expectations from Sir John Fastolf? There would be many more discussions but this one was testing the matrimonial waters.

As my mother finally drew breath, my suitor turned to me.

'Are you willing, Mistress Elizabeth? Would you be content to become Mistress Scrope?'

Before I could even think of a reply my mother, drawing a second breath, supplied it. 'She is. My daughter is very willing.'

And there it was. I tried not to flinch when Master Scrope once more saluted my fingers before he bowed and departed. My gaze followed him as he walked with a pronounced limp, one foot dragging a little across the polished boards, that I had not noticed on his entrance. My mother returned to where I still stood, still trembling, awaiting her in the parlour.

66

'You can at least look accepting of this first meeting,' she admonished.

I was weighing the hope of escape from this house against the prospect of marriage to this disfigured man, for whom I could find so little compassion. Would I become Mistress Scrope, dreading every night in this man's bed? Would I flinch from his touch?

I was ashamed of my reaction, but he had repelled me.

'No!' I said. 'I will not.'

I could not believe that I had made that denial. Had I really said those words? I shook inwardly, for I knew that I would pay dearly for what I had done.

'By the Blessed Virgin, Eliza! Have you lost your wits? You will do as you are bid. He will be a good husband. I swear you will not get better. Now keep a still tongue in your head. We must be sure that he has sufficient stable income to provide for you, unencumbered by the demands of his children. We need to see it written down, not just from his knowledge of it. Men can prove to be untrustworthy when wills and inheritance are not to their taste.'

'Master Scrope is not to my taste,' I said, yet knowing the hopelessness of it.

'That will be decided by your brother.'

Which I knew meant that it would be decided by my mother, as John would be more than willing to shirk the responsibility.

★

I was punished for my denial of Master Scrope, kept in close confinement as if I were a prisoner in a castle. If I went to market or to visit with our neighbours I was under strict supervision, a female servant following my every step. Not a male servant. Mistress Agnes even watched my conversations with our own servants, as if I might organise a flight with one of them and cast our family into scandal.

'I will not wed him,' I repeated.

But by then I knew that she would break my spirit by one means or another. The blows and the beatings started once more. A crack, a slap from whatever was in her hand. I had not told Margaret the worst of it, about when her temper erupted and she took a cane to my sides, breaking the skin. She had been careful not to mar my face, which would have caused comment.

Nothing ever came of that letter I sent to Mistress Elizabeth Clere, a family friend and cousin of long-standing, begging for her aid. My mother continued to work out her temper on my shoulders and ribs when she was not content with a slap against my cheek.

'We will drag you to the altar, if we must,' she said. 'Better a reluctant bride in the family than an unwed spinster draining our livelihood whilst giving nothing back. You are a burden on me, Elizabeth Paston. I wish with all my heart that I did not have to live in the same house as you.'

I did not believe that she had any heart at all.

And then, I was summoned. I thought it would be to be told the date of my marriage.

'You will not wed Master Scope,' my mother informed me, satisfaction strangely warring with anger as she tore a document in half and consigned both pieces to the fire where they fell into ash in the hot flame.

I could not believe it. 'Has he refused me?'

'The Pastons have rejected him. How fortunate that we

discovered in time. Master Scrope's daughter has a claim on his estate which might be to the future drain on his own finances and to the security of a new wife. He did not tell us that, did he? We want no financial commitments elsewhere, and so I have rejected his offer for you. We must look elsewhere.'

He no longer came visiting, but my mother continued to chastise me. The bruises and welts continued. No one was willing to go behind Mistress Agnes's back to rescue me.

Thus I continued to be still unwed, to be offered to the highest bidder.

In moments of grief when my body was sore, I thought that I would have taken Master Scrope despite my physical revulsion and the span of age between us. Given his unstable health, I might have become a young widow, which would not have been without its merits. But no further offer was made.

The story of my failed chance of wedded bliss as Mistress Scrope.

Chapter Four

Margaret Mautby Paston

Norwich: autumn 1448

I had been thinking about Gresham, and I had a plan. John would not like it, but I considered that it would have its advantages.

'John! This is what I want you to do for me.'

'What?'

John was preoccupied, once more stuffing legal documents into a pannier to be tied to his saddle. I could swear that our married life was determined by that one action. He was planning to return to London, unable to neglect his legal business there any longer. The Gresham affair had taken up far too much of his time, with no change in the circumstances. Moleyns's servants with their military supporters continued to harass our tenants and collect rent from them. We could do nothing to stop it.

By the time that autumn arrived and John was fired up with new possibilities for Sir John Fastolf's increasing tally of estates, I was out of all patience. I could not bear the distance from my tenants any longer. I could not sit at home, alone except for the children, and allow Moleyns to smirk at our failure.

'Rent a house for me in Gresham,' I said.

'A house? Why? What use would that be?'

My husband was not moved to discontinue his task, until I clutched his arm to stop him, taking a sheaf of documents from him and placing them on the table, so that he must perforce listen to me.

'When you go back to London, I am going to move into a house that you are going to rent for me, in the centre of Gresham. The old manor house there is unoccupied. It is in bad repair but it is available. I am going to sit on Moleyns's doorstep, a permanent Paston presence to remind him that he is a charlatan. Any weakness in Moleyns's armoury, and I move back into our castle.'

John looked at me as if I had lost my wits.

'You can't do that, Meg.'

'Oh, but I can. And I will.' The more I thought about it, the more it seemed to be an action of exceptional logic. I would not challenge Lord Moleyns. I would do no more than remind him that his claim on my land was not just. And if I could keep the loyalty of my tenants strong, then all well and good. 'You must keep up the legal pressure in London, John. I will present a Paston voice in Gresham.'

'Not too loud I hope!'

Which persuaded me that John was weakening. 'Of course not. Moleyns will not harm me physically,' I added, 'and it will put heart into our tenants. Have you thought of that?'

Of course he had. But he had never thought that I might take this initiative and go and live cheek by jowl with my own castle with its hostile household.

'The old manor house will be large enough for my household and our two sons and our daughter, as well as the servants. We will live quietly but I will be sure that Moleyns's people will not forget me. Gresham is mine and I'll have it back. It is held only by a small group of Moleyns's servants and a Steward. What's more, I will demand that our tenants pay their rents to me rather than to Moleyns.'

John looked sceptical.

'I don't like that you could be putting yourself in harm's way.'

'There will be no danger. I will take a goodly escort to augment my household and send you frequent letters. It might just force Lord Moleyns to show his hand and come to court. When he does, you will argue our case.'

The frown was heavy on his brow.

'I think it's a bad idea. My mother would agree with me.'

'That is why we are not asking your mother. I can think of nothing better. Courage, John. It seems to be our only hope.'

'It's not courage I lack. How can I protect you if I am in London and you are in Gresham?'

'I will not need protection. What can Moleyns do to me? I swear he will not wage outright war on a woman.'

I sensed a weakening.

'What will you do if I refuse?'

'I might just send our Steward to Gresham to take the manor house and arrange the rent for me.'

A faint smile touched his mouth. 'I believe you would too.'

'And I might take Eliza with me,' I continued. 'It will do her good to get from under your mother's feet. Eliza is unhappy and your mother has no compassion in her. She can come to live with me for a little while. When you have arranged the house, you might turn your mind to a husband for her, now that Scrope has disappeared from her horizon.'

He thought it over, shuffling the documents before him. Would he agree? I knew it would be impossible for me to do this thing if John was not in accord with me.

'I will get you the house,' he said at last.

'And Eliza?'

'I'll think of Elizabeth when my mind is not full of Gresham. You must promise me that you will keep your doors locked.'

'Of course.'

'Do nothing to antagonise Moleyns.'

'I will be most discreet.'

I smiled and kissed his brow. How could I keep my doors locked? How could I be discreet? It was my intention to be seen and heard in Gresham. I would make a lot of noise that Lord Moleyns would find impossible to ignore.

*

Thus on a bright autumn day in October I, my sons and my new daughter, together with a not-conspicuously-reluctant Eliza and my household, augmented by some strong men, all moved into the large house in the village of Gresham, next to the church and little distance from the castle that was mine. It was all so familiar with its well-fortified towers and its moat. Down the length of the village street, past the church, I had a perfect view of the entrance. Did I have any fears of the repercussions of what I was doing? I do not think that I had.

I studied the house where I had chosen to make my challenge. It was sturdy, constructed of wood and roofed with thatch, large enough to accommodate us all with a hall and four chambers accessed by a dilapidated staircase. A number of outhouses offered storage, the kitchen was dark and low-beamed, yet all could be made comfortably habitable by a resourceful woman. But there was no moat, no drawbridge to keep us safe. And, on entering, every surface was redolent of neglect. It was exceedingly dirty, with a strong stench of mould and damp, which gave me something to occupy my mind. I instigated a regime of cleaning and sweeping and washing. Fires were lit, our supplies unloaded. The solar was soon set up with my bed, and there were chambers for Eliza and the children.

As I had expected, even before we were settled, my arrival stirred Moleyns's Steward, a portly man appropriately named Partridge, into activity. I became aware of him at the gates of the castle, watching my door, quick to assess the comings and goings of his new neighbour. In defiant reply I stood there, to look back at him, raising my hand in a formal little salute. There was no response. His fists were planted on his hips.

Would he come on a welcoming visit, for I knew that he had seen me?

Of course he did not.

In the following days, boxes and large packages of what I could only presume were weapons and items of armour were driven on carts past my door and delivered to the castle. Enough, I considered, to repel a siege. Or launch an attack. I took my sons to the gate of my erstwhile home, holding their hands to deter their investigation of the moat.

'This house is mine,' I informed them, 'even if I am not allowed in. One day I will return here and you will come with me and see it for yourselves. It is a Paston house. One day it will be yours.'

There was much activity to entertain them. The windows were being fortified with bars, with wickets placed at every side of the house behind which soldiery could hide, to fire arrows and handguns at the enemy. At me, I presumed. A passing villager, one of my tenants leading a plough horse, halted to join me in my surveillance.

'They're carrying in much ordinance, mistress. They've no intention of giving it up.'

'So it seems.'

'If I were you, I'd make my own defences, mistress.'

'That is good advice.'

'It wouldn't do for you to be driven out of a second home in the village.'

There was a glint in his eye. Did he seriously foresee this possibility? How humiliating that would be.

'What do you think?' I asked Eliza who had followed to stand beside me.

'Look to your own defences,' she said. 'I've no wish to return to my mother's guidance for at least a month.'

'Then come and tell me what you think I will need. I am not in the habit of ordering ordnance.'

'And you think that I am?' She laughed, a rare occurrence.

I would take my own fortifications in hand. I would preserve an outward appearance of confidence, to mask my anxiety. Within the day I sent off a letter to John.

★

To my very honourable husband,
    Send reinforcements. Merely for my own peace of mind since we have little to protect ourselves. Here is a list of what I need:
    Crossbows

75

Two or three short poll-axes to keep inside for protection
As many jacks as you can lay your hands on for the protection
of my household

★

Not that it would be good to worry John overmuch. I added a list of household items as if there were nothing uncommon about my situation.

★

It will please me if you order for me, and send:
one pound of almonds
one pound of sugar
Your busy wife M PASTON

★

All I could do now was sit tight and see how events would unfold. It was a relief when the crossbows arrived. I hoped that Partridge had seen them and knew that I was prepared. I also hoped that John would send a written reply but he did not. I could only presume that he had confidence in how I might use the armaments. Instead there was a verbal comment from the carter.

'Master John says to tell you to be sensible and keep your head down.'

It was my intention to do no such thing if I came under physical threat.

Events began to unfold and in the most astonishing of ways. Master Partridge devised a plan to cause me strange discomforts. It displeased me enormously to watch him invite guests to the castle where he held feasts and great dinners, proclaiming his master's future intentions. How dare he celebrate in my hall, using my kitchens, squandering my hams and ale and cheeses that had been stored there? How dare he sit on the dais and lord it over all my tenants who were invited, as if he would win them over? How dare he employ minstrels to sing and make music, filling my hall with jollity and celebration?

When the wind blew in the right direction, I could almost smell the roasting meats: mutton, beef, even, I could have sworn, venison. I heard the raucous celebrating from my own chamber.

'And it is my tenants who are having to provide all of this,' I complained to Eliza who clucked in sympathy. 'In effect I am paying for their debauchery!'

My head ached with a need for revenge.

It displeased me even more to be accosted in the church-yard, after one of those feasts, by a man who was my tenant as I returned to my own house from evensong, in Eliza's company, with a manservant. Master Partridge's liberal use of my ale and food had had an inebriating effect on the man. To my horror, he cornered me and ranted that I should accept what was obvious to everyone in Gresham. Moleyns was lord here, and would be for ever and a day.

'Get you gone!' he advised. 'And take your household and your foolish weapons with you. It is unseemly for a woman to threaten the incumbent lord. Tell your husband that there is no room for him in Gresham any longer. There is certainly no room for you! What can a woman do against Lord Moleyns?'

'You remain my tenant,' I replied, fixing his wavering eye with mine.

'I renounce my tenantry, mistress.'

'You cannot legally do that.'

'I advise you to have a care, mistress. You might regret it if you attack Lord Moleyns's people.'

There was ale on his breath, but I thought that did not account for his venom. He had come under the evil influence of Partridge. I wondered how many more of my tenants would say the same to my face. Even if they did not, I knew that I could not rely on them to come to my aid. They would keep their heads well below the parapet, or risk retribution from Lord Moleyns. Nor would I put them in such danger. I had already decided that there was no gain to be made by encouraging my people to pay their rents to me; indeed it would place them in more danger than they deserved. I must fight this battle on my own. Now I held my ground, even when my tenant lumbered towards me. He positively smirked.

'You'll not win, mistress.'

'We will see about that.' I took a step towards him, relieved to see that although he hesitated for a brief moment, he stepped back. Eliza took hold of my forearm and drew me away.

'Perhaps you should recommend that your husband in London buys himself a new piece of good-quality body armour, mistress.' His final words followed me at a distance as I walked smartly, keeping my knees firm. 'The streets of London are not safe, and Lord Moleyns has a strong arm and a bottomless purse. A knife can slide through leather as easily as through butter.'

Had I misheard? I glanced to Eliza. She had heard it too. Which frightened me more than all the rest.

'I think you should tell John,' she said, quickening her footsteps.

So did I. I was reluctant to worry him, but that had been a nasty threat, far more potent than Wyndham's petty tyranny. John must be warned.

★

I was not without support in my hour of need. At the beginning of November we had a welcome figure that was neither scowling, shouting obscenities, nor bearing arms other than for his own protection. My wealthy uncle Philip Berney, tall and angular, impressively clad and usually grumbling, came to visit me. No sooner had he crossed the threshold than his jaw dropped and his brows climbed almost to disappear where the brim of his velvet chaperon was pulled down to keep out the cold. He pulled off the elegant folds as he looked round.

'Your husband suggested that I come and see that you are comfortably established, Margaret. What's all this?'

'Uncle Berney,' I greeted, stepping forward to draw him into the parlour where a fire offered welcome heat, passing his heavy leather gloves and hat to Eliza. 'We are so pleased to see you. We have been short of visitors. Of a welcome kind, that is. I presume you are in good health, since you have ridden this distance.'

The greeting was not returned.

'Why are your servants wearing helmets? And jacks? Even in the house?'

I could not hide the situation from him, even if he passed the information to John.

'Because we are threatened with reprisals for living on the doorstep of my old home.'

He spent the afternoon in a twitch of apprehension. When I invited him to eat supper with us, he accepted but ate as fast as may be, refusing all but the plainest of dishes that he could devour swiftly. Barely had he chewed his way through the final mouthful of bread and roast mutton than he was donning his heavy cloak and the velvet chaperon once more, sending instructions for his horse to be made ready. He would go home immediately.

'I'll not stay. I don't like it, Margaret.' He pulled on his gloves with some force. 'But I will visit again next week if you are still here.'

'I am certain that we will still be here.'

'I don't like it!' he repeated. 'I will tell John that all is amiss. Does he know that you expect an attack at any minute?'

And with that he was mounted and gone.

A week later he had not returned, but one of his servants had, with a sad tale to tell. Uncle Berney had been kicked by a horse and so with a broken hip he was unable to come to Gresham, which was enough to rouse my compassion, so much so that I considered asking Mistress Agnes to visit him with a basket of autumn fruits and herbal remedies. Until I received a letter from John.

★

Don't waste your pity on your uncle. It was all a tale so that he need not put himself in danger by a second visit. He is seen to be fairly nimble and spry around Norwich for a man with a broken hip. Is your situation so dangerous that your uncle would refuse to visit you again? I hope that you will retreat if you come within any great peril. I have to put my trust in your good sense.

★

I read the note aloud to Eliza. I looked at her and she at me. We began to laugh. It was a relief to laugh at something.

'What will John say when he learns that you have not exactly been truthful about the dangers of our position?' Eliza asked.

'I doubt it will be complimentary. All I can hope is that we remain safe and John's delivery of armaments will protect us. I do not see that we are in any danger. We are an annoyance to Partridge, not an outright threat.'

I became aware that Eliza was watching me with worry on her brow. I regarded her quizzical look.

'What are you thinking?'

'That it might be peaceful living with Mistress Agnes again.'

But there was nothing to laugh about by January.

Gresham: Tuesday 28th January 1449

'Mistress. Mistress.'

There was a hammering at my chamber door, enough to raise the dead.

It was early, before we had even broken our fast, when I was still clasping my keys at my waist, much in the manner of Mistress Agnes, which made me smile with grim appreciation. I was becoming a matriarch in my own household. We had yet to say our household prayers. I heard Eliza moving around in her chamber next to mine. I could see no need for such urgency, unless the well was frozen or the ale had turned sour overnight.

'One moment.'

Fastening a final pin to my coif, I cast a glance around. All was as it should be in the chamber of a careful tenant. I took a deep breath, prepared to face the day.

The knocking on my door came again.

'Now, mistress! Now. I swear it's more than urgent.'

My Steward was most peremptory. I opened the door, intending to upbraid him for his strident tones, but he grabbed my arm in his distress, pulling me to follow. Seeing the wild emotion writ large on his face I made no complaint.

'Come and see, mistress. What do we do?'

He urged me into another of the upper rooms where my children slept and all was awry with the detritus of the young; my maid having abandoned her domestic tasks was peering through the window. The room provided us with an excellent view of the gate and entrance from the road. I expected it to be quite deserted at this time of day except perhaps for one of the villagers driving his oxen to the fields, or the priest making his way to the church. What I saw brought me to a moment of sheer panic that gripped my throat.

I thrust open the window and leaned out to take in the full scene.

There, congregating before my door, was a force of men in Moleyns livery; the complicated melee of black and white stripes and gold chevron against red and green was more than clear. Beneath the livery I could see that they were wearing every sort of warlike protection. Cuirasses, jacks, brigandines, all topped with salets that gleamed in the late-rising sun. So many men that I could not count them. Where had they all come from? They must have gathered under the protection of darkness to achieve this element of surprise, all armed to the teeth. They stood quietly as if waiting for a signal. Leaning further and looking down, so much so that my Steward grabbed my arm, I could see before my door the man who was in control of this nightmare.

I withdrew inside again.

'They surround the house, mistress. On all sides.' My Steward announced the appalling news, releasing me.

I tried to marshal my thoughts. My Steward was looking at me for direction. We had a mere twelve men in our household to protect us. We could not possibly hold this force at bay. I was left with little choice: flee in ignominy, to be taken captive in my garden, or sit tight, refuse to open the doors, and force Moleyns to show his hand.

'Well, mistress?'

He almost hopped with anxiety.

A Paston did not flee. Neither did a Mautby.

I walked onto the upper landing and raised my voice so that all would hear.

'Make sure all the doors are locked. Arm every man. Keep clear of the windows in case they decide to use arrows against us. Then we wait to hear the demands from our neighbour.'

How I wished that John were here. What did I know about repelling what might become a siege? But John could not save me. Nor were any friends near enough. Master John Damme was a good mile away and he might well be in London too.

'Eliza!' I called.

And there she was beside me, her eyes wide with horror but her voice strong.

'Do what you must,' she said. 'Leave the children in my care.'

I squeezed her hand in gratitude as she set herself to dress and feed them.

Meanwhile there was a stir in the force gathered below me. They were bringing forward a hefty tree trunk that left nothing to my imagination. They were going to batter down my door.

The captain looked up, his attention drawn by my leaning from the window once again. He grinned.

'You see the force drawn up against you, mistress. Do you and yours come out? Or do we come in and drive you out?'

'This house is mine, and I will stay here.' I slammed the window shut so that I could not hear his response. Would I order my men to attack? It would do no good. It would only bring down certain death on them. Twelve men against dozens would have no impact. It would be like casting a handful of pebbles to prevent a landslide.

Then, because there was nothing more for me to do, I stood in my parlour with Eliza and my children and waited, aware of a shattering silence which was all the more menacing. I found myself praying for a miracle of deliverance, knowing in my heart that it was impossible. There would be only one outcome here this day.

I lifted little Margery into my arms when she became fractious, then flinched, instinctively covering her head with my hand. The vicious crash was the first signal that the ram was being applied. And again. The whole house shook. And again, followed by the crack of wood and a victorious cheer and the hacking of axes against the doorframe. The clatter of feet as men rushed into my hall.

And then a hammering on the wood and plaster wall of my

parlour where we had taken refuge with the door barred. Axes were still being swung with enthusiasm. They were going to break through the wall. A key in the lock and bolts on the doors would not keep them at bay. Dust and plaster fell in a shower on our heads, dislodged from the walls and ceiling.

A hole appeared in the wall. It grew bigger, the wooden laths shattered.

I could do nothing but push the children away towards the window and wait. I had challenged this man, and here was the answer to my challenge. I sat in my chair beside the fireplace, as if I were the Queen herself waiting to welcome a foreign ambassador, and summoned all my courage. I watched the hole grow bigger with every blow, in horror at the lengths to which this man would go. He was destroying my house around me.

I wiped the dust from my face with my sleeve.

The breach in my wall was now large enough to allow a man to enter. And another. Then the captain of the force, with others behind him who proceeded to demolish the wall in its entirety.

Still I sat, the mistress of the house, even though it was falling down around my ears. Eliza stood with the children, my daughter now transferred to her arms. We remained silent.

'Mistress Paston.' The captain bowed before me with empty courtesy, removing his salet and slapping the debris of plaster from his sleeves.

'Well?' I raised my chin. 'By what right do you trespass on my property? By what right do you destroy my property?'

'By the right of this, mistress.' He raised his sword.

'And will you use it against me?'

'No need. I do not kill women – unless they stand in my way.' His grin was feral. 'You are to come with me, Mistress Paston.'

'I will not. This is my home. I have the documents of legal tenancy. It will be common assault to remove me from my own hearth.'

'I'll not bother to deny it, mistress. I'm not here about legality. You are a nuisance. Documents or not, we are here to ensure that you leave Gresham. And since you refuse to walk from here on your own feet ...'

He signalled to one of his men.

'Bring that woman and the children.'

And then to two more of his henchmen, who approached me, leering from ear to ear, enjoying my helplessness. One on either side. They lifted the chair with me in it as if it weighed nothing, and bore me out through the space where my wall had been.

I was breathless with shock, frozen with fear.

Then here was no time for dignity. Here was no time for the good manners that had been bred into me since my childhood. Clenching my hands into fists, I belaboured my two gaolers on heads and shoulders, using all the force I could muster. I kicked out with my feet, too, delighting in the contact when one of the men hissed in pain.

To no avail.

'Easy, mistress. You wouldn't want to hurt yourself.'

I did not stop. I caught him a blow across his ear.

'I'll not be the one who is hurt!'

They laughed, pinned down my legs by simply wrapping my skirts around me and manoeuvred me out of my house into the garden where they set the seat down amidst the herbs and winter grass.

'Now stay there and let us get on with this.'

Fury had replaced my initial fear, now that it was clear that they would not kill me.

'Send my children out to me,' I demanded. Would they keep them as hostage for my good behaviour? But there they came, Eliza pushing the boys ahead of her and still carrying Margery, her composure remarkable in the circumstances.

'We do not wage war on children, mistress,' the captain growled.

I was on my feet, clutching the boys to me. They had harmed no one, not even my armed men beyond a blow or two.

'Here's the penalty for being a nuisance on the doorstep of my master.'

I stepped forward, unable to just let it happen, But Eliza grasped my wrist.

'Do nothing,' she said. 'To retaliate will only bring worse punishment down on your head.'

'Excellent advice, mistress. Take it.'

I knew that Eliza spoke from her own experiences. Their patience with me might evaporate and my people might suffer if I resisted further. I nodded and she released me.

By now we had an audience from the village, agog to see what was amiss. Their silence surprised me. Many of them were my tenants but fear kept their mouths closed. There would be no help here.

Surrounded as we were by this hostile force, we were made to watch as they lavished destruction on the house that had been my home for so many months. The posts were cut so that the walls collapsed. All the chambers were entered, the contents rifled, the coffers borne out. All my possessions snatched away by Moleyns's minions to be picked over and squandered.

The house was uninhabitable when they had finished. I was without both clothes and household artefacts. All were gone, and there was nothing I could do but bear witness to this terrible destruction. I sank back onto the chair and noted every possession that was carried from the wreck of my home. So little time it took to make of me a beggar.

'You have robbed me of everything.' It was all I could say in the end.

'Take yourself off out of Gresham, mistress, for the good of your health. You're a brave woman, I'll say that, but there's no place for you here and my lord Moleyns is not a man to tolerate further opposition.'

I looked at him, but pity was not what I wanted.

I had only one choice since the villagers, through fear for their own families, were in no mind to be helpful. I rose from my chair, the only piece of furniture in one piece, gathered my children and my household and set out for the sanctuary of the manor of Sustead, a mile away, on foot, with all the remaining dignity that I could muster. It was not far, but far enough for me to experience all the agony of the destitute. We arrived at the door of our friends John and Elizabeth Damme like vagabonds with nothing but the clothes we stood up in. The humiliation was unbearable. Gresham had meant so much to me. I chided myself for my foolishness in believing that I could successfully defy Moleyns, but my defeat hurt me like a blow from a bladed weapon.

★

Without any words of endearment I wrote starkly to John about my present whereabouts. This was a matter of business and my heart was a cold lump of ice in my chest. I needed to see him, to learn what we could do next. More urgently, I was in need of his comfort. After all the uproar around us, it was a necessity to feel his arms around me and to be able to rest against him, just for a short time. I would like some words of affection.

John arrived at Sustead, cold, windswept and not best pleased, wrapped around in a heavy cloak which he shed abruptly into the arms of a servant. He regarded me, where I stood at the opposite side of the chamber. Mistress Damme and Eliza had tactfully faded from the scene, sensing a domestic interlude.

'Oh, John!'

He regarded me for a long silent moment. 'You look as if you have not suffered greatly.' He lifted his head, listening. In the distance Elder John was shouting, Young John, who had fast become Jonty within the family at my insistence, simply because of too many complications, replying with laughter. 'My children also appear to be safe.'

Had he feared for my safety? It did not seem so.

'They are safe, but we have lost everything, all we owned in the Gresham house. All was stolen from me.'

'Tell me its value.'

I should have expected that question before all others.

'I say one hundred pounds. Moleyns's man says twenty pounds, which is just foolishness.'

John scowled at me. Loss of money always made him scowl. 'I said that you should not go to Gresham.'

'But I did. Who is to support our tenants if I do not? Moleyns has an army at his beck and call, some say a thousand men, cast loose from the wars, and so prepared to serve any man with the money to pay them. Our tenants suffer. Their complaints are ignored. They are threatened with beatings, with losing their homes and land and all their possessions.'

'What good did you do?'

I took a deep breath and confessed. 'I could do nothing. And I don't regret it.'

'Well, I do.'

'We are not harmed.'

'We are weaker than ever, because you pushed Moleyns to retaliate.'

There was no comfort to be had. There was no resting in his strong arms while he reassured me.

'Are you going to come any further into the room,' I asked, 'or will you leave immediately?'

John grunted and complied, coming to warm himself by the fire, but still as chilly as the weather beyond the walls.

'I persuaded the Earl of Oxford, who is Justice of the Peace in Norfolk, to demand recompense from Moleyns's men,' he said.

'So that is good,' I suggested hopefully.

John was gloomy. 'No. The Earl went to Gresham, but Moleyns's thugs barred the gates against him and refused to let him enter. No threats or entreaties could get Oxford past the door.'

I knew that as a good wife I should touch his hand, soothe his concerns. I remained at a distance.

'Then we have failed. What do I do now?'

He thought for a moment.

'Stay here if Mistress Damme will allow it. Just in case I can manoeuvre a change in the Gresham situation.' Then, as if it were an afterthought, 'I regret that you were put in this position, Meg. I should have had more care for you. I should have forbidden you to come in the first place.'

The first sign of mellowing, perhaps even of a touch of guilt. It made me hopeful.

'Yes. But in truth you did warn me, and I insisted.'

I mellowed too.

I walked towards him and at last his arms closed around me. Here was the comfort of which I was so in need. For a little while we simply stood together, the house safe and quiet around us as if nothing were amiss. Until another shout from Jonty broke the idyll.

'I would be pleased if you did not frighten me again before the end of the year,' John said, releasing me so that he could look at me. 'I have no wish to lose you quite yet.'

'I have no intention of becoming lost!'

My sorrow at the distance between us ebbed and I returned his kisses.

I waved John off the next morning after a night together that had seen some good measure of reconciliation. Yet our future loomed. His expression was grim, but then so was mine. Nothing had been settled.

★

All came to a head at the end of the month of February when water lay on the fields and the tracks were well-nigh impassable. A word came to me. A whispered word, from one of Mistress Damme's servants as she discovered me inspecting linen for mould. The damp weather encouraged it to grow; the linen needed to be turned and sprinkled with a mix of lavender and oregano to remove the black spots. It was a soothing task, if anything could soothe my mind.

'There are rumours, mistress,' the girl said.

'I no longer listen to rumours,' I replied, more sharply than I had intended. There had been no change in our circumstances here at Sustead.

'There's a plot to kidnap you from Sustead and take you captive, mistress, back to Gresham.'

My attention was caught. 'Kidnap?' I whispered back. *Kidnap?* 'To what purpose?'

All I received was a shrug as she hurried off, leaving me to consider. The intention might be to hold me captive to force John to give up his pretensions. Or it might be one designed to create malicious entertainment. I found myself looking out of the window, expecting to see a body of Moleyns's armed men come to drag me away. And what would become of Eliza and my children?

'Have you heard any disturbing rumours when you have been in the village?' I questioned Eliza.

'Only the Gresham tenants who are having to dip deep into their bags of coin to keep Moleyns content. He is a hard man.'

'Any rumours about me?'

Eliza managed a tight smile. 'Only that you are as hard as Moleyns.'

'Ha! I'll prove them right!'

But that did not prove that the threat against me did not exist. I must write to John. But what good would that do? It would take too long and what would John advise that I could not devise for myself? In a small corner of my heart I knew that on this occasion I could not rely on him to rescue me, and so I must make my own preparations. I considered the secrecy of the message, passed by a servant. Were there other servants in Mistress Damme's household who would work for Moleyns? Whatever my plan, I must not announce it for fear of alerting the enemy. It would not do for me to be captured on the road.

I must not even tell Mistress Damme.

Thus with a devious care for detail that I had always suspected in me, I made my plans. Yes, I could definitely be as single-minded as Lord Moleyns.

Packing the meagre possessions lent to me and my children by Mistress Damme, I announced that I would take my children to Norwich, to have new clothes made for all of us, including Eliza. I would return to Sustead in less than three weeks, if Mistress Damme were willing to accommodate us further. I kissed her farewell and set out at dawn with my little household, before most people were awake. Not a whisper that I was leaving for good. Not even to Eliza.

'Why do we leave so early?' she asked, yawning in the gloom of the late dawn.

'To make good time,' I replied. Time for what I did not explain, even when she slid a suspicious glance in my direction.

Every inch of the journey, 1 listened for signs of being followed. I urged on the horses that pulled our borrowed wagon. I resented any halts that we had to make. Only when Oxnead came into view behind the trees did I allow my senses to relax.

Mistress Agnes was as welcoming as it was possible for her to be. She eyed Eliza.

'So you have returned.'

'Yes, mother.'

'You will have to work far harder here than you have been used to at Gresham. There is no place for leisure here.'

'There was no leisure at Gresham,' I replied in her defence. 'Eliza has been of great use to me, not least in her courage when under personal threat.'

'If you say so.' Mistress Agnes was in a sour mood. 'What can I do for you, now that you have finally accepted that Gresham will never again be yours? A pity that my son could not get any of his fine friends in London to stand against Moleyns and the Duke of Suffolk. Why was the Fastolf knight not shouting for your cause? Why could he not send you sufficient armed men to drive Moleyns off?'

Which ruffled me but I would not show it. 'I know nothing of Sir John's thoughts in this, but your son has not abandoned the cause,' I said. What else could I say? Eliza vanished into the fastness of the house without a farewell beyond an agonised glance in my direction.

'Why did you not wait for my son to rescue you from Sustead, rather than riding about the country on your own, open to attack?'

My patience was now stretched too thinly for a polite reply.

'Because I could not rely on my husband to come and get me. So I am here, and I hope safer than I was.'

The result of my exchange of opinion with Mistress Agnes was that she offered the use of the Paston Norwich house for as long as we needed. A weight of worry dropped from me. What would John say, knowing that I had left the scene of our failure? I was past caring. Haunting me was the returning nightmare of my being carried from my home by violent men, being made subject to such cruel humiliation and lack of dignity. I did not think that I would ever forget it.

Chapter Five

Elizabeth Paston

Oxnead: 1450

Alone in my chamber in Oxnead, I was dragged low with a raw melancholia. Gresham had not been a happy experience. We seemed to live in fear for much of the time, but I had enjoyed Margaret's company and there had been no demands on me to behave in a certain manner or watch for my mother's presence. I had enjoyed it. It taught me what family life could be, with warmth and compassion and tender care for the children in their midst. Margaret did not strike her sons. She did not beat her daughter. Even the attack at Gresham had made my blood race with excitement. What a strange balance, between fearing for my life, yet feeling so alive and free from blame.

Soon Margaret would be on her way to the Paston house in Norwich, taking the children and the promise of a new babe, leaving me to Mistress Agnes. Since there was nothing I could do about it, I must set myself to tolerate my drab existence, becoming invisible if I must.

I changed my garments to an over-gown of plain, hard-wearing wool in some drab, dark colour that I barely noticed, tucking my hair into a coif, both suitable for the task of polishing two new coffers that my mother Agnes had bought, doubtless for the safe storage of her coin. But then, driven by memory, I opened the lid of a small oak chest where items of fine linen and embroidered girdles were stored. Removing the layers, putting them aside, I revealed what I had hidden below, shielded from view. From my mother's view. I would not wish her to know that I repined over lost chances.

For there had been other offers for my hand in the years since the disaster of Master Scrope's visit. The Paston family had not been neglected by those intent on making a valuable marriage alliance. Here, wrapped in cloth and dried lavender flowers, was a wretched collection of tokens of those men who had sought and failed to gain my hand. I would not shed tears over them, for there would be no purpose in it, but they tugged at my heart a little.

There was a knock on the door. Immediately I closed the lid on the coffer, keeping my hands splayed there. But it would not be my mother. She would not knock. She would enter as if hoping to discover me engaged in some sin even if it were merely sloth.

I crossed the room to open the door. There stood Margaret.

'I thought you had already gone.'

'I came to say farewell. And to thank you for your help and companionship.'

'I did nothing.'

'You did everything. I am sorry you were not made welcome here.'

'It is not new to me.'

'Shall I ask that you come with me to Norwich?'

'No. Better that I remain here. Come in.' I closed the door after her. 'Thank you for taking me to Gresham.'

Margaret smiled. 'Even if you lived in fear of your life.'

'I felt alive.' I admitted what I had been thinking, as I would to no one else.

'What were you doing? You had an air of guilty conscience about you when you opened the door.'

'Reliving my past hopes, and the death of them.'

I opened the coffer once more. There was no reason why Margaret should not see. I laid open before her the bare bones of my life.

After the Scrope disaster, we had been approached by Master William Knyvett, a man of means from Suffolk. He had been promising. Another widower, his wife and child dead, he was heir to the family land and so seeking another wife. Not without income of his own, and with no claims on his money or property, he had seemed suitable enough, even to Mistress Agnes. In pursuit of a betrothal, he had sent me a length of fine lace to trim a new gown.

Now I held it lightly in my hand, smoothing the delicate threads, before handing it to Margaret who lifted it to the light, clicking her tongue at the slight discolouration along on edge.

'I never met Master Knyvett,' I explained. 'Nothing ever came of it, after that first enquiry.' Did my mother drive too hard a bargain, or refuse me a suitable dowry in spite of my father's will? Had John not given it his full consideration, allowing my mother to do as she pleased? 'Perhaps Master Knyvett had not possessed sufficient income to fulfil my father's terms.' I sighed a little, when I had promised myself that I would not give in to the fierce rejection of that slighting. 'Master Knyvett faded from my life before he ever truly entered it, apart from this fine edging which, you have seen, is showing signs of yellowing. I have never used it, but it is really too exquisite to remain secreted away. Master Knyvett had desired me enough to give me something of value.'

I retrieved the lace from Margaret, refolded and replaced it. Perhaps I should make use of such fine handiwork, but my heart was not in it.

'Have you any remedy for removing such signs of age?' I asked.

'Soak in white vinegar,' Margaret replied promptly in house-wifely mode, her interest now elsewhere. She lifted out a pair of gloves with gilding around the cuffs. 'Now these are very fine. What man of distinction gave you these? I had no idea that you had been sought after by a man of such means.'

'Why would you, since nothing came of this either? These were the gift of Sir William Oldhall, no less, chamberlain to the Duke of York, a distinguished man even if he was as weighed down in years as Master Scrope. Again I never met him, but I understood from John that he was not scarred. I was willing enough, indeed proud that so important a man would even consider me. It had seemed that so were John and my mother willing to enter into negotiations. Any connection with the Duke of York, so powerful at Court, would not come amiss.'

Although perhaps a Beaufort connection would have been even more advantageous since the Duke of Somerset was highly regarded by the Queen and both were intent on destroying any power the Duke of York might claim at Court through his royal blood. But neither connections had worked for my benefit. I pulled on the gloves, smoothing the soft kid over my fingers, imagining them as the hands of Dame Oldhall.

'Sir William did not suit the high Paston standards of unentailed land and income any more than Master Scrope had done,' I explained.

I sighed and stripped off the gloves, refolding them with care for the gilding.

'I would have liked the opportunity to flaunt my superiority over Mistress Agnes Paston,' I admitted.

Margaret laughed. 'I am sorry that you could not.'

For a moment regret almost brought tears to my eyes. I mopped them quickly away with my sleeve.

'And then, after Sir William …'

Here was a folded document, now much creased and dog-eared from constant reading, with *Mistress Elizabeth Paston* written on the fold in a florid hand. A poem. A love poem. If I smiled at this memory, it was a pitiable one, although the verse was sweet enough.

I read it out aloud:

★

You belong to me: I belong to you:
That you must regard as absolutely true.
You are locked in my heart,
Lost is the key,
And there you must remain
For all eternity.

★

'Well!' Margaret was impressed.

'Did John ever write to you such a poem, when you were first wed?'

'Never. He would be more likely to send me an order of replevin to deal with.'

'And what is a replevin?'

Margaret clicked her tongue against her teeth, as if every Paston daughter ought to know such intricacies of estate management. 'A case to reclaim some piece of property wrongfully taken.' Which forced me to smile, it being so apposite. 'You must know that property takes precedence over poetry in John's head.'

'How true. And what value poetry?' It was a dismal reflection for me. 'How fanciful a thought is expressed here.'

'I doubt that he wrote it himself, although I agree it is not in a clerkly hand.'

Margaret, rarely driven by soft emotions, refolded the note. Although patently untrue, I had enjoyed the sentiment of Master John Clopton, a young country squire making a name for himself in Norfolk as a lawyer.

For a few weeks Master John Clopton was my hope of rescue. I appreciated his romantic turn of mind. I admired his age and appearance, and the manner in which his dark hair curled against his cheek, for this was a suitor that I had seen when in Norwich. Master John Clopton was young and personable which was all I could ask for. How my hopes had risen, to greet me every morning as the sun rose.

'So why did nothing come of it? The Cloptons are a good family.'

I shrugged a little. 'I know not. A marriage settlement was drawn up between my mother and the groom's father, William Clopton of Long Melford. I began to plan my marriage clothing. I held my breath that it would all come to fruition and I would exchange vows with him. Why was the planning abandoned, when it had gone so far along the path to fulfilment? Certainly I did not repulse him. I could see no problem with his rank in Norfolk society.'

'Perhaps he was simply not rich enough.'

'Or perhaps he met another woman who could bring him a better advantage and he changed his mind. Mistress Agnes turned her back on the Clopton family and the proposed settlement.'

I took the poem from her and returned it to the coffer. I admitted to knowing it by heart.

Margaret tried to bolster my spirits. 'So many invisible suitors, but you would not be the only girl to be courted in this manner, until the marriage documents were signed.'

'You are very kind, Meg, but I do not believe it. I am no longer a young girl.'

We were interrupted before she could make another trite reply.

'Elizabeth! Come down here! Are you wasting time? What are you doing?'

I replaced the linen and closed the lid, letting it drop with a little thump, as my spirits fell into an abyss of despair. Was there any hope? As my family became more and more desperate to find me a husband, my mother's accents became sharper. I must not linger in my room when she summoned me in such a tone.

Why had they all failed? Because my suitors were not wealthy enough to meet Paston expectations. Because my mother would prefer to keep my dowry of two hundred pounds under her own greedy eye, with the result that I had come to the anxious point in my life when I would marry almost any man, no matter how decrepit in years or ill-favoured. I was well into my twenty-second year with no prospect of a husband. I would live and die a spinster, firmly under the hard hand of my mother, until her soul left this earth and that particular hand was stilled for ever.

'Why does she dislike me so?' I asked, full of anguish and not for the first time.

'Because you are the evidence of her failure, and your mother does not like to fail. That is all.'

Margaret was regarding me with a mix of compassion and impatience.

'Well, Mistress Paston?' I asked with no attempt to hide my lack of hope. 'What is your advice now?'

'Does she still beat you?'

'Yes.'

'Then take any man who offers. However old, however great his afflictions. In fact, the older the better. Your best hope is to become a rich widow. I will talk to John again.'

'If John can bring any gentleman to this door, with an estate that is halfway respectable, I will fall on my knees in gratitude and kiss his feet.'

Chapter Six

Margaret Mautby Paston

Norwich: 1450

This was a year of troubles for us. When all grew to such immense proportions that it was too much for me to bear, it drove me one morning to take refuge in the Cathedral. I rarely worshipped there, and knew not the priests, but I could not make confession to my own priest, and certainly not to Master Gloys. I had a deep desire for anonymity in the vast impersonal space of the arches, in the great pillars that hemmed me in, in the musical angels in the windows, splashing vibrant colour on me and the stonework. It was silent except for a distant murmur of priestly voices as I made my way towards the Lady Chapel where I knelt before the statue of the Blessed Virgin. The vestiges of incense hung in the air.

'Blessed Virgin.'

I raised my eyes in supplication.

But this was not what I wanted. The Lady's robes were stiff with gold from neck to hem, encrusted thickly with gems, ropes of jewels entwining her throat, rings sparkling on her fingers as she held out the Christ Child to be adored. Her veil was rigid with precious stones, framing a face that was distant and cold. This was the Queen of Heaven, resplendent in her saintly glory and power. How could the Queen of Heaven have any interest in listening to my worldly anxieties?

I stood, ruffled at my own presumption, bowed in apology, and moved quickly into a dim and empty side chapel dedicated to a saint I did not know. This is what I wanted. Once again, I knelt before a statue of the Blessed Virgin, this time in all her simplicity as a Virgin and a Mother. I studied the eternal tranquillity of her face, the simple blue of her robe, the pristine whiteness of her veil, the gold of her halo. Wearing no jewels, her hands were held out, palm up in supplication towards sinners who could approach and make confession. She would listen to me. She would understand. She would give me peace.

I began my petitions, raising my eyes no higher than the hem of her robe.

'Hail Mary, full of Grace, the Lord is with thee

Blessed art thou among women, and blessed is the fruit of thy womb, Jesus.'

I took a breath. Where to begin?

'Edmund is dead,' I said. 'I pray for his soul.'

John's brother Edmund had died at Clifford's Inn where he had been engaged in law, following in the footsteps of all the Pastons. A fever they said, and he only twenty-five years old. All that promise, all that energy, obliterated in a matter of hours. We mourned him, as a beloved son and brother should be mourned. For once, briefly, Mistress Agnes was without words and took to her chamber in her grief. Edmund was laid to rest in London where he had died.

When I looked up the Lady's eyes were full of sorrow which encouraged me to continue.

'Gresham is still a problem. You know all about Gresham, Blessed Lady.'

Gresham remained as ulcerous as a boil on our scullion's neck, for which I applied the root of the cuckoo-pint, beaten up with hot ox-dung, to the affliction. I wished the abscess of Gresham was as easy to cure, in spite of my suffering scullion's shrieks of pain. The Blessed Virgin did not need to know about that.

'I pray that Gresham could be returned to us. I pray for your protection for our tenants who are punished and live in fear. I ask your guidance for the Bishop of Winchester who has failed miserably to move anyone in our favour. And I ask for your hasty retribution against our enemy Moleyns. We cannot move him. Perhaps a blast of righteous anger will bring him to his knees.'

So many petitions. I was not yet finished.

'I ask forgiveness for my lack of tolerance, Lady, but Mistress Agnes is a constant irritant. Does she need to gripe quite so consistently about Edmund leaving all his wealth to his brother John rather than to her? She needs patience too.'

The Lady looked severe. Yes I was intolerant.

I felt anger raise its talons to scrape and grip hard.

'And if that is not enough there is the Duke of Suffolk!' I said, more loudly than I had intended.

A passing priest slid in my direction.

'Can I be of help, mistress?'

I shook my head, bending my head as if in fervent prayer, as indeed I was. For behind and above all those who would attack and belittle us, like a sinister cloud, billowed the powerful influence of the de la Pole Duke of Suffolk. We had no such influence on our side. I raised my eyes to the calm plaster face, for here was a concern that ate at me night and day.

'Blessed Lady, I am afraid for John's safety. It would be so simple for an enemy to cut him down in the street in Norwich, even in London, or slip poison into his cup when he frequents an alehouse. Will I see him carried home drenched in blood or vomiting from some noxious substance?'

I could read no reply in her still repose. I clenched my hands around my rosary in final petition, placing at her unshod feet all the rest of my concerns as rapidly as I could for fear that she might lose patience with me.

'All my thanks, Blessed Lady, for the blessings that are so often hidden from me under the layers of tribulation. I pray for my children, that they will be kept safe, and for the new child, a healthy boy whom we have named Edmund. I pray for Elizabeth that she may find a husband. I offer thanks for such good friends as John and Elizabeth Damme.' And then as a loyal subject: 'I pray for King Henry and his new Queen Margaret, that they will be blessed with a son and heir before too long. They have been wed five years now. I imagine she is becoming anxious.'

Standing, I bowed and lit a candle. And then another, for my litany of complaint seemed to demand more than one, and when my conscience was touched with guilt, I retraced my earlier steps and lit a third before the mighty Queen of Heaven, the small flame bringing the precious gems into flickering life. The Blessed Virgin always listened, whatever her raiment, even if she did not always reply as instantly as I might hope.

As I opened the door into my hall, stepping into the warmth of a patch of sunlight as the sun moved round on its daily course, a thought came to me. What we needed was a change in direction, a way to safeguard John's inheritance for our children. It would be a radical change. Would it reap any benefits for us? John would not relish it, but it seemed to me that he must do it. I would tell him, although it was not a prospect that I would commit to paper. He must come home, but how to achieve it?

In my chamber I took up pen and paper and began to write, for once dispensing with a clerk.

★

Our little son Edmund is suffering from a fever. I know that you still feel the recent loss of your brother, his namesake. I do not fear for the child's life, but I would appreciate a visit from you, to assuage my maternal anxieties. Your mother, full of tales of death and suffering, does not make good company, and Eliza has no experience of raising children. I am in need of your presence here at the first opportunity.

Have pity on me, your troubled wife, and on your young family.

★

Dishonest as I knew my device to be, it was the only means I could think of to lure John speedily back to Norwich. If we did nothing, we might just lose all we had. If we followed the unlikely path I had in mind, victory might well be ours. It seemed heartless, even callous, but nothing else would bring John from London with alacrity after receiving my plea, and bring him I must.

★

When John arrived as expected within two weeks, I welcomed him with kisses. He observed the children who clamoured to be noticed, including young Edmund who squawked in his cradle. When, having kissed each one, he sent the older ones off with a package of honeyed figs he had brought with him, we were at last alone.

'Edmund looks remarkably well,' he said.

'Indeed. He had recovered almost before I had sent the letter. My prayers to the Blessed Virgin were answered with great speed. The fever cooled almost overnight.'

'How remarkable.'

'So I thought. But it was too late to recall my messenger.'

'Of course it was. Well, I am here.' We sat side by side on a cushioned settle before the fire in the quiet of the parlour, my hands in his. I knew that he had forgiven me for demanding his time. 'Now that I see that none of my household is in danger, perhaps you will tell me why I am summoned away from important business?'

He was moved to award me with a kiss to both my cheeks.

I did not hesitate. 'I have a suggestion.'

The door opened. In came Mistress Agnes, to plant herself in front of her son. There was a missal in her hand. Mistress Agnes did not often find the need to resort to urgent prayer in the middle of the day. She had arrived in Norwich the previous day in some agitation about the affair of the Paston wall, but would not talk about it in any detail with me.

'I need conversation with you, my son.'

John stood, awarding his mother a little bow. 'I thought you were at Oxnead.'

'I was. There is a problem that needs your time.'

'Can not my brother William deal with it?'

William was fourteen years old. He was already following in family footsteps, learning the law as a student at Cambridge and with as much ambition as the rest of them.

'No.'

'Will you sit?'

'No. I will not sit.'

'Then I promise that I will give it my time.' John sat again. I felt his fingers tighten around mine, and I responded, afraid that I would be put aside for whatever it was that had recently ruffled Mistress Agnes's feathers. John responded suitably, to my pleasure. 'But first I need a little time alone with my wife.'

'Then it seems that I must wait.'

She turned on her heel.

'I have earned another dose of her hostility. It is not hard to do. Is it so urgent?' John asked.

'I think it will be the critical matter of the wall and the road at Paston, her ongoing dispute that you renegotiated with the rector.'

John breathed out slowly. 'The wall again. Very well.' I saw as his legal mind switched from his mother's problems back to mine. 'Your suggestion, Meg. You are always full of suggestions. Why not write it to me?'

'Not this one.'

'Tell me then. Why do I have a sense that I will not like it?'

'It is about a patron.'

A furrow appeared deep between his brows.

'Have you approached anyone recently?' I asked.

'No.'

It was now or never. I launched into my idea, trying not to

recall that my last strategy in Gresham had not gone particularly well for us.

'We need a man with political power. You must talk to the Duke of Suffolk.'

'Suffolk?' I read disbelief in every line of his face. Had I expected him to receive this suggestion with joy? 'You have brought me all this way to Norwich, under the pretext of my son's ill health, to suggest the Duke of Suffolk? By the Rood, Margaret!'

'Yes, I have.' I released his hand to grip his cuffs, noting that they were a little worn around the edges and that he would need a new houppelande unless he was to appear nothing but an underpaid drab lawyer at Court. 'The mighty Duke, who governs all things in this part of the world, is our only hope. The man who has more influence in his little finger than any other local magnate will ever have in his whole body.'

'To what value will my approaching him be? Moleyns has his ear.'

'You must persuade him. The Duke of Suffolk is the only man who can change this mess of Gresham in our favour. He is the only man who can give us some stability. Without a patron of his status, John, you are vulnerable to every thief and trickster who crosses our path.'

'I will not bend the knee before Suffolk. He will laugh in my face. Or kick me out of his house on my arse.'

I would not retreat. I had discovered all I needed to know about pursuing a policy at Gresham.

'It is either the Duke of Suffolk or the King,' I said. 'There is no value in approaching the Duke of Norfolk who, as you say yourself, is as untrustworthy as a hound-hunted boar.'

The Duke of Norfolk, now Earl Marshall to the King, was

often to be seen in Norwich, as ostentatious as Suffolk in his clothing and entourage but lacking his talents.

'And the King will listen? It has been proved that neither man will listen to me.'

'You have too much pride, John.'

I could see him resenting the fact that all his attempts had failed. He despised the fact that we were at the mercy of those who could manipulate the courts with threats and handouts. He despised the fact that his wife took him to task, and his mother would do likewise within the hour about the petty matter of a wall.

I ran my hand over his hair, smoothing it, smoothing his hurt feelings.

'I know it will be hard, but I have every confidence in you. Try this one last chance John. You can be persuasive. It might just work. I have faith in you. If he wants peace in Norfolk, this is the way for Suffolk to help us. To heal the divisions between Paston and Moleyns. He might wish to be seen as a peacemaker. Think of the weight it will bring to his reputation, like the gilding on a statue of a saint in the Cathedral. Suffolk will not waste any opportunity to win the good wishes of the King.'

I had my arguments well-marshalled.

'Well, I might.' John caught my hand and held it to his chest, but he was not convinced. 'I foresee failure. Not that I don't think you have a good argument. But there are troubles at Court that might impact on us. Suffolk has fallen somewhat from favour.'

'Oh.' It was indeed news to me. So much for my plans. 'Is it serious?'

'I think it will be.' John leaned back, stretching his legs as he prepared to inform me of Court matters. 'Someone must take the blame for our recent failures against the French. Our troops have been forced out of Maine and Normandy. Who would be the best scapegoat to carry the blame for our ignominy? The Duke is like to be charged with corruption, bribery, and treason. He is detested for directing much of the King's money into the pockets of his friends. If he is found guilty he will fall from grace and so be no use to us, or anyone else.'

'Well, until he is so accused, I still think you could approach Suffolk. Nothing else works to our favour. One day the King will undoubtedly smile on him again.'

His lips twisted in dry acquiescence.

'You have the voice of a shrew, Meg.'

'But a well-intentioned shrew.'

'And one that I find most endearing. But nothing is certain. Who's to say where the King will give his affections?'

'More certain than our hold on Gresham! And now you must go and talk to your mother about a wall.'

He groaned. 'I still think I will let William cut his eye-teeth on this one!'

He departed to hear his mother's complaint. I left them alone, for in truth there was nothing that could be done about the wall that Mistress Agnes had had built at Paston, a gesture typical of her to re-stoke the dispute with the church and villagers. The wall had been pushed over and Mistress Agnes accused of enclosing more than her entitlement, and was consequently found guilty of trespass and fined. Guilty or not guilty, she was refusing to pay the six pence demanded of the court. Silently I wished John well of the problem. The court was threatening to seize Mistress Agnes's property to pay the fine.

The Duke of Suffolk as a Paston patron, as long as he was not declared guilty of treason, was of far greater importance.

★

My thanks to the Blessed Virgin!

The news seemed promising. The Duke of Suffolk was pardoned and restored to good friendship with the King.

Which taught me a lesson. Never believe rumours, however reliable the source.

My suggestion to catch the ear of the Duke of Suffolk might have had its advantages; the rumour that he had been pardoned by the King might have had some merit. All hopes collapsed around us when the Duke was banished from England, the King bowing to much pressure to find the Duke guilty of bribery and corruption even if he was innocent of treason.

The Duke of Suffolk had too many enemies.

On a bright May morning in 1450, our possible patron, the noble Duke of Suffolk, grasping, ambitious, opinionated, was taken captive on his way to Calais. After a summary trial on board the *Nicholas of the Tower* he was vilely done to death, his head hacked from his body, so we heard, with a rusty sword. Stripped of his gown of russet and mailed velvet doublet, his body was left exposed and without dignity on the sands at Dover, his head set up on a pole beside it. The revulsion was widespread. The Duke became far more popular in grotesque death than in tyrannical life.

'I never thought that I would drink a toast to the death of any man! And yet tonight I will do so with a joyous heart.'

A callous comment, but John's eyes lit with an inner fire when the news reached us.

'Should we not say a prayer for his soul?' I asked, even as I raised my cup to mirror John's toast.

'By all means. I detest the manner of his death and would wish it on no man.' He drank, wiped his mouth on the back of his hand, and smiled, if so savage a twist of the lips could be called a smile. 'The removal of the Duke of Suffolk could just work to our advantage after all.'

Thus the hard-headed lawyer who saw only Paston gains and losses.

Norwich: February 1451

John and I rode to Gresham on a frosty morning when a pale sun glittered on the frozen puddles on the road, turning it into a jewelled pathway towards our future. The winter hedgerows offered a haven for flocks of twittering sparrows. It was impossible to feel downhearted, whatever my fears of what I would find at the end of it. Even so, we rode in silence for much of the way, but it was not an uncomfortable one.

'Moleyns's forces have gone. Gresham is ours to reclaim, with or without a final settlement in the courts,' John had announced.

The Duke of Suffolk's murder on the beach had brought us respite. Without his chief patron to stand at his back, Lord Moleyns's courage had deserted him.

'Will our tenants be pleased to see us, do you suppose?' I asked at last as we came within view of the village.

John rubbed his nose, considering our past difficulties with our tenants. 'Who's to say where their loyalties will lie, if they decide we had abandoned them? They suffered enough in our name; at best their properties searched and despoiled, at worst they were beaten and left near death. They may consider Moleyns a stronger landlord. Even a fairer one.'

'I dispute that!'

'I thought that you would.'

As we passed, he pointed out broken fences and gates. The fields were winter-empty but rank weed infested the margins and the hedges grew apace. The wall around the church was in need of repair. There was a dearth of animals close to the cottages. When we rode past the remains of the old manor house that I had occupied for such a short time, I could not look at the desecration of its old walls, all fallen in a heap of wood and plaster.

'See the signs of neglect.' John was mentally taking note of every speck of evidence against Moleyns. 'Our tenants may well lay it at our door.'

'Then they would be wrong,' I argued. 'This is all Moleyns's doing.'

What would we find when we reached the house? What if Moleyns had, at the last, left some of his men in permanent occupation?

It proved to be a peaceful return, in crude comparison with my departure from Gresham. John and I entered our disputed home with no one to deny us. We stood together in the courtyard, our servants remaining at a distance. A robin sang somewhere over to my left where I knew a herb garden and arbour to be. It should have raised my spirits but happier memories, before it was taken from us, were difficult to resurrect when we tallied up the results of our absence.

At first sight, it looked to have survived in one piece, unlike the rented house that had been razed to the ground. It still had its towers and strong walls and the drawbridge over the moat in good repair, the living accommodations still stalwart. But that was a kindly welcome before we saw the truth of what had been done within.

The soldiery had used it hard, or neglected it, or deliberately taken revenge before they left. Grass now grew between the once well-tended cobbles in the courtyard. Window frames were broken, the panes smashed. I suspected, from the activity when we first rode in, that jackdaws had taken to nesting in the chimneys. The main door hung out of true on its ruined hinges.

All reparable but what would I find inside?

John took my hand.

'Let us go in. We may as well see the worst.'

It was worse. Far worse. I walked from room to room, unable to speak, not wishing to touch any surface. Of course it was dusty, the floor grimy with the wear of many boots, but the damage went far deeper than that. It seemed to me that my home had been thoroughly looted and damaged beyond repair. Many of the floor-tiles were cracked. The wooden structure of the staircase was hacked about, the stair treads dangerously unstable. Walls were black and greasy from the torches that had lit the feasting. And all looted, robbed out of anything of value. Nothing remained of my furniture and furnishings. Had the stools and coffers been used for firewood? My bright tapestries had vanished.

Upstairs the scene was even more grim, where the beds were despoiled and the panelling smashed in the solar. It was too heart-wrenching to remain long. The whole place reeked of piss and ill-use. Rats scurried between holes that I had no memory of.

The rank state of the kitchens disgusted me beyond words. My herb garden was a place of true desolation. I dare not even approach the orchard, where the lack of trees was evident even from a distance.

'Oh, John.'

He took me into his arms, so that I could rest my forehead against his shoulder. Tears came. How could I weep for a castle, a house of stones and mortar? But I did. My heart was sore with the loss.

'Don't weep.'

The tears would not stop.

'It has been savaged, and with such malice. How could they do this to so fine a place? I do not think I can ever live here again.'

'It can be put right.'

'Only if Lord Moleyns pays damages. How much would it cost?'

He regarded the room that once had been our bedchamber, before turning away, as dispirited as I.

'Well over two hundred pounds, I would think.'

We did not have that sort of money to hand. I saw no hope.

'There will be one more advantage from Suffolk's death,' John announced as we turned our faces towards Norwich. 'The friar Hauteyn will slink back beneath the stone from which he emerged without Suffolk whispering in his ear. I wager there'll be no more claims against Oxnead.' He scowled at the road between his horse's ears. 'At least not until some other form of vermin surfaces.'

John's bitterness coated us both.

What we saw that day was a grievous memory of the lovely manor, when we should have been rejoicing that John had held his own and the property would one day be ours again when the courts confirmed Moleyns's legal departure. There was no rejoicing in my soul as I turned my back on it. I would not live there again. I remained in Norwich while John decided to put his efforts and some coin into a new building project at Mautby, to extend the manor house I had inherited there into one more suitable for a growing family.

It was kind of him, and I knew that he did it for me.

Norwich: April 1452

'We will have fish today,' I said, standing in the middle of my kitchen, ticking off items on my fingers. 'See what is good and fresh in the market. There are enough fishmongers to provide what we need, such as more salt cod. And a quantity of white herrings. Nothing curling at the edges or I will send it back.'

'Yes, mistress.'

'I must remember to ask Master Paston about the cost of spices in London. Pepper, cloves, saffron, and cinnamon, of course.'

'Yes, mistress.'

'Are we in need ...?'

I never finished my query. I lifted my head, ears pricked.

There was rarely any peace when living in a town house with comings and goings in the road into the centre of Norwich, particularly on a market day. Today it was a commotion at the door onto the street, but I thought nothing of it. Perhaps our two eldest sons engaged in some difference of opinion, which I supposed I should investigate before it came to flying fists and feet.

'John?'

I raised my voice. It would elicit a response from any one of three. There was no answer.

The fear engendered by Gresham had leached away from me. I was settled in Norwich; the Mautby building was progressing well and soon we would live there. We were thriving. John had made a name for himself for civic duty in raising a petition with the Norfolk gentry to rid the town of a notorious band of thugs. Eliza was still not wed, still living at Mistress Agnes's mercy, but I had tweaked John's conscience often enough. Mistress Agnes had still not paid her fine over the matter of the wall, but there seemed to be no way of making her comply other than sending her as a debtor to the Fleet Prison. She would have to be carried bodily, complaining all the way.

Contentment had a habit of settling over me, when I sat at ease after supper, or rose from my bed, or took the servants to task in the smooth running of the household. I was pleased with my life. John was here in Norwich for a few weeks, I had recovered from the tears I had shed over Gresham. No use weeping over what could not be changed.

It seemed so short a time since I had worried over our copious failures. We had swum to the surface of that particular pond, like carp seeking midges on a summer day. Suffolk's death had had no damaging effect, and the rebellion in Kent under the leadership of Jack Cade, taking to arms and advancing on London to complain of high taxation, had not spread to Norfolk.

'And I wish you to see to the purchasing of a barrel of oysters,' I said, returning to the task in hand. 'Take Thomas with you to carry them home.'

'Thomas is with Master Paston in the town, mistress.'

'Then find one of the stable lads. Master John is very partial to oysters. They are not to my taste, although better a fresh oyster than rabbit in a thick onion sauce which is Master John's favourite.' I had failed to wean him from this Paston family favourite in all our married years; I was forced to steal myself against the pungent aroma and could eat none of it. I wrinkled my nose, considering instead the buying of—

A splintering crash destroyed my pleasurable anticipation of what the market might provide. This was no childish difference or disagreement. The noise was that of our door flung back to crash against the wall, so loudly that it all but shook the house. There were raised voices. Shouts of pain.

This was no sociable visit from Norwich townsfolk.

Was it the paid ruffians, against whom John had stirred the local gentry? Were they come to attack us in our home? Memories of Father Gloys and John Wyndham, blades drawn against each other, came back fast enough. But surely Wyndham would never attack the house.

As the noise increased, those old memories of Gresham returned to flood me with panic. The thoughts and fears ran together through my mind as I gathered my skirts and strode in the direction of the noise, my Steward already with me, gripping a knife that he had snatched up from the kitchen. One of the manservants emerged through the cellar door, brushing cobwebs from his hands and sleeves. And there were our three sons, jostling together to see what was amiss.

I pushed the boys towards the servant, relieved that Margery was somewhere above stairs where one of the maids would surely be aware. 'Hide them,' I ordered. 'Hide them in the cellar if it is necessary. They must come to no harm.'

For without doubt the attackers, whoever they might be, were inside the house.

I wrenched open the door into the hall to find one of my maids, eyes wide, mouth stretched in fear.

'What is it?'

'There has been an attack on Master John!' she gasped. 'I am sent for water and linen.'

My blood ran cold.

'Is he dead?'

'There's blood on the floor. Pools of it ...'

I would get no sense out of her. 'Fetch your weapons,' I commanded our servants. But they were already prepared, as we always were, with swords and knives.

My fear for John was billowing like smoke from a badly swept chimney. We had parted with no presentiment of trouble after breaking our fast, John going to a meeting with fellow lawyers, to be followed by a visit to the Cathedral, safe in the environs of Norwich in the broad light of day, where we were so well-known, and in the holy sanctuary of the Cathedral.

I swept through the hall to the entrance.

It was as if we had been butchering carcasses at Martinmass. John was crouched on the floor, head bent.

'John!' I all but shrieked.

And then breathing out in relief as my husband, who had been kneeling on the tiles, rose to his feet, bellowing his fury.

'This is what I have to contend with. In my own town. On my own doorstep. God help me, I'll have blood for this!'

'It seems to me that there is enough blood here already.'

At last he saw me. My face must have been ashen, for he lurched across and took my hands in his. They were covered with blood. So were his sleeves.

'There is no need to fear. I am unharmed,' he said.

'Then whose blood is this?'

I was astonished at how calm I sounded when my heart was thundering in my ears. There was John: dusty, dishevelled, favouring one arm and shoulder, but unhurt as far as I could see.

'Thomas's blood,' he said.

I saw now that John had been kneeling beside Thomas, a young man brought from Paston, who was sitting, propped against the wall, holding his head in his hands, blood on his shirt and jerkin, and in a trail from the door. Releasing my hands, I sank down at Thomas's side, tilting his head to see the damage, even when he hissed with pain, leaving John to dispatch our armed servants back to their normal routine with calming words. Thomas's wounds were unpleasant, bleeding copiously, as head wounds so often did, but were not vital to his health. The cut to his arm was deep and equally bloody, but was not a serious injury and could be bound up.

'What is this?' I asked, looking up at John.

'This is an attack on me in the street.' He looked as if he could barely believe what had happened so close to home. 'This is an unwarranted assault on my person!'

My face was no doubt colourless with shock; his was pale with fury.

I beckoned to the maid who had appeared with a bowl of water and clean linen.

'Are you hurt?' I asked my husband as I began to remove Thomas's jerkin, ignoring his groans of pain. The sooner we stopped the blood flow the better it would be for him. I took a cup of ale from my maid and made him drink it. Now that the danger was passed my control over my emotions and actions returned.

'No!' John snapped at me. 'More by chance than anything else. They held me by my arms while they hit at me.' Anger flushed his face from white to red as he gently investigated his ribs. 'At the door of the Cathedral itself. They polluted the sanctuary with Thomas's blood, until priests and townsfolk came to our aid and drove the rabble off.' He drew his hands down over his cheeks, wincing, where I could see a bruise beginning to develop. 'Are we not safe in our own holy sanctuary? They would have been carrying me home, a dead man, if the priests and our friends had not come to my aid. Poor Thomas paid a high price.'

At close quarters I now noticed the abrasions on John's face where at least one blow had landed.

'Who? Who did it?'

'A band of five or six ruffians, all masked. They had swords and bucklers and daggers, as if they were expecting me to be fully armed. You don't attack an honest citizen with so many weapons to hand unless you intend to cause him real harm. Why would I be armed to visit the Cathedral? And why attack me?'

'Who paid them?' I asked, the obvious question.

'I'd wager they were of the Duke of Norfolk's affinity, although I saw no livery.'

I sat back on my heels, leaving my maid to continue the staunching of blood while I poured out another cup of ale. 'Are we at odds with Norfolk? I did not think it.'

'Neither did I.' John's brow was furrowed, as it so often was, the lines becoming all but permanent in the last year. 'We met in London two weeks ago. There was no animosity in him. I had hopes of a good relationship with him now that Suffolk is no longer clouding the local waters. Nor to my knowledge have I crossed the path of any of his household.'

He drew me to my feet, and then into the parlour, leaving the servants to their ministrations to Thomas whose colour was returning, already being consoled by an engrossed audience and a second cup of ale. I sent our Steward, the knife still tucked in his belt, off to the market, with orders to keep his ears and eyes open as well as buy fish.

'Why Norfolk?' I asked again when we were able to speak freely.

'I don't know. Know your enemies is an excellent maxim to live by but in this case I do not, which makes me vulnerable.'

'I fear for you until we do know.' When I touched his temple he winced. 'You will have a blackened eye come the morning.'

'Better than a knife in my ribs!'

All my tranquillity of the morning had been crushed.

'Life would be far more comfortable if you were able to make friends as readily as you make enemies. There is no spirit of compromise in you. Not at all.'

'Compromise?' His earlier anger had returned. 'What value compromise when my enemies hide in dark corners to inflict damage to my person and wound my servants? I will never compromise, Margaret.'

John ate the oysters with relish. My appetite was much diminished.

★

By the end of the day we knew well enough the source of the antagonism. News was brought to us that my uncle Philip Berney, my uncle of the suspect damaged hip, had been ambushed by a band of ruffians similar to those who had attacked John. John had escaped lightly. My uncle Berney and his escort had not. Shot at with arrows, their horses wounded, my uncle, although physically unscathed, was taken prisoner and called a traitor, although accused of no actual crime. When they finally let him go he was so afraid that he took refuge in the newly built Caister Castle where he was put to bed to recover. Such intimidation proved to be terrifying for an ageing man who had never committed a crime in his life.

'What is this?' I asked, my fear growing again.

'I know not, but I will discover it.'

124

'Do you have to return to London?'

'Yes.'

'Will you write to me?'

'Of course. Do not go alone in the streets without an armed escort. Keep the children close.'

'And do not you play fast and loose with your life in London,' I retaliated. 'I think you are no safer there than here.'

Before he left me, I stood in front of him, administering a reluctant caress to his untidy hair with non-too-gentle fingers, for I had been truly afraid and knew not where to put the blame. 'Will we ever live without this? Will we ever live together for a whole year? Nay, even a month. We have not done so for all of our married life. Will there never be peace?'

'I cannot see it.'

'Is there nothing we can do?'

'I am doing all I can.'

I hoped for a word of endearment, an encouragement, as he saluted my cheek. Instead: 'I thought the ale we drank last night was not of the best. You might decide to buy it elsewhere. We have enough brewers in Norwich to purchase the finest.'

In spite of a little breath of sadness that cooled my flesh, I laughed. Had I really expected any different?

'I will do that, John. And I will pray to the Blessed Trinity for your safekeeping.'

'As I will pray for yours. You are always in my heart and mind, Meg. Look after the children, and yourself.'

I pushed him on his way, turning back into the house, stopping when he called after me.

'I'll not let you be harmed, Meg. You mean too much to me.'

I smiled. The little wound to my heart was quickly healed.

Well! John's letter proved to be something of a relief. We had done nothing to antagonise the Duke of Norfolk. The dispute that provoked the attack on John in the Cathedral involved an altercation over a parcel of land. One of the parties in the squabble was a cousin of mine, with whom we had little communication. We had done nothing to merit the attack except by family connection. Not that it allowed me to return to my previous ease of mind. We seemed to be fair game for any local dispute.

You may rest easy, John wrote. *The Duke of Norfolk is not our enemy.* I replied forthwith.

★

I may rest easy, but my uncle will not. He is ailing. If you will buy me a pot of treacle in London I will send it to him with our prayers for his recovery. They say that the flesh of roasted viper, and the other ingredients, as well as the forty days in its preparation, is excellent in unblocking the intestine, curing fevers and heart murmuring. Mistress Agnes says that it is excellent at counteracting the effects of poison.

As well as sending a pot to me, I suggest that you keep some beside you at all times. Take twice a day in clear wine or ale.

I would be grateful if you would send me word – quickly – if you want your new livery to be red, or if you have decided on some other colour. Also if you would be kind enough to send good-quality hats for your sons. The last you sent are too small.

Have you made any progress in finding us an influential patron?

★

The answer was clearly no. In passing I noted that there was not one word of affection in my correspondence. But did he not know that my heart was his? It did not need to be written.

Chapter Seven

Margaret Mautby Paston

Norwich: April 1453

I was standing in my bedchamber, clad in stockings and linen shift. My hair still needed the attention of a comb and pins.

'What do I wear?'

I asked the question of my cousin and close friend, Mistress Clere, who was opening the lids of the coffers I had brought with me to the Paston town house in Norwich, frowning at their contents. It was vitally important that I make the most of this visit of Queen Margaret to Norwich.

'What have you got?' Mistress Clere was turning over some of the garments, running her fingers over the cloth, searching for anything with fur or embroidered decoration on bodice or hem or sleeve. There was little to satisfy her.

'Nothing here to make an impression,' I admitted.

It was to be a notable reception for all the women of status, this visit of the Queen, wife of King Henry VI, to the town of Norwich, to which I, as a Paston, a name to be noted throughout

Norfolk and Suffolk, although not always with sufficient respect, was invited.

For a moment I wished John was here with me, to bolster me with his own brash confidence, but John was in London. Since I must make my curtsey to royalty alone, I was determined to do it well.

'What about this?' Mistress Clere was lifting out a loose-fitting gown of the finest woollen weave in autumnal russet.

'Too plain. Russet does not become me. I will not cry poverty on the family,' I said. It was a depressing sight. I had clearly had too little time to spend on my clothing. The garments were well-worn and lacked any nod to fashion.

My cousin and I surveyed the possibilities.

'I have to say, Margaret. How many years has that bodice seen?' Mistress Clere was brusque and incorrigibly honest. 'The one advantage is that Queen Margaret will not notice what you wear when you curtsey before her. Her mind will be too set on the miracle that is this child to be born to her and the King.'

'As well it might,' I agreed with a grimace. They had been wed all of eight years with no child to herald the King's royal power and the Queen's fecundity. Now her fervent prayers had been answered.

'Do you suppose the child is Henry's?' said Mistress Clere, always willing to indulge in Court gossip.

'They say that he is incapable.'

'Not a problem from which your husband John suffers,' Mistress Clere said.

'Not that you would notice,' I admitted with a prim twist of my lips, and some pride. 'I sometimes wish he had less ability to burden me with yet another offering of his affections. When he returns from London, his energies are prodigious.'

I had carried four children for John in thirteen years of marriage, all healthy and growing fast.

Mistress Clere's eyes glinted. 'And if not King Henry's child, then who might have fulfilled the Queen's dearest wish?'

'No one outside the royal bedchamber will know the truth of it,' I suggested. 'We must share the Queen's joy that this is indeed a royal child.'

In maternal joy, the Queen had already made a New Year offering in gratitude for the blessing, so we were told, of a gold tablet engraved with an angel bedecked in jewels. Now she was coming on her own private pilgrimage to Walsingham to give thanks at the shrine of Our Lady, stopping in Norwich on the way. Our Lady had a reputation for smiling on women who were carrying a child. Queen Margaret would be anxious for a successful accomplishment.

'I wish her well,' I said, casting aside the bodice that I had been examining. The King and Queen had enough to worry about with the threat of the ambitious Duke of York to their royal power. In private my husband thought that he had much to offer in good advice that was not totally self-seeking, unlike some of those magnates who hovered like carrion-hunters around the King. Like the Beaufort Duke of Somerset.

Searching the coffer once more, I sighed.

'Queen Margaret might not notice what I wear,' I announced, carrying to the window a gown of rich blue wool, the skirt flowing from a high waist, the sleeves banded with narrow strips of pale vair, to see if the bright light highlighted any encroachment by the moth, 'but the gentlewomen of Norwich will certainly do so. I imagine them smirking behind their hands.' I lifted the weight of the skirts. 'It was made for my wedding. It will have to do, but it lacks something. I have no intention of allowing them to look down their superior noses at me as if I were a bondswoman.'

Mistress Clere laced me into the offending garment and handed me a girdle trimmed in similar squirrel-pelt. She stood back and regarded me.

'Not too bad. Something to enhance the neckline perhaps.'

'I have nothing but my rosary beads, and they are not of the finest quality. John bought them for me when we were first wed and coin was in short supply. I'll not wear them and draw comment.' I turned my head to look at my cousin.

'What is it?' Mistress Clere was busy tugging the fall of my skirts into seemly order, before taking issue with my hair and the veil of my heart-shaped headdress.

'I was recalling a jewel that John inherited from his father.'

'Where is it now? Have you not brought it with you?'

'John sold it. It was a fine thing, a beautifully chased silver crucifix, all set with dark sapphires. I wish he had not. It would have been enough to close the mouths of the Norwich harpies.' I cast an eye over her own finery for the royal visit, dwelling on the intricately wrought gold chain set with gems that rested on her shoulders. I watched as her brows rose in a query.

'I can read your mind,' she said.

'So you can. *You* could lend me something, my dear cousin.'

'I could. But I'll have it back when this is finished!'

Mistress Clere was protective of her own property, but then so was I.

★

131

I attended the reception for Queen Margaret in fine style. The Queen was resplendent and glowing with health and achievement, although I admitted to a disappointment. Never before having been in the same chamber as the Queen of England, all I had in my mind's eye was the image painted by gossip and rumour of her arrival in England for her marriage to the King. Then she had worn, so it was said, a white satin wedding dress embroidered with silver and gold marguerites in honour of her name. In the days of celebration to follow she had paraded before her new subjects in violet and crimson cloth of gold, trimmed with a hundred and twenty pelts of white fur. On her hair had rested a coronet of gold, richly set in pearls and glittering gems.

Queen Margaret's appearance in Norwich was much muted, with no gold coronet or ermine to be seen, but still one of splendour in robes of scarlet and blue, stitched with the royal coat of arms to impale her own. There were no outward signs of the pregnancy.

She had left her husband the King at home.

We, Mistress Clere and I, would not disgrace our family. My gown was enhanced by an enamelled chain set with garnets. We curtsied, a sway of bright colour beneath the tapestried walls of the great chamber in the Guildhall in the centre of Norwich, a new addition to the town of which we were suitably proud. By far the largest building of its kind in all England, except for those in London, the glass in the windows kept out the draughts to the comfort of all. Now it was suffused with the all-pervading intensity of lavender that the women of Norwich had used in their coffers over winter to keep the mould and mildew at bay.

I was by no means first in the line to be presented to royalty, but I had not expected it for the Duchess of Norfolk and the

Duchess of Suffolk were both present. But at last the Mayor of Norwich called me forward before the Queen: 'My lady, this is Mistress Margaret Paston.'

I sank into an obeisance. 'My lady.'

I rose to see her assessing me, her chin tilted, a smile warming her features. The Queen was about my own height, neither tall nor short and of slight build. A handsome woman but not a beautiful one. Her nose was straight, her lips firm and with a rounded chin that did nothing to detract from the overall impression of a woman of some strong character. The Queen's hands were small, smooth-skinned, heavily jewelled. Mine were not. Her narrow feet were encased in gilded leather. There was such a wide gulf between a Queen and a commoner such as I, but I must leave her, for John's sake, with a sense that the Pastons were a family to be remembered and perhaps encouraged. If we could not achieve a patron amongst the great magnates, then at least the Queen might remember us.

'I have heard your husband spoken of at Court, Mistress Paston. He is making a name for himself in the legal world. We understand that he does useful work for Sir John Fastolf.'

Her voice was soft, still holding to its French accents, and yet I imagined that it could command obedience when needed.

'Indeed, my lady. My husband is the most loyal of subjects. And the most hard-working.'

'And Sir John Fastolf is a relative of yours, we understand. We know Sir John. An exceptional soldier in his youth.'

The Queen was well-informed. My heart beat a little faster, my cheeks flushed, as it became clear that we were not unknown in Court circles.

'Yes, my lady. Sir John Fastolf is a cousin, on my mother's side.'

'It is good to make your acquaintance, Mistress Paston. It is important that we have loyal gentlewomen, with clever husbands, settled in our towns. Do you have sons?'

'I do, my lady. Two sons, of eleven and nine years, and a child still in the nursery. I have a daughter too.'

She was not interested in my daughter. 'I envy you, Mistress Paston. I hope to have a son within the year, and many more to follow. Send one of your sons to Court when he has a few more years to his name. It will be good for his education and it will be an honour for you.'

'I am indeed honoured, my lady, that you should consider it.'

I felt a little ripple of warm pleasure around my heart. The Queen had done our family a great service by this slightest recognition, to remain speaking with me, to invite me to send a son of mine to Court. If the Pastons were good enough for the royal circle, they were good enough for Norfolk society. I would make my place amongst these women of Norwich. There was no one here who could now question our worth.

Then the Queen had moved on; the event was over but left me deep in thought as Mistress Clere and I strolled back to the Paston house on Elm Street in companionable conversation over the Queen's graciousness in promoting a marriage for her. Mistress Clere was much gratified and inclined to be loquacious over the Queen's compliments, but I was becoming distracted.

'What are you thinking now?' she asked, smoothing on her gloves.

'Two things,' I replied promptly. They were foremost in my mind. 'It would be good policy for me to spend more time here in Norwich to build our reputation. I am thinking of renting a house here, for myself and the children. It will cost less than buying one.'

'Will John object?'

'Not he, if it will bring him an advantage. Besides, I won't tell him until it is done.'

'A brave woman! Would you not find it simpler to continue living with Agnes in Elm Street, or at Paston or Oxnead? It would be at no cost on your purse.'

'No. Not permanently.' I wrinkled my nose at the prospect. 'We need more space and I would like a town house of my own, where I can step out of my door and greet my neighbours without Mistress Agnes calling foul. I would enjoy ordering my own property with a kitchen and buttery laid out to my own wishes. Mistress Agnes is too dogmatic and domineering.'

Mistress Clere slid a glance in my direction. 'Thus speaks another domineering woman.'

I did not disagree. I was well aware of my liking for managing my own household.

'What is the other issue on your mind?'

I knew that I was frowning. There seemed to be many issues that made me frown of late, and this was a far more difficult problem to solve. I pulled Mistress Clere to a halt, before we reached the Paston doorstep.

'John's sister, Eliza,' I said.

'The situation for her gets no better, does it?'

'No. She is very unhappy.'

'She needs a husband.'

'And her mother Mistress Agnes treats her ill. She beats her. But you know about that.'

'Yes. Eliza wrote to me, and I took John to task for not protecting his sister. I presume he has done nothing to stop it.'

'No. It's not that he does not care. He simply becomes preoccupied, so Eliza is left to fend for herself.'

'Then you must do what you can for her.'

'But what that can be, I have no clear idea.' It would be easy to turn a blind eye to Eliza's problems. To confront Mistress Agnes over them would simply lead to more bad blood between us. She would see it as an interference in matters that were not mine to discuss, and John would not want me to stir the already troubled waters between him and his mother. But I could not quite shrug away Eliza's ills.

'I will broach it again with John,' I said. 'If I tell him how warmly the Queen speaks of him, and how well-regarded we are becoming in Norwich, he might be moved to do something useful for his sister.'

'And I will write again to him, more forcefully than I did last time,' Mistress Clere promised, to which I agreed, although I had little hope of her success.

Returned to the Norwich house, I removed my turban and veil and my shoes that nipped my toes, and sat with a cup of warm spiced wine, contemplating the recent hours. I decided that I had done all I could to remind the Queen of the existence of the Pastons. I smiled, sipping slowly, enjoying the costly aromas of cloves and cinnamon. I would remind John that he might owe me at least a gold chain, if not two, for my efforts on his behalf. It was not seemly that I should have to borrow.

Chapter Eight

Elizabeth Paston

Oxnead: 1454

It had been five years since Margaret and I had escaped from Gresham and there were no changes for me, so that a visit to Oxnead from John and William – unusual to have both brothers together – spurred me into desperate action, such that I dragged John from the door into the stable before he even entered the house. I pulled him into the stall where he had just left his horse. I hated that I was so powerless to determine my future but, as a daughter of the house and so under his ultimate dominion, there was no escape for me unless John took a hand in my affairs. Could he not overrule Mistress Agnes if he so wished?

'Have you found me a husband, John?'

'And there I thought you were merely pleased to see me.'

'I am. I will be even more delighted if you have found a man who will pass all my mother's tests and exchange vows with me at the church door.'

He looked strangely sheepish for John, uneasy perhaps, but then he rallied with affectionate bluster.

'And what a pleasure it is to see you, Eliza! You look in good cheer.'

I knew that I did not, but concurred, as he gripped my shoulders and planted a kiss on each cheek, before handing me the leather pouch to carry. So he was here for business. I returned his embrace but would not be deflected, pushing aside the animal that had come to nuzzle my shoulder in hope of something to eat.

'I am not accosting you here in the company of your horse for the good of my health. I can bear this no longer. Is there no one within your acquaintances?'

'Well ...'

He rubbed a finger down the length of his nose, a habitual gesture that Meg would have recognised, when John was in a quandary or left with no road of escape.

'John! Have you given it no thought at all?'

'I have.'

'I mean more than a thought since you broke your fast today.'

For a moment he looked hurt. 'It may be that I have come bearing good news.'

I did not like the sudden sharp gleam in his eye.

'You have discovered a man of means who will offer for me!'

'It is possible.'

'Do I know him?'

'You have met him.'

An awful sense of the past attacked me.

'Not Master Scrope!'

'Now that you talk of him ...'

Our mother, receiving news of John's arrival, appeared in the doorway to pick up this gem of information.

'What are you doing out here? Come into the house. This is no place to discuss family business, for every groom and servant to hear.'

Dutifully we followed her, as if we were children still, until the door of the parlour was closed, when she turned with a swish of her dull skirts to face us.

'Good day, mother,' John said to cut through the hostility, but with little effect. Brother William, standing with his shoulders propped against the wall beside the fireplace, grinned behind her back. William was proving to be astute and clever but with an uncomfortable air of mischief that he had not outgrown in his eighteen years. I thought him to be even more ambitious than John with an eye to Court preferment.

'Good day to you, too, my son. So it's Scrope again, is it? Is he still unwed? After six years since he last made an offer?'

'Master Scrope is still available,' said John.

'Why would we consider him a second time? And why is he still not wed?'

'I know not, but his family connection with Sir John Fastolf makes him still a worthy husband, despite the disadvantages that moved you to denial last time.'

'By God! Bring it to an end.' Mistress Agnes clapped her hands together in irritation. 'Surely it is time. Will she get any better?'

We had all remained standing since our mother chose to stand. We faced each other in an uneven circle, the atmosphere heavy with dissatisfaction from my mother, despair from me and a determination to bring this matter to an end from John. William was engaged in studying the edging on his gloves.

'I have been talking with Sir John Fastolf of late,' John said. 'He hopes that we can make a conclusion of it between Scrope and Eliza. And there have been developments. I have heard, thanks to William here who has been in London, that the offer is made again.'

'It is,' William affirmed.

'Thus,' continued John with a degree of pomposity, 'I think that we could possibly bring it to a settlement, for your sake, sister.'

His smile for me was kindly meant although the content of it did not warm my heart. Once again I was faced with a union with Master Scrope, who I doubted would have improved as a marital prospect in six years. Moreover I considered John's interest in making close ties with Sir John Fastolf far more important than Master Scrope's suitability as a bridegroom for me.

'But is his financial situation any better than six years ago?' My mother echoed my thoughts but for different reasons. 'Is his daughter still dependent on him?' she asked. 'Will she be a claim on his estates when he is dead? If his finances are still encumbered, we are not interested.' I detected a sniff. 'He must be desperate if he has not wed in all this time.'

'Many in London have a hint of desperation, looking for brides to produce an heir,' John agreed. 'William here says there is pestilence in the city again. Hovering death makes men look to the future.'

'So that is why you have left the city. I wondered, William, what had brought you here after so many months of absence, and with nothing to say for yourself.' Mistress Agnes considered her younger son with disfavour. 'But the pestilence is an irrelevance.' She plucked at a piece of lint on her cuff, then aimed her dissatisfactions once more at John. 'I don't know, John. Scrope may still be the best offer that we can get after all this time when we have done no better. Do we wish Elizabeth to remain under my roof into her old age? I do not wish it.'

'Then will you hear his offer?'

'If I must. Arrange it for me.'

All I could recall was Master Scrope's heavy scarring, his aged limbs; the drops of moisture from his nose, which he had wiped on his sleeve. In spite of everything, in spite of Margaret's advice, and my own declamation that I would wed any man who would take me, I could not bear it.

The conversation was continuing over my head, until my attention was caught. John was introducing a new turn in this particular wheel.

'I still think that Scrope may be a lost cause, however keen Sir John Fastolf might be to make the alliance, and however valuable it would be for us to please him. We will keep Scrope in mind as a last resort, but I have a new offer that I think we should consider first.'

'Who?' I demanded, my attention fairly caught with a sliver of hope.

'A relation of Lord Grey of Ruthin who contacted me.' John was looking smug. 'A high-born gentleman with excellent connections. He seeks a well-dowered wife and is willing to consider a Paston. He compares well with Master Scrope. He is young, unconnected to any legal demands on his estate, and is considered comely, all in all. He rides and dresses with style, so I am told.'

'Have you seen him?' I asked, my experiences rendering me suspicious.

'Has he wealth?' Mistress Agnes demanded.

'I have not seen him and so know of him only by repute. He has an income of four hundred marks a year. Lord Grey seems to think it an urgent matter and is most accommodating. I have replied to his first enquiry, to say that we will consider it most warmly.'

Which would all seem to be perfection. My heart began to lift, until I watched my brother's eyes slide from mine. 'What is wrong with him?' I asked. 'If so well-born and high-bred and so wealthy, would he not look amongst the Court aristocracy for his bride?'

John's reply was as smooth and bland as new whey. 'Nothing to my knowledge. What should there be wrong with him? The young man is keen to be associated with us.' I did not believe a word of it.

'But who *is* he?' My mother asked the question before I could. John was losing patience.

'I do not yet know his name. I have not yet met him. I only hear what is said of him, and there is nothing to his disservice. The suggestion came from Lord Grey himself.'

'Then discover it. We must ascertain all we can. I will not wed my daughter to a nameless man who might prove to be unsuitable, no matter how elegant he might be or how good his seat on a horse.'

But for the first time for many months I had hope. Here was a real possibility. Lord Grey of Ruthin was both courtier and notable landowner. 'This is how it stands,' John was explaining to our mother. 'I have said that Eliza will be neither married nor betrothed to any other man for the next two months ...'

'As if that were possible!' I huffed a breath.

'During which time,' John continued with a warning glance in my direction, 'I need information on the gentleman – his name, where he lives, and whether he is a widower with children. Only if this is satisfactory will we continue with Lord Grey. Does that put your worries to rest?'

'It must. And if that's all you have to say …'

My mother stalked out, the keys at her belt clashing together, while I turned on my brother John.

'Margaret tells me that you have suggested that your daughter Margery should marry Fastolf's cousin Thomas Fastolf of Cowhaugh. Margery will not be old enough to wed for another decade. She is barely six years old. Why not let me take Thomas Fastolf?'

John's spine stiffened. 'Fastolf and I have talked only of Margery.'

'Then talk of me. What is it that you want, John? The Fastolf boy's wardship? It could come to you as head of the family, whether the bride is your daughter or your sister.'

'This marriage is not offered to you, Eliza.'

'No. As you said, I can always have Master Scrope as a last resort.'

I felt emotion building that would erupt if I allowed it, until William, so far having stood behind me, detached himself from the wall and put his arm gently around me. 'Don't fret so much, Eliza. Yours is not a hopeless case.'

'Don't fret? Not hopeless? I am twenty-five years old. I will be past the age of childbearing, and then I will remain a spinster at my mother's beck and call for ever.'

'We'll bring you a husband on a silver platter. A man with such distinction that our mother will be unable to refuse,' he assured.

'We will do all we can,' John agreed. 'But if I bring a gentleman to the door, don't regard him as if he were a black beetle dislodged from the woodpile.'

Had I done that when Master Scrope had visited? I did not think so.

'I would not,' I said.

'You might.' William was inclined to be mischievous. 'Encourage him, do not scowl. Even if it is Master Scrope.'

I bared my teeth.

★

In his own mind Master Scrope, it appeared, was neither a lost cause, nor a last resort. Undeterred by either John or William, within a week he was riding up to the door at Oxnead where he dismounted with stiff lack of agility. I was watching from my chamber. The years had not been kind to him. There was more of a stoop to his shoulders, although the intricate folds of his velvet chaperon masked any further lack of hair and shaded his scarring from my sight. I heard the knock. The door was opened. I made my way quietly down the stairs to the parlour where he had been shown in to wait for my mother, who met me at the door, approaching from the opposite direction.

'What are you doing?'

'Master Scrope is waiting to see you.'

'I have been told. Go to your chamber. I will deal with this.'

As she watched, I retreated to the stairs, until she had entered the parlour, then I stepped quietly back. I remained and listened to the low exchange of greeting for my mother. Anticipating a short visit, she had not quite closed the door. And then …

'If I could but meet with your daughter, Mistress Paston, it may be that she would accept my offer. A woman still unwed, so many years after my last visit here, would surely see the value

144

of this marriage, even though I must provide for my daughter. Mistress Elizabeth will have her own household and lack for nothing. I have sufficient income to ensure that. Would you agree to my having a conversation with her?'

I was troubled by his determination after such a brutal rejection of his previous wooing. My mother was touched by no fine sentiment.

'My daughter is indisposed, sir.'

'I believe that we could make an excellent arrangement.'

'You must talk of this with Sir John Fastolf. If your financial position is no different, and Sir John is not willing to fund you, we can offer you no settlement. You have wasted your time, Master Scrope, in undertaking this journey. There is nothing more to say between us.'

'And yet there might be something for me to say to Mistress Elizabeth. And she to me.'

Such courage in the face of rejection, how admirable he remained in spite of such discourtesy. My mother had not even offered him a cup of ale after his journey.

'Mistress Elizabeth has nothing to say. She will be obedient to me and to her brother.'

Thus the conversation appearing to be coming to an end, I took refuge in the kitchen. However much I might flinch from marriage to Master Scrope, my heart had softened at his willingness to face the Gorgon and take me as a bride. I could not let it go unremarked.

Moving swiftly through the kitchen, past the closed doors of the scullery and pantry, I entered the courtyard and waylaid him as he prepared to ride away. He was already mounted so that I had to look up. The scarring was as evident as before, but at least on horseback his infirmities were less obvious. He held the reins lightly in gloved hands.

'Master Scrope …'

Surprised, he smiled down at me, although with a quick glance towards the house as if my mother might appear at any moment.

'Mistress Elizabeth. It was you whom I came to see. Your mother said that you were indisposed.'

'I know. I was listening at the door. I felt that I must come and say this to you. Thank you for your thoughts for my predicament.'

'I had hoped …'

'It is hopeless,' I broke in, wanting no more humiliation for either of us. 'But you are very kind.'

The ruined face softened. 'I would have enjoyed taking you as my wife.'

In that moment I think I would have taken him in spite of his scars.

'It was generous of you to try again.'

'Are you certain, that you will not persuade your brother to listen to my offer?'

I knew how impossible it would be. 'Yes. I am certain. He is looking elsewhere, I believe. Good day, Master Scrope. I trust that you will find a bride who will suit you better than I, with a family who will be more generous to you.'

Reaching out, he took my hand in his, bending awkwardly, raising it to his lips.

'My thanks, Mistress Elizabeth. I wish you well.'

He inclined his head, released me, and rode away, while I walked back to the house by way of the kitchen, ushered in by one of the scullions who closed the door after me.

'Your mother is counting hams in the larder, mistress,' he

whispered, nodding towards the door. 'If you're quick you'll be gone before …'

I was not quick enough. My mother's sudden appearance, a large ham in her arms, caught me before I could disappear to my chamber. I fled, leaving the scullion to face her wrath; her loud complaint was followed by slamming of doors that echoed through the house.

Within a day, the scullion had been packed off to William to work in his London house. Did my mother have so little thought of my morals, suspecting that I would make a liaison with a scullion? I doubted that she did. It was simply one more example of her petty cruelties, allowing no servant who had any degree of compassion or a kind word for me to remain in our household.

She beat me that night.

Thus the Scrope betrothal was consigned for all time to the midden and all my hopes lay with the Grey of Ruthin relative who was exhilaratingly young and elegant and wealthy. We heard nothing, but these things took time. I was not downhearted.

Until a letter was delivered to me by my mother. She had already opened the seal and read the contents. She could have destroyed it, but my mother was scrupulous, not without a conscience in matters of business. I was an affair of business, rather than a matter for affection and concern.

'You may as well read it.'

She watched me as I did so. It was a seal that I did not recognise but why would I? I looked at the signature at the end. A name I did not know, but the content of it I now understood. Here was the outcome for the negotiations with Lord Grey of Ruthin. I smoothed the single page and read, keeping my face expressionless through long practice although my heart was beating fast.

★

Mistress Elizabeth Paston,

I regret any hopes of our marriage that might have been raised in your emotions. It cannot be.

Although he may not have made this clear to your brother, John Paston, I am the ward of Lord Grey of Ruthin. It is Lord Grey's scheme to arrange this marriage with you, with the sole purpose of claiming your dowry for his own ends. It may be that we would prove compatible but I refuse to wed at my lord's dictates, purely to further his own pecuniary interests. I am his ward and any dower appertaining to my marriage would end up in his coffers. I cannot approve of being married to any suitable lady to further my lord's desire for more income.

I would wed you but the dowry must be mine. I doubt my lord will support me in this. I think the negotiations between my family and yours are thus at an end. I must wed a bride of my own choosing, and I may not do this until I come of age to dispense with the wardship.

I write this, believing that you deserved an explanation from me.

With regret.

★

I folded it. Handed it to my mother when she beckoned with her fingers that I should. Such a beautifully worded letter. So courteous and thoughtful, seeing a need to apologise to me, an anonymous woman he had never met, for any false hopes that had been raised in my breast. He did not know the length and breadth and height of it.

He sounded very young but I could accept that, as I could readily understand his desire to dictate the path of his life.

I must wed a bride of my own choosing.

'He sent you this.'

My mother held out a leather-wrapped package that looked as if it might be a small book. Another gift. Of no value, but he had thought about me.

'Thank you.'

I climbed the stairs and added it to my little collection of pitiful relics. I did not even unwrap it to see what the gift might be.

My position at home became worse when John failed to discover any other possible husband. It was as if they had all dried up under the summer sun, like the saltmarsh at Cley, leaving a flat infertile plain, of no value to anyone. My mother's temper became shorter. It boiled over like a pot on the fire when I forgot to order a quantity of dried salt cod from our local purveyor of fish.

She slapped me.

'There now! If I want it done, I must do it myself. You are of no value to me here. I would be rid of you!' It was the first time that such words had actually been spoken. 'You do not try hard enough,' she said. 'I could wish that you lived elsewhere.'

I did not know whether she referred to my discovering a husband or my failure in the ordering of comestibles.

'The problem of my moving to another household is not mine!' I responded, stepping swiftly out of the range of her hands. 'I would willingly leave here.'

Would I ever become accepting of my life in this cage? I was trapped like the singing finch that John had given to Margaret in a moment of foolish light-heartedness. Did he know that Margaret had allowed it to fly free? It would enjoy its freedom;

Margaret would not have to feed it and clean up after it. Like that dejected caged bird I could sing and stretch my wings, but I could not fly. Even more fearful, would I one day become accepting of my prison through my inability to do anything but what I was ordered by my mother? One day I might lose any courage. One day perhaps I would not dare to step beyond our door, my wings truly clipped, so strange and distant and unwelcoming the world outside had become.

Chapter Nine

Margaret Mautby Paston

Norwich: 1454

'Margaret.'

I looked up from my platter of bread and ewe-milk cheese and the pippin that I was paring, to John who sat opposite me. He had been reading a letter from his brother Clement which as usual seemed to be a political comment on the state of King Henry's Court. John's eye caught mine, then slid away.

'What is it?' I asked brusquely.

After a heavy pause, he announced:

'News of Lord Moleyns.'

This was not the news I had expected him to deliver, a matter over which I felt considerable resentment. I managed to keep my tone light, interested. 'And what is Lord Moleyns doing now?'

John grunted in satisfaction. 'In prison, God be thanked. He felt compelled to fight in the English army in Gascony. When we were beaten at Castillon, our friend Moleyns was taken prisoner.'

'Excellent news,' I agreed, finishing the slices of apple. 'May he remain incarcerated in France for many years to come. I will pray for his good health to enjoy his lack of freedom.'

The visit of Queen Margaret was now over, merely a pleasant memory, although I still awaited a collar or neck adornment in case there was a repetition. Gresham remained a disquieting memory but we engaged in the lifestyle of a reasonably affluent Norfolk family, with no outward threats against us. John found time to leave his books and charters and litigation in London and come to live with me and our four children in Norwich. We attended church. Our servants visited the market. John met with his legal associates, and I took ale and sweetmeats with their wives, all without any bandying of crude words or physical violence against us. Perhaps that was now to be a thing of the past. We found a new brewer whose ale met John's exacting standards.

No contentment for my Uncle Berney, who did not recover from the attack despite my having sent on to him the pot of treacle. However highly recommended, it did not save him, who suffered more from the shock rather than any physical sickness. He would no longer stir from home. He would not use the chamber that was set aside for him in our new house in Norwich which I had duly rented, for more than I wished. It was a fine half-timbered house over a brick-vaulted undercroft, and I was determined to rent it to have the independence of my own hearth.

Except for Uncle Berney, the rest of the family thrived. Our sons, Elder John and Jonty were now twelve years and ten years and had learned their letters well. Our plans were that they would follow their father into the law. Margery was a sturdy six years and John was already casting around for a suitable betrothal for her. Edmund was four and intent on following his brothers, whatever they might be doing. He had an unnerving wilfulness that took him into mischief. All were healthy, not prone to childhood diseases, which allowed me great satisfaction.

During these days of unheard-of placidity, the first of my married life, I thought John looked inordinately pleased with himself, as a cat might that had filched a herring from the pantry. He said nothing so I let the matter lie. He would tell me eventually when he had worked out what it was that he was planning. I hoped that it was nothing unsettling, but feared the worst since he was attending far more meetings in Norwich than was usual.

'Margaret,' John said, again.

At last! Once more I looked up and this time his eyes caught and held mine. This was what he wanted to say, and I did not think that I would like it.

'There are some local people who would encourage me to stand for parliament.'

Now here was news to me, and news that was in no manner pleasing. For a long moment I let it lie in my mind as I considered the good and the bad of it. Oh, I knew why John would seek such an honour, of course I did, but he would seek it without thought of his family. Would it be of any advantage to the Paston family? I was certain that it would be of inestimable worth. But I was not won over by the prospect.

'Parliament, forsooth!' I did not guard my tone. It was decidedly combative. 'And how long has this been in your mind?' I pushed my platter aside, no longer interested in food.

I was aware that I sounded much like the shrew that he had once called me.

'A few weeks,' he admitted.

'You have decided to tell me at last.'

'I had to make the decision. Why raise it before I had decided?'

'And will you accept the advice of *some people*? Rather than discuss it with your wife?'

'I am discussing it now. It would be an advantage to us for me to be elected.'

John was regarding me with exasperation, knife clenched in his fist, but all I could see were the repercussions for us as a family.

I would try to be amenable; I folded my hands, one on top of the other on the table.

'I understand the need for your ambition being recognised, John, and I also understand how you would wish to accept the honour.' I drew a breath. 'But I see you less and less often as it is. I have to send to London to discover both the state of your health and your clothes.'

It was becoming increasingly difficult to be amenable.

Meanwhile John fought hard to keep his expression benign.

'You would be content enough with the status it will bring us in this town,' he said.

Which was true enough. I frowned down at the neglected food on the platter. What would grandfather Clement Paston have said if he had seen his grandson sitting in parliament with the great and the good in London? Both he and Justice William would have glowed with pride. I should do so, too.

'All very well to speak of status and standing,' I said. 'What value is that to me in the permanent absence of a husband? I am no better than a widow. Except that I am burdened with this.' I placed my hand on my belly where a new child now grew with ferocious energy, another consequence of John's presence in the household. 'Will this babe ever know its father when it is born? Will it recognise him, unless I point him out at Christmas and Easter?'

'It's not as bad as that.'

'It most certainly is!'

'It is not as if you cannot run the household and business dealings without me.'

'That is not the issue. When we wed I expected to see my husband at my board more than a dozen times in the year.' I poured a cup of ale and smacked it down in front of him so that it splashed onto the wood. 'And you're only here now because you are discussing becoming a member of parliament. I would like to think that it was because you enjoyed my company.'

John ignored the offered cup and strode out, as I knew he would. Sometimes he was very like Mistress Agnes, walking away from an argument he was losing.

The next commotion I heard, an hour later, was his shouting for his horse to be made ready and then he was riding back to London, leaving all uncertain between us. I deliberately did not present myself to bid him farewell but watched from my chamber.

At the last moment I opened the window and leaned out.

'John!'

Shouting from my chamber window might not be worthy of Mistress Paston, but I was in no mood to be dignified.

He looked up at me but made no effort to approach.

'If you are going to London, and if you by chance remember the present affliction of your wife, you might send home a dozen oranges.'

He rode out without a reply.

He sent the oranges but no letter with them, and although I enjoyed the eating of them, I nursed my resentment like the unborn child, under a black cloud.

Mautby: 1454

I moved to my newly built home at Mautby, not yet quite complete but sufficiently so that living there could be considered, where I was paid a visit by Mistress Agnes who had, to judge from her accompanying baggage, come to stay. I met her at the door.

'You will need some help around the house when this child comes.' She assessed the swell of my belly and the building still progressing around us to extend our living accommodations. The Hall was complete along with my solar and some of the bedchambers, but we were surrounded by dust and the smell of newly sawn wood, as well as the clamour of hammering with the frequent oaths of the men building the tie-beam roof and crown posts. 'Not long now, I would say. And I presume that John has no plans to return.'

Rumours of our falling-out had reached Oxnead.

'You are welcome here if you can put up with the noise. And no, I know nothing of your son's plans.'

Her stare was baleful. 'You wrong him, Margaret.'

The fact that she unexpectedly took John's part against me stirred my annoyance with both mother and son.

'I don't see him often enough to wrong him. And such criticism does not come well from you, Mistress Agnes. You are quick to complain when John does not do your instant bidding. You cannot now take me up for disagreeing with him.'

Which Mistress Agnes ignored in lofty refusal to accept any criticism.

'It will be good for the Pastons if he becomes a member of parliament.'

Obviously she had heard the cause of our dispute.

'It will be good for me if he finds the time to write to me, much less visit.'

'You must concentrate on matters at hand.' She waved her hand at the posts being carried past us, almost brushing our skirts. 'He relies on you.'

'Yes. Too much. I swear this child will be born on the road if I have to collect more overdue rents. There is rebellion in the air and our tenants are quick to tie the strings of their money bags tight.'

Mistress Agnes surveyed the room. 'He has spent liberally.'

'I know.'

'You have your new property in Norwich to take your interest.'

'Yes.'

'And the new child. You can deal with all of this without John's dancing attendance.'

'Why should I always have to?'

I was ashamed that my voice was becoming increasingly strident.

'There is no good in stirring him to hostilities.'

'Hostilities?'

'He does not find it easy to ask forgiveness for things he should not have said.'

'I know it.'

'Write to him, Margaret. And when you have finished kneeling in penitence, tell my son that we have need of some commodities from London. I will give you a list.'

'When I have finished over-looking the rent returns, only then will I consider kneeling in penitence! As for the list ...'

I left her to her own devices, running her hand over dust-laden surfaces. The child stirred in yet another energetic tumble beneath my girdle, its impatience as strong as my own. Undoubtedly it was the pregnancy that was making me so short of temper.

I sent his mother's list to him with no endearments.

★

Three yards of purple schamlet.
A bonnet of deep murrey.
A hose-cloth of yellow carsey.
A girdle of plunked ribbon.

★

And for myself I added:

★

Three pairs of low pattens, long enough and broad upon the heel.
Do not pay too much for them.

★

John could make of that what he wished.

★

The weeks passed. I enjoyed another packet of oranges, and the toothsome dates that accompanied them, sent by John, again without a note. He had been thinking of me after all, if only to send out a servant to make the purchases for me. Perhaps I had been less than tolerant. I also gave birth to another child.

Confined to the house until my churching, I wrote again to

John. An apology. I would have to do it, if the silence between us was not to grow and fester until Christmas. Oh, it was difficult to write. It felt clumsy and without elegance but I wrote it anyway. This was not a letter to dictate to the clerk or Master Gloys who had recently been restored to my household.

★

I beg that you will not be displeased with me, John. It is not my wish to do or say aught that will cause you displeasure. I am sorry and will amend my conversation in future. I beg that you will forgive me and bear no heaviness in your heart against me. Thought of such heaviness weighs with me.

★

I smiled wryly and applied my pen again, slowly. I might as well kneel in penitence.

★

I understood that you would wish to be a member of parliament. It may make your path to finding a reliable patron easier. Ambition, as Mistress Agnes has been quick to remind me, is strong in this family.

★

I paused. Should I break the news to him in this manner? It was the only way he would discover it.

★

I have been brought to bed of a child. To reassure you, we are both well. I know that it was your wish to have the baby called Henry after your brother who died many years ago soon after his birth. Our new child is a daughter. I think that she should be called Anne, after Saint Anne, the mother of the Blessed Virgin. I am sure that you will approve.

I will remain here in Mautby until I am churched, if you can find your way to make the acquaintance of your new daughter.

★

And finally, with gritted teeth, pressing hard so that the pen all but snapped under the pressure.

★

I will support you in your decision to stand for parliament.

★

There! I had done all that I could.

After I was churched I would turn my mind to the completion of this new building at Mautby. I was so proud of the comfort of higher ceilings and wide fireplaces, and not least the tile floors that John had promised me, but the purchase of joists and boards, as well as the interminable hammering, was giving me a headache.

★

'Will these be enough to feed the family?' I asked.

'Right well they will, mistress.' My cook beamed at me. 'If I add a side dish or two of Buttered Wortes and Cives d'Oeufs. And then perhaps Wardons in Syrup for those of a sweet tooth. Little Margery will enjoy them. Might I suggest, mistress, that you install a dovecote such as Mistress Agnes has at Oxnead. Squabs are always a good addition to a meal ...'

The door into the kitchen from the inner courtyard was pushed open, John bringing a surge of vigour with him. I had not heard him arrive. I turned slowly, wiping my hands on a bloodied cloth, determined to hide any pleasure that I might feel.

'Were we expecting you?' I asked, not unfriendly, but not welcoming.

'No. But here I am.'

His colour was high, his eyes bright as he caught me in his arms and lifted me so that my toes swept the floor. A kiss was planted on my coif.

'What's afoot?' I asked with a false smile.

Lowering me back to my feet, he eyed my gown. I was not at my best. I had been helping our cook in plucking chickens with the result that I was covered with small white feathers. Now so was John.

'Before God!' He brushed them off his own garments.

'What do you expect?'

'Not to see you working in your own kitchen. We are going on a visit. Change your gown.'

I made no move to do so. 'Might you wish to set eyes on your daughter first?'

'Yes, but quickly.'

I led the way to the room that had been set aside as a nursery where our daughter lay in her cradle, quite a plain affair and without ostentation since it had been made in grandfather Clement Paston's day, used by all the Paston children. John leaned over the baby; she looked up at him in silent contemplation.

'She is growing,' he said.

'How would you know? You have not seen her before today.'

'She looks like Margery.' He stroked a forefinger down her cheek.

'She does not look like anyone at the moment!'

I could not resist the urge to pinch at him.

'If you are to be a member of parliament, perhaps you should have a new cradle made for your daughter. One that does not look as if it has been brought in from the cow byre.'

'I may well do that.' He smiled down at the child who stared solemnly back. 'There. I have met my daughter and admired her. Now will you change your gown and make yourself ready?'

'To whom do we offer the honour of our visit?' I asked.

He followed me back into the kitchen, seizing my hands with a grimace before I could plunge one into the innards of the fowl.

'We are going to visit Sir John Fastolf.'

Which instantly caught my attention. Despite our cousinship Sir John and I were not on regular visiting terms. I was already unfastening my stained over-gown with its burden of feathers.

'Where is he?'

'At Caister Castle, of course. We are invited. Now if you could make yourself ready.'

'I will be with you in a half hour!'

I ignored his snarl of impatience, giving a passing nod to the fact that not once had he made any remark about our disagreements, nor had he accepted my written apology. It was as if all had been swept behind the kitchen screen, no longer to be given recognition. Well, I would remain silent also. I smiled at the prospect of a visit to Caister Castle and used my half hour well.

Austerity was abandoned and the blue robe with the fur trim donned, my hair confined in a blue and silver striped confection. Handsome? I would like to think so. And as a handsome matron I would do all I could to further my husband's ambitions, even if it still rankled that he would seek another position in London.

'Take him a gift,' Mistress Agnes advised as I settled the fashionable heart-shape low over my forehead, level with my brows.

'Why would he need a gift from us, when he owns innumerable manors and has made a fortune in the wars?'

'He doesn't need anything, but make him remember you with kindness. Smile on him. Business is all well and good, but a woman's pleasure in such an invitation is also of great value. Sir John might be an old soldier, but I expect he was never averse to flattery.'

'I have nothing to take that he would value,' I said. 'If he invites us again, I will embroider him an altar cloth. For now I must go empty-handed, and I don't believe he will think it remiss of me.'

★

An excitement built in me. Invited to Caister Castle indeed, whose tower could be seen during its construction, growing almost daily, from our new house at Mautby, although I was not aware that Sir John Fastolf had as yet taken up residence there but rather remained in Southwark until the building was complete. As

John and I rode the short journey together, since I had mellowed considerably, I asked him about this growing association, and he was quick to tell me. Of course I knew that he had had dealings with Sir John Fastolf over the years, but not to the width and breadth that had recently developed. It seemed that John had become the ageing knight's right-hand man.

'Does he not resent the Scrope situation?' I asked. 'He might think that you should have done more to bring it to pass.'

'It does not appear so. Sir John appreciates my legal knowledge more than he resents the lack of a marriage contract.' I decided that my husband's smile was excessively complacent. 'Who is the most powerful man that we know? I will strengthen my ties to him in every way possible.'

'Are you thinking he will be your patron? Would he have the ear of the King?'

'I believe so, and that of the magnates at Court. His reputation goes before him. And since he now owns Caister Castle he will be a power in Norfolk, too. Thus here we would have a rich and generous patron to protect us against local hostilities. And, even better, one connected to us through family as your cousin.' He was still glowing with his success. 'It is my ambition to become indispensable to him.'

John looked more light-hearted on that journey than I remembered him for some years. I hoped that his desire to be chief counsellor to Sir John Fastolf would replace his inclination to stand as a member of parliament, or at least for a space of time. And if he was to spend more time at Caister at Fastolf's whim, then I would have the pleasure of more of his company.

My cousinship with Sir John Fastolf was not of a close nature given the difference in our rank and our age. Our status was too dissimilar for our families to mingle frequently. My mother knew him better than I, but now it seemed that all would change.

What did I know of him? Sir John Fastolf was now over seventy years old, a goodly age. Before this substantial building at Caister, I presumed that he had lived alone in one of his various estates since his wife, Millicent Tibetot, an heiress at least a dozen years older than Sir John, had died a decade previously. He was well-known as a man of letters, a collector of books, an open-handed patron.

'Few castles are now built,' John was expounding at my side, as men do, 'but Sir John had ambition to mark his family importance by building this edifice on the site of his old family moated manor. All financed by plunder and booty from the French. Now he has moved in and is enjoying the costly accommodations, intent on living out his days in comfort, paid for by his years of hard labour with sword and shield. They say the work has cost him more than a thousand pounds.'

'Have you been here?' I was curious.

'No. All my work for him was done from his house in Southwark. This we must regard as an honour.' He looked sideways at me. 'I know you will do all you can to win his favour.'

'Of course.'

'And don't mention Master Scrope.'

'I will not. And I am willing to be impressed.'

And so I was. As we approached one of the two gatehouses with its bridge that led into the outer enclosure, John explained what he thought I needed to know, whether I did or not. All was built of brick with stone dressing, the bricks made locally, the clay from pits just north of the castle.

I looked around, weighing up what I saw against our recent

renovations at Mautby. It did not bear comparison, of course, either in its size or in conception. Here was a castle to rival any in the country. There was a squat tower to my left, at one of the corners, with a flat roof to bear a cannon to protect the whole. It made me smile, recalling my vulnerability in Gresham where the walls of my house had simply been hammered down by a tree trunk. Here was all power and security that would safeguard the occupant from any attack or siege.

And comfort was here, too, in two rectangular courtyards, the Outer and Inner Courts, lined with efficient ranges, supplying all the domestic expectations for a life of refinement, and all completely surrounded by a moat. Curtain walls protected the storerooms, the pantries, the buttery, and the stables, from which fine horses were being led by grooms dressed in the Fastolf livery of gold and blue with three silver shells.

We were welcomed, I was helped to dismount, and the Fastolf Steward, who made himself known to me as Master William Worcester, escorted us into the great keep where, in his private chamber, Sir John Fastolf rose from his chair beside the fire and turned a smile on us.

'Master Paston. And Mistress Margaret. You are welcome here in my new home.'

'We are honoured to be invited.'

'Forgive the warmth in here,' he said. 'My old bones feel the cold these days. The years of campaigning have taken their toll.'

It was indeed as if the years at war had drained all his strength. He was slight and spare, his face austere and much lined, his hands as gnarled as the trunk of an old oak, but still I sensed an energy in him. A gold cross and chain hung from around his neck, valued at two hundred pounds, John told me later. A great pointed diamond set upon an enamelled white rose was embedded in a collar that rested magisterially on his shoulders. The light glinted and shimmered from the heart of the gem.

He saluted my cheek. 'Cousin Meg. You have a very efficient husband when it comes to the detail of the law.'

'As I know. He is also one of the most hard-working.'

'I am sure he will be well rewarded. What do you think of my new home?'

'It is a jewel indeed, Sir John.'

'Would you care to investigate, while your husband and I discuss a matter of business? I am very proud of it. I enjoy any opportunity for a guest to explore and admire.'

'It would be my pleasure, Sir John.'

So under the guidance of William Worcester, I set myself to satiate my appetite for domestic details, to discover the quality of my cousin's home over five storeys of hexagonal rooms. Forty chambers, I was told, although we did not visit all of them. There were two halls for entertaining, a chapel, a buttery, and a pantry. And most miraculous, for Sir John's own use, a room with bowls, a bath and a water tank for the comfort of his ablutions. The Great Hall was festooned with tapestries, stitched with religious subjects, hunting and dancing, as well as bloody warfare.

'We have more than forty of them,' Worcester explained with some pride. 'Sir John likes to change the scenes in here. His mood dictates whether we eat surrounded by dancing maidens or martyred saints.'

Walls were plastered and painted. Some of the tiled floors were even furnished with tapestries, which made me shudder that their fine surfaces should be trodden on. Fireplaces and garderobes, set into walls and embrasures, were in generous supply. Many windows were large with painted glass, allowing the sun to scatter coloured patterns across the floor. There were timber shutters to protect the precious glass, as well as the inmates, in case of attack.

Indeed it was a jewel of a place, with even a pleasure garden where a lady might walk in the cool of the evening.

'Did you give suitable admiration to the diamond in Sir John's collar?' Worcester asked as he opened the door to return from the gardens and the fish pools into yet another room.

I laughed. 'Does he wear it every day?'

'Only when he receives visitors. It was bought by the Duke of York for four thousand marks and given to Sir John as payment for a loan and a reward for his loyalty. He sees it as an honour to wear it.'

I walked past Worcester into what must be a library. Books that did not interest me overmuch lined the walls although I enjoyed the leather bindings, the gilding, the vivid painted pages. Such wealth was beyond my imagining. And I knew the books, some of which lay open to be admired, to be of inestimable value, hand-copied in Latin and French and in English. Histories of England, *The Romance of the Rose*, a book of King Arthur, which Worcester was pleased to pull down from a shelf and open for me.

I made suitable responses, wondering how many servants Sir John must employ to keep such a vast dwelling free from dust.

We returned to eat dinner at noon from gold and silver plate decorated with gilding and enamel and adorned with lively figures of some heraldic significance, or with scallop shells, Sir John's own device. The food was plain, no rich sauces here or fanciful creations. Sir John had made no bow to the fact that he had invited guests, but the bread and meat were of excellent quality and there was no lack of dishes.

We stayed the night even though it would have taken no time to travel back to Mautby. Nothing would have persuaded me to step back from the offer to enjoy one of Sir John's bedchambers, sleeping under a silk canopy, with silk and velvet pillows beneath my head and the bedcovers embroidered with gold. Or to make use of one of the bowls providing water and perfumed soap from the east. A young serving maid helped me disrobe and plaited my hair before I slid beneath the sheets. My clothes were taken away to be cleansed before next morning.

I sighed with sheer pleasure, stretching my legs.

'While you discussed legal niceties, I swear that I have walked miles today,' I said.

'Were you suitably entertained by Worcester? He can be uncommunicative when the mood is on him,' John observed as he sat on the edge of the bed, tugging off his shoes, casting them aside.

'He was most informative. I expect that he approved of me since I asked all the right questions and admired Sir John's taste at every opportunity, even when I did not. Do you think that he will leave us one of his tapestries in his will?' I asked, leaning back against the silken pillows, studying the expert stitching of eagles and exotic flowers in the bed-hangings.

A slide of his eye in my direction aroused my suspicions that John had something in mind that was more important than a single tapestry. 'He might.'

'Tell him I would like the small one in the Great Hall, by the dais.' I traced the fine stitchery of the bedcover with one finger. 'It will hang well in one of our new rooms at Mautby.'

John remained silent.

'Does he entertain all his guests in this fashion?' I asked when no more was forthcoming.

'Why, yes. He has the wealth for it. More wealth than we can ever dream of.' He climbed into the bed beside me apparently oblivious to the rich furnishings, but then he had stayed at the Southwark house on more than one occasion. 'The diamond,' he said. 'It cost the sum of nine Suffolk manors. He has bags of gold coin as well as silver plate, more than we supped off. Most of it is stored in safekeeping at St Benet's Abbey.'

'He values you.'

'It is my ambition for him to value me even more. And I will make it my aim to become an ally of William Worcester who is close to Sir John. I can serve Sir John even better than I do at the present and reap the rewards.'

My heart lifted as I lay under the fine wool coverlet, too overawed to sleep. Life might just become a little easier with such a patron.

We parted company with our host after breaking our fast with bread and meat laid out on silver platters.

'Come back tomorrow, John, when you have delivered your lady wife home.' My cousin once more kissed my cheek. 'We have a contest to win, about which we must speak at length. I am of a mind to purchase the wardship of one of my young relatives. It will not be cheap or easy to obtain, but we can do it.' His glance towards me was keen. 'You have a very able and cunning husband, Meg.'

He placed his hand over John's when we were mounted.

'You are the heartiest kinsman and friend that any man could desire, John Paston. I know that we will continue to work well together, to our mutual benefit. I am old in years but there is much life left in me.' He turned to me with a smile which was all mischief. 'I have arranged a gift for you, Meg. You will find it waiting for you at Mautby. Treat it well. I do not think that you will be disappointed.'

He raised his hand in farewell as we rode away. John was very contemplative, and I was considering what the gift might be.

'Are you hoping for more than a small tapestry in Sir John's will?' I asked.

'Yes.'

'How much more?'

'Who is to say? By the by, Sir John is keen that we live at Mautby, which will be convenient for him.'

I could see nothing wrong with this. 'Then it will be convenient for me, too.'

John left me to my own thoughts. I would indeed stitch an altar cloth for the chapel in the castle. And it might get me a tapestry for my new hall after all, although I would never consider displaying it on any of my floors.

John's satisfaction in his developing vision of his future at the hands of Sir John Fastolf spread to me. We would be strong and secure, impervious to our past enemies.

Home again, I made the acquaintance of Sir John's mischief. A crate stood in the courtyard at Mautby amidst the stacks of joists and wall panels. It was a surprisingly large crate that shivered and hissed as I walked slowly to peer between the bars, black beaks stabbing through as if to wound any who came too near. I kept my distance. Here was no costly wall-hanging.

'What is it?' John asked, coming to join me. 'Birds, I presume.' He squatted to look at our new possessions, keeping his fingers clear.

'Swans,' I said. 'Four of them. What do we do with four swans?'

'Clip their wings and release them on the mere, where they will look after themselves, I suppose. They come from the moat at Caister.' John looked up at me. 'A gesture worthy of our new status, but it cost Sir John nothing to make it. I should tell you that in some quarters he has a reputation for parsimony.'

'Perhaps if I don't clip their wings, they will fly back to him.' I really could do without them. 'If they are any trouble to me, we will feast on them at Christmas!'

There was still business to be settled between us, John and I, and I could wait no longer. I put out my hand to restrain him when he straightened and began to walk towards the stables.

'Have you forgiven me?' I asked.

I thought that it needed saying.

'For what?'

I took a breath, knowing that I might be stirring up this hornets' nest when it did not need the stirring. 'For objecting to your becoming a member of parliament and spending too much time from home.'

He looked at me. I regarded him. It reminded me of our early days together when we were still discovering each other. And then he smiled. 'Oh, Margaret. Has this been a worry on your heart?'

'Yes. I do not enjoy being at odds with you. Am I forgiven?'

He linked his arm within mine, leading me towards the stable. 'Yes, my incomparable wife. You are. You were probably right in the first place.' And he kissed me so that I perforce must kiss him in return. It did not impinge on our dignity as a married couple of many years. There were only the swans to see us.

★

The months rolled on through the seasons, through mild summers when the sheep grew fat, into wet autumns when Mautby was threatened to be inundated with floods that turned the marshland into water meadows and our shoes grew mould with the perennial damp. Our household might have been settled, but not so the country. News of most of the doings in London and in the Court we gleaned from a distance, for little of it touched on our county of Norfolk. Another severe bout of pestilence broke out in London, William informed us, which brought him once more hot-foot home. The King emerged from his months of mental stagnation, meeting his baby son and recognising him for the first time, before sinking back into an inability to think or act in a kingly manner. Queen Margaret's visit to Walsingham had had a desired effect in producing an heir, but not in restoring the King to good sense.

I had no such need of a pilgrimage to Walsingham, coming to bed with another son whom we called Walter. I enjoyed more visits to Caister Castle and the altar cloth was duly completed with gold thread to enhance the tendrils that anchored the lilies around the edge. It was much admired.

The country remained in a state of imminent upheaval. When Henry first resumed his royal powers, the Protectorate of the Duke of York was brought to an end. The Beaufort Duke of Somerset was released from the Tower and returned to office at the King's side. This caused much hostility, York and the Nevilles solidly in alliance against the power of Somerset, who was equally intent on destroying York.

We were told of the battle fought at St Albans where Somerset was killed; King Henry was fortunate to suffer only a slight arrow wound to the neck. We gave thanks for his survival when we heard that the skirmish was fought without mercy through the streets of the town with much blood-letting. I could imagine the horror of the same in Norwich, the streets full of the dead and dying. York was made Constable of England. Queen Margaret, it was said, despised him and would continue to work for his downfall.

'Will there be battles here?' I asked John.

'I doubt it. None of the local magnates are sufficiently moved to march into battle.'

I enjoyed John's company, his sharp wit and comment, and my growing family. John returned to his thoughts of standing as a knight of the shire, to my regret, but was warned off by the Duchess of Norfolk who wished her Howard cousin to take the position. The Howard cousin, thin-faced and ambitious for power, was not well-liked in Norwich, but John saw the sense of not opposing him. Besides, as he had hoped and planned, he was becoming more and more shackled to the ambitions of Sir John Fastolf who kept him hard at work.

'What is it this week?' I asked.

'Which would you like to hear? It's all to do with money. Damages owed to him by the Duke of Suffolk's heir. His losses in France which he would like to reclaim. Loans to the King that have not been repaid. Henry has probably forgotten all about them. Claims against the estate of the now-dead Duke of Bedford. They go on and on. Sir John's fingers dabble in more pies than are served up at a royal banquet.'

'Are you well remunerated?'

'Of course. Sir John is generous to me.' But then John laughed. 'Not to everyone, though. Sir John is charged by many with avarice and cupidity. He does not like what he is hearing, so I am sent to be his close ear to the ground. When I was at the merchants' dinner in Norwich, the conversation ran like this: "Where shall we go to dinner? To Sir John Fastolf's – only he will make us pay for it even before the eating." Sir John would like me to give him the names of such men who he sees as his enemies.'

'And will you do so? I would not.'

'No, I think my time over the next month will be taken up with helping him to draw up his will. He has no direct heir and his fortune is large. He wishes to have a perpetual chantry set up at Caister to pray for his soul. But it will need a royal licence to grant land to a religious body. Impossible in the King's current mental state. I must apply again to the Lord Chancellor, our friendly Bishop Waynflete, who proved helpful in the past. Other than that we must offer up prayers for peace and wait to see what the Duke of York will do when faced with a hostile Queen. I smell the taint of battle and bloodshed in the air.'

'And where will you give your allegiance?' I asked him. 'If it comes to a war.'

He thought for a long moment, studying the document that he was writing.

'I do not know. King or York? There will be many in this realm as divided as I.'

I hoped it would never happen. Meanwhile, I picked and pounded pennywort into a green paste to smear on the feet of John and the children. Chilblains were a constant irritation from rooms that were either very hot or very cold. John complained more than his sons.

I had no compassion.

'If that is the worst you have to worry about, you will be well blessed!'

★

'You will be pleased to know, Meg, I have taken steps to assuage your worries.'

My husband had listened to my complaints of the burdens he had placed on me, and would continue to place if Sir John Fastolf had his way, and arrived one afternoon at Mautby with a young man in his company.

'Allow me, Margaret, to introduce to you our new bailiff, Richard Calle.'

Master Calle was tall, fair-haired, with a pleasing open countenance and neat garments that suggested a comfortable income, if not of the highest rank of townsfolk. He bowed to me with precision.

'Good day, Master Calle.'

'I am grateful for the welcome, Mistress Paston.'

He spoke softly with a Suffolk intonation. He had clearly received an education.

'Master Calle is now in our employ,' John said. 'I have need of a new bailiff, and I find him well suited to the task.'

A capable bailiff would certainly add to my own comfort. I expressed my satisfaction at his future place in our household, until he had left us to take possession of his new accommodations. I wondered why John should employ someone we did not know, from outside our own circle of acquaintance, but I knew better than to appear openly critical.

'He is very young,' I said.

'But highly experienced, so I am told.'

'What is his family?'

'They sell commodities of various kinds, in Framlingham.'

Shopkeepers, in effect. I pursed my lips. 'Does he have the necessary experience?'

John looked askance. 'He comes highly recommended. By the Duke of Norfolk himself.'

The Duke of Norfolk owned Framlingham Castle and so would know of this family. We would soon learn if John was satisfied with Master Calle's handling of recalcitrant manors and tenants who refused to pay their rents. He would have to prove to be intelligent and capable or he would not hold the position long. But being curious, I accosted Master Calle, inclined to discover for myself. The Duke of Norfolk's opinion was one thing, but I would make my own judgement.

'Tell me about your family, Master Calle.'

'My brother sells dried goods in Framlingham, Mistress Paston.'

'And you did not wish to continue in the business?'

'I have four brothers, mistress. Nor do I wish to work on the family farm in Great Waldingfield.'

'Is it a large farm?'

'No, mistress.'

I sounded like Mistress Agnes, question after question, concerned with the status of the man. But if John would not ask, then I would.

'You seem far too young to me to be appointed as our bailiff. Are you well educated?' I asked.

'I am.' He was confident, too. 'In Framlingham with the monks. I can read French and Latin as well as English. I can keep accounts.'

'Excellent.' What other questions could I ask? 'What is your ambition, Master Calle?'

'I would make money to buy land of my own.'

'So you have come to us.'

'The Duke of Norfolk pointed me in your direction.'

'And you were happy to come.'

He regarded me. I regarded him. His appraisal was steady and direct, but not without respect. Here was a man who knew his own mind. But would he fit into our household? His reply was forthright.

'I had little choice, mistress, if I am to make anything of my life. I followed the Duke's direction. I would say that my family is an old one, and has earned much respect with the townsfolk of Framlingham and its environs. I will work well for you. I will earn your trust.'

Which put me in my place. There was one more matter that slid into my thoughts.

'Can you oversee the care of four swans, Master Calle?'

He did not even blink. 'I expect that I can, Mistress Paston. I doubt they are much different from geese in their habits, of which I have some experience.'

Thus Richard Calle joined our household. We would see what we would see.

Chapter Ten

Elizabeth Paston

Oxnead: spring 1458

'I have instructed that your clothes be packed. You will be leaving tomorrow.'

My mother had sent for me. There had been no warning of this, so my throat clenched and my heart thumped out of rhythm in the face of what I did not know. What had she done? I knew with every difficult breath that this would not be the easy move I had prayed for. I could think of no household other than Margaret's where I would be welcomed.

Fear built rapidly. 'Where will I go?' I asked in a tight voice.

'It has been arranged by John, at my behest, that you go to London. William will meet you there. I am sending you to board with Lady de la Pole.'

My mother did not once look at me, instead shuffling the sheets of documents of rent agreements into a tidy pile. It was not unusual to send daughters to board in the house of some important personage, but even so I felt my heart give another heavy beat of dread.

'I do not know the lady.'

'It is not necessary for you to know her. She is willing to take you. She is the wife of Sir Thomas de la Pole.'

I considered this, recognising the name. The de la Poles were the family of the Dukes of Suffolk; Sir Thomas must be some distant cousin. Did we have enough influence that this titled lady would receive me into her house?

'Why will she take me?' I asked. 'When we do not know her?'

I might question it, but in my belly fear had been replaced by just the faintest kernel of hope, beginning to grow. Would this be the escape that I had dreamed of? Would this take me to London and a noble household, where I could live a different life?

'The lady is willing because I will pay her twenty-six shillings and eight pence for your board,' Mistress Agnes snapped as if she begrudged every penny of it. 'Your brother has negotiated it.'

So much. I could barely believe what I was hearing.

'Can you afford it?' I asked. Which perhaps was not wise.

Taking a swift step, she slapped at me, catching a sharp blow to my arm.

'I expect you to earn your keep, daughter. If you behave well, it will make a valuable connection for our family. You must use yourself readily, and help yourself as other gentlewomen do. I expect you can make yourself indispensable in such a household. You will leave at dawn.'

As if I were a child, not a woman of twenty-nine and a wretched one at that. Residing in London, of which I had no knowledge since I had never travelled there, might indeed be to my advantage, if it meant I could find a husband. I stood and met my mother's stare, defiance building within me, and with it that courage that I had thought lost for ever.

'Yes, I will ready myself, and I will use my time well in the house of Lady de la Pole. I will work hard for her. As for this house, I will leave Oxnead with joy. It has not been my home for many years, just a place where I must eat and sleep and work. You are my mother, but you have used me ill. You will chastise me no more.'

'I have given you food and clothing since the day that you were born.'

'But no affection. I swear that I will never again return to your dominion.'

My mother's lips thinned.

'What will you do if Lady de la Pole no longer needs you?'

'I would rather be one of the harlots who earns her keep in London than return here.'

An empty threat, but I turned and left the room, my mind full of possibilities. How would I find my new mistress? Would she have a kindly disposition? Would she beat me? But I was not a servant. I rejoiced at the prospect of a change of scene, of a different household, a new world. I expect that my mother did, too.

I was later to read her letter to William where my arrangement was mentioned after a list of errands for my brother. The payment for my board was placed below the making of six spoons for Mistress Agnes, carefully noted to be of eight ounces troy weight, well made and double-gilt. Thus was my value.

I left behind the tokens of my past life: the lace, the gloves, the letter. They were of no importance. What was the value of my living in the past? Sometimes the power of memory was too painful, and I would not encourage it.

My mother did not embrace me before I left.

★

In London I was met by William on Ludgate Street, my baggage strapped to a packhorse, two stalwart Paston servants to accompany me and my maid for protection.

'Eliza! At last!'

He had come from the Inns of Court, full of haste and self-importance. With all the energy of youth, William lifted me down from my mount and saluted me with a kiss to my cheek, at the same time dealing efficiently with the coffers and horses. I was impressed seeing my younger brother take charge in such a manner. I should not have been. If he could argue a case and win it in the courts, he could disperse my coffers and servants. His hand gestures were confident, his dispensing of small coin liberal.

'Come on. Don't linger.'

He drew my arm through his to lead me the short distance to the house where my new life would begin, while I was overpowered by the size of the city, the raucous noise, the stench of crowded humanity. There had been nothing in Norwich, where the raw reek of the tanneries was bad enough, to warn me of what I would find here. My initial excitement had early been replaced by a trepidation.

'I am surprised that you have found the time to meet me,' I said as my brother strode on, all but dragging me with him, his dark hair stuffed beneath a plain woollen cap, his eyes burning with some unexpressed zeal.

'It was not easy.'

I would not be high on his list of business for the day. I liked him, but had to acknowledge that William was driven by an ambition even stronger than John's, an ambition that was to be achieved in London, as close to the Court as possible and whichever magnate had the King's ear. There were seven years between us, fifteen years between John and William. William still had all the exuberance that John had lost in his struggles over land and disputed inheritance.

'Are you using your time well in London?' I asked, to quell my growing sense of abandonment.

'Better than any man would expect. When we are not suffering a dose of the pestilence.' I must have shivered. 'There is no need to fear. There is none at present to make you go home again.'

'Nothing will make me return to Oxnead!' I said.

He cast a glance over me as he led me round a puddle of unspeakable filth. Looking at his shoes, he was not always so careful. I tiptoed carefully so as not to arrive on Lady de la Pole's doorstep with ordure seeping into the leather.

'Nor need you if you prove indispensable to Lady de la Pole. You look in good heart.'

'My heart is better for escaping from our mother. Is it always as noisy as this?'

'Yes. My advice, dear sister, is to make the most of your escape.'

'So I have been told. But how will I do that?'

'You will discover when you see how the household works. Take time to watch and learn. You are a sensible girl, I think. All Pastons are sensible, except perhaps my brother John who sometimes has no sense at all …'

I gripped his arm as townsfolk pushed past us, ignoring his animadversion on our brother's obsessions with his own glittering future. 'I am no longer a girl. And I have no wish finally to go to my lonely grave with a reputation for being no more than sensible.'

'No, but you have the good sense to see what will be of

value to you. Be helpful, obedient and cheerful. Do not linger in corners. Your position here is paid for so you have a right to be here. Lady de la Pole will not be as difficult to satisfy as our mother. And if a husband crosses your path, snap him up. John and I will support you, even if Mistress Agnes does not.' Our route was now into an area of more substantial houses on both sides of the road, all leaning inwards so that the sky was almost blotted out. 'No one will help us if we do not help ourselves. Nor can we waste time.' As we crossed the road between two large wagons, I saw the little frown between his brows. 'I'll not waste time when I decide to wed.'

Which surprised me. This was a very personal line of thought from William. I had not heard of his approaching nuptials.

'And have you decided?'

'I have yet to set my eye on a young woman who will further my career.'

'Or one who might have an eye to you?'

He smirked, full of confidence, but offered no comment.

'I presume that she must be a bride of high value,' I suggested.

'More than you could ever guess at.'

'You are still young with much before you.'

'I will not always be so. My brother wed an heiress. I will make a name for myself and do the same. I cannot wait for ever. Remember this piece of advice: do not hesitate in approaching anyone who will be of use to you.'

'Easy for you to say. You are a man.'

'And you are a resourceful woman.'

'No, I am not. I never have been. I have been cowed all my life.' Now that the moment came for parting, I felt like gripping

184

his arm even tighter. He seemed to be my last anchor in a strange world. 'I have nothing to recommend me in such a fine household,' I said, fear mounting.

'If you make an excuse even before we arrive, you will achieve nothing. Look to the future. You do not want to make that return journey to Oxnead unwed. I would not wish that on you for all the wealth in the royal coffers.'

William came to an abrupt halt.

'Where are we?' I asked, looking around.

'The Strand. And there is the home of Sir Thomas and Lady de la Pole. Pluck up your courage, Eliza. This will be your home.'

The de la Pole house on the Strand: spring 1458

On the strength of the promised payment from Mistress Agnes, or perhaps it was because my brothers were becoming known at Court, I was made welcome, discovering that it was an easy household into which to settle. Lady de la Pole, older than I but younger than Mistress Agnes, proved to be kind and not demanding other than that I should bear her company. She had servants enough to carry out the menial daily needs of her household, so it was not an onerous existence. I prayed with her. I read with her. I carried her missal to Mass. I stitched with her. I became used to female gossip, about the family, the discussion of the events in London and at Court. I did not find it easy to express an opinion, having so little experience of it in my life, but Lady de la Pole was blessed with an ability to laugh, to entertain and to be entertained. She was easy to like.

So was her house on the Strand.

I was used to the comfort of the Paston dwellings, but nothing could have prepared me for this. Built on an elegantly vaulted stone undercroft, here was the luxury of space and fireplaces, of windows with efficient shutters, of chambers rising up over three storeys. The carved beds were curtained in blue and gold wool, the colours of the de la Pole heraldic badge. The walls of the Great Hall that occupied the whole of the first storey were awash with a riot of leaves and flowers, all expertly stitched, from which peeped eagles and lions and popinjays. I wished Margaret could see them for I could imagine Caister Castle having no finer. Over all was the pleasant scent of herbs used by a careful Steward who kept the property as well preserved as its owners would wish.

In such surroundings I soon discovered that my garments were not acceptable to those who would be clad in the height of fashion. Nor had I the money to remedy it. To my pleasure, Lady de la Pole was generous to a fault. I was donated a hood here, a length of veiling there, a pair of fine gloves, numerous shifts and a cote-hardie in finest wool, even a fashionable houppelande in the softest of velvets and another in rich satin. My mother would have decried the vibrant hues of verdant green and dark amethyst, the extravagance of gold stitching and fur cuffs, but I revelled in it and in the affection handed so liberally to me, a beggar after years of near starvation. I was not humiliated, merely grateful, for I knew how important it was to impress.

I soon became far more politically aware than I had been under Mistress Agnes's aegis since little occupied her thoughts other than the state of the Paston properties. It soon became clear to me that John de la Pole, the present Duke of Suffolk, blighted by the political fall and subsequent murder of his father who had been a significant opponent of my family in their fight to hold onto their estates, had wed one of the daughters of the Duke of York and

186

his wife Cecily Neville. Although he was not inclined to take to the battlefield, this marriage put him firmly into the Yorkist camp, and thus so were Sir Thomas and his lady. So, by acquaintance, was I. I was careful to match my political opinions to those of Lady de la Pole. Never had I been so conforming in my thoughts, but my heart was at rest and I was not unhappy. I was never beaten. Sometimes I was awarded a kiss to my cheek, or a smile. I had to learn not to flinch if by chance she stepped close to me.

As the days passed into the second month, I wondered how long I would be able to remain. It could not be permanent, but I learned to cling to every hour of my freedom. William had said that I was clever, but how to use my cleverness?

'What you need, Elizabeth, is a husband,' Lady de la Pole observed one day out of nowhere.

'So my mother believes.'

'You would make a most competent wife for a man with land and dependants. You are amiable, most capable, and would fit well into any household.'

'I have learned to be quiet and accommodating.'

She laughed indulgently. 'You decry yourself, Eliza. I think you have a stronger will than you realise. Your age is against you, of course.'

'So I fear.'

'I will bend my mind to it,' she promised.

★

Lady de la Pole had a well-deserved reputation of welcoming visitors into her house. I learned to attend such gatherings, to acquire confidence, to talk if I was addressed, shuffling aside my usual quiet demeanour. My acceptance in such society had much to do with brother John's business alliance with Sir John Fastolf. Who would have thought that the old gentleman would have eased open the door for me in this company? It was on an afternoon in the warmth of July that I was part of a group of a few friends and family.

'There is a gentleman here whom you might care to meet, Eliza.'

I read a gleam in Lady de la Pole's eye. At least it was a kindly one.

'Are you attempting to find me a husband, my lady?'

'Of course. As I said, it is long past time.'

It reminded me of William's thoughts, that so much of my time had been wasted, but I was not full of hope, even if Lady de la Pole took a hand in the matrimonial game. The old fears raised their multitude of heads.

'Tell me he is not very old, my lady. Or lacking sufficient income to please my mother. Or has too many dependants. Or is ...'

Her hand on my wrist silenced me and she smiled. 'I will tell you nothing. Come and meet him, as a friend and as a favour to me. You will see for yourself.'

I walked beside her through the chattering groups where the conversation was much about the continuing clash of will between Queen Margaret and the Duke of York which must surely result in more bloodshed before the year was out. The Battle of St Albans had solved nothing except to remove Somerset from the scene. York still had ambitions, perhaps even greater than before: the Queen would do all in her power to thwart them.

'Does he need a wife, my lady?' I asked.

'I think that he does.'

I thought about this reply.

'Does this gentleman know that he needs a wife?'

Lady de la Pole chose not to answer as she ushered me towards a gathering of men drinking wine and talking loudly with her husband by the window. With a brief apology, she took the arm of one of them and drew him away, towards me.

'Robert, allow me to introduce a guest of mine. Mistress Elizabeth Paston.'

He bowed.

I curtsied.

'She is newly come to London. She is sister of John Paston, the lawyer. The family is well connected to Sir John Fastolf. Eliza, this is a family friend of ours, Robert Poynings. He is not from your part of the world but from a Sussex family. He is a member of parliament.' She patted his arm. 'Eliza does not have a wide acquaintance here. Entertain her for a little time, to please me.'

Robert Poynings obediently led me to a cushioned stool, away from the gossiping throng, and found me wine while I watched him. I had no notion of his financial situation, nor his family. I would enjoy the moment, to simply talk to a well-dressed man of less than forty years with not a scar on his face and an admirable physique. He returned, gracefully presenting me with a cup of wine before taking a stool at my side.

'Lady de la Pole says that I must entertain you.'

'I would be grateful if you would. I find gatherings where I know no one very hard.'

He looked around. 'I think that I know everyone here.'

Which I thought to be a typical male comment, full of easy confidence. 'Then you are fortunate, sir. You will not understand my discomfiture.'

His smile was sympathetic. 'Forgive my lack of compassion. Tell me about yourself, Mistress Elizabeth Paston.'

So I did.

What did we talk about when my family connections had been covered to his satisfaction? My impressions of London. His home in Sussex. My knowledge of Norwich. Was I enjoying my sojourn? All irrelevant matters, requiring us to leap across many pauses, wondering what next to speak of. As soon as this trivia could be spread out no further and the wine drunk, he gallantly escorted me back to Lady de la Pole, bowed, once again joining the men who were still exchanging opinion on when and where there would be another battle, and would they present themselves on the field, even though to oppose the combatant Queen would be tantamount to treason.

'What do you think?' Lady de la Pole asked without preamble.

I considered before I replied. There was a cool reserve about Robert Poynings, a self-containment that was new to me since my Paston family were outspoken and boisterous. His long features were smoothly carved, his brown hair holding a touch of russet when caught in a sun's ray. There was a quiet eloquence about him and I decided that he knew his own mind and would be chivvied into nothing that he did not wish for.

'That he is a fine gentleman,' was all I could say.

'He makes quite an impression, does he not?'

'He dresses well.'

His thigh-length houppelande, figured in deep green and black, was cut from better wool than John ever wore, his hose so well woven that they might have been silk. I thought that the accoutrements on his belt were made of gold.

'Is that all you can say, Mistress Eliza Paston?'

'No. He is polite. He was very kind and talked to me when he would rather discuss the situation between York and the Queen. He is too good for me, my lady. He will want a woman who is more well-informed and better dowered from a family of good blood and high repute. He will look higher than a Paston.'

'Perhaps.'

What I had learned in our brief conversation was less than encouraging to a woman from a newly emerging family, who might consider him as a possible husband. Sir Robert Poynings was the second son but now the heir of the fourth Baron Poynings, with a younger brother and a half-sister from his father's second marriage. A man of considerable means and some political ambition. He might be under some pressure to be wed, but he would look to a family of his own status. He would look for wealth, land, and useful connection, probably in Sussex.

What had he thought of me, with neither colouring nor features to recommend me? I was in his eyes little better than a servant, wearing borrowed clothes.

But he had been good to talk with, even for so short a time.

★

One morning Lady de la Pole and her household made a pilgrimage. A short journey, our objective was the most holy shrine of Edward the Confessor within the great abbey at Westminster. There we would pray for the deliverance of our city from the terrible effect of the pestilence that came to assail us in frequent waves of suffering and death. We left our horses and our shoes at the door in the care of the de la Pole servants and walked barefoot the length of the abbey to the structure behind the high altar that contained the much-revered bones of the saintly king. We were not alone. There were many who felt the need to seek the saint's blessing.

There we knelt, full of penance, shivering in the chill, our feet cold and dirty, and offered petitions for God's deliverance. At the same time we prayed for the good health of the King, his weak mind allowing dissent to wrench open the unity at Court. Lady de la Pole considered that the two camps needed our prayers in equal measure.

There was no sign that the saint in his magnificently carved shrine heard our petition, but we had faith that he would as we retraced our bare footprints with a lighter heart.

Lady de la Pole had not abandoned her project to see me with a husband. By her design, as I supposed, I found my mount ambling beside that of Sir Robert Poynings as we returned to the Strand.

'Did you realise, Eliza,' Lady Pole queried ingenuously, 'that Sir Robert has only recently returned to our company after an unfortunate imprisonment, which he did not deserve?'

'I was not aware.'

'If you ask him, he will tell you about it.'

Without subtlety she urged her horse to quicken and left us together.

'You must excuse her ladyship,' Sir Robert observed, his solemn face creasing into a smile. 'She thinks that we would deal well together. I am sorry if her obvious methods displease you, Mistress Eliza.'

'They do not displease me, Sir Robert.'

Indeed it pleased me that he had abandoned formality and used my more intimate family name. But what would we talk of now? We had used up all the trivia of new meetings. But Sir Robert was of a mind to be expansive.

'Are you shocked that I was imprisoned?'

'I don't think so.' Perhaps I was a little. Whatever the shadowy roots of my own family, no one had been in prison. 'Will you tell me?'

'I have bored my own friends with the stories of my recent history.'

'I promise I will not be uninterested. Perhaps I can claim to be a new friend who will gladly listen.'

A man who had been imprisoned but was now restored to acceptance. He intrigued me. I was astonished at my boldness. Perhaps it was the courage engendered by the new gilded crispinette that contained my hair most flatteringly.

'Tell me when I have said too much.'

'I promise that I will.'

He returned my smile.

'It's a simple enough story to tell. I joined Jack Cade in his rebellion. You know of it?' When I nodded, he continued. 'The men of Kent feared that the King planned revenge on them for the Duke of Suffolk's murder on the beach at Dover. I have manors in Kent and knew Jack Cade. I had sympathies with his cause, to assuage the lot of the common people, and I served as his sword-bearer when he took up arms.' His eyes lifted to mine. 'Do you find this tedious?'

'By no means.' I thought I would if it were John giving me a lesson in Kentish politics, but there was a winsomeness about this man. I had discovered that I knew very little about Jack Cade.

'You are very kind to bear with me.'

'I am interested in why you ended up imprisoned.'

He shrugged one shoulder, as if perhaps he did not wish to remember too much. 'It was very simple, if bloody. The rebels failed. Jack Cade was wounded in a skirmish and died on the road. His corpse was beheaded at Newgate. A lesser fate was reserved for me. I was imprisoned and outlawed. I spent time in the Tower and then in Kenilworth Castle. No great hardship was imposed on me, I was no martyr, it was merely the loss of my freedom that I had to accept. Last year I sued for a pardon which has been granted since the King has decided that his mercy will win friends to the House of Lancaster. So you behold me, restored to grace and to my lands and re-elected as a member of parliament. And I am received once more into the households of my friends.'

All coolly and unemotionally recounted, as if it had brought no suffering, although I thought that it had, if only to his self-esteem. He had also lost a friend.

'Did you fight?' I asked.

'Yes, there was a battle of sorts through the night on London Bridge. It came to nothing and we were defeated.'

'I expect that you were very brave.'

'No more than any man faced with such a situation.'

'Why would you risk your life and your property in a rebellion that would never succeed? How could you hope to move the King to listen to your demands?'

'It seemed a cause worth fighting for.'

I knew from the brusque reply that he would say no more.

'It must be a relief to you that it is all over.'

'Of course. But now there is much family pressure for me to find a wife and produce an heir for the Poynings estates.'

As I had thought. 'I doubt you will have difficulty, sir.' I surmised he would have no difficulty at all. What a personable man he was.

'Perhaps not.' A little silence fell between us. 'But let us talk about you, Mistress Eliza.'

'I have nothing to say, sir.' I felt my senses close down, dulled like an old tapestry, my tongue become tied.

'Do you stay for long with Lady de la Pole? Does it satisfy you to be here?'

'It satisfies me greatly.' I looked across at him, at his severe profile. Why not be honest since he had been so with me? I had nothing to lose. 'I stay as long as my mother continues to pay for my board. And as long as it takes for my lady to discover a husband for me. I do not know who will give up soonest. I suspect that it will be my mother, since money is close to her heart. Then I will be summoned home again.'

'Do you not want that? To be with people that you know? I recall that you said that you disliked gatherings where you knew no one.'

He had listened to me. He had remembered.

'I do not wish to go home.'

If he registered my blunt denial, he made no comment. We steered our mounts round an obstruction in the road where a cart had lost one of its wheels and shed its load of pungent leather.

'Has it been so very difficult to achieve a husband for you? I find that hard to believe,' he continued when we were free once more to converse.

'Inordinately. My family has high standards when assessing a new husband's financial state. My mother rejects any man who seems unworthy.'

'I would have thought that your brother John Paston would have seen an advantage for you in a good marriage.'

'He is more involved with hanging onto his own acres in the face of great hostility. A sister's betrothal is not high on his list of necessities.'

'Do you have no dower?'

'I do. I was left the money for a dower in my father's will. Unless my mother has spent it to ameliorate Paston problems.'

We rode on in silence for a little way. I was beginning to regret my honesty. What would he think of me, of my family? I should have had more discretion.

As the de la Pole residence came into view, offering me an opportunity to escape, Sir Robert asked: 'Do I understand that Lady de la Pole considers me as a possible husband?'

I was startled into a blunt reply: 'Yes. But that does not mean that you have to be compliant. I imagine you are considering any number of more suitable women to fulfil the role of Dame Poynings.'

How could I have been so outspoken?

Sir Robert laughed softly. 'No, I do not believe that I am noted for being a biddable man, as Lady de la Pole well knows.'

He helped me dismount at last, and I was sorry that our acquaintance of the morning would come to an end. But there was Sir Robert Poynings picking up an earlier conversation, as we stood close together.

'Would it be too unpleasant, Mistress Eliza?'

'To remain with Lady de la Pole? Why no, as I said—'

'To wed a man such as I.'

I was robbed of words. Then, 'Why would you even consider it? I have nothing to recommend me. Nothing to offer a man of your status.'

For the first time he truly smiled, showing his teeth, rather than the previous polite curl of his lips. 'I like honesty in a woman.'

'As I do in a man. But Sir Robert Poynings needs more than honesty in a bride.'

'Perhaps he does. I am pleased to have met with you again, Mistress Paston. I am surprised that no one has courted you.'

'Oh, they have. They have. And failed abjectly.' Had I truly said that? 'Is your income quite unencumbered, Sir Robert? It is your only hope.'

Now he laughed aloud and kissed my hand in the manner of a Court gallant. I had never received so warm a tribute.

Lady de la Pole, as we parted company from our prayerful companions: 'Well? What do you think?'

But I had not changed my original thoughts. Sir Robert would look elsewhere, and I watched with regret as he rode away. There would have been no love in such a marriage, but honesty and respect. Successful marriages were built on much less than that.

Meanwhile, as the days passed all was quiet in London, the progress of the Duke of York and his Neville allies simmering in their quest for power but bringing no further outright clash of forces. I heard nothing from my brothers or from Margaret. Nothing from my mother. Nothing at all from Sir Robert who had probably returned to his Sussex lands. Any little flame of hope in that quarter slowly flickered out and died.

★

'There are movements afoot,' Lady de la Pole announced, setting a stitch in a girdle, the leaves and flowers twining in green and deep rose and gold thread, with a hint of citrus yellow which I thought did not enhance the whole.

'To what purpose?' I presumed that she meant some further development between York and the Queen. 'Has there been another battle?'

'That is not my meaning, Eliza. Master William Worcester, Steward to Sir John Fastolf, has been much occupied on your behalf.'

'Worcester?' I dropped my needlework to my lap. There was no bright yellow in my stitching. 'I do not know this man, although I think I have heard my sister talk of him. He escorted her around Caister Castle on her first visit and pointed out every item of value which she should admire. Why would he have any interest in me?'

'He is an associate of your brother John Paston since both work closely for Fastolf. Your brother has spoken of your plight to Sir John, with the effect of Master Worcester becoming a busy man. He travels between your brother and Sir Robert Poynings to achieve negotiations pleasing to both.'

I truly could not believe what I was hearing. A negotiation: it could only mean a marriage settlement. Viciously I quenched all hopes, for we had been here before.

'How has this come about?' I asked as if it were of no importance.

'By pure chance, but what an excellent opportunity. Your brother is a master at making opportunities work for him. Sir Robert, so it seems, twice saved the life of a man called John Payn, one of Fastolf's servants, from the blood-letting in Cade's rebellion. Payn had been left in charge of Fastolf's house in Southwark. He stopped it being burnt to the ground but was taken prisoner by the rebels and threatened with a summary execution.

Sir Robert rescued him and set him free. Thus Fastolf owes Sir Robert a severe debt of gratitude and is generous in showing an interest in the choice of a wife for Sir Robert.'

'But why me? Sir John is willing to support me?'

'So it seems. If Fastolf can reward Sir Robert, he will be well pleased, and at the same time glue fast his association with your brother. Everyone will come out of this smelling of victory, not least yourself, dear Eliza.'

'Then I trust that Worcester will be successful. But I still do not see why Sir John Fastolf's good intentions to reward Sir Robert should have settled on me.'

Lady de la Pole's smile was wry. 'We have to accept that Sir John Fastolf has no real personal interest in you, my dear Eliza, merely that here is an opportunity to tie your inestimable brother John Paston close to him through another debt of gratitude.'

It was not a flattering thought, but, oh, I hoped that Master Worcester would succeed. In my chamber I fell to my knees and offered fervent prayers to the Blessed Virgin, even when I did not believe that my prayers would be answered after so many years of heavenly silence. I wished a fleetness of foot to Master Worcester as he rode back and forth, and a long life to Sir John Fastolf. I prayed that my brother John would not tell my mother until all was settled. I prayed that Sir Robert's money coffers would be overflowing.

And still, through long disappointment, I had no hope.

★

My marriage settlement was agreed.

'It is done,' John advised me on a rare visit, brother William again in his company.

'Does my mother agree?'

'Not easily, because of difficulties in Sir Robert's ownership of some of his estates in Kent, but she will not speak against it. William and I have stood as guarantee that Sir Robert will give a bond of one thousand pounds to Mistress Agnes, that he will produce a jointure for you. It has sweetened our mother beyond belief. In return she has agreed that she will raise the money promised for your dower. You and Sir Robert Poynings will be wed.'

I let the words settle into my mind, to spread their honeyed sweetness. I was worth one thousand pounds to Sir Robert. Such wealth.

'I cannot believe it.'

'You will achieve a titled husband, your own home, a family,' William said. 'And an escape from the perpetual sense of failure at Oxnead. Did I not say that you were resourceful?'

I kissed him, surprising us both with the excess of emotion, but was not my mind enthralled by the idea? Then to John, 'Will she do it? Will she keep her word, or change her mind again?'

I could almost believe that Mistress Agnes would wait until the last moment before she dashed my hopes.

'I believe she will keep it,' John reassured, patting my shoulder as if I were a favourite mare. 'We have worked hard to get this far. Besides, this is due to Fastolf, and I will not allow our mother to sabotage this settlement. Fastolf wants it to happen, so happen it will.'

I breathed out slowly as I read John's determination to have his own way in this.

'You cannot believe my gratitude.'

'And you will be happy.' It was almost a warning that I must not throw away this chance. 'You will not turn away from this marriage.'

Did they not trust me? 'I will. I swear it. My thanks to you. Both of you.'

William's lips curved in a smirk.

'I am considering marriage also.'

Both John and I turned to stare at him. We had heard nothing of this. When I had last asked him he had denied an interest in anyone.

'Who is the fortunate lady?' John asked.

'I will bring her to meet with you when her family has accepted my offer.'

'Do you not need your brother's agreement in making a settlement?' John asked.

William's reply was unnervingly terse.

'Not I! What help have I ever received from my family?' But when he read the sudden shock in my face at such rancour, he lapsed into good humour. 'I will make my own way in the world. I will amaze you all with my talents.'

'Did you know that William has a bride in mind?' I asked John when William had departed about his own concerns, making his bow to Lady de la Pole.

'No, I wonder if it should worry me. It all seems to be swathed in secrecy. But then, much of William's career is, until he reveals his success. Sometimes it is as if there is a resentment in him that he inherited no Paston estates from my father. And then he supports me in some difficult case and I think I am mistaken.'

William might be a master at hiding his thoughts, but it seemed to me that he bore a well-honed grudge. Where it would lead I had no idea.

★

I had little faith in this marriage settlement until I was summoned by Lady de la Pole to meet with Sir Robert Poynings in her parlour. She was kind enough to leave us alone.

'Sir Robert.'

'Mistress Eliza.'

Thus the courtesies.

'I think that you have expected this visit.'

'I have not dared to do so.'

'Now you may dare. My family and yours have come to an agreement that we will be wed.'

'I hope that I will be worth the bond that you had to pay to persuade my mother.'

It was all I could think of to say, and perhaps not the reply he had hoped for. Sir Robert waited for a long moment, his eyes searching my face.

'If I may say, Mistress Elizabeth, you have an air of unease about you. I will never persuade you into a union that you do not desire. Are you sure that this is what you wish for? I should say that, financial consideration apart, it will be my pleasure to bring you happiness in our marriage.'

I regarded him, his solemn countenance, his perfect composure, while my heart thundered in my chest. Could I trust this man whom I had known for so little time when trust had never held a central place in my life? As I acknowledged in that moment, my mother was cruelly self-interested, my brothers too concerned with their own affairs, Margaret compassionate but buried under estate matters in John's absence, Mistress Clere too distant a cousin.

'No one has ever had a concern for my happiness, Sir Robert. I have never been asked what I might wish for.' I took a breath and continued with the enormity of this confession. 'I find it difficult to trust people. I think that you should know this before we take another step.'

Trust! Trust for me was like a carp in one of the ponds at Oxnead. It could be solid enough between my palms, but too quick to slither away when I lost concentration, to disappear for ever amongst the reeds. Leaving me to explain to my exasperated mother my failure to secure it.

'I do not ask for pity, Sir Robert. Just for understanding when I do not respond as you might like.'

He took my hands in his, such a warm clasp as if he understood all my anxieties. His reply proved to me that he did.

'You need never go back to Oxnead again, Elizabeth. It will be a comfortable life for you as my wife. We will do well together. I will never expect more from you than you are free to give.'

And I held onto those hands, hard and calloused as they were from sword-play, as if I were a drowning woman grasping the one who had come to save her from certain death.

'Are you sure, Sir Robert, that of all the women you know, you want me for your wife?'

'I am determined on it.'

I nodded as if he had cleared the path for my decision.

'Then I promise to be an efficient and honest wife, Sir Robert.'

'I have no doubts. I do not seek your hand in marriage out of pity. You will never receive ill-treatment at my hands. That is what I promise you.'

I wondered how much John had told him of my past experiences. I had been tight-lipped, unwilling to exhibit my shame. Now I found that I was smiling. It might have the appearance of a business transaction, but for me it was a moment of true delight.

'May I say, Mistress Eliza, that when you smile you are quite beautiful.'

I did not believe him, but it was as much and more than I could ever have hoped for. Sir Robert Poynings knew well how to put a woman at her ease. I was astonished when he kissed my fingers and my palms before holding them flat against his chest where his heart was beating as rapidly as mine.

'I will wed you with joy in my heart,' I said.

'As there will be joy in mine.'

*

We were wed in London, a quiet ceremony before a priest arranged by brother John and by Lady de la Pole, who spoke her regret at losing me from her household while I expressed my undying gratitude. My mother did not attend, but it pleased me that John and William managed to find the time to witness our exchange of vows.

There was no feast to mark the occasion, no celebration other than Sir Robert pushing a plain gold ring onto my finger before we began our journey to my new home, but I felt that I was dressed as a bride in a high-necked, fur-trimmed houppelande in azure velvet-damask, with rippling sleeves that all but swept the floor – a gift from Lady de la Pole, as well as the little rolled turban that gave me status. The ruby that shone on the brim was a gift from Robert. For the first time in my life I felt treasured, worthy of the good fortune that had fallen into my damasked lap.

As we rode across London Bridge to Robert's house in Southwark, the sun managed to illuminate us for a brief second before the clouds closed in again. That moment of brilliance I felt to be a good omen. When we reached the house, Robert stood back, allowing me to walk in first, alone, through the gateway and the courtyard, a lady into her new home. There I stood in my hall, enclosed by the grandeur I had seen in the de la Pole house. I clutched my happiness to me, as if it might be snatched away. I could not believe that I was Dame Poynings with a home of her own. This was now mine. I would treasure it and care for it and, in God's infinite mercy, provide an heir to inherit it.

I turned to Robert who had followed me to stand by the door, silently watching me.

'Thank you,' I said. 'Thank you from the bottom of my heart. I will be a good wife to you, Robert Poynings.'

'I know it, Eliza Poynings.'

He kissed me. The first time that any man had kissed my lips in all of my twenty-nine years. I was not disappointed. His hand was secure around mine, our fingers interlinked, as he led me further into my home. No, there might not be the passion of courtly love between us, but I would exchange such extravagance any day for this glorious affection that curved its protective wings around me. And around Robert.

There I stood, my hand in his, waiting for my future to begin.

I had come home at last.

Chapter Eleven

Anne Haute

Bishopsbourne, Kent: 1458

I am Anne Haute. In this year I am four and ten years old.

'One day you will make an advantageous marriage.'

My mother, Lady Joan, informed me of this in the weeks before she died.

My family, as I understood, was one to be noted in the county of Kent. My father, Sir William Haute, and his father before him, and perhaps many generations before that, were members of parliament for the shire of Kent. My father had also served in the English garrison in Calais and so had acquired a reputation as a soldier. I was not interested in history. My lessons, beyond learning to read and write a little, as well as setting fair stitches, were a struggle. My thoughts flew beyond the windows to what the future might hold for me.

They flew far beyond Kent.

I was taught, before my mother Joan died, that I must marry well. Marriage connections were much discussed in our household in Bishopsbourne and the other Kentish manors where we were raised. Joan was my father's second wife, and not the heiress that he might have hoped for. His first wife had come with a large dowry, bringing wealth and land into the family. We were not poor, I understood, but it was important to marry well, to improve our status and the number of estates to which we could set our name. It would not do to take for granted our good fortune, but we were a comely, fair-haired, grey-eyed family who made good marriages.

Because I had four brothers and four sisters there was much to be planned. I was neither the youngest nor the eldest, but somewhere in the middle. My brothers would inherit the Haute estates, of course. William the heir would claim the bulk of it. Richard would step into Ightham Mote, inherited from our grandmother. Edward and James would make their way in law or at Court.

As for the girls, there were already discussions for Alice and Joan and Elizabeth. Margaret, the baby still in the nursery, was too young – which left me. We would all have dowers to attract families looking for suitable wives for their heirs.

'Although with five of you to provide for, your dowry will not be as large as we would like,' my mother Joan informed me.

'Who will I wed?' I asked, for this was far more important to me as a child than the extent or otherwise of my dower.

'We do not yet know.'

'Will he be rich? Will he own land?'

'Of course.'

Which raised an important point for me.

'When I am wed, will I still have to wear my sisters' clothes?'

As my older sisters grew, their shifts, skirts and bodices

became mine. The wool was of a fine weave, the dyeing of good colour. I had come into possession of a particularly sumptuous over-gown from sister Joan, rich in a deep-blue figured velvet and only to be worn on such occasions as saints' days and gift-giving. From sister Alice I inherited much that was green, her favourite hue. I did not like green.

'You should be thankful for what you have, Anne.'

I thought that my mother looked weary, her skin pallid. She had only just risen from her bed after a prolonged bout of fever. Knowing her patience would be thin, I decided to abandon the question of my garments and appearance.

'Will he live in Kent?' I asked. 'Or will I have to go and live far from here?'

'You must wait. Nothing is arranged yet.'

'Will he perhaps be a gentleman of the Royal Court? Will he mix with the King and Queen and the great magnates of the realm?'

Except for my father as a member of parliament, we had nothing to do with the Court. That was not our world, yet, knowing nothing of it, it was my ambition to be part of it with all the glamour and magnificence of which we had heard tell when the King and Queen travelled in our vicinity. Royal pilgrimages to Canterbury gave much food for gossip.

'You ask too many questions,' my mother complained.

'But when will it be arranged?'

I received no answer to satisfy me. Instead my mother sent me to stitch an altar cloth to repent of the sins of pride and covetousness. It did not succeed.

★

One day I rode the short distance to visit Ightham Mote with my brother Richard. He was full of schemes.

'I love this place,' he said. 'But I will improve it and enlarge it.'

It looked a fine house to me, built on four sides of a square, looking inwards into a courtyard where we were standing. A servant had taken our horses to the stable, leaving us to investigate as we wished. Richard did not yet live here, but I knew that it would not be many weeks before he left home. He was twenty years old now. I would miss him. He allowed me to wander round after him, tolerant of my youth, talking to me as if I were of an age with him.

'I will rebuild in stone, Anne. It will last longer than timber and plaster. And I will add more rooms.' We walked through the accommodations, pausing to look out of a window here, to investigate a small chamber there. 'It is no longer enough to have just a great hall and a solar and a chapel. I think that I would like a tower. I would like my neighbours to be aware of me and my fine home.'

I thought about this. 'I would like a tower, too,' I agreed. 'Will you keep the moat? Does it not make some of the rooms damp?'

There was definitely a chill that made me shiver, even on this day of summer heat.

'Most certainly I will. Why drain it?' Richard was pushing on ahead of me as I stopped to look into the solar with its cavernous fireplace and a window that was larger than most in the house. 'This is a lawless time, Anne. King fighting against subjects, magnate against magnate. Why remove a good defence? And I think that my tower should be crenellated, if I can get permission.' We were back in the courtyard where the sun warmed me. 'A squint will be useful to see who is at the door before we open it.' He waved his arm expansively. 'And an open walkway here, with perhaps a gallery above, so that I don't get wet walking from the hall to the gatehouse.'

It seemed fine planning, but would it not take many years? I thought I would be impatient with so many men working in wood and stone around me, with all the dust and grime and inconvenience.

'Are there not enough rooms already?' I asked.

'Not when I wed and have children of my own. I will make it a house to draw attention in the area. Everyone will know of Ightham Mote. You may come and visit me,' he added graciously.

'I will have such a house of my own one day,' I replied with a tilt of my chin.

'I am sure that you will. You can persuade your husband to build you one.'

He was laughing at me.

'I will. I will wed a courtier who will build me a house and take me to Westminster.'

'There is nothing like ambition, little sister. But don't set your sights too high.'

'Why should I not?'

'Because Mistress Anne Haute is not important enough to attract the most wealthy of husbands.'

Which might have cast a cloud over my youthful ambitions if I were a girl of weaker temper. I knew exactly what I wanted.

'I will set my sights high,' I informed my brother, marching ahead of him.

'Of course. I will be surprised if you do not wed the King's son himself and become a princess.'

Richard was laughing at me again as we remounted and

prepared to leave, bidding farewell to the Steward who cared for the house.

'I am not so foolish,' I said.

'Women are always foolish when they fall in love.'

An inflammatory statement that I chose to ignore.

'Will they allow you to build as you wish?' I asked eventually as we paused to look back, Richard still planning his improvements.

'When I am of an age I can do as I like.'

It was a thought that remained with me as the years passed by but no husband was forthcoming. I could do as I wished when I came of such an age that my opinions and desires would have an audience. But what could a woman do without a husband? What could a woman do alone if she were not an heiress? I had no thought of taking the veil, even if my father would allow it. In spite of all my boasting, I could foresee nothing of my future except one that was bounded by my family and our Kentish manors.

Chapter Twelve

Margaret Mautby Paston

Mautby: early summer 1459

'John, they're here.' The clatter of many hooves had drawn me to the window. 'Are you not going to come and look?'

'You don't expect me to stir myself to my feet, to spy on my own brother through my own window?'

John did not raise his eyes from his desk festooned with pens, ink and legal documents. He was seated in a chair brought over from Caister, given to him by Sir John Fastolf; high-backed with carved arms and a cushion. At his elbow was a cup of ale, his body loosely clothed in an old houppelande that had seen better days. So had his shoes, the sole that I could see showing the suspicion of a hole. It was rare that I saw him so much at ease, even when working, without somewhere to go or people to meet.

'It's not your brother that's the issue. It's his betrothed that might spark your interest.'

'I'll meet her soon enough.'

'In about two minutes, by my estimate,' I suggested. 'You

should at least find some interest in this marriage that William is contemplating.'

Despite John's laconic approach, here was a domestic interlude of some note. And a welcome one. Events in our lives were now submerged in the cataclysm of war when Englishmen took up arms against their English brothers. Dispute at the English Court was nothing new and affected us little, but for the participants to face each other on a field of battle was a source of much anxiety. But not as much for us as many. There was no Paston engaged in this conflict. Nor did the field of battle stray far into the east. Why would we worry overmuch? The great magnates would fight it out between them, leaving us to grow and prosper.

'Why would I?' John queried. 'William may wed where he will. As long as the King and his counsellors can maintain law and order, as long as the lords and their retainers stay away from Norfolk, that will suit me well enough. It's hard enough to cling onto our acres as it is, without armies rampaging over them and reducing them to desolation. I am praying that they keep clear.'

And so far they had. The Battle of St Albans, four years ago now, where authority had changed hands from Somerset to York, had little direct influence on us. The Beaufort family fell with the death of the Duke of Somerset; the Duke of York was on the rise, taking the office of Lord Protector to rule in the name of the King. Meanwhile the King remained ignorant of what went on around him, but the Queen was fighting hard to keep her hands firmly around the reins of power. William considered that the Duke of York, with an excess of royal blood in his veins from both parents, might have a strong argument for his position of authority, but would have to watch his political step. Enemies were easy to make and none more dangerous than

Queen Margaret. Without doubt a complicated weave of power and ambition, but what was this to us, who rose and who fell? Nothing. Or so we thought.

Meanwhile, William had found for himself a notable bride. It was enough to take our concerted breath away.

'I like not such ambition for my son,' Mistress Agnes announced into the silence that had fallen after John's pronouncement. 'I see no good coming from it. Better to take a solid merchant's daughter from Norwich for a wife.'

'But not too solid,' John smirked in my direction before admonishing his mother. 'You would find fault with the Blessed Virgin herself!'

So here was William come to introduce the lady to his family. As he helped her down from her horse, it crossed my mind to hope that he had warned her of what to expect.

'It is quite an entourage for a woman with no money for an impressive dower.' I was watching from the window of the newly completed upper range in our Mautby house as they entered the inner court.

'Come away, Meg,' John suggested, still refusing to join me although I would swear that he was as interested as I.

'Shall I describe what I can see?'

'No.'

I did anyway. 'An escort dressed in smart livery, all blue and red and gold with lions and fleur-de-lys. Good horseflesh. Two women in attendance. I can make out little of the bride. Do you think she will think less of me, for peering down at her?' I asked.

'She probably thinks less of us already,' Mistress Agnes said, having descended on us the previous day to cast a proprietorial gaze over William's choice of wife. 'Not that she has a right to do so. Nothing more than a disgraced offspring of an illegitimate side-shoot of the House of Lancaster.'

'Yet you will make her welcome in my house, Mistress Agnes,' I warned.

'It is only the quirk of fate that has put her into the path of my brother,' John acknowledged. 'Such is fortune, which is one thing she does not have. I still do not see how William did it. Not that it will bring him any advantage, unless the political climate changes. As long as York is Lord Protector and Constable of England, the family of this little bride had better watch its step.'

I wondered what the bride thought of such a dramatic descent from her birth-status to wed a lawyer. I wondered what I thought of such an alliance. I remained where I was, only stepping back when the lady looked up, as if aware of my scrutiny. Did she see me? Perhaps, but I refused to be embarrassed in my own household.

William led her into our upper chamber, her duenna following with a maid who carried her cloak and a missal, as if she might need it at any hour of the day. I wished that I had taken more care with my own appearance, but my girdle was expanding again and I was dressed for comfort in a loose robe.

William ushered in the bride.

'I would introduce you to the lady who has agreed to wed me, Lady Anne Beaufort.'

John bowed. Mistress Agnes and I curtsied. So did the lady.

At that moment as I took in her slight figure, her smooth features, she had my compassion, although I might have resented her unsmiling, keen-eyed assessment of me. Did her family see her as a sacrificial lamb? Was a Paston the best they could achieve for her?

For William was to marry one of the once-mighty Beaufort family, a daughter of the Duke of Somerset, a bride far beyond the dreams of a family such as ours. And would we wish to be dragged into their troubles? The bride's father had been cut down in the battle at St Albans, casting his family into political banishment with the rise of the Duke of York.

Nonetheless it was a glamorous match, and a significant coup for William Paston who had only just reached the age of twenty-three years. They had royal blood in their veins, descended from the illegitimate union of John of Gaunt and Katherine Swynford, even if it had later been legitimised. Edmund Beaufort, Duke of Somerset, royal counsellor, closely related to the Lancastrian King by blood, had been firmly placed at the side of King Henry, whispering in his ear until the disaster at St Albans.

Now a Beaufort daughter would become a Paston.

'You are kind to welcome me to your home.'

Her voice was light and without inflexion, as if it were a greeting which she had learned by rote. Perhaps she had said it often since the Beaufort fall from grace.

'It is our pleasure, my lady,' John replied.

John and William drew apart, leaving me to carry the social discourse. Mistress Agnes remained uncompromisingly silent.

'Will you not sit?' I gestured to the chair in the window embrasure where she sank at her ease, disposing her expensive skirts and embroidered over-sleeves. Her hair was completely confined in a soft roll, but her brows were dark, her lips unsmiling. William might see the value of this marriage but I wondered what she thought of him. There was no reading her bland expression.

I sat, too. The duenna and the maid withdrew to the far wall where stools had been arranged for them. Mistress Agnes stood by the fireplace. The new chamber, large by our standards, was suddenly very crowded. The Beaufort lady looked around. However protective of my Mautby house I might be since the building was our own, it would not compare favourably with her home, which I imagined was as luxurious as Caister Castle. Regretting the plain linen of my coif and the undecorated wool of my gown under such aristocratic scrutiny, I noticed that on my fingers there was the suspicion of ink-stains, but my life was one of business, not of indulgence and ease. I would not hide them from the gaze of William's betrothed, however critical she might be.

'William was anxious that we should meet,' she announced.

'Of course. When you are wed, we shall be sisters.'

'I have many sisters of my own. I have five. It is necessary to find husbands for us.'

'You are fortunate,' I said. 'I have none, nor brothers. I have often wished for a confidante.'

'But my family is not fortunate.'

'No.'

What else could I say about the disaster that had struck her family? I had not expected her to introduce it so early in our conversation. I wondered if her brother, the Beaufort heir, was plotting a return to power at the expense of York. Was this a marriage the Beauforts might regret? But that was not a subject to fill this social silence.

'Some of my sisters are already wed and have their own households,' Lady Anne said.

'Do you miss them?'

'Yes. But it is important that I marry. If it had not been for the battle that was fought at St Albans, my family would never have considered William as a husband.'

'No, I don't suppose that they would.'

'I am now twenty-four years old. It was thought by my family that it was high time that I should be wed.'

It was difficult to know what to say. Mistress Agnes was no help. Lady Anne had summed up the dilemma for her family with absolute precision, and remarkable courage. Lady Anne continued, explaining with the supreme confidence of noble birth.

'My father was hacked to death after the Battle of St Albans, you understand. It was a running fight through the streets when he emerged from his refuge with an axe to fight his way to freedom. It took four of his wicked adversaries to bring him to a most undeserved bloody end. My brother Henry was so badly wounded that he had to be carried away in a cart. He now fears further retaliation at the hands of the Duke of York. We have lost all our standing at Court and all my brother's offices have been given to our enemies. It is hard to find husbands for my remaining unwed sisters. It was hard to find one for me.'

Such clear-eyed acceptance of disaster earned my admiration.

'But your family approves of William, I presume?'

I was interested to know what she would say.

'My family believes that William has a gift for the law,' she announced, again as if she were repeating a family decision. She glanced across to where William was in conversation with John, the pair warming themselves beside the fire. There was no affection in her eyes, but neither was there any trace of resentment for this husband that was unlikely to be of her choosing. 'They think he will make a reputation for himself. And a fortune.' Briefly she pressed her lips together. 'They agree that they will overlook his antecedents.'

'And what do you think, my lady?'

She hesitated. Her fair brow furrowed.

'I was brought up to be an obedient daughter. I do as I am told. I will try to be a good wife, and William will be a good husband and provide me with a house and a household of my own. One day we will have children.'

I hoped that she would not be disappointed as she rose and I summoned a servant to show her and her duenna to a chamber where she would spend the night. Mistress Agnes decided to accompany them, while I hoped that she would guard her tongue.

'A coup indeed, brother.' I joined the menfolk as John gave his opinion. 'If I did not know you better, William, I would think that you looked smug.'

'I should think I do!'

'What I do not understand is why they would even look at you,' I said. 'A younger son from a parvenu family.'

William refused to rise to my bait. 'My answer, Margaret, is because I am regarded as a man of ambition and many gifts. Their loss at St Albans is my gain. I am a man considered to have a future. I will have wealth and land. While you are gripping hard to the Paston acres here in Norfolk, I will make my fortune by giving sound advice to Court magnates. And with a Beaufort wife at my side, what can go wrong?'

'I hope that you will not live to regret this contract.'

'What will there be to regret? Do I not need to snatch at every opportunity that crosses my path?' It was as if the question, innocuous enough, had reminded him of an old grievance. A frown suddenly dispelled all William's previous pleasure. His tone became distinctly combative. 'I have to make my fortune in some manner. Was I not robbed of what should have been mine in my father's will?' He turned a hard-eyed stare on John. 'You declared the verbal will to be invalid, brother. You should have upheld it and I should have received the money and land due to me. You dispossessed me of my due rights.'

For a long moment John was silent, his face registering shock, then resentment at such an accusation, until he responded, clasping a hand around his brother's arm.

'The will was invalid because it was not written down,' he said, clearly not expecting this attack from a friendly quarter. 'It was your mother's ill-considered dream to furnish you all with Paston estates, a fantasy that would have spread our inheritance so widely that we would have sunk back to the lowly depths of tillers of the soil.'

'But I was the one who lost, not you.'

'I paid for your education.'

'And I should feel grateful? I am your brother ...'

'And I have always supported you.'

Since the room was becoming hot with their anger, I leapt in before this could go further, although truth to tell I was as astonished as John at the level of William's invective. 'You will make your own way, William. One day you will be richer than all of us.'

'But with no help from my brother.'

'You know that is false!'

'Do I? I am aggrieved at past slights from my own family.'

'But is a bridal visit the moment to air those slights?'

'No. Perhaps not.'

The anger left him as quickly as it had arrived, and he kissed my cheek, perhaps in gratitude that I had stopped more damaging accusations. Nor did it resurface for the rest of the visit.

The next morning they prepared to depart: Lady Anne, the

entourage, her duenna and maidservant and William, leaving me to decide that I knew no more about her than when they had arrived, other than that she had an uncomfortably clear view of her family's demotion. I thought that I detected a deep remorse within her, but no malice.

'You have a fine new home here, Mistress Paston,' the lady observed with studied courtesy. 'I hope that I may visit again. Perhaps you will come to see us in London when we are wed.'

'I will be honoured to receive an invitation.' I did not tell her that I rarely visited London. She would not understand the demands on my life here in Norfolk.

I could not quite push aside a worry, but I was impressed. We were all impressed. Our future looked bright. A Beaufort wife for William, Eliza now Dame Poynings and Sir John Fastolf as our patron. What could go wrong for us? I prayed daily for Sir John's continuing good health.

'What do you think?' I asked John when Mistress Agnes had, still grumbling about marriages that would bring no benefit, left us alone. 'Will it harm us to be dragged into Court intrigues? Of what value would that be if you and William end up on a battlefield in Beaufort livery?'

John's shrug suggested that it would take a clap of doom to get him to a battlefield. 'William is pleased enough with her.'

'That is not what I meant.'

'I know what you meant. Will a Beaufort bride be an advantage or a danger to the Pastons?' There was a crease between his brows as he explained his thoughts. 'If I were a man predisposed to a wager, I would put my gold coin on the Duke of York rather than the Beauforts for the future. But who's to know? William thinks it a bargain worth making.' And then: 'I had not thought him to have held such a grudge all these years. Once I suspected that he was not accepting of what was done, but that is the first time that he has ever accused me of deliberate unfairness towards him. It appears to be a dissatisfaction that runs deep.'

And I felt it behoved me to agree and offer a warning. 'I have not seen such dissatisfaction in him before, John. I think you need to have a care in how you work with William.'

'Perhaps. Another self-interested Paston!' His smile was wry.

My compassion for the little bride was reborn. Many women knew what it was to be wed for their dower or their inheritance. I hoped that Lady Anne Beaufort had not accepted this betrothal with dreams of romance springing up from such a barren landscape, as so often happened in the lays of minstrels. She would be sure to be disappointed.

'When this child is born,' I placed my hand on my flowering waist, 'if it is another son we should call him William. It may help to heal whatever rift there exists between you and your brother.'

'If you say so, Meg.'

John's knit brows suggested that he had no faith in such a move. I tended to agree with him. We could try, but sometimes, so it seemed, family divisions were buried deep and were beyond healing.

★

It was in June of that same year that our lives were to be turned inside out. One new life emerging into the world and one old one departing. Our son, duly called William, was born while Sir John Fastolf, now almost eighty years of age, showed signs of great weakness, so much so that, when he was struck down by a hectic fever, seeing the end of his days fast approaching, he made his will. Of the ten executors, some of the most high-born and powerful in the land, John was one, as we would expect.

If we had not already understood, for had he not talked about it for months, we learned that the whole of Sir John's mind was fixed on establishing a college through the offices of the Abbot of the Abbey of St Benet of Hulm, to honour his name. Six monks and seven poor men would pray for Sir John's soul and that of his long-dead wife, in a daily round of services and perpetual prayers. Clearly the sins of his life were weighing heavily on his mind. To achieve the college, Sir John determined that his properties should be sold to pay his debts, reimburse his servants and provide for the college. Sir John also expressed his desire to be buried in the Abbey Church itself.

We talked about this, John and I, about the work it would bring John, as one of the executors, to establish the college which would be no easy matter. The remuneration, although considerable, would not offset the loss of our patron. Sir John's death would be a severe blow to us.

Then in October came a change. Sir John, still hanging onto life as a good soldier would, added a codicil. An utter surprise to everyone, he signed over all his moveable goods to two executors: to John and Sir Thomas Howes.

'Why would he do such a thing?' I asked.

Was this a good or a bad move on Sir John's part? I did not know. All the rest of the original executors were demoted to advisers only. It crossed my mind that they would be displeased. Would they question what had been done? If they did, I could foresee trouble ahead. On his return from Caister to give me the news, John was unsettled, his features grimly set.

'It is the establishment of the college again that is preying on his mind. Sir John cannot rest easily until he is certain that it will happen. He is doing all in his power to make it so. He has no heir to name in his will, so he has decided to leave the whole to me and Thomas Howes, believing that we will ensure that the college will indeed come about.'

And he explained: Sir John was afraid the three mighty lords, Viscount Beaumont, the Duke of Somerset and the Earl of Warwick, originally named as executors, intended to buy Caister once he was dead. If this happened, the whole property falling into the hands of any one of them, the college would never be established. There was still no licence from the King to establish the college. The bargain Sir John was now pursuing was to leave the Fastolf inheritance to John and to Thomas Howes, in return for the college being established as he wished, as soon as that licence could be procured.

'So he will make a bargain with me and Thomas.'

'Will you do it?'

'I will try.' John still looked more than gloomy. 'First to keep it out of the hands of the land-grabbing lords. If one of them buys Caister, I doubt he will be satisfied with it. He will be looking at other manors in the vicinity. At Paston manors, I expect, and I have no intention of losing Mautby. So Thomas Howes and I will take on the task and gain the licence if the King sees fit to give it.'

'It will be worth a vast sum of money to you.'

'Yes it will, and it will demand a vast amount of work.'

★

Sir John took a turn for the worse. John, in London, was sent for by the Fastolf priest, Friar Brackley, while I visited Sir John as he lay in the great bed at Caister, struggling for breath. His skin was grey, his face sunken. His chest was painful, he said. He looked like a man at the very door of death; there was only one thought in his mind as I placed my hand on his and sat beside him.

'Margaret.' His breath caught on every exhale, ending in a dry painful cough that racked his whole body. 'God send me soon my good cousin John Paston.'

'Your priest has sent for him.' I tried to raise him against his pillows but he pushed me away with surprising strength. 'He will come, I have no doubt of it.'

'But will he be here before I depart? There is much that I need to say to him.'

'He will do his best.'

Sir John was growing weaker by the day. I brought a decoction of St John's Wort to bring him some ease and a lightening of spirit but to no avail. It was the same question every morning when I entered his chamber where the light was as dimmed as the figure in the bed.

'Is my cousin John Paston arrived?'

'Not yet, Sir John.'

'John Paston is the best friend and adviser I could wish for. Urge him, Meg. I trust none but him.' For a moment his eyes closed. Then he opened them and he was quite lucid. 'What can I leave you as a bequest in my will?'

I recalled my first visit, how admiring I had been, what I had hoped for. I smiled ruefully.

'A tapestry, Sir John. I would like a tapestry to remember you whenever I look at it.'

Sitting on the edge of the bed, I folded his gnarled hands, scarred with old sword wounds, around mine. They were as cold as the metal of his own sword that he had insisted be brought to lie beside him on his bed. An old soldier who had fought all his life, he would not be parted from it.

'It shall be yours. More than one, if you wish it.'

'But not too much bloodshed. It would not suit my rooms at Mautby.'

'No hunting scenes. No holy martyrs pierced by arrows either.' He tried to laugh with a rumbling cough.

'No.'

'You have no idea what I have planned for you, Meg. You could not begin to imagine.'

His breath failed him. The tapestry could wait. I prayed that John would arrive to give him peace in his final hours.

When John finally rode into the Inner Court at Caister, I was at the door to meet him, William Worcester standing stolidly at my shoulder.

'Does he still live?'

'Yes, but barely. His priest is with him.'

John did not need Worcester's urging: 'Go to him. He talks of you often.' He was already climbing the stairs two at a time.

We gave them time alone, then I entered the room with Worcester to find that the priest had been dismissed and John was there, seated beside the bed, leaning forward so that his ear was against Sir John's whispering lips. Beside him a parchment. A pen was in John's hand and a single candle rested dangerously on the bed to give necessary light for the rapid writing as Sir John spoke. All was silent except for the hoarse voice and the scratch of the pen in that room redolent of brooding death. If Sir John had been given the last rites, we did not know.

We halted just inside the door, but John, alert to our entrance, frowned at us, waving us away. We departed. Whatever was to be said there was clearly for John's ears only.

*

Sir John Fastolf died on Monday, the fifth day of November, falling into a deep sleep from which he could not be woken. John remained at his side, protecting him from those visitors, mostly tenants, who tried to gain access, demanding settlements and decisions from the dying man. He was too weak, John said. He should not be disturbed.

I had no speech with John during these difficult hours. My task was to work with William Worcester to keep the activity in the home of a dying man as smooth and peaceful as I could. It was much as any other day in such a household with servants to feed and horses to be shod, the local washerwoman sending clean linen. I received capons and dispatched a cartload of malt to Yarmouth. I greeted men who claimed connection with Sir John's family, hoping for money. Some were allowed in, more were not, Worcester standing guard at the door. The priest said the daily service alone. Sir John would never say prayers with him again. I remembered that day clearly, a day of brooding sadness but with all its habitual hustle and bustle as if nothing untoward were to happen other than the commemoration of the life of a great man.

*

On the evening of the day that Sir John Fastolf died, John summoned the most important members of the household to meet with him in a private chamber, Sir John's body finally at rest, his soul assoiled, still lying above in the great bed. John looked exhausted, as if he had lost his own father all over again. I recalled the difficulties over Justice William's will. Surely Sir John's would be straightforward enough. He had made his wishes quite clear in the weeks since ill health had struck him down. I placed my hand on John's shoulder, then stood back to take a seat against the wall. I knew this was not for me, but neither would I leave the room. Here were William Worcester, Thomas Howes and Friar Brackley. They sat around a table, all eyes on John.

'I have to tell you. When I arrived here on Saturday, Sir John was weak but clearly in his right mind, as Friar Brackley will testify.' The priest nodded in agreement. 'Sir John expressed a wish to change his will. On that day he dictated a new one to me. I read it through to him and he agreed with what I had written.'

Here was John at his lawyerly best as he placed the document before us. Even from a distance I recognised John's neat hand. There was no seal that I could see on the document.

'What does it say?' Worcester asked. 'Why did he need to make yet another will?'

John picked it up again and started to read. Within all the legal wording, Sir John had made changes. John was now named as principal and sole executor, even Thomas Howes demoted.

My fingers curled, my nails digging into my palms. My heart thudded in my throat and I shivered in the cold room, for no fire had been lit.

John continued in flat tones, as if he had no personal interest in the proceedings. I had to concentrate to take in the vastness of what had been written down in that chamber of death.

All the Fastolf manors and lands and tenements in Norfolk and

Suffolk were given to John alone, in which to dwell and abide and keep household. Everything was willed to John, in return for a payment of four thousand marks to the other executors in biennial instalments of eight hundred marks. Those executors who were no more. In return for this inheritance, John was to provide the college that Sir John had so much desired, as well as pay minor bequests to his servants and to charity. A word of warning was included. If the college was not founded by John, then the castle in which we sat would be pulled down, every stick and stone of it.

There was a silence in the room after the will was read. Worcester and Howes exchanged glances. Friar Brackley studied his hands while I breathed so quietly that the flame of the candle at my side barely flickered. Such an inheritance was beyond anything we could have dreamed of. I had asked for a tapestry. I had got a castle in its entirety and all the Fastolf land with it. I had coveted a wall-hanging. Instead I had been given a legacy of unbelievable wealth.

'I had no idea of this,' said Worcester. 'Why did he not tell me?'

'Yet it was said to me by Sir John.' John was all business. 'Father Brackley, if you would copy this correction onto Sir John's original will and then make copies for all of us. We will keep the will together in this box with Sir John's signet ring, which I have taken the liberty of removing from his finger.'

He placed the heavy gold circle on the table beside the written instructions.

'Did not Sir John apply his seal to his wishes?' Worcester asked.

'No, he was too weak to do so.'

'That is true,' agreed Howes. 'It remained on his finger until he had taken his last breath. I was there at his bedside at the end.'

Howes had been late in arriving but had said his farewells to the dying man.

'Were you there when the new will was dictated and written?' Worcester asked, still seemingly juggling the legalities of what he had just heard.

'No, I was not. It was already done.'

John raised his chin but he kept his voice low and calm, no hint of hostility. 'Are you questioning my honesty, Worcester? Do you suggest that I would change the will in my own interests and lie about Fastolf's involvement?'

'No, but ...'

'I hope that I have always been honest in matters of the law, Worcester.'

As I listened to the authoritative timbre of John's voice, I realised that this was the first time in all my life that I had seen him at work in his role as lawyer. Never had I sat in a court of law. Never had I watched him argue and persuade as he must do now. His demeanour was without doubt impressive as he demanded the attention of this small but potentially critical audience, and so was his appearance. Dressed in muted greys and black, John was in his finest raiment of rich silk and wool.

Why had I not noticed before? John had changed his garments between the death-bed and this crucial meeting. He had come into this chamber to impress and make these men accept the weight of his counsel and his judgements. The leather of his belt was exceptional, with a hint of gold in the fastening. He wore rings on his fingers, a fine gold chain enhanced his shoulders. Here was a man of property and wealth and erudition. How cunning he could be. I was impressed even if they were not. He would inveigle them into believing that every word he spoke was the truth. And why would it not be? But it was a heavy thing to present to them that John alone had been privy to the new will. His smooth competence must win the day if Fastolf's people were undecided on the legality of what had taken place in the death-chamber.

'I think that we all accept your integrity in legal matters, Paston,' Thomas Howes stated. 'There is no need for this.'

'Are we then content with the legality of it?' Worcester asked.

'I am,' said Thomas Howes.

'And I.' Friar Brackley, who had taken pen and ink, was already writing the codicil beneath Sir John's original will.

So there it was.

I continued to watch John, solemn but with a flush of colour on his cheekbones, as he accepted the victory he had just won. With their agreement he was thus transformed into the owner of the Fastolf lands throughout Norfolk and Suffolk, and some elsewhere. He now owned a major dwelling in Southwark. *We* owned it. His unceasing efforts on behalf of Sir John Fastolf over the past fifteen years had been rewarded more fortuitously than we could ever have believed. There were no words to express my feelings. And beneath it all lurked a little knot of anxiety that so much had happened in so short a time, at the expense of so many who had had their own hopes dashed.

I studied my hands that lay lax on my lap. The hands of Mistress Margaret Mautby Paston of Caister Castle, no less. And yet. And yet ... I looked up at the other occupants, suddenly aware of the continuing tension in the room. I could have wished that the Fastolf will had been drawn up with seals and witnesses. But then, what did I know about the law? Worcester and Howes still looked uncomfortable, but all I could see in John, in the deliberate drama that he had created here, was his imperturbability, his certainty that all was as it should be.

Later John and I returned to the death-chamber, to stand one on either side of the bed where Sir John Fastolf lay finally at peace. His face was waxen, the flesh pared down to the bone, the sharp eyes closed for ever. I made the sign of the cross, but John looked at me, his indomitable will shining in his face.

'This will be the making of us, Margaret. This will herald the rise of the Paston family.' He turned his gaze on the earthly remains of John Fastolf. 'How many steps can we climb up this ladder that our benefactor has created for us?'

John's eyes were bright, his face alive with possibilities. Until that moment I had not understood the magnitude of the ideas that had taken root in his mind with Fastolf's death. Had he not always been ambitious? Now he was looking far beyond the sturdy advancement of a Norfolk family desiring gentry status. Now I was beginning to understand the scope of his dreams all too well.

I straightened the coverlet on the bed, smoothing away any creases as disquietude became an uncomfortable companion.

'What are you saying?' I asked, needing all to be made clear, knowing that today, when strong emotions ruled, John would not tolerate any criticism from me.

He did not hesitate. 'Do not the great magnates of this land look as high as they choose? Does the Duke of York not look to the crown itself? How much power did the Beaufort Duke of Somerset covet at the King's side, before his ambition was curtailed in death? Where do you consider the Earl of Warwick is setting his sights for the Neville family? There is no curb on their ambition, when the King is weak.'

It was an unnerving explanation.

'But can you compare such men with us?' I asked. 'They have royal blood. We do not.' I shook my head in denial. 'It is a royal game that they play.'

John was not to be intimidated by such realism. 'It may well be a royal game. But our ambitions are the same.'

'It is a dangerous game, John. It is not for such as us.'

'Why not?' He walked round the bed to stand at my side, to take my hands in his. I felt the heat of his driving purpose in his grasp. 'Yes, it has become a royal game, to challenge and win and achieve. Do we not follow their example? No, we are not of high blood, but why should a man of ability and education not be enticed by aspirations to make more of his family? Should we always be curbed by our birth, by our family origins? If that were so, we would still be serfs, dependent on our lord for every acre of land we farmed, still working a mill as my grandfather Clement did. Your days would be spent between the butter churn and the feeding of chickens. We are better than that, Meg. The Pastons are better than that. Why should we not seize every opportunity to make our own bid for power?'

It was an attractive proposition, of course. To look ahead, to what might be.

And yet ... I pulled my hands away, tugging until he released them.

'It will make us enemies. Powerful ones too.'

'So it will. But it won't stop us. We will face them and defeat them.'

With a hand of warning on his magnificent damask sleeve, I spoke the one immediate worry in my mind. 'Will the old executors raise objections at the making of this new will, at the manner of its creation?'

John shook his head. 'Why should they? Its legality is unquestionable.'

★

'We will bury him in all splendour and honour. Everything will be done as he wished it to be done,' my husband decreed.

Thus Sir John Fastolf was buried with gravity and extravagance, the weight of coin spent on his obsequies as befitting the old soldier in death as in life. As heir apparent and sole executor of his will, much of it was placed in John's hands, although he apportioned some of the detail to William Worcester. I was relieved that, despite our cousinship, the domestic arrangements were not left to me. All I had to do was to be present with our household, and rejoice in what Sir John had done for us.

As instructed, the requiem for the dead was held eight miles to the north-west of Caister, at the Abbey Church of St Benet of Hulme, Sir John's body interred next to that of his wife, Millicent. Foreseeing the day, Sir John had built a new aisle to the south of the chancel to accommodate them for the sum of more than six hundred pounds.

'It is a fine show,' I whispered to John when we stood in the church and marvelled at the results of Worcester's organisation. 'Sir John would approve.'

Worcester had been busy with Sir John's money. Down the length of the nave and in the arches above our heads, banners and pennants moved in the chill air every time the door opened, displaying Fastolf's arms and those of his parents as well as images of saints and the Blessed Virgin. Every inch of space proclaimed the presence of Sir John Fastolf's earthly remains.

We Pastons were all there, of course, as family, friends and employees. And John as the great man's heir. I smoothed my hands down my new skirts, enjoying the sensation of fine woollen cloth. I knew that hundreds of pounds had been spent by Worcester on black raiment for the mourners. We would make a significant statement in the congregation as the words of the Mass rolled on and the candles flickered over the neat heads of our children who would in the fullness of time come into a great inheritance.

'I see Judge Yelverton is also here,' I observed as we knelt in solemn reverence. Justice William Yelverton, one of the original ten executors of the will, now demoted, had brought his dour little wife and fourteen servants. I could not fault their mourning-raiment of fine wool since that too had come from Worcester's organising. 'He'll be wanting something from you as heir.'

John grimaced. 'As soon as the man is buried, I expect I'll find out. But Yelverton and I are friends of long-standing. Have we not supported each other in local disputes time out of mind? Of those I mistrust, Yelverton does not even appear on the list.' A thought clearly crept into John's mind. 'Unless he resents my achievements and covets them for himself.'

Which was quite possible. Ambition could strike hard at any man, as I knew from my own experience of every Paston I had ever met.

I allowed my mind to settle on the dark ceremony.

Agnus Dei, qui tollis peccata mundi: dona eis requiem sempiternam.

I glanced at John's face. It was smooth, with no trace of doubt. Yet there nibbled at my mind that rat of concern, as it had when we faced each other over Sir John's body.

As the obsequies rumbled on around us, my reticence deserted me.

'John ...' I whispered.

'What?'

'Are we certain that you are the heir? Is the will a truly legal document?'

'Of course. And all done as it should be. Everything as Sir John wished. William Worcester would never allow anything that smacked of illegality.' I was aware of John's spine stiffening infinitesimally. 'Are you questioning my integrity, Margaret?'

'No, I am not.' I did not think that I was. 'But I think that many will. I think that you know it, too. Am I not right? The executors will not like it. Did you not need a witness for so important a change? To hear the words spoken by Sir John at the end?'

He did not reply as we settled into silence as the ceremony moved into its final solemnities.

Libera me, Domine, de morte æterna, in die illa tremenda ...

It was not a question that he ever found time to answer and I resisted asking him again. Later I wished that I had done so, but it was a day of mourning, not of domestic strife.

'What now?' I asked, when it was over.

'I go to London tomorrow, for the probate hearing in the court of the Archbishop of Canterbury.'

'Will you be with us for Christmas, John?'

'I think it unlikely.'

His acceptance of it ruffled my temper.

'And I shall think myself half a widow, so infrequently are you at home.'

★

How wrong John had been, that the will would not be questioned. There were consequences of it before we had even left the Abbey. After I had collected together the children and the household, I went in search of John through the rooms of the Abbot's accommodations. There I was surprised to hear raised voices, the sharp clash of anger that was inappropriate for this day of mourning. I followed the accusation and counter-accusation, opening the door into a sunlit parlour. There was John with Justice William Yelverton, Friar Brackley hovering on the edge. The argument did not even hitch its breath as I entered.

'Whoever says that of me is a liar!'

It was Judge Yelverton, red in the face. Judge Yelverton, long-time associate and friend of the Pastons. There was no friendship in his stance today.

Nor was there in that of my husband. 'Yet it is being said,' John replied. 'Are you denying that there is truth in it?'

'There is none.'

'Why then have I heard that you are implicated in questioning my honour as a man of law, if there are no grounds for it?'

'Sirs …' Friar Brackley tried to intervene but was brushed aside. I did not even try.

'I thought that there was trust and long friendship between us, Paston,' Yelverton growled. 'Yet you would believe a calumny against my name.'

'Yet you will not explain how the story came about.'

Two angry men, arguing about personal honesty and trustworthiness. No, there was no hope for my intervention. Yet silent I would not be. 'Your dispute can be heard at a distance,' I warned, raising my voice. 'Do you wish to spread this abroad, on so solemn an occasion?'

Judge Yelverton glared at me. 'I will say no more. There is nothing more to say in the face of such treachery, Mistress Paston.'

The Judge stalked out. The friar followed him, raising his hands in the hopelessness of the case.

'What has he done?' I asked, my heart sinking. They had been invited into our home to eat and enjoy festive occasions for many years.

By now John had calmed a little. 'It is said that he has instigated a claim for possession of Caister Castle, from Lady Elizabeth Heveningham.'

It had begun.

'Who is she? Does she indeed have a claim?'

'No. But it will interest you to know that her recently acquired husband is John Wyndham, an old enemy who will do all he can to get under my skin.'

'But is it true? I heard the Judge deny it.'

'Of course he denied it.' John fell into step with me as we made our way to join the children. Before adding: 'He is intimating that the will is a forgery and that my claim to the inheritance is fraudulent. Almost before Sir John is laid in his grave.'

'I warned you this might happen.'

'So it might, but I will fight it every step of the way. If Yelverton and the rest of them will seek to take Caister from me, they will find that they have a battle on their hands.'

There were our children and our horses, a knot of mourners making their farewells in the outer environs of the abbey.

'Try not to glower at everyone,' I suggested.

To do him justice, he tried hard, even bowing to Judge Yelverton and his family, but I had a presentiment that this would only be the start of it. If this were to be the pattern of the future, it seemed that we were to lose some good friends.

Norwich: Christmas 1459

John would return to London, as he must, which left me with a dilemma: how to celebrate Christmas at home in Norwich, where we had moved the family. In a time of very public mourning for Sir John Fastolf I must take care not to ruffle local feathers with a lack of respect. And yet I had five young children who would expect to celebrate at Christmas. Elder John and Jonty were old enough to accept the need for a time of quiet reflection, even if reluctantly. William, little more than a newborn, Willem to his family, would do nothing but sleep in his cradle. But what of the rest of our family?

I looked them over as they sat in church at my side, from youngest to eldest. Walter was three, Anne five, Edmund nine and Margery eleven. They would look forward to some seasonal jollity. My maternal heart was unwilling to rob them of the anticipation.

'What do you suggest?' I asked Mistress Agnes.

'What need to celebrate at all? It would save money if we simply drew a mourning curtain over the whole.'

'And make the family miserable.'

'They will survive, and thank you for it.'

No help there.

'I doubt it. But we must keep the festival sombre to all outward appearances.'

I had an idea and summoned Elder John and Jonty.

They were stalwart young men now, both well educated,

but with no position in which to hone their legal knowledge as yet. They needed a place at Court or in the household of some magnate. I acknowledged that this had been neglected with John's endless battle to secure the Paston inheritance, and now there would be another increasingly fraught foray to make sure of the Fastolf lands. It would be good for them to visit our neighbours in Norwich, with courtesy, in search of good practice.

'I have an errand for you both,' I said. 'To discover what might be acceptable Christmas arrangements in our household when we are in public mourning, taking into account that we have five young children under our roof.' I turned my attention to seventeen-year-old Elder John, the most unreliable of the pair when it came to fulfilling tasks. His own interests, the fashionableness of his clothing and consorting with his peers in the town, often with visits to the alehouses, tended to take precedence. 'I wish you to visit Lady Morley. When her husband died just before Christmas ...'

'But it was seventeen years ago,' Mistress Agnes interposed.

'What has changed?' I continued with my instructions. 'Ask Lady Morley what she found appropriate.'

I turned to Jonty, at fifteen as reliable as the present days were short. 'You will go to Lady Stapleton and discover the same. Between them we should have a pattern that will worry no one. If they invite you to take refreshment, accept. Remember above all the good manners with which you were raised. I expect you home before the streets are too dark to detect any trouble. We have enemies still.'

Their report was what I had feared.

'No mummers or disguisings,' Elder John reported.

'No music,' Jonty added. 'No harping, no playing the lute, no singing.'

Which did not sound encouraging.

'And no loud games.'

'What if the singing is carols?' I asked.

Elder John shook his head. 'And no lewd sports.'

'We are not in the custom of entertaining lewd sports,' I declared. 'Your father would not allow it.'

Elder John laughed. 'Our father will not be here to see.'

Which made me determined to keep a close eye on our first-born.

'Is there anything we can do?' I asked.

'Quiet games. Backgammon or chess or cards.'

'But no decorations in the house,' added Jonty. 'Not even greenery.'

'What about food?'

'Be abstemious, Lady Morley says. And don't invite the neighbours.'

Which put a final blight on our festivities. I did not think that Sir John Fastolf would be in agreement with such a mean Christmas and New Year, but we would do nothing to dishonour his name.

'Were you polite?' I asked.

'Yes, mother. I was given ale and a pasty,' Elder John assured. 'Lady Morley said that she would pray for Sir John Fastolf.'

And Jonty: 'Lady Stapleton has sent you this. You will get your cook to make use of it to make mince pies, she said. They would be acceptable, even if a rich pudding is not.'

A packet of spices indeed. A fulsome gift from proud Lady Stapleton. It was hard to quash the sardonic thought that our acquisition of a castle should be rewarded in so condescending a manner. I stifled a shrug. Our little coffin-shaped pies would benefit, although John could be relied on to send all the spices we needed. I must take care not to be remiss in sending my thanks to Lady Stapleton.

'You have done well,' I said. 'Your father would be proud of you.' I looked at Mistress Agnes; she looked at me. 'I revere the name of Sir John Fastolf, but it will be a sorry Christmas for the young ones.'

I looked down at Edmund who stood at my knee. He loved mummers. With a good voice he sang the carols robustly. Margery could already play the lute with some skill. What to do? The decision would be mine since I had no hope that John would be with us to approve or otherwise.

★

We marked Christmas with admirable solemnity, attending both the Angel Mass and the Shepherds' Mass. At home we forwent the decorations of holly and ivy and anything green. We ate capon and sweetmeats and puddings but we invited none to join with us. If we sang the old carols, it was quietly. If Margery sang to the music from her lute, there were none to hear and comment adversely on our lack of respect.

We played games. Elder John and Jonty taught the children to enjoy the simple counter-game of merrills and the more complicated fox-and-geese. The young ones were not beyond enjoying a hearty bout of hoodman blind.

By Twelfth Night I had decided that I would not let this occasion go overlooked, engaging Agnes who still had dextrous fingers and also Margery who was of an age to keep a secret. Crowns of holly and ivy were plaited, and one with the addition of spangles and hellebores cut from the garden, while I spent an hour or two with our cook. We would have at least one festivity that the young ones would recall.

Before the Twelfth Night supper, when we all wore our crowns, even Walter managing to sit still enough to keep his intact, I brought in a cake and a knife. Rich with raisins and spices and almonds, its appearance was cheered. I cut it into portions.

'Who will be King or Queen of the Bean this year?' Mistress Agnes and I served it up. 'Eat carefully,' I instructed. 'There is a bean to be found in one of these. Margery, keep an eye on Walter or he will choke.'

They ate with enjoyment and much laughter, even the older boys. I knew immediately when Jonty found the bean in his piece of the cake. He looked at me. I looked at him. There was no need for me to say a word. He leaned over to Anne.

'There is a large raisin hiding under your platter,' he said.

'I cannot see it.'

Jonty lifted her platter up to discover the lost fruit, and in doing so slid the bean beneath the crumbs while she sought the invisible raisins on the table. It was a kind thought that warmed my heart. Would Elder John have done the same? I did not think so. He would have enjoyed the victory for himself. There was a depth of generosity in my second son. Meanwhile Anne crowed with delight and wore the hellebore crown as Queen of the Bean. She insisted on wearing it for the rest of the day, and it sat by her bed when exhaustion pulled her into sleep.

I wished that John had been there to share the moment with us. It was an empty festivity without him.

Chapter Thirteen

Elizabeth Paston Poynings

Southwark: late November 1459

Was I happy? Margaret wrote to ask me, the only one of my family to do so.

I was surprised that she could find the time to write at all since she had acquired a castle of her own. Yet in spite of all the issues over that inheritance which trickled my way in local gossip, Margaret asked and I was much gratified.

I considered the reply I might make as wife of Sir Robert Poynings, a man with a reputation for honesty and fairness in the counties of Kent and Sussex where he held his manors. How could I not be content? I had no need for a castle as grand as Caister. My marriage had given me my own household: a dozen manor houses and a smart town house in Southwark where we spent most of our days. I now had a baronial family forsooth, with servants to undertake my every need. As I learned to enjoy the leisure appropriate to Dame Poynings, the shade of Mistress Agnes Paston faded from my existence. I would never again have to answer to her for my failures. A quietness engulfed me. Eventually I stopped thinking that I might be punished for some unacceptable sin of which I had not been aware.

Not that I was not quick to exert my authority. I knew full well how a household should be efficient and peaceful, obedient to the wishes of the lady of the house. What I had not learned from my mother, I had seen in the hands of a skilful Margaret. I would never have her confidence, but I knew the pattern to follow. Engage the loyalty of Perching, my Steward, win over the good-will of the cook, allow no partiality in all dealings with the servants, keep an accurate accounting of outgoings and, most important of all, keep one's husband content.

When I quickened with a child, Robert's joy lit a flame to a candle in my own heart. This was not the love of the troubadours; my heart did not shiver on every occasion that I set my eye on him. Nor, I think, did his when I walked into a room. But he smiled at me and we lived well together. We were, I supposed, compatible, at ease in each other's company. We did not argue. Sometimes he held my hand, or drew it through his arm to walk in the garden that he had given to me for the planting of herbs and sweet-scented flowers. I had not been raised to complain and demand. I suppose that I was the perfect wife. And this child would be the most loved.

I learned to smile, too.

Yes, I am happy, I replied to Margaret. Yes, I am content. How could I not believe in my good fortune? I hoped that she would not become too grand to reply.

Yet I was aware of ripples below the surface of my new life, even an impending gloom. Robert might not discuss it with me, but living for most of my life in a household where a tight grip on property had been a matter of discussion at every meal, it was not a problem to absorb the difficulties with some of Robert's inheritance. He rode out frequently, staying away from home when his travels took him into Sussex and into Kent, returning with a grave face.

'Will you not tell me?' I asked. 'I see something troubles you.'

'There is a dispute over some of the Poynings manors.'

'Can the law not solve it?' I recalled John's frequent call on the local courts.

'It was caused by my father's will, so it is difficult to argue against it.'

He was unwilling to say more, but remembering Margaret's frequent assaults on John I chanced another question.

'He left the manors to others?'

'Yes, four manors in Kent: Tirlingham, Newington, Eastwell and Westwood.' They meant nothing to me. 'They are valuable manors, too. And as things stand it behoves me to keep an eye on the other Kentish manors that still remain to me. I fear that they, too, might be threatened.'

And he would not elaborate further although it clearly caused him much heartache. Robert was not from a household where women took it upon themselves to have as much to say about family affairs as the menfolk. He did not know my mother or my sister-in-law well or he might have expected a more opinionated wife. I would have dug deeper, but there was a more immediate cause for anxiety. The conflagration at Court was beginning to burn fiercely, the Duke of York proclaiming his right to be Lord Protector during the King's ill health, while the Queen resisted, determined to take the power into her own hands. There had already been bloodshed at St Albans: there were fears that more battles hovered on the horizon between those who supported the Duke of York and the adherents of the Queen, battles where Englishman would face Englishman and spill blood.

On hearing a clattering, a shuffling, a loud thud accompanied by some oaths, I found Robert and his body servant turning out the contents of a number of large coffers in one of the store-rooms. On the floor between them lay pieces of armour, two swords, a dagger, a helm, all in need of scouring to remove rust. When had they last been used?

Would Robert don this armour and go and fight? Would his livery be seen on a battlefield? For the first time it brought the dangers home to me. My family had never been engaged in fighting, John claiming a lack of skill and too many demands on his time. I entered the room, stooping to lift one of the swords, running a finger along an edge that was not as sharp as it might be.

When Robert took it from me, returning it to its place in the arrangement, I possessed myself of a pair of well-worn gauntlets.

'When did you last wear these?' I asked, working a finger through the broken strands of an embroidered Poynings coat of arms.

'Cade's Rebellion. Not that I wore them with any honour, or success.'

Robert took them from me, instructing me to gather up the tabard proclaiming the Poynings colours of green and gold stripes, opposite quarters patterned with fleur-de-lys, and dispatch them to the laundry with instructions to cleanse them carefully. Then I waited until we were alone, the servants carrying the pieces away to begin their restoration.

'Will you fight?' I asked. I had to dig for every piece of infor-mation. Why could he not be open with me? Meg complained about John's reticence, yet in comparison with Robert, John was a chattering magpie.

'It may be that I will.'

We sat on the storeroom's window ledge, Robert brushing cobwebs from my sleeve. His reply was unusually brusque.

'But for whom will you fight?'

I did not think that it would matter but suddenly all was uncertain. Should I have a loyalty to King Henry, rightfully crowned? Our old enemy in Norfolk had been the de la Pole Duke of Suffolk who had been Lancastrian and knelt to the King and Queen, but his son, the new Duke, through marriage to York's daughter, would undoubtedly change his political affiliations. I did not know where John and Meg or the rest of my brothers were giving their allegiance; I did not know where Robert's loyalties lay. It had not been a question that was asked when we were wed in the de la Pole household; they would follow their family connections and don their armour for York without any doubt. How complex it all was, and now I was personally involved.

'For York,' Robert said without hesitation. 'I think he has the stronger argument in this dispute. What about your brothers?'

'They will support whichever magnate will uphold their position in Norfolk,' I admitted. Sir John Fastolf was dead and John was waging his own battle to secure the estates left to him in the will. 'I must pray that it does not come to a conflict. Or at least not until this child is born. I would not wish our son to be ignorant of his father.'

At least it made Robert smile.

'I have no intention of being killed on a battlefield.'

I prayed that he would be safe. I must stitch for him a new

pair of gloves, praying that he would never have to wear them in conflict. For a time it seemed that it would be so.

★

I discovered the depth of ill-will in Robert's manorial disputes. He would have continued to remain silent about it, all buried beneath the rumble of discontent in the country, but it was revealed through a visit that began an undermining of my new world. A handsomely appointed litter pulled by four horses drew into the inner courtyard of our Southwark house as evening shadows doused it in dark colour. Servants leapt down to hold the horses, draw back the embroidered curtains. A young woman of my own age was helped to descend. Assured and dressed in the style of the Court, she stepped down in gilded shoes, her damask hems held up from any dust that might contaminate them. There was a coat of arms emblazoned on the right shoulder of her travelling cloak. For a moment she stood and surveyed the house. I had the impression that she knew it well. And then she moved out of my sight, into our hall, with all the confidence of a woman who owned the property.

'Who is it?' I asked Perching who passed me on the stair as he hurried down to receive her and apprise Robert of her arrival. I felt reluctant to face this lady of such countenance; I sensed that my ignorance would tip me into her elegantly gloved hands. Mistress Agnes would undoubtedly have slapped me for my reticence in my own home, and rightly so. Yet I lingered on the stair.

'The Countess of Northumberland, my lady. We did not expect her.'

An important visitor indeed. Was she a connection of the family? I was certain that she had not been at my betrothal or my wedding. First I returned to my room to appraise my appearance, exchanging a linen coif for a soft-rolled turban and short veil. I was woman enough to wish to make a good impression on this well-dressed visitor. My gown would have to do. At least it could boast some embroidering to mark the high waist. Then I trod quietly down the stairs.

She had been shown into one of the parlours where Robert had joined her. The tone of the exchange was not a pleasant one. For my sins I stood beside the door to listen, moving silently as a hunting owl. Had I not become adept at eavesdropping in my mother's household?

'I expected a more effusive welcome, sir.'

'I would feel more welcoming if you and your husband were more careful of the legality of my claim to the Poynings manors in Kent. I dislike being branded a thief.'

A harsh reply, I thought, to give to the Countess of Northumberland.

'We hold what was indubitably left to us by my grandfather.'

'And your lord desires so much more than was willed to you, if my suspicions are true. Do I have to scrabble to hold what is mine against the might of Percy ambition?' There was a pause, broken only by the sound of a chair being pushed back on the wooden floor. 'We should not argue, Eleanor. Unless that is why you have come here today. To what do we owe the honour of this visit?'

There was another pause, as if the lady considered her reply.

'I hear that you are wed.'

'I have been wed for some months.'

'News travels slowly. And in time of war some news is less important than others. I suppose that you hope for a son and heir to inherit your acres. Or what is left of them.'

'Such spite does not become you, Eleanor.'

'Not spite, sir. Just surprise. Did you indeed wed a Paston? What possessed you to look so low for a bride?'

'You will be courteous when you meet her.' Robert's voice had adopted an edge. 'Or your visit beneath my roof will be shorter than you had intended.'

'I suppose it was money,' the lady persisted, undeterred. 'How much did her litigious family lend you?'

'Enough!'

'Is she ugly? Did you have to lessen your expectations in a wife for the sake of a loan?'

I could feel a flush of colour sweep into my cheeks. This was embarrassment indeed. I did not wish to hear Robert's reasoning for our marriage. It might be too uncomfortably honest, and I would rather not dwell on the truth of it. I thought that it was time that I made an entrance, particularly as Perching was standing behind me listening, too. I looked up at him and grimaced. He smiled, nodded and urged me forward with a tilt of his chin. It reminded me of how invaluable loyal Stewards could be in a household. 'It is your home, your husband, my lady,' he whispered. 'Go and claim them.'

Thus I took a breath and I stepped forward to meet the Countess of Northumberland. Robert turned at my step, which I made forceful enough. I would not creep into my own parlour.

'Eliza.' He looked across at the lady. 'Allow me to present my wife, who was Elizabeth Paston.'

By now I had my composure pinned tight, thick as a winter cloak. I was my mother's daughter after all, I discovered. I imagined Margaret making her presence felt in any situation. I would do so, too.

'Eliza.' Robert took my hand to draw me forward, deliberately so. 'Here come to visit is my niece Eleanor. She is the daughter of my elder brother Richard and is now wed to Harry Percy, Earl of Northumberland. Thus the glory of her apparel for a family visit.'

I could not mistake Robert's cynicism but replied in good style. 'You are right welcome, my lady.'

I curtsied. She returned it. I summoned Perching who was still waiting at the door and who now bowed with rigid formality to me and brought us wine in an enamelled ewer, of Italian design, accompanied by matching cups. He had assessed the situation perfectly. We too would impress.

We sat.

It developed into what could only be called a chilly meeting. Robert and his niece talked of family affairs and connections, people unknown to me, although Robert did his best to draw me in. Nor was I unwilling to be so encouraged. This was my home. I would not sit silently, I would not feel discomfort inflicted by any woman, no matter how well connected she might be by marriage.

'Who will you support in the coming conflict?' the Countess asked Robert.

'My mind is in conjunction with the Nevilles and the Duke of York.' It was the first time that I had heard him state it so unequivocally in public.

'My lord will, of course, uphold his loyalty to the King.'

'Then we will of necessity be at odds over the outcome on the battlefield as well as over the Poynings manors.'

'My advice would be to give your support to the rightful King.'

'The rightful King is incapable of ruling. And I like not his advisers. Or the powers now held by the Queen.'

'So you will declare yourself traitor.'

I decided to manoeuvre into this, as any good wife should, to draw the sting.

'You will be pleased to rejoice with us, my lady, that we expect a child imminently.'

Her eyes narrowed, travelling over me, although I knew that my voluminous houppelande hid from curious eyes any outward sign of the child.

'You are to be congratulated, madam.'

'My thanks for your good wishes.' And here was an opportunity to heal at least some of the wounds, whatever the cause. 'As my husband's niece, perhaps you will stand godmother for the child.'

She inclined her head in a stately manner, in what might have been agreement, but she did not acknowledge my invitation.

'Do you stay with us, my lady?' I asked.

'For the night.'

'Then allow me to show you to your chamber. I will send whatever you need to refresh yourself after your long journey before you join us for supper.'

She rose to her feet. 'There is no need. I know the house well.'

'But there has been some renovation, according to my own wishes, since you last came here,' I chided gently. I thought that by now Margaret would have shown her to the door. Instead I escorted her to the chamber set aside for visitors of some status.

'It must be very different from the arrangements that you are used to,' she observed, actually running a forefinger over the edge of the bed where the carving was heavy. I knew full well that there was no dust.

'Not entirely,' I replied, smoothing my hand over the counterpane although there were no creases there.

'I understand that your grandfather was from humble stock.'

'Indeed he was, but my father used his talents to make his way in the world, as perhaps you yourself did, my lady. Marriage is a valuable commodity. My father married an heiress. So did my brother.' I continued: 'This manor is larger than the one in which I habitually lived. There are more rooms to be cared for, more furniture to be dusted.' I smiled at her, rewarded by a hint of colour along her sharp cheekbones. 'But I can be instructed in nothing new about household management. In Norfolk my family owns more than one manor. My brother is now in possession of Caister Castle.'

'I heard of that. Undoubtedly a step up in the world for your family.'

'As I assume that yours was a momentous leap when you wed the Percy heir.'

She stiffened as if she had been struck.

How had I gained such confidence?

'But there is a dispute over Caister, I understand.'

I was not deterred. 'When is there not dispute over property? I have been raised in the middle of it. As you said, the Pastons are a litigious family.' She flushed an even deeper pink as I made it clear that I had been listening at the door. 'The only difference for me as Dame Poynings is that now I have more servants to do the work for me, rather than taking it on myself. Which I assure you I am quite capable of doing. If you have a need of anything you must tell me, my lady. I will send a maid to wait on you.'

I left her.

I would not look forward to supper, but I would ensure that nothing could be criticised in my kitchen or my selection of dishes, or the fair cloth that was spread on my table. Candles of good-quality wax were lit. A minstrel, who happened to be passing, touting his skills, was invited in and paid to accompany our meal with dulcet tunes. I had heard worse.

We survived in what might have been interpreted as amity. Until Robert asked the one pertinent question. I wished that he had waited until they were alone, but this was what he needed to know, and I, too.

'Why are you here, Eleanor? Why have you travelled all this way?'

She fidgeted for a brief moment with a knife which she had used to pare an apple before raising cool eyes to Robert's face.

'My lord intends to make a claim against all the manors in Kent.'

'I see. And why would he have the power do that, when your grandfather's will left you only four manors? Does he not have enough with the Percy acres in the north? He is already Baron Poynings through your right as your father's heir.'

'My lord's motives are not your concern. Enough that you should know that he will claim them by right of gavelkind, of course.'

Beside me Robert inhaled deeply. 'His motives are most definitely my concern. Why would he send you rather than come himself?'

'He is well occupied in support of the King. He is also collecting a force of our dependants. He thought that you should know, since he will use them to guard against any conflict in Kent if you decide to protect the manors with your own liveried men. You may challenge it if you wish, but I doubt you will get anywhere in the courts, or by force of arms. The Percys are a powerful might. And of course the King will support a Percy in any venture.'

'The King lacks the wit to support any man. My thanks for the warning. I will resist with all the power of the law behind me.'

Eleanor showed her teeth in a semblance of a smile, glancing towards me.

'You have a tame lawyer in the family now.'

'I have, with two sons who will be just as capable. They have the law and landownership at their fingertips.'

'It will make no difference. My lord will keep them occupied to the tips of their low-born fingers when he takes possession. For once there will be no Paston success in law.'

Robert stood, unable to sit any longer. 'I will resist, Eleanor. I have no ambitions for power at Court or at the side of the King, but I have all the ambition in the world to hold fast to my lands.'

Which brought to an end any further discussion. We retired to our rooms and the Countess of Northumberland left on the following morning with unsmiling visage and no amicable agreement.

'This is a grave concern,' I observed as we watched her depart.

'It is not good.' Robert turned to step back into the house, but I stopped him, a hand to his arm.

'Why did she visit us? Why warn you of what was to come?'

'Perhaps to overawe me into compliance. If so, she failed.'

'Why does the Earl of Northumberland have the power to disturb you so greatly?' I continued to fire questions.

'Such a question for a Paston. You have suddenly become very interested in the laws of inheritance.' It was a grim smile, but at least it was a curve of his lips. There was no softness in his eyes.

'But what is gavelkind? Does he have that right?'

'Yes, it is a Kentish thing. All land in Kent is held by gavelkind unless proved to the contrary. An estate can be passed on to a female. Percy is claiming all the Poynings estates through

Eleanor being my brother's sole direct heir, even though I inherited the bulk of it as the next male in line.'

'So this is a threat to your whole inheritance?'

'Yes.'

I followed him back into the house, into the chamber where we had broken our fast with the sullen but beautifully presented Eleanor. He poured a cup of ale and drank it off. Then with a grunt of apology poured one for me, which I refused. He sat amongst the debris, brushing crumbs on the cloth into a neat pile with the edge of his hand.

'Will the courts not uphold your right to the estate? Will my brother help?'

'He might.'

I thought that he seemed reluctant. 'Have you asked him?'

'No, but in the light of Eleanor's visit, it will behove me to do so.'

Here was truly a threat to Robert, to me, to our unborn child. My contentment destroyed by one blow from a pair of elegant be-ringed hands. Robert must have read my fear before I turned away.

'There is nothing for you to worry about.'

But I did. Of course I would worry.

Restlessly he pushed to his feet and strode to the door, coming to a halt before he reached it. 'There is one thing you could do for me.'

I was surprised. If it was a discussion with my brother over the inheritance, would not Robert wish to deal with it himself?

'I will do whatever is needed. Unless it is to return to stay beneath my mother's roof. That I will not do, not even for a se'enight.'

He laughed, more at ease now. 'There is no need to go so far. But you might write a letter on my behalf.'

'To my mother?' And instantly I knew. 'Can I guess?'

'You might well. I gave my bond for a thousand pounds to Mistress Agnes with your brothers standing as guarantee that I would produce the jointure. I am finding it difficult to meet the payments. Because ...'

He halted, hating to have to make the admission.

'Because my mother has failed to make the payments on my dower,' I finished for him.

'Yes. Nor, it seems, has she made the payments to Lady de la Pole for your sojourn with her before our marriage.'

Humiliation washed over me. Once again my mother had placed her love of money and financial security before my happiness and my relationships with others. I felt tears well in my eyes at such perfidy, but again turned away. Robert did not need me to weep over him, or over my mother. I detested the need to do it, but I had promised and so I would. My hand was not good enough to write this myself so I made use of Robert's clerk, biting down on the shame that I must send such a letter.

How to address her? I settled on the purely factual, hoping that she would prove to be my tender and good mother.

How to describe my husband? My best beloved, because indeed he was.

And then the gist.

Do not fail to pay to us the hundred marks as you promised with the remnant of that which was left to me in my father's will. Do not fail to honour your debt and pay Lady Pole for all her kindness.

Would she comply?

I thought not, or not readily, but I would ask, for it was

wrong that Robert should be disgraced with this debt because my mother had failed.

I would have asked John, or Meg, to intervene, but their minds were caught up in their own inheritance. My dower was now small meat to them, I feared.

Southwark: late December 1459

It seemed for a little time that my fears were ill-founded. Even though we received no reply from Mistress Agnes, and no money was forthcoming, life smiled on us after all.

I bore a son, in the cold dark days before the turn of the year. A healthy child with strong fingers that gripped mine and good lungs that he used readily when not smiling at the new world with toothless gums. I could see no resemblance in him to either the Pastons or to Robert. His eyes were the dark grey of a winter storm cloud, his hair a fair swirl of curls. His limbs were straight and firm as he kicked against the covers in his carved crib. Here was the Poynings heir.

Robert was delighted, holding him tenderly, so I was told, when my maid carried him out of my chamber for his father to admire. I poured all the residue of my love into that child in the solitary days before I was churched and restored to the world of men.

'What will be his name?' I sent the message with my maid-servant.

Robert came to stand outside my door.

'Edward,' he said, his voice strangely hollow through the panels. There was no such name in my family, nor from all I knew in Robert's.

'Would you not wish to call him Robert, for yourself and your father? Or even Richard for your brother?'

'Too many Roberts in one household will make for complications.' I could hear the smile in his voice, acknowledging the problem of the many Johns in my own. 'We will call him Edward in honour of the Duke of York who I trust will bring this country back to good government. His eldest son is Edward. So will ours be.'

So Edward he was.

'We will restore all the Poynings lands to him so that he will never have to fight the Percys for every acre,' Robert added.

As the dark year tipped over into the next, I was content, as was Robert with the return of the Duke of York from his exile in Ireland after the debacle at Ludford Bridge when the Duke and his Neville allies had been forced to flee for their lives, to take refuge across the sea. Now he was returned to London, proclaiming his royal lineage through the lines of Clarence and York, sons of the third King Edward. The Act of Accord had recognised the Duke of York as the heir to the throne after King Henry. Many frowned at York's ambitions, but there were few who would openly support Queen Margaret in her determination to hold on to royal hegemony in her husband's name. In a spirit of optimism I sent another letter to my mother to inform her of her new grandson and demand the payment of my dower.

And yet with the turn of the year of 1460 into 1461, our delight in our healthy son became overshadowed and we became a household in mourning, as did all adherents of York. The cause of York seemed to be dead with the Duke of York and his son Rutland and his Neville ally the Earl of Salisbury at the Battle of Wakefield. We waited for news, as the future rested on the shoulders of the experienced Earl of Warwick and hung in the youthful hands of Edward, Earl of March, for whom our son was called. Every day in Southwark we looked for the arrival of Queen Margaret with her wayward forces, dreading the pillage of London. March's victory at Mortimer's Cross in the west was welcome but did not put our fears to rest, even though King Henry was now a prisoner of Warwick and Queen Margaret was still to reclaim her husband and her capital.

'Now we look to see what the Earl of Warwick will do,' Robert said with conviction that he too would be victorious. The Wheel of Fortune was turning to bring the House of York back to pre-eminence. It spurred Robert into instant action.

'There is no time to lose. The Queen must face Warwick since her allies in the west have been put to flight.'

Thus Sir Robert Poynings, as I had feared, rode out to war. Before he went I completed for him a new pair of gauntlets. With every careful stitch of gold and green, and the bend gules across the whole, I sewed in a prayer that the Blessed Virgin would keep him safe and bring him home. Then I added another prayer with the gilt edging to the wrist-guards:

'Blessed Virgin, if it may be that there is no battle, I will light candles in your honour every day until the day of my death.'

I presented the gauntlets to Robert as he came to mount his horse, a mettlesome grey named Grisone with the reputation of courage when under pressure. The liveried entourage drawn up behind Robert made an impressive showing. I had no experience of expressing intense emotion but on that morning it overflowed.

I kissed his hand. 'God keep you safe, my dear husband.'

'And may He keep you close, my inestimable wife. I will

return. And when I do I swear that Edward of York will be King of England.'

I did not greatly care, only that he should return, enabling us to live out our days in placid harmony when we had defeated the Percy claim on our son's inheritance. Perhaps there would be more children. I held Edward high in my arms. Robert stroked a finger down his cheek, laughing when the boy grasped the cuff of the new gloves and attempted to test his new teeth on the gilding.

'I will write when I can. I have made provision for you in my will. Your dower is safe.'

I reached up and placed my fingers over his lips.

'You will return to fight for what is yours. I will pray for you.'

It was always the lot of women to remain at home and worry. We would hear alarms and rumours so far from the clash of arms. Momentarily I wondered if Margaret was in the same situation. Had John finally been moved to raise troops to resist the Lancastrians and their allies in Norfolk? I did not think that he would. He would claim that the law took up too much of his time.

I did not care who ruled England, whether York or Lancaster. This conflict had destroyed my hard-won happiness. For a moment I wished that Robert could be so easily persuaded as my brother that affairs at home took precedence, but he would not be the man I knew if he turned from this deadly clash of ambitions.

Chapter Fourteen

Margaret Mautby Paston

Norwich: New Year 1460

Sometimes as I awoke I could not believe our good fortune. I might mourn Sir John's passing, but his death had provided us with a solidly constructed ladder. John was firmly and competently climbing up its rungs, fending off any man who might see this as a chance to feather his own nest in the dangerous space between Sir John's death and the issuing of probate. Such men existed, quick to take advantage of a high rank and a position of influence at Court. So many eyes had been cast over Sir John Fastolf's possessions, so many ears had twitched to hear news of his death without an heir. There were evil forces at work.

I visited Caister Castle again, now my own property, walking around my new possession, slowly, contemplatively, seeing it with different eyes. Mistress Agnes came with me, but for the most part I walked in silence. The rooms I had first seen with William Worcester were now mine. A magnificent bed, all carved wood with a tester and arras hangings. The little golden lions with red eyes particularly caught my foolish interest, romping over the silk and linen coverlet. There were books in French and Latin and English, which did not interest me as much as the household necessities, ranging from costly silver candlesticks in the public chambers, to the pewter chargers and brass ladles in the kitchen. From the mundane to the magnificent.

All the tapestries now belonged to me. I examined them, touching the silk stitching, enjoying the intricate scenes. A lady clad in stitched brocade sitting in a chair, a little dog at her feet. I had never had such a fine gown but now I owned it in this tapestry. Here was the Coronation of Our Lady, her cloak the blue of heaven and embroidered with stars. Here the Assumption of Our Lady, full of golden angels singing to welcome her into heaven. And there was Lancelot and Guinevere beneath a leafy glade.

'Thank you, Cousin John Fastolf,' I whispered.

I was lady of Caister Castle and all it contained.

'Fine feathers! Fine feathers!' Mistress Agnes muttered, refusing to be impressed. 'Let us hope that the will is proved and that you do not lose all this before you can fully lay claim to it.'

I would not speak of my disappointment. Claims had already been laid to Sir John's splendid house in Southwark, with all its goods and possessions, with no legal authority whatsoever to do so. The great magnates did not need legal authority. All they had to do was march in with their liveried retainers and occupy it, which they promptly did. I had never even seen the house for myself. All I had was John's enthusiastic description of its walls and towers and its wharf onto the River Thames. Now it was gone. What a home that would have been, almost a rival to Caister Castle.

'Can you not get them out?' I asked John.

'By God, I will!'

'And if you cannot, do I need to hide *all* of Fastolf's treasures from any thieving fingers? Where do you suggest?'

He ignored my flippancy.

What caught my interest in the cellars at Caister, provoking a disquiet, was the store of arms that we discovered, a private armoury, in fact. Body armour, salets, guns and crossbows, not all in good order, probably due to their lack of recent use. I was aware that the castle was well fortified, but would we ever be called on to defend it? I lifted one of the rusted plates of armour, letting it fall with a clatter, praying that my sons would never be called on to wear it.

Leaving Mistress Agnes to prowl the chambers I climbed to the wall-walk, to overlook our acres. Somewhere on the manors in Norfolk we had inherited three thousand sheep as well as horses and cattle. Here was true wealth.

I frowned at our distant flocks that might never be sheared in our name for there had emerged a real threat of the Pastons being linked with the supporters of the Duke of York who had raised arms against the King. We had never proclaimed ourselves for York but were so labelled because of our perennial disputes with the Duke of Suffolk. To oppose Suffolk equated to being Yorkist, and attainder was a fearsome thing. Any day now we could be dragged off as traitors and our property, including our newly acquired sheep, stripped away and apportioned to royal favourites. It was a fear that kept me awake at night, and John too, although he would be loath to admit it.

A familiar hissing and beating of powerful wings below, warning of an arrival, took my attention. Peering down between the crenellations to the moat, I had a foreshortened view of more creatures to which I could now lay claim. I owned far more than four swans. The burden on Richard Calle's shoulders had multiplied. I hoped that he would enjoy the burden. Unless they too were forfeit under attainder.

I discovered that I was smiling as the visitor was forced to fend off the vigorous attack from the moat. In spite of attainders and swans and Mistress Agnes's carping, a supreme satisfaction kept me company on my perambulations up and down the stairs. Caister Castle was the jewel in the Paston crown. I had to believe that it would remain so.

Back at Mautby as Mistress Agnes and I rode into the court-yard, it was to discover that John was on the point of departure. From the corner of my eye I caught a glimpse of Elder John and Jonty, slipping quietly into the stable with a large sacking bag. Out with snares after rabbits, I presumed, and now intent on keeping out of John's line of sight since he would demand to know what they were doing. I did not draw attention to them. Let them have their moment away from business.

'I have been surveying our acres,' I said as I slid down from my mount while John helped his mother.

'And did you enjoy it?'

'Immeasurably. If we are allowed to keep them.'

And there it was! At last, as he came towards me, I read relief in his face.

'We were not named,' he said. 'Our property is not forfeit. We are not traitors.'

I cast myself into his arms. I had not realised how much fear had been eating at me.

'Oh, John. I am so pleased to hear that.'

'About me or our property?'

'Both, I think.'

'Dear Meg!' The relief made him grin, an expression I had not seen for some weeks. 'Can I leave the local affairs in your hands?'

'Of course.' Did he need to ask?

He beckoned to our two eldest sons who had now emerged, clothes brushed down to remove any incriminating evidence, to bid their father a dutiful farewell, as if they had been engaged with estate affairs since breaking their fast. Their smiles were superbly ingenuous and I did not betray them.

'You will be a help to your mother. You will be obedient and do as she tells you. You will be a credit to your Paston family. You will put your very expensive education into practice. Do you understand?'

They had listened gravely enough to the list. Both nodded. I had more faith in Jonty than his elder brother who already had a strange kick in his gait when challenged. I might have to use cajolery rather than instruction when their father was gone, but to give them a handful of tasks to fill their days and keep them out of mischief in Norwich would be no bad thing.

So John departed and I took my sons in hand as the vital inquests over Fastolf's lands were to be held at the villages of Acle and Bungay. Jonty had a good hand with a pen. I knew what I wanted from him.

'You will be my clerk,' I informed him. 'When I say write this down, you will write it. I will give you a book to keep my notes in. And you will not scrawl nonsense in the margins. This will be an official record of our inheritance.'

'Yes, mother.'

'And you,' I turned to Elder John, 'you will help me in the administration of the manors when we have proved our right to them.'

He preened a little at his duties being some days in the future. Did he think that I could not read him as well as I could my psalter?

'And, if you thought to escape into Norwich, I have a task for you now.' Also, a parting shot to both of them: 'I do not wish to have to seek high and low for you when I have a task for you. If you choose to go out after rabbits and such, I do not wish to know unless it is in a dish for supper.'

They exchanged glances but Elder John followed me to John's room where there stood the great standing chest in which he kept all the pertinent documents for the Fastolf inheritance that were not with him in London. I pointed to it.

'Lift the lid.' And when he did so, with all the anticipation of finding treasure within, 'There are three large canvas bags. Lift them out.'

He did so. They were weighty with documents.

'I need you to search through these titles of ownership.'

'All three of them?'

I could see the horror on his face. 'All three. We need to find a copy of a particular document relating to the manor of Drayton. It may be needed when one of the writs is heard.'

His face had fallen as if he had been faced with the pestilence. I knew how to remedy that.

'It is a difficult task,' I said, 'but it needs to be done with care so that not one document is overlooked. If you prove your worth, who knows? It may be that you will earn your father's gratitude and a place at Court where you can use your talents more widely.'

Which cheered him momentarily, but not after the hours it took to shuffle and read through every document.

As evening fell I returned to find him still occupied, surrounded by candles, his hair disordered by hours of apparent failure. His head was bent over the remaining documents that he rolled and unrolled, scanning them before tossing them into the chest at his feet. For a brief moment it made my heart ache. This was not what he would choose in life, yet there was no doubt that he had a strong will, a persistence even when the task did not please him. How could I not admire him, his handsome profile, the dark fall of his hair? Regretfully Elder John had more interest in the quality of his boots and his hose than this mundane but essential task. I knew that he saw himself working at Court, as William did. Perhaps I must talk to John about this. I thought that my son was unhappy. We must keep him in the Paston fold or he might escape to pastures new and more fertile.

'Acle and Bungay, by God!' I heard him mutter. 'Do I want to spend my life dealing with the doings of Acle and Bungay? And with damnable writs *diem clausit extremum*? Who knows what they might be!'

'It's a writ to allow the decision of who is to inherit,' I said. I think that it surprised my son that I should know. 'One for each county in which Sir John held property. They are vital to our secure holding of the land.'

Elder John turned his face away. No, a lawyer was the last thing that he wanted to be, burdened with Latin clauses and legal battles. Jonty would do it, but the Paston heir had his ambitions set on horizons far distant from Norfolk and the narrow world of legal disputation.

I walked forward and placed my hand on his shoulder. He looked up.

'It is not here.'

I did not question his judgement. Despite his lack of

willingness I knew he would not have made a mistake. I planted a kiss on his brow, ruffled his hair even further, and rewarded him with a cup of ale and a plate of bread and cheese which I had left just within the door. It amused me that there was already a cup at his elbow. He had clearly charmed one of the maids to keep his thirst at bay. And there were sweet crumbs of some delicacy.

'Well done, anyway,' I said. 'I will tell your father. He needs to look through the remaining documents in London.'

'I might wish that he had done that first.'

'I know. But you have proved your efficiency.' There must be some way I could encourage him. 'You will make a good lawyer.'

'But do I want to be one?'

Which confirmed all I had feared. 'Do you?' I asked him, a hand lightly on his shoulder. No one had ever asked him. It had always been presumed by his father that he would follow the family tradition into the law.

'No!' How brusque he was. He shrugged my hand away.

'Your father expects it,' I added, distressed at his vehemence.

'Do I have no choice of my own?'

I shook my head, wishing that I might not agree. He saw himself as a courtier, or a soldier at the King's side. I hoped that he would not live to be disappointed. My heart ached for him, and for the clash of will that I already foresaw between my husband and his heir.

★

The Mayor of Norwich and his lady invited themselves to dine with us at Hellesdon, one of our new Fastolf manors just outside the town. Here was acceptance. Here was recognition even though I had little time for the self-important Mayor or his wife. Such an honour to be paid to us, to mark our rise in status as owners of a castle. The distinction was helped along by the fact that John had at last been elected as member of parliament for Norfolk in November of the previous year. I had come to terms with the worry that it was merely another drain on his time.

John might be a lawyer in every bone of his body, he might publicly accept this honour with gravity, but in private he preened.

'What would my grandfather Clement have to say about this?'

'He would probably shrug aside the Mayor on his threshold and take himself off to plough one of the pastures.'

'I think he would secretly have been pleased.'

'He would have cared more for the working of his mill!'

'But to have his grandson step into the first society of Norfolk?'

I relented. 'He would have broached a keg of his best ale and toasted you from dawn to dusk.'

In a cynical moment I considered my husband to be the equal of Robert Toppes, Mayor of Norwich. Was I not more than worthy of associating with his lady wife? Yet it was indeed a great honour for us to be singled out and I would not be churlish. When I sought a suitable garment in my clothes presses, I chose a patterned gown in figured velvet that John had bought for me in London at great expense, as he often reminded me. As for jewels, I had the Fastolf legacy to choose from. A cross of gold, glittering with a diamond and ruby and three pearls, would do more than impress Mayor Toppes and his wife. The crispinette that confined my hair gleamed with gold wire as I stood by my door when the Mayor's servant arrived in the middle hours of the morning with a cart. I could now play the great lady with ease.

They began to unload. My own servants were there in smart new Paston livery to greet them, to take the dishes and boxes and carry them to the kitchen. They might have invited themselves to dinner at eleven of the clock, but they had been considerate of us by sending on the food ahead, that they would not be a trouble to me and my household. I was gratified that my own preparations should be so augmented when I followed the dishes in. Ridiculously I felt a sense of excitement. John emerged from his chamber to see what the fuss was about.

'Shall we take a look?'

We lifted lids, opened boxes. Sniffed flagons.

'Well!'

I slapped Jonty's fingers away.

'There will be no pieces missing from that crust, or I will know the reason why.' I smiled at Richard Calle who had supervised the unloading. 'I would be obliged if you would keep an eye on the children.'

He already had young Willem's arm in a firm grip.

'Take note of this, Meg,' John advised. 'One day you may have to do the same. You may as well learn from Mistress Toppes who probably does this every week.'

'I could do better. I would not serve so plain a dish as capon. Guinea fowl,' I said. 'Or at least pheasant.'

The arrival of the Mayor was less of an excitement than the food to my sons, but we sat down in our parlour which had been set for the occasion and we ate of the dishes. The conversation ranged, as at any such meeting between neighbours, from the weather to the state of unrest on the streets of Norwich. We stepped nimbly around the subject of Caister Castle since Fastolf's will still hung in abeyance. Instead the chatter turned towards the state of the realm and the ambitions of the House of York. We all agreed that there would be more clashes of interest before the year was out.

'You must be thankful that your name was not included in the list of attainders,' Mayor Toppes observed as the meal drew to its end.

I nudged John's arm as I passed him a platter of cheese and sweet cherries.

'We thank God daily,' he replied, amazingly bland.

Since we were uncertain of the Mayor's political affinity it was wise not to commit ourselves to any sympathy with York, or indeed with Lancaster.

The Mayor had a speculative gleam in his eye. 'If you are offered a knighthood, Master Paston, will you accept it, to enhance your new position in Norfolk?'

'By Lancaster or York?' John did not take the bait. 'I will wait for it to be offered.'

It was a surprise to me. Had there been any mention of a knighthood? I found that I was smiling at the prospect, as I looked down at my hands in my lap. Were these the pampered hands of a wife of a knight of the realm? If I dreamt of it ever happening, it would be a long time in the coming. Recalling the visit of Lady Anne Beaufort, now my sister-in-law, a soft-fingered lady cosseted from birth, I considered the evidence of hard work before me, not from shame but from a bleak acceptance of my lot in life, allowing my smile to fade as our guests departed. The Mayor's lady took her empty platters and dishes with her.

'Well?' John asked as we stood alone amidst the detritus of the meal.

'I have never spent a more tedious few hours,' I said. 'The

Mayor trying to decide whether you are a traitor or not, whether he should continue to associate with us, and his wife assessing the value of our silver plate.' And then: 'Would you accept a knighthood?' I asked. I had decided that I might enjoy being Dame Paston.

John thought about this. The seed had been sown.

'Don't worry your head about it, Meg. Who would offer me one when the Crown is being fought over? Pastons are small fry in these political days.'

Norwich: January 1461

Knighthoods were indeed soon far from our thoughts. Lawless times hovered over us like a nightmare that would not be dislodged, no matter how many meals we might share with the worthy of Norwich. Nor did our tenuous connection with the House of York bring us good fortune. We might have been encouraged to know of the Yorkist victory at Northampton where King Henry was taken prisoner by the Earl of Warwick and the Lancastrian forces put to flight, but any supporter of York would be dismayed by the Duke of York's death on the battlefield at Wakefield, his head impaled on Micklegate Bar in York – mocked, it was said, with a paper crown. The Yorkist cause seemed to be dead with the Duke. John's young brother Clement kept us informed when he feared that the uprisings might spill over into Norfolk.

Raise troops in Norfolk, John. Arm yourselves.

His advice was trenchant. John's reaction equally so, his mood unreliable.

'Raise troops? Arm myself? Do I present myself on a battlefield?

Before God, I cannot do this,' John responded, his voice loud enough to echo in our hall at Elm Hill in Norwich where we had moved so that John could be at the centre of the present legal wrangling. 'I have neither the time nor the money. I am spending all the hours in a day on trying to prove that Fastolf's will is not a forgery. So many of Fastolf's servants have suddenly emerged to question it. William Yelverton is hostile. Even William Worcester, whom I thought to be my most loyal supporter from Fastolf's household, is muttering in corners.'

'The problem is, John, that you were on your own with my cousin when he changed his mind.'

John glowered, unable to dissent. His frustration drove him to snap the pen he carried. He dropped the pieces on the floor.

'I am accused of robbery, by God.'

I bent to pick up the pieces before he stamped them into the tiles.

'But what if ...' I began, envisaging our eastern counties war-torn and desolate, and the Paston family without protection.

'What if? There are so many what ifs. If troops appear on the horizon, I promise that I will arm our household.'

I had snatched the letter from John's hand and managed to read it well enough.

'Clement says the people of the north rob and steal and will come south to pillage.'

'There are enough people living not too far away from us who are prepared to rob and steal and pillage, without hordes from the north.'

'But we have sufficient arms at Caister, do we not?' I remembered the contents of the armoury there. Did John know how worn some of the salets and breastplates were? How much it would cost us to replace them?

'Yes. And they will stay there. I have no plans to appear on a battlefield in Norfolk or anywhere else.'

When we heard of the Earl of March's victory at Mortimer's Cross in the west, our spirits rose from their depths after Wakefield. And then, after Warwick's battle at St Albans, our hopes sank again with his defeat. John shuffled between one task and the next like a restless hound. He could settle to nothing.

'Go and visit your mother at Oxnead,' I suggested to get him out from under my feet.

'Wanting to be rid of me?'

'Yes.'

'It's March. It's too cold for travelling.'

'Nonsense. You have a new cloak with a fur lining.'

He thought about it. 'Then I will go tomorrow.'

'Take the young ones with you. It may be safer for them.'

The nightmare of the northern lawless army descending on us would not leave me. John looked askance but did not demur. But before the next day dawned we had the expected letter from William.

'What do you think?' John, determinedly cynical, shook the single page as if to shake the words free. 'Will this give our local lords free rein to grab another estate from me?'

I took it from him. 'We will never know unless someone reads it.' It was long, with a substantial list of those who had died and those who had fled the recent battle, a list that did not greatly interest me and one that John could peruse for himself, but I relayed the pertinent sentences.

'Lancaster is defeated and King Henry is fled to the north. It was a bloodbath at a place called Towton in the snow, while we were kneeling in church on Palm Sunday to give thanks to

God for his blessings on the Paston family. Edward of York will be King. William thinks the Yorkist victory can bring nothing but good for you.'

'Is William certain?' John was already holding out his hand for the letter, but I was still reading.

'Yes. And you might be interested in the final comment. From his underlining, William seems to think it is of some vast importance.'

'What is it?'

'He has recorded the death of the Earl of Wiltshire. He was captured after the battle, his head displayed on London Bridge for all to see. Is he important to us?'

'Well, let us say that's one death I will not regret,' John said, his mouth twisted in sour pleasure. 'The Earl of Wiltshire is – was – Lord Treasurer to King Henry. He had set his officials to discover any legal means possible to take all of Fastolf's property for the Crown. To take it all from me. So he's dead. It may make my life easier.'

Mistress Agnes would not set eyes on her eldest son this side of the summer solstice and neither would I. He would be London-bound by the morrow, I knew it.

★

For once I was wrong about John's length of absence. Within the passing of two months he was returned, almost gaunt with exhaustion, his hair uncut, unless hacked about with a blunt knife, but overall there was a suspicious gloss of self-worth. And I knew exactly why that would be.

'You look like a cat with the cream, or a fat rat,' I said.

'Why would I not? The Fastolf inheritance still belongs to us.'

'I'd say that it is more than that!'

Did I not already know which way the wind was blowing? John had kept the secret until his own good time for its telling. Once it would have irritated me beyond measure. Now, with age and experience, I accepted it. I had my own sources. Both William and Clement proved to be excellent suppliers of information.

'William tells me that our new King Edward plans to confer a knighthood on you at the time of the coronation.'

He looked disappointed that I already knew, but should he not have told me himself? I was not in the mood to be charitable. If John's ties with the Court became stronger, I would be called upon to shoulder even more of the responsibilities of our manors. Sometimes I was simply tired. Sometimes I would just like to rest a little in my own home and deal with petty domestic crises such as the depredations of the fox in my hencoop. I knew it would never happen, and did I not enjoy the authority given to me? But sometimes I would appreciate sitting with a cup of ale with friends in Norwich that did not entail disputes, tenants who would not pay their rents, and threats of violence in the streets. Sometimes I would just wish to sit with my husband and savour the moment. I would exchange being a knight's lady for the assurance of my husband's whereabouts any day of the week. Sometimes I was ground down with dismay and loneliness.

But not today. My temper was stirred. Today I would take my husband to task for his neglect of me.

'Yes, he did,' John admitted. 'But did William tell you that I refused it?'

Now that I did not know, which stopped my complaint before it was uttered.

'No.'

'Well, I did.'

I watched John's face but he was giving nothing away. Why would he refuse? All his life he had sought a patron, a recognition of some power higher than his own. And here it was, offered on a royal golden platter. An open-handed gesture of a knighthood. And he would refuse it?

'Why would you do that?' I asked.

'I do not want it.'

I did not understand. He had clearly thought about this and made the decision, with or without my advice.

'Why would you not want it?'

For a long moment John studied the floor at his feet, then, looking up, said:

'I have ambition for my family, for the future, but not through a knighthood for me; I am too old for that. I foresee a place for me in our new King's household, which will give me the King's favour and the King's ear in any local disputes. But not a knighthood. We will survive without my being a knight.'

Which was all very well, although I did not see the logic of his argument. Was death haunting him? He had thirty-nine years to his name. In the bright light of the window that threw his face and figure into sharp relief, he looked older, the constant work and worry not good for him, undermining his strength. Still, perversely and in good legal manner which he would appreciate, I made the case for accepting such a reward.

'What if I would like to be the wife of a knight? What if I would like to be addressed as Dame Paston and make an entry in Norwich circles with drums and fanfare?'

He shrugged. 'I did not think that you would care.'

'Tell me the name of any woman of your acquaintance who would not wish her husband to be a knight? When I am dead I would like such recognition on my tomb. I would like Mistress Toppes to curtsey to me when we pass in the street. What woman would not?'

'You will survive well enough without.'

'But it is such an acknowledgement of your favour with the House of York! By the Virgin, we need it, John. Now that England is settled into peace, the Duke of Norfolk will make a bid against Caister. And the new Duke of Suffolk will do the same. Why refuse a knighthood?'

My mind had already begun to work.

'Now what are you thinking?' John asked. 'I have to say that I would have liked more of a warm welcome from my wife rather than an attack on all fronts.'

'I would have liked my husband not to leave me in ignorance, so that I have to come by my information from his brothers.' Yet I relented a little. 'As for what I am thinking, if you have no ambition to become a knight, why not persuade the King that it would be an excellent reward for our family if our eldest son became a knight instead?'

Why had he not thought of this? Because all his focus was on the Fastolf will.

'And you could suggest a place in the King's household for Elder John to further his education and acquire some social niceties,' I continued. 'What better than such an opportunity to make friends amongst the other squires about the King?' I recalled Elder John's complaints over the document search, his lack of ambition in the legal world. 'Your heir needs some polish. It would curb his terrible restlessness.'

For a little time, there was silence in our hall. Then:

'You are a woman of great cunning, Margaret Paston.'

'I am a woman who has learned well from being married to a Paston. What I did not learn from you, I learned from your mother. Is it a good idea?'

'It is an excellent idea.' At last he reached to take my hand, his smile outrageously sly. 'I had already thought of that. I have already suggested it to our new King. Did you think that I would not have seized this golden opportunity for the Paston family?'

I could have snatched my hand away but did not. Of course he had thought of it, and I was a fool not to have realised.

'And?'

'King Edward was not averse to it. My heir will become a knight.'

Elder John would go off to Court, he would become a courtier, to make friends and make use of his legal education at the same time.

'And what about Jonty? What will you do for him?'

'We need to find him a place where he can make his name.'

So I still had my clerk to write at my dictation. All was as good as we could hope for, even if it caught the attention of John's enemies that we were growing stronger. Which gave me something more to worry over. John's safety as well as my eldest son's demeanour and progress at Court. I was not confident about either.

John folded me into his arms, rubbing gently at the crease between my brows.

'Are you not content?'

'How could I be otherwise?' I replied and kissed his lips.

I was content, but I became aware of a despondency in my heart: I would lose my eldest son to the heady world of the Royal Court.

Chapter Fifteen

Elizabeth Paston Poynings

Southwark: February 1461

In the month of February in the year 1461, two years after my marriage, when my little son had gained his feet and seemed set to be a soldier like his father, a man could be seen riding up to the door of our Southwark house. It was barely dawn, a cold grey morning with the threat of snow. I had heard no word of conflict, only the rumour of armies manoeuvring. I was there in the inner courtyard before he had dismounted.

It was not Robert. Was it then a message from him? I had received no letter to tell me of his situation. Had there been a battle? Who had seen victory? Queen Margaret or the Earl of Warwick who still had King Henry under his control?

Please let it be a victory for the Earl of Warwick, who owned Robert's loyalty. Let him come home. Blessed Virgin have mercy.

It was Thomas, Robert's squire, who slid down from the saddle of his hard-ridden horse, his young face severe with new lines as he turned to me. My heart shuddered, my throat dried. It was impossible for me to do anything but fear the worst, for he was leading a horse that I knew to be Robert's, the courageous grey. Grisone's saddle was empty. I faced him, sensing that Perching had come to stand behind me. My shivering was not from the cold.

'Tell me.'

'The forces met at St Albans, my lady. Queen Margaret against Warwick. The second battle to be suffered by that little town.' He halted. Swallowed. 'It was not a victory for the Earl of Warwick.'

'What is the situation now?'

I watched the movement of his throat as he swallowed again, painfully, noting the gleam of moisture in his red-rimmed eyes.

'My lord Robert was cut down on the field. My lord is dead. I have ridden hard to tell you because ...'

His voice dried.

'My lord is dead.'

I repeated it but the words seemed to have no meaning.

'Yes, my lady.'

'And Warwick?' Although I did not care. It was not important when my life, so new, so precious, lay in ruins at my feet.

'Alive to fight another day, but his army was in rout when I left. Queen Margaret's forces were marching on London. They'll not be far behind me, I wager. They were out for blood and plunder. She'll not hold them back.'

It did not matter what Warwick was doing. Robert was dead. Robert had been dead for days and I had been unaware, living in hope that all was well. How could I not have known? I was a widow before I had even slipped into the security of a bride, into married life. Edward had lost his father. Aware of him come to investigate at my feet, I lifted him into my arms and buried my face against his neck.

My thoughts were awry. Robert was dead. I was a widow. I was alone. What would I do now?

Lifting them from where they had been tied to Robert's saddle, Thomas laid two items at my feet: Robert's tabard covered with blood, and his sword. I did not know what to do with them, simply looked in horror.

'My lady.' Perching placed his hand lightly on my shoulder, bringing me back to the present. If I had ever shown determination in the past, I must do so now.

What would Margaret do? It seemed that she stood beside me, a shadowy figure but one that gave me strength. First I must be practical. I must do what had to be done. Time for mourning and tears later. I shrugged off Perching and stretched out my hand to clasp Thomas's shoulder. He could have been one of my younger brothers.

'Go to the kitchens. Eat and drink and then sleep. We will take care of the horses.'

By the time that I lifted a hand to run it down Grisone's neck, Perching was again at my side.

'What do I do?' I asked him.

'You fight for your son's inheritance.'

'Of course.' In a moment of insight I lifted Edward even higher to place him in the saddle that Grisone still wore. He crowed with delight, clasping the high pommel. 'I can do that. We can all do that,' I said, holding tight to my son.

I remembered when Perching had strengthened my spine, and my courage, when Eleanor had visited. By the Virgin, I needed that strengthening now.

'Be brave, mistress. You are not without friends here. Take your son. I will arrange for the horses to be cared for.'

I watched as the weary grey was led away, favouring one of his forelegs, then inside I placed my son in the centre of the hall.

'Edward,' I said. 'Your father is dead. This now belongs to you.'

He did not understand. The burden of this family was now his. So young. So vulnerable. My happiness had lasted so short a time.

Crouching before him, I pressed my lips to his forehead. There was still no resemblance to Robert. He was too young, his features still unformed. His hair was darker than Robert's, perhaps now more Paston than Poynings. My heart felt cold and numb in my chest, empty, scoured by this loss.

What to do now? Would our lands be secure? To whom would I turn for help?

A touch of conscience pricked me that these first thoughts should be of my son's inheritance rather than Robert's death.

Leaving Edward in the care of Perching, who led him off to the kitchen where he would be fed on some sweetmeat, I went to my own chamber where I wept for my personal loss. Where was Robert buried? What had been done with his body? It was the most important question in my mind. Ridiculously, I imagined him still lying in his vibrant livery on the battlefield, until I remembered that his battle surcoat had been returned to me, and it was covered with blood.

⋆

Robert was dead, his heir a child, just learning to walk, while I, the widow, had no experience in dealing with the inevitable defence of an important inheritance. After a night of misery, morning brought counsel. As soon as Eleanor and the Percy family knew of Robert's death, they would make their claim against the full extent of the Poynings's manors. That must be stopped. They must be hampered at all costs. I summoned Perching. I stood in the room frequented by Robert, the hearth cold behind me, while I held one of the leather-bound ledgers in which Robert made an account of his manors and the rents due to him. I clasped it to my chest.

'We will come under threat,' I said.

'I know it, my lady.'

My mind sped off towards Norwich. What would Margaret do?

I seemed to ask the same question again and again, and I had no time to write and await an answer. Margaret had taken the matter into her own hands and glared at the enemy in Gresham. Margaret had taken the war over property to the enemy's threshold. Margaret would be at John's side in the war of Fastolf's will. Margaret had the courage and tenacity of a wolf at bay when her family was threatened. Could I have the same?

What would my mother do? How would Mistress Agnes react when her property was threatened? I swear that she had still not paid the fines over the encroachment of the wall, even after so many years of litigation.

'My lady?'

Perching was still waiting for me to explain why I had summoned him.

'I was thinking of my mother …'

'Do you wish to see her?'

'No. No.' Hers was the last advice I would seek and I would assuredly receive no compassion. 'Send if you will for my lord's man of law. I must enquire into the state of my son's inheritance.'

Once I knew, I could decide if I too could be like a wolf and hold the hunters at bay.

Meanwhile, I sent Thomas back to the battlefield at St Albans to discover where Robert might lie.

★

Robert's legal adviser, a man in his middle years named John Dane whom I had not as yet met, arrived with grim visage and bleak condolences. He clasped my hands with true comfort which I welcomed, but nothing must turn me from the cataclysm that faced us.

'Thank you, sir. I need to know the detail of how Sir Robert's lands are left. I need to know the contents of the will.'

He withdrew documents from a leather pouch, spreading them over the table. I invited Perching to join us. It seemed important that he be there. He had been long employed in Robert's service, and I knew his loyalties were engraved in stone. I noted that he had had the fire lit, when I had taken no heed of the seeping cold in the room.

'It is simple enough, mistress,' John Dane explained. 'Your jointure is assured as the widow of Sir Robert.'

How cold, how unfeeling the word sounded. Both of them. Jointure and widow. I was determined that my life would not be encircled by them.

'And the rest?' I asked. 'Please sit.'

We settled around the table, the documents spread between us.

John Dane began to explain in clear words. 'All of Sir Robert's estates have been willed to his son, as you would expect. Until the child is of an age to take on the management, the control of all the estates, both your jointure and those now belonging to your son, are under your jurisdiction. It is within your power to take all the produce and profits to pay for the needs of your little

287

son, to pay any debts. And to pay for any need to protect the legal right of ownership and title of these properties.'

He looked across at me.

'Do you envisage such need for my protection?' I asked, knowing full well the reply before it came.

'I do, my lady. And so, I believe, do you. We know the difficulty posed by Sir Robert's niece, the Countess of Northumberland.'

'Yes. She will immediately be hovering like a buzzard over a carcase, to strip it clean. What do we do?'

'This is what I suggest, my lady. For as long as we can, outside these four walls we will deny Sir Robert's death. We will allow no weakness. We will proceed as if he still lived and you, with my aid, will run the estates.'

It was not the reply that I had expected. I regarded him in astonishment.

'But what is the value of that?' I asked. 'Sir Robert's death must be known soon. Surely there were those who saw him fall on the battlefield.'

'All too true,' he replied, leaning forward in his urgency, lowering his voice as if to be overheard in this house was a danger. 'One day we must be open about this, but until then we will mourn in secret. As long as Sir Robert is believed to be alive, or even if his death is still a matter of uncertainty, there will be no claim on his estate and we will be safe. We can put up with cattle-rustling and theft but not a full-scale occupation of the properties if that is what the Percys decide to do. I trust they will be too occupied with their own difficulties. All eyes will be focused on the battle between Warwick and the Queen.'

I thought about this, studying my hands that I had placed flat on the table. How short a time it was since Robert had given me the gold ring as a symbol of our lasting affection. Was it a plan that could be carried out? I saw the sense of it, but how could we pretend that Robert was alive, when he was not?

'Would it not be better to admit the whole and wait for the attacks from the north?'

'I think not. If nothing else it will give us a little time,' John Dane advised gently. 'The longer we have to prepare, the more successful we will be in guarding the estates, even if it is a matter of a mere number of weeks.'

I raised my eyes to his, aghast at such a strategy.

'Do you agree with my suggestion?' John Dane prompted when I failed to reply.

I looked across at Perching, who nodded.

'Then yes. I agree because I can see no other way, although my family will swear that grief has fouled my wits. We will do as you suggest. And pray that we can keep the Poynings land intact for my son. I hope that you will stand with me as we explain the situation to my household.'

I would be the wolf to hold the ravaging huntsmen at bay.

★

The household was sworn to secrecy. I stood my little son on a chair at my side, holding him firmly upright, as if he were a symbol of hope for the future. On the table before me I had brought Robert's tabard, still ruined with the bloodstains. It would never be cleansed. On it lay his sword. My small household stood before me, silent in the awe of this event, the air still and cold on our flesh. It was as if the events of the battle had come amongst us, forcing us to accept the terrible consequences of that field at St Albans.

I looked around them, the faces that were now well-known to me. This was my household, and I would demand their compliance. I would beg for it if I had to. I spoke, my voice low and even.

'We will honour my husband, we will mourn his loss, but we will not broadcast his death beyond this house,' I announced. I knew I needed to explain, even though I despaired at having to admit to our precarious situation. 'We fear for the estates. As long as Sir Robert's death is a matter of speculation, there will be no claims made against us. When it is assuredly known that he is dead, there will be a deluge that we may not be able to withstand. If you honour your late master's name and that of his son, you will help me in this.'

A rustle of movement, a shuffle of fear, eyes slanting from one to the other.

'It would not be right that Sir Robert Poynings's estates be seized by anyone but his own direct heir,' I continued. 'He is here in our midst, Edward Poynings. It is our duty to protect him and revere the Poynings name. We will let no one, man or woman, steal what belongs to this child.'

My plea was impassioned. They knew to whom I referred. 'I know that you will support this child, in his father's name.'

'It can't be kept secret for ever, mistress.'

The one voice expressed the bewilderment of all. I had expected this. We were all aware of the problem in this strategy.

'I know that ultimately the truth must be told. But the longer we can deflect any claims on the estates, the stronger we can be. So says John Dane, who has given me much counsel, and I believe him.' I glanced across to where he stood beside the door, accepting his brief nod of agreement with a faint smile. 'No, we cannot remain in foolish ignorance for ever, but we can simply deny all knowledge. As long as you do not gossip or whisper our secrets abroad, this child will be safe, and so will you. If these estates are taken over, your positions here might well be in jeopardy. I will not be able to guarantee your security here. The new owners may well bring in their own people, whom they know they can trust.'

'Aye, my lady.' Perching spoke up in my support. 'That is the truth.'

It was agreed. I knew, I hoped, that I could rely on their total discretion.

It was Perching who raised the other thought in my head. He waited until we were alone and the household dispersed.

'You could approach your brother for help in the courts, my lady, when it comes to a legal battle.'

My reply was sharp with disappointment.

'If you knew how many times I have approached my brother on personal issues, with no response when it conflicted with his own affairs in the courts, you would not hold out any hope. I swear I am far at the bottom of his list for legal necessities. We will do this ourselves.'

I was determined.

By now, since Thomas's return, I knew that Robert's body had been taken to the Abbey at St Albans. I did nothing for a while. It smote at my conscience, but at least he was at peace in holy ground. One day I would erect a memorial to the man who had rescued me and given me my first sip of happiness, but until our son was secure in his inheritance, Robert must wait. I knew that he would understand.

John Dane set himself to seek out every item of document and binding inheritance. Nothing must be left to chance. There must be no difficulties over Robert's will. All was legal and I was without question the sole executor, but I must be sure that I could hold all in the name of my son.

★

I received a letter from my brother John. It was predictable, offering nothing but platitudes, even though it was the first time he had found the need to contact me since my marriage. I detected Margaret's hand in this sudden interest.

★

Margaret says that I should be concerned. Is it not true that Sir Robert died on the field at St Albans? Yet we are told that you act as if you know nothing about it. Even as if he were still alive and might return at any moment. Although how Margaret would know this, I have no idea.

Is this true? Are you quite well? And your little son? Is there anything I can do for you?

My advice is that you accept that Sir Robert is dead. You cannot pretend any longer.

Mistress Agnes says that she would come and give you support if you would need it, in coming to terms with the truth of Sir Robert's death.

★

The prospect of it sent a shiver through me. I replied promptly, in uncharitable vein since I was not deceived into thinking that

292

John would ride to my rescue, even if he was in London and I was in Southwark. Could he not have come to my door and offered me his legal authority? I enjoyed my rebuttal of his help after all the years he had left me without hope at Oxnead.

★

What could you possibly do for me, John? I doubt you will think of me again within the year. Do you have either the time or the inclination to devote to my affairs, however difficult they might be? You have no knowledge of the problems I face.

I am in good heart. My son thrives.

I know full well what I am doing.

Do not send Mistress Agnes to me. It would not be good for either of us.

I would be grateful if you did not discuss Robert's fate at St Albans with anyone.

★

In that moment I wished that I might have Margaret here with me in Southwark. I would talk to her as I would to no one else, but Margaret rarely came to London. I could not help but feel bereft despite my relief when my mother made no move in my direction.

But one lady, predictably, came to Southwark. Eleanor, Countess of Northumberland, rode into the courtyard on a fine mare, escorted by a groom and a servant, probably from no further than Westminster since she had seen no need for her previous equipage.

'What do I do?' I asked Perching, panic rising to grip my throat. 'What do I say to her?'

'You do what you wish to do, my lady,' he replied gravely.

What would be best? How could I be so indecisive? I could invite her in. I could keep the door locked and pretend not to be at home. Neither was satisfactory. I could send a message with Perching. All seemed to be actions of sheer cowardice. As I watched her dismount, her self-importance as impressive as her wired veils, I summoned all I had learned as Robert's wife, knowing in that instance what I would do. I had no duty towards this lady who presumed to demand admittance into my home.

'Come with me.'

I walked out, Perching a stalwart support behind me. The Countess and I faced each other.

'My lady.' I curtsied. I would not be completely lacking in good manners.

'Dame Poynings.' She inclined her head. 'I think I have business with you.'

She was clad as impeccably as she had been before in layers of velvet and fur against the cold. If she noticed anything about me, it was that I was not in mourning.

'Why would that be?' I asked.

'My uncle is dead.'

I replied with neither yea nor nay, even though it would have been foolish for me to deny it, faced with her certainty. 'You have no business with me, my lady. My son's affairs are in the hands of our legal people.'

'But are you not the executor of his will?'

'Indeed. I am named executor in Sir Robert's will.'

'I think we have much to discuss.'

'I am sure that we have not.' How confident I sounded, how comfortable in my own status as executor for the Poynings heir. Only I was aware of the thud of my heart and the dryness of my throat. 'I know your purpose here, my lady. I have nothing to say.'

'Do you not invite me in? Do we discuss legal affairs like common folk in the market square with all the world to listen and wonder at? Is that what Pastons do?'

I ignored the deliberate jibe. 'I do not invite you in.'

'Sir Robert would expect you to show me courtesy.'

'Sir Robert would not expect you to lay claim to lands that are not yours.'

For the first time she appeared disconcerted, as if she had never envisioned that I would simply refuse to talk to her, to listen once again to what she had to say.

'Is that it?'

'That is it, my lady. I have nothing more to say. I would be grateful if you would leave my home. My Steward will help you to mount if you have need of him.'

Perching stepped forward with a bow, but the implied threat was apparent.

'Very well. I will go, but you know that one day I will return, perhaps with my husband's armed men, and I will take possession of this fine house.'

Eleanor's groom helped her to remount and, without further words, she rode away.

'Well done, my lady.'

'Do you think so? I could not pretend to be friendly and hospitable. And what good would it have done?'

In a mood of blind fury that shook me by its intensity, I sent for Thomas. Now I would hear it. Now I would face all that he could tell me. I had resisted for far too long. Now my courage was high.

'Tell me what you know of Sir Robert's death.'

I had not asked until now. I had feared to know.

'What would you know, my lady?'

'How it happened. What you saw.'

But there was so little to glean from Thomas. 'It was in the attack,' he said simply. 'He fought with bravery. He was cut down. Who did it, I know not.'

'Did he suffer?'

'He died on the battlefield. It was a terrible blow that hacked at his neck and shoulder. There was no hope of staunching the blood. By the time I reached him he could no longer speak to me.'

So little knowledge to be gained, when all around must have been noise and the thunder of battle.

'Is that all?'

'It is all. War is cruel and short, my lady.'

'Thank you.' It would have to be enough. I would hold it in my heart.

★

The days crept on towards the end of March, the sharp cold, icy roads and frequent snow showers keeping people in their homes. Perhaps this helped us to survive our self-imposed isolation. We kept the estates intact. There were no claims against us. Those who might take them were too involved in their affairs in London to secure the throne. The new Duke of York might occupy the city but he had not yet taken the crown. All it seemed was yet to play for and the Earl of Northumberland might have his own loyalties uppermost in his mind. He fought for Lancaster so it would be ill news that York was in the ascendant.

Robert would have prayed for the Duke of York's success, and so did I, a loyal widow. Every morning and evening I lit a candle in his memory. But how long could we remain as if nothing had occurred? I knew that we must accept reality and face the Percy legal men on our doorstep. I hoped it would be their lawyer and not another visit from Eleanor.

Margaret wrote, with an urgency that pleased me.

★

Tell me that you are still secure.

If there is any problem over the inheritance, ensure that you have a trustworthy man to stand witness as to what is said and what is signed. It could mean all the world to you.

Clement said that John should raise troops in Norfolk and join the Duke of York but as usual John found every excuse for staying in London. I am not sorry. Your own position, alone and without protection, is not to be envied.

May God protect you and send you His blessing with mine.
M Paston

★

And my reply?

★

I will take your advice and ensure a witness. I have a Steward,
Perching, that I would trust with my life. His loyalty to young
Edward is beyond question.

I continue to pray that warfare will take the mind of the Percy
family away from us. I think it is a sin, but my son and his
inheritance mean more than the country at peace. I waited long
for this marriage and the hope of a child of my own. I will fight
to the day of my death to preserve what is his. There, Meg, I can
be quite warlike. You gave me an excellent example when I lived
under your roof. Give in to no man. Or woman.

By your sister-in-law,
Elizabeth Paston Poynings

★

When there were whispers of a conflict in the north between the
new youthful Duke of York and Queen Margaret's followers, John
Dane rode to Southwark to tell me. He was made welcome and
brought to me. I bid Perching stay, as I always did. I had taken
Margaret's warnings about a witness to heart.

'Is all well? Seeing you always puts fear in my heart.'

'Yes, my lady. I am careful in saying it, but I believe that all
is well, for you and your son.'

He carried no papers for me to sign or peruse but there was an
air of excitement about him. Not a smile, but then he rarely did.

'Do not tell me you are going to join the armies in the north.
What would I do without your support?'

'That is why I am here. I thought that you might have heard
from your family.'

'I hear little from my family. There has been a battle?'

Since Robert's death the vagaries of the Court factions meant much less to me. Robert had been the one who brought news into the household.

'There has been a battle, at Towton, a place near York. I wondered if your brothers had been involved. I hesitate to rejoice at the death of any man on a battlefield, but this will lighten your burden. At Towton, on Palm Sunday, in the midst of a snowstorm, there was a Yorkist victory of the most bloody nature.'

So who had died? It was not John or William or Clement, and my nephews would not have gone without John's permission.

'It is far away,' I said. 'My own family were not involved.'

'It is far away. But it could have long-lasting results. For you.'

'King Edward rather than King Henry.' Had not the Duke of York already been accepted as King after his victory at Mortimer's Cross, where the Lancastrians were routed? All that was needed to complete his hold on power was the sacred anointing and crowning. After such a victory at Towton, Edward of York would assuredly have every right to wear the crown in place of the hapless Henry.

'What effect will that have on me?' I asked. 'Be plain, sir.'

'It may well be of an advantage to you, my lady. Your brothers will stand well at Court, I think, with Edward of York as King. But that's not it. One of those killed on the battlefield was the Percy Earl of Northumberland.'

'Oh.'

It was a shock, even though death on the battlefield was something we were all coming to accept. Eleanor was now as much a widow as I. I tried to search for compassion, but my thoughts were racing, full circle back to our own predicament. The Percy claimant was dead.

'It may ease your fears somewhat, my lady.'

'It may indeed.'

'Perhaps the constriction on the Poynings lands will be loosened at last. The Countess of Northumberland may well pursue your manors, but she may be much concerned with keeping the Percy lands safe for her own son if the Yorkists decide to take revenge. She may decide to abandon the difficulties of her Poynings claims.'

I felt tears begin to gather in my eyes. The relief was so slight. The dangers had not gone away but we might at last be safe from incursions.

'Thank you,' I said, clutching his hands. 'Thank you. All does not seem quite so bleak.'

And I went to tell my son, even though, occupied with a little metal knight on horseback, he would have no understanding of what had occurred.

Now I would take a journey to St Albans to seek the final resting place of Sir Robert, with some measure of peace in my heart.

Chapter Sixteen

Margaret Mautby Paston

Norwich: October 1461

The Duke of Norfolk struck at us hard and fast.

In all matters of the War of Fastolf's Will, as many called it with cynical amusement, John proved to be right in his reading of the future for us. The Duke of Norfolk made his bid for Caister Castle through the courts. John put in a plea for redress. The Duke claimed that we were not the rightful owners. And yet the evidence of our ownership proved to be too strong in the terms of Fastolf's will. Caister remained ours.

Time to draw a breath before the next onslaught.

The Duke of Norfolk tried to purchase Caister but John appealed to the new King Edward who chose to smile on us, probably intent on gaining as much support as he could after the bloody Battle of Towton and the insecure start to his reign. The Duke of Norfolk withdrew. All remained a morass of uncertainty, but I found myself thinking that this was a war that we might win without much fuss. If King Edward was of a mind to be gracious then our adversaries must retreat and leave us in peace. I seemed to live my life in trepidation of another claim against us, yet for a little time it was assuaged.

Until a letter arrived, in brother Clement's neat hand. It was addressed to John, but since he was somewhere in Norwich, about some business of which he had not seen fit to inform me, I opened it. It was marked urgent, and when Clement wrote with urgency it usually proved to be the case since he, of all the Pastons brothers, had developed the facility of discovering what was afoot. I would apologise later to John but I would argue my case that without me his business would rarely thrive.

I read through the single sheet. And then again. By the time John came in all my anxieties had returned threefold.

★

News of your altercation with Sheriff Howard in the Shire Hall in Norwich has reached the King. And with it many complaints from the Duke of Norfolk, who still has his eye on your castle at Caister and will not let the matter rest. The Duke of Suffolk is also vocal in his vilification of you and that damned Fastolf will. The King says that he has sent you two summonses to appear before him, both of which you have ignored.

The King is not pleased.

★

Blessed Virgin! Without a word I handed over Clement's letter. 'Is this true?'

'Is what true? If you mean my altercation with Sheriff Howard, you know it is. He objected to my being re-elected to parliament.'

'Yes, I know all about that.'

There had been some disgraceful grappling in the Shire Hall, and two of Howard's minions had struck at John with a dagger. If he had not had on his good new doublet he would have been stabbed with more than a flesh wound to his arm. How easily we accepted these conflicts. It frightened me that it should be so, and that I should bind up John's arm without a second thought other than the blood dripping onto the tiles. My squeamishness when tending to Master Gloys when he was attacked on our doorstep in Norwich was now far distant.

'And I imagine the Duke of Norfolk will make all he can out of it, in support of his cousin,' John said, laconic enough to disturb me further. Sheriff Howard was unfortunately a close relation of the Duke of Norfolk.

'Yes, but John, Clement says that the King is full of ire.'

'I doubt it can be all bad. The King in his wisdom was ready to support me against Norfolk when he tried to purchase Caister. Why should King Edward be stirred by a squabble in the Shire Hall in Norwich?'

'He'll be stirred because you have not leapt on your horse to answer his summons. Why defy him in this manner?' What could I say to spur John into action? 'It is a perilous situation to be in, to stir the King to wrath. And before you tell me differently, I know you have ignored two previous royal summonses.'

'Yes, Meg, I have.' I saw the stubbornness building in the set of his jaw. 'I have spent every hour of every day trying to untangle the problem of Gimingham Manor, not to mention our son and heir's problems in setting his Paston nose to the grindstone in our interests.'

Elder John had been sent to join the Court of our new King. Youth joining youth. To his father's wrath he seemed to do nothing but spend money, admire the assets of ladies of the Court, and participate in jousting. When a court roll from Gimingham had surfaced, declaring that the Pastons were originally bondsmen there in that manor, it had been sent to the King by one of our meddling rivals. Elder John, instructed to get his hands on it before the King did, had failed. John was displeased, both at the imputation against this family, as well as his son's lack of application in retrieving this vital evidence.

'How do I have time to go to London?' John was now building to a full complaint. 'Now if Elder John would seek out that troublesome document ...'

I saw as his eye travelled down the page and then fell on Clement's final warning.

★

The King says that he will send another summons, and by God's mercy, if you fail to answer it, you will die. No man has the freedom to disobey a royal writ.

I advise you to get to London as fast as a horse can take you.

I suggest that you have your excuses ready. My lords of Norfolk and Suffolk complain daily to the King about you. They would like nothing better than for you to be stripped of all Fastolf's manors and for them to fall into their hands.

The King will make an example of you if he must.

John's jaw tensed further, then he dropped the letter on the floor and began to struggle out of his smart town paltock.

'Why are you taking that off?' I was already there, gripping the cloth to prevent him. 'You need to be in London. And take an escort.'

'Why must I rush now? All can wait until tomorrow.'

'Wait?' I all but screeched. 'Why did you let it come to this? To defy a newly crowned King is surely bad policy!'

'I let it come to this because there are only so many minutes in the day, as our King will already know. I need to sleep. All my life is taken up with guarding our possessions. As for my son, all that legal training has gone for nothing …'

'Nonsense! You will move heaven and earth to keep this inheritance safe for your sons, and your heir will soon come to know how to go on, when you learn to have patience with him.' I allowed him to take off the paltock. 'Come and drink a cup of ale before you set off. And eat.'

'I'll not go today.'

'We'll talk about it …'

I thought he looked weary to the bone but chose not to say it. There was no one to take this burden on his shoulders. Our sons were too young, their experience not great enough, their contacts not strong enough. I would make sure that he left before the end of this day with food in his belly and a good escort, no matter what argument he concocted against doing so.

'I will wait to hear from you,' I said as he prepared to ride off an hour later, a picture of disgruntlement, paltock back in place. 'Do not antagonise the King further.'

He managed a peck on my cheek and a rueful smile before he mounted. I had no idea when I would see him again.

★

I was forced to wait with patience. No news, I had learned, did not necessarily mean good news. There was a surfeit of Howard gossip in Norwich although the Sheriff who had arranged the attack on John was also in London where he was up to no good, adding his voice to that of his cousin the Duke of Norfolk. The Sheriff's wife, however, enjoyed making further mischief at our expense. Our paths could not fail to cross when I went with our cook to the market to oversee the purchase of fish. I did not always trust my cook's keen eye in the matter of brightness of a fishy eye or the shine on the scales.

My greeting with the Sheriff's lady was the essence of politeness.

'I hear Master Paston has gone at a gallop to London, mistress.'

I gave a brisk nod of my head, neither discourteous nor friendly. 'My husband does not gallop, mistress. It is bad for the horses. But in truth he has gone to London. I expect that most of Norwich knows by now.'

'I am surprised that he risked the dangers of the journey.'

I smiled tightly. 'Could it be more hazardous than being struck at by two of your husband's underlings? Sheriff Howard should be ashamed to employ such as servants. I would not trust them in my household.'

'My husband rules his household well.'

I left our purchases to my cook.

'Should he not also keep the peace in the town? It seems to

me that he stirred up more trouble than necessary over a petty jealousy. He almost had a murder on his hands. Could we expect justice if my husband had been killed in the Shire Hall? I doubt it.'

She snapped back, the merits of the various fish offered for sale abandoned. 'Your husband's life will not be worth a penny if he falls into the hands of the Howards. I trust he has travelled with some protection. A padded doublet will not serve if he is caught on the road. Or in the back streets of London.'

It stoked my fears for John's safety even higher. Such a brazen threat and it was impossible to warn him. But before I could think of a reply that would preserve my dignity, one of my kitchen lads pushed through the crowd to my side. His face was alight with excitement. Or perhaps it was some species of horror.

'Mistress Paston! Mistress Paston! It's the Master.'

Seeing Sheriff Howard's wife expressing more than an interest I pulled the lad away.

'Why have you been sent here? Do you have to announce our business to the whole market? What is it?'

His eyes widened under the grip of my hand on his arm.

'Mistress?'

'What about the Master?'

'He's in prison.'

Prison! That was the last thing I had expected, but perhaps I should not have been surprised given John's flouting of royal authority. At least he was not dead. Relief and foreboding warred within me.

'Are you sure? How do you know?'

He thrust a grubby letter into my hand. 'The courier told me.'

Couriers should have their tongues clipped, gossiping to all and sundry, I decided, ripping it open to discover yet another letter from Clement. Extremely brief. Even more frightening.

To tell you, sister, the King was out of all patience with my brother after he was late for the third royal summons to answer complaints made against him by the Duke of Norfolk. As a result John has been taken to the Fleet Prison. The Howards are gloating. More later.

Was my life to be forever bound by letters to, from, or about my absent husband? At least he was free from a Howard dagger, but to be thrown into prison made me sick to my stomach as I returned home as fast as I could manoeuvre through the market-goers, dragging the kitchen lad with me, although he was only the bearer of the bad news. My cook must make what he could of the fish.

Mistress Agnes had come to see what the commotion was as I entered in a hurry, dispatching the unfortunate boy back to the kitchens with a flea in his ear about speaking loudly of my affairs in public. I explained in brusque detail what had occurred.

'Do I go to him?'

Why ask Mistress Agnes? She would give me her opinion anyway, and in the end I would make up my own mind.

'What good will it do? What would you do in London?' Mistress Agnes was adamant. 'Remain here, is what I would say. There is no one else to hold our adversaries at bay. Besides, John can take care of himself. When did he ever need our help?'

Not a well-reasoned response, but expected since she had still, all these years later, not forgiven him for his stand over Justice William's will. I frowned, collecting together in my mind what I knew about the Fleet Prison. It was enough. A noisome place by all accounts, but at least the Fleet was not a desperate dungeon crowded with thieves and cut-throats, rather it was used for lesser offenders of the upper classes, especially debtors. It was the only relief I could find, and little at that.

'I still think I should go. I will do as I wish.'

'As you always do, Margaret. You have never taken advice.'

My temper flared, exacerbated by fear.

'And there speaks a woman who has done nothing but follow her own wishes throughout her whole life. When did you ever take advice? Certainly not from your son who had your best interests at heart.'

She stood, as straight-backed as she had ever been. 'I will not stay to listen to such discourtesy.'

'Then go back to Oxnead, if you so wish.' I was out of patience and not in the mood to make apologies although I accepted her argument that to travel all the way to London might not be best policy. 'Very well,' I said. 'I will stay here. There is one thing I can do.'

I wrote to Clement.

★

If you have not already done this, give money to the gaoler for food and bedding for John. I will reimburse you. A little bribery will not come amiss. Also appoint a servant to attend him, a man well-known to you who will be reliable. I believe that you will be freely admitted to speak with your brother. Please visit.

★

Our enemies were victorious in Norwich. I tried not to listen to the gleeful speculation that John might remain in the Fleet for the rest of his life, but after two weeks of no news of his whereabouts or his health my patience was at an end.

'I cannot abide not knowing. I'll go and lodge with William and his wife.' Was John in health? Was he being treated well? Would I know if he had actually died? Only if Clement wrote to me. A black shadow pursued me day after day. 'I cannot in all conscience remain here in ignorance.'

John's mother, who had not returned to Oxnead, was no more accommodating.

'If William's Beaufort bride cannot get him out of the Fleet, what can you do, other than trample up and down there, much as you are here? Go and sort out the unpaid rents at Hellesdon where I hear rebellion is being stirred up by the Duke of Suffolk. John will thank you for that when he returns.'

It never failed to astonish me how critically Mistress Agnes could keep her ear to the ground for insurrection and dissent. I too feared for the safety of Hellesdon, one of Fastolf's most vulnerable manors, yet I was on the edge of packing a coffer and taking myself to London when another letter arrived from Clement. I hardly dared open it.

★

Our friends have obtained John's release, at the same time black-ening Sheriff Howard's name. We have shown the King that he has been fed dubious accounts of the situation in Norwich. King Edward is now aware of the hostility towards John. Sheriff Howard has been committed to the Fleet, on the same day as

John is released. A new Sheriff from the royal household has been appointed to Norfolk. You should get justice in all things now. You will be relieved to know that John is in good health.

★

'Praise to the Blessed Virgin!'

Mistress Agnes merely grunted what might have been approval.

This might promise well for the future, but I could not be merry. Indeed I knew that John would be more at risk than when he was behind strong walls. The Howards had long arms and sharp knives, and might just take revenge. I lived in constant dread as I looked to see him return home, but he did not come. The balm offered by an increasing number in Norwich who expressed their love and respect for John to offset the dire predictions of the Howards did not soothe.

Come home, I instructed Master Calle to write. *There are many here who will welcome you.*

John did not come.

But when he did, in the first week of December when we were keeping Advent-tide, he was full of bright energy, with a plan in mind, as well as a fully laden sumpter horse which might promise bolts of cloth and other necessities, as well as perhaps a gift for his long-suffering wife.

'I have an idea.' His first words on dismounting.

'Good day, Master Paston,' I replied.

At least it made him aware of how long it had been since we last spoke. His imprisonment had had no effect on him at all to my eye.

'Good day, Mistress Paston. As I said, I have an idea.'

John had many ideas. I sighed. I must have looked more than sceptical.

'Of what we can do with Jonty.'

'You make him sound like a parcel.'

John saw nothing amusing in this. 'And so must be trussed and sent to where he can best represent the Paston name. He is now of an age to be of use to us. The Duke of Norfolk is dead.'

'Which is not news to us here in Norwich,' I said. 'Since the Duke of Norfolk was firmly in the ranks of the enemy, you will not expect me to wear a mourning veil.'

'No, but I thought you might see the opportunity here. What do you know of the new Duke?'

I thought about this. 'Nothing of any moment. I suppose he is built in the same mould as his father and will not wish us well. I expect that he too will want Caister. How old is he?'

'Little more than a boy. Seventeen years.'

'And, as I said, probably as grasping as his father. Since when did age make a difference? King Edward was only eighteen years when he won the Battle of Mortimer's Cross.'

'The new Duke may well be rapacious.' John was striding up and down the hall, as if all the energy pent up from his days in the Fleet was still there to be released. 'But if he forms his own household, will he not seek younger men than those his father used? Jonty is much the same age. Now if my brother William might put in a good word for him at Court …'

'The Duke of Norfolk employing a Paston? It will be a miracle enough to bring the citizens of Norwich out into the streets.'

'But not an impossible one, I think.'

Here was John, for once building bridges rather than destroying them, and it would bring Jonty into contact with the Royal Court, too. I saw the value of it and must accept that the days were coming when I must say farewell to both my elder sons. What would be the new Duke of Norfolk's gain would be my loss. I would lose an excellent clerk, but for Jonty it would pave an enterprising path to the future.

'I think it is an idea worth pursuing,' I told my husband since he was still awaiting a reply. 'Now come into the parlour and tell me all about the Fleet. Then I will tell you about affairs in Norfolk.'

He was walking beside me through the house. It felt good to have him home again. We stopped to exchange an embrace for we had been apart too long. Surely for once affairs of Paston business could wait?

But not for long. 'What about the problem of the rents from Hellesdon?' John asked between surprisingly warm kisses.

'I will tell you of that, too.'

I must make the most of the time that he would stay with me and rejoice at the plans for our sons. Both, for once, were in good heart with their father, even Elder John. Long might it last.

Norwich: May 1463

'What have you done?'

How many times had I asked him that one question? My eldest son, now Sir John Paston, stood before me, bristling with self-righteous anger, so furious that he could not speak to answer my question. The ride from London had not tempered it to any perceptible degree.

'Why are you here?' I asked, to nudge him into some response. Not that I was not pleased to see him, but my suspicions were instantly roused. They often were when my eldest son appeared with no good reason.

I risked an embrace but he stood in my arms as unresponsive as a block of wood.

'I have been ordered home from Court by my father!'

'To what purpose?'

'I know not. You must ask him. If I have failed to achieve what he wanted from me at Court, it is all his own fault. And I resent having spies set on my tail, to report back to him the detail of what I do every day of every week!'

He turned to stalk out with plenty of fire in his eyes.

'Come here and talk to me,' I said before he had quite closed the door, which would undoubtedly have been with a thud to shake the rafters.

'I will not. But I will speak with my father.'

There came the thud, the noise reverberating, followed by a distant one as he shut himself into his chamber.

Immediately I sent for John, ending my letter: *In haste, in all haste.* Did I ever not write a letter to him in haste? But this was a serious affair. There were troubled waters here beyond my soothing. I warned John to expect disobedience from his heir which he must handle with subtle care if he wished to retain a Paston voice at Court. I was unsure that John was capable of such subtlety, but a father's voice was needed.

It should have been an excellent year with great honour for my eldest son. A coming of age and a knighthood so that he became Sir John Paston. Now, to my pride, any mention of Sir John in the family was of my son, not Sir John Fastolf. I was not present at the knighting and so dependent on a sardonic letter from William.

★

The Pastons have been honoured indeed. How will we be able to live with it? Sir John, as he now is, made an excellent figure when the King knighted him. He knelt with commendable elegance to receive the flat of the sword-blade on his shoulder. You would have enjoyed it, Margaret. Has John complained yet about the cost of his garments? I hope that the touch of the sword will endow him with some dignity as well as a sense of duty. I would not hold my breath. He drank considerable toasts in fine Bordeaux after the ceremony. I trust he will recall the thick head when tempted to repeat such debauchery.

I have to say that he has already acquired the requisite Court swagger.

★

Although I never spoke of it, I wished that I could have been there to see so momentous a ceremony. Instead I would hold William's description close to my heart. Sir John Paston. It had a fine ring to it.

Such a sense of gratification, of fulfilment, that we should have had in our son and in his position at Court. Indeed we heard nothing but good things. He was well-liked with the lawyers and the courtiers. He had set himself to further the Paston claim to the Fastolf inheritance with goodwill, even persuading the influential Lord Essex to intervene with the King in the matter of the manor of Dedham which had been claimed from us by others. What more could be expected of a young man taking his first steps in the Royal Court, even if his pride and his enjoyment of wine sometimes overcame his good sense?

There had been areas of concern in his style of living, his extravagance, in his falling in love with the tournaments, but nothing that would not be expected. He was still trying his wings. Perhaps I was more tolerant of my son than John was inclined to be, but I saw nothing in him that worried a mother. Yet here he was, summoned home in what could only be disgrace and less-than-knightly fury.

John eventually put in an appearance, having ridden in from Caister, as outraged as his son, demanding a conversation with him as soon as he had set foot in our hall. What a chilly affair it started out to be when John kept our son standing, while he sat. I stood midway between them, hoping to lessen the chasm. I was not sure that a mediator would do well here, but this stoking of ire was not good for our family.

'Why did you summon me home?'

Unwisely, Sir John lost no time in expressing his anger. I should have warned him to wait and let his father have his say, but I had the experience that my son did not.

'Because you are wasting your time and our money at Court with no benefit for the family.'

'Which is an untruth. And I resent being summoned in so humiliating a fashion. I deserve more respect. It was an embarrassment for a man of my standing to be ordered home by his father!'

The colour was again high along our young knight's cheekbones.

'Respect? I heard the rumours about you as soon as I rode into Norwich this morning,' John replied, pushing aside his hat and gloves that he had piled on the table before him, his hands fisted on top. His accusations were driven home like bolts shot from a crossbow. 'Our neighbours informed me that you failed at

Court because of my niggardliness. Our neighbours informed me that it was all my fault in not providing you with enough money to fritter away. Is that what you have been saying, when drinking ale with your friends in the taverns? I see no respect between father and son. I object to being taken to task by men of little worth because you cannot keep a still tongue in your head. Have you not learned? You do not speak of Paston business in public!'

Sir John straightened his spine. 'I have told the truth.'

'Then explain it to me.'

'You kept me short of money. Without money what can be achieved at Court? You must know how impossible it is for a pauper to have any influence. You know how liberal spending works. And yet you humiliate me. I have to count every groat that you have deigned to give me.'

I could see it in his face. It had hurt him. It was so easy to forget that he was not just our son, but a knight of the realm. John frequently forgot. His expression was implacable under the barrage of accusations from his errant son.

'Pauper? I see no pauper. Tell me the sum you had to pay out for that houppelande. Is plain wool not good enough for you now that you are a knight? All I hear is that you are spending your time in jousting at the tourney with the likes of Anthony Woodville.'

'I have done that.' Sir John was unwise enough to grin with recognition of his new talent. 'I am thought to be a talented jouster. Or at least an improving one. You should be proud of me, but you have never found the time to come and watch. When has a Paston ever won acclaim at a joust? And who better to joust with than one of the foremost jousters of the realm? Do you not realise, father? When we hold tourneys at Eltham, I fight with Lord St Leger, Lord Hastings, Sir John Woodville and many more who are notable at Court.' His brow clouded. 'I joust when I have the money to pay for my mount and my armour.'

'I do not give you money to be thrown away in frivolity.'

'You do not give me money at all. How can I make a place for myself? There are other gentlemen's sons with far less reputation for legal ability and sport than I, who have ten times more to spend. It was your intent that I make a name for myself in London, but you will not give me the coin to do it.'

His spine was still as rigid with fury as when he had first arrived.

'So you went as a beggar to your Uncle Clement,' John accused, knowing full well that was exactly what he had done.

'I did when I got none from you. What's more, Uncle Clement sent me one hundred shillings. Is that not better than borrowing from a stranger? Would you rather I was in debt to a courtier who would spread the word of it to the four winds?'

'I will not have you in debt to my brother. Or to anyone else.'

I moved to stand behind John and placed my hand on his shoulder with a light pressure as I had done many times before, hoping to temper his replies.

'Then give me what I need as your heir and a knight of the realm, to uphold our name. If I am to travel with the King the length and breadth of this kingdom, I need the resources to do it.'

'Well, you will not be travelling with him now,' John growled. 'You can stay here until you learn thrift and to dedicate yourself to the work of this family. I have a list of manors that require an immediate visit from a Paston.'

'But you have always lauded the need of a patron, to put forward our name at Court. Why not me?'

'You are obviously too young. Some experience under your belt in Norfolk will stand you in good stead.'

Sir John took up another bone of contention. 'You sent William Pecock to spy on me, forsooth!'

'And you sent him home, without my permission.'

'I did not need your permission. I refuse to employ a spy as my servant, reporting back to you about everything I do.'

'Master Pecock said that you were too slow in settling down to business.'

'Master Pecock lied!' Sir John's reply rose to a shout. 'I'll not have him work for me again.'

I pressed harder on John's shoulder, to no effect.

'Yet he will remain in Paston employ, whether you like it or not.'

'There is no talking to you!'

Sir John Paston stormed out, ill-using the door for the second time.

There was no moving either of them. I had sympathy with both. I understood the humiliation of my son, but it was not wise to antagonise his father in this manner.

'I have no patience with him,' John said, as if it needed saying, his hands now spread wide and flat on the table.

'As you made clear.'

'I'll not tolerate such disobedience.'

'He is no longer a child, John.'

'He acts as irresponsibly as if he were still a boy.'

What to do? 'Give him a task, John. Give him more to do than collecting rents from Paston manors; Richard Calle can take on that task. Don't leave your son to malinger or to spread even more local gossip. It will not be good for him or for us.' I hesitated but I would say it anyway. 'You will lose him if you push him too hard.'

319

'Have I not already lost him? He is not the obedient son I would have wished for.'

'He is like a colt newly put to the bit. He needs tolerance and careful handling.'

'And you, Margaret, are too quick to give support to his misdeeds.'

'I do not support him, but I would find a remedy rather than a punishment.'

John's expression did not suggest that he was in agreement with me to any degree. 'What do you suggest, that will keep him out of the alehouses?'

'The manor of Cotton has been stolen from us by Justice Yelverton, in the name of the Duke of Suffolk. Yelverton is probably sitting there at this very moment, in smug satisfaction like a toad on a muck-heap. Send Sir John with a small force to repossess it. He will enjoy the experience, I swear.'

'What good would that do? The last time we petitioned for it, we lost. I have no faith in my son's ability to negotiate. Or to lead a band of armed retainers successfully.'

Neither, to be fair, had I. Cotton was another of Fastolf's manors, giving us many headaches since it was isolated in Suffolk, a good distance from most of our lands. 'Then give your son a larger allowance and send him back to Court. Or get him a marriage with a woman with a dowry.'

'Like you?' He surveyed me from under heavy brows. 'I would like to think that you are in agreement with me in my disapproval of our son, but you seem to uphold his disobedience.'

How sour he was. I ignored the mocking taunt, even though it hurt me.

'Why not find him a suitable bride? It is high time. Heiresses are very useful. You have done well by my acres all our lives together.'

'He does not deserve it. Who would have him? And I have not the money for an alliance with a family with an heiress on offer. He will stay here and earn his keep under your direction. And you, Margaret, will ensure that he does not slack in his efforts.'

I sighed, regretful of the hot words between us, and went to find the culprit who was predictably in the stable, grooming his horse with short angry strokes that the animal seemed to enjoy.

'Is there any moving him?' he demanded as soon as I set foot in the stall beside him. 'If you can't, no one can.'

'Not yet. I will uphold your cause but try not to anger him further.'

'I'll not say a word to him. I have no wish to hear about the value of Jonty settled in the household of the Duke of Norfolk. He can do no wrong. I, it seems, can do no right. I cannot even afford to purchase an animal to carry me in a tournament.'

I felt like soothing him, as he was soothing the horse, a grey raw-boned animal that even to my inexperienced eye was not the mount of a tourney knight.

'Are you hungry?' I asked. Food in my experience often helped to settle a raging temper.

'No.'

My eyes focused on his left hand splayed against the horse's flank as he brushed with his right. I stretched out my own to touch it.

'What is that?'

There was a deep and ugly scar that ran from the base of his thumb to his wrist, still red and not quite healed.

'A tourney wound. It was bad but is almost healed now.' It was said with such ridiculous pride that I could have wept for him.

'You were fortunate it was not worse.' The dangers of life at Court struck me but I must let him have his way.

'I was. It was a good fight and I held my own.' His anger was cooling. 'Did you mention food? It will be good when my father goes back to London.'

I thought he might be right. We walked together towards the kitchen, in some level of restored harmony, where my cook was prepared to spoil the heir with some favourite dish. I thought that my reconciliation with an angry husband might take considerably longer.

★

It was an uneasy time. John returned to London, our parting devoid of any noticeable affection; Sir John approached local Paston affairs with little devotion; I took up residence in Caister Castle. Until, after six months of being aware of every hoofbeat on the road, expecting an invading force from the new youthful Duke of Norfolk at any moment, in spite of Jonty being firmly established in his household, my daughter Margery found me with the Caister accounts spread before me. I barely looked up.

'Tell Sir John that I want him to ride over to Drayton with a message that—'

'I can't.'

Now I looked up, caught by her tone. She stood before me with a mix of shock and admiration writ large on her face. Her composure was adult, her grey eyes steady, everything about her neat as a nun's stitching, but her hands were tight linked in the folds of her skirt as if she were still a little girl.

'Why not?'

'He's gone.'

I stood, the pen dropping from my hand, scattering blots of ink on the page.

'Where has he gone?'

'I don't know. He has packed his belongings and left. He did not take his armour or his jousting horse. He couldn't, of course. It's lame.'

'Ha! London, I expect.' I was suddenly suspicious. 'Did you know he would do this? Did he say goodbye to you?'

'No, Master Calle has just told me.' She flushed brightly. I wondered why when her eyes fell before mine. 'He saw my brother ride off, but he was already on the road and no words were exchanged. He has not returned. Master Calle thinks that he has gone for good.'

Master Calle had read the signs perfectly, and I knew for certain by the following day when a letter arrived from Sir John, written from King's Lynn. My son had fled his home to join King Edward's Court travelling north into Yorkshire, leaving me to inform John of his son's absconding. Reluctantly, I dictated my letter to Master Calle.

Our son has returned to King Edward's side.

'Try to make it sound better than it is,' I said. Master Calle scribbled an extra phrase or two.

The outcome was not a happy one, with letters flying in three directions. John blamed me, accusing me of encouraging our son to go, while I was of a mind to blame my son for creating a dissention between me and my husband. As for John, why could he not find some spirit of compromise? All I could do was dispatch a letter, suggesting that Sir John write to his father with as much humility as he could garner, beseeching his forgiveness.

Would Sir John not be valuable to the King who was putting down the northern rebellion? That was the best argument I could advise. And if he could find the time he might also write to Mistress Agnes who missed him and wished to know how he fared. And write to me without his father discovering. I was in enough bad grace as it was.

And what should I do with the grey horse he had left with us? It was lame. I sent it to the farrier who said that it would never be any good for ploughing or carting, and it was certainly not fit to ride. Who was to pay for it, eating us out of house and home, when it was of no value to us? Should I sell it? What had hurt me most was that Sir John had left without telling me, giving me no chance to say farewell with strong words of advice. He had not thought that it would matter. The years were passing, he was a man grown, but indeed it mattered to me.

I hid Sir John's armour from his father. What he did not see could not stir him to wrath. Neither father nor son was aware that my loss of both of them, obdurate husband and arrogant son, made me sleepless with frustration when I retired to my bed. Neither would wish to know. And what use was my fretting? I sat up, lit a candle and set myself to make a list of recalcitrant rent-payers at Hellesdon.

Chapter Seventeen

Margaret Mautby Paston

Hellesdon: September 1464

Drayton. Cotton. Hellesdon.

Three Fastolf manors. Now three Paston manors. Until they were taken from us.

I swore that those names would be engraved on my heart. Or in the space not taken up by Gresham. They were to cause me just as much heartache.

Who was to blame for our troubles? The co-executors of the will, of course, led by Judge Yelverton who was intent on proving its invalidity. If he could prove it, then John would revert to being only one of the executors, if not altogether cast out as a cheat and a fraud. Yelverton brought forth a case that the will was fraudulent: John had no right to Caister, or the rest of the Fastolf lands in Norfolk and Suffolk.

It was a matter that troubled me constantly. Was that will truly an honest representation of what Sir John Fastolf had decided in those days before his death? Only John had been present when those final words had been uttered by the dying man. Only John had gained from it. And what benefits it had given to us.

I knew that questions were being asked. Who were the witnesses? How had the document been sealed? Were there copies made of it? John had an answer to every accusation but that would never satisfy Yelverton. Even Howes and Worcester, once firm friends of ours, were becoming lukewarm in their allegiance. Worcester's wife avoided me when our paths might cross in Norwich.

On this premise, that Fastolf's will was not legal, indeed a true malpractice, all the attacks began. By autumn we were reaching a crisis enough to demand a family council held in London, because Judge Yelverton was not our only enemy. Far more disturbing was John de la Pole, Duke of Suffolk, the powerful son of the man who had died so gruesomely on a Kent beach, now claiming that the Fastolf lands were rightfully his, long before Fastolf's death.

Was this true? Did John know of this?

John was adamant: he claimed that the estates were legitimately purchased by Fastolf, when he first had the money from his campaigning days, but there had been plenty of bad blood over these manors. Now Suffolk wanted them back. Why would he not reclaim Drayton and Hellesdon, when they were so advantageously positioned on the opposite side of the river facing the Duke's great mansion of Costessey?

So we began attack and counter-attack. Writs and distraints. Replevins to order the return of goods wrongfully seized. Horses, sheep and cattle driven off on both sides. I made no apology when I, in a fit of temper, confiscated the draught horses of a troublesome tenant. Our tenants themselves were bullied with threats that they would be thrown off their land if they duly paid their rents to us. Drayton was occupied by the Duke of Suffolk's minions, suffering the same fate as Cotton. Personal threats were issued, servants arrested. Squabbles with sheriffs and judges became commonplace. Richard Calle was imprisoned, threatened with trial in London. How would I manage without him?

As for John, any patience he might ever have laid claim to flew out of the window. He accused Richard Calle of conspiring with his foes. He neglected the few friends that he had. He wrote a stream of letters to the Lord Chancellor in less than diplomatic terms. Fortunately, reading them first, brother Clement refused to deliver them. Meanwhile, I was left to hold fast to our inheritance, the burden of it increasing daily. Some mornings when I rose to face the next tribulation, I felt that it was too weary a life to withstand, and told John as much, not that it had any effect. In all the years of our marriage, these were the most difficult, when I felt a distance growing between us, and not just in the miles between Norwich and London.

Yet I would not be intimidated. I took up residence at Hellesdon which seemed to be the most vulnerable of our manors, sending Sir John, now back in the familial fold, having accepted my advice and made a temporary peace with his father, to Caister; Jonty I sent off to the Duchess of Norfolk in a desperate bid to ask for aid, and we secured Richard Calle's freedom. In all we did, the tiny achievements, the clouds grew blacker. I was inundated with fear.

★

'Good news or bad?'

Should I have been more welcoming? I did not feel welcoming, and I was used to it being bad. Except that John had found the time to come home. He smiled.

'Good.'

'Praise God. Come and tell us all some good news. We are short of it.'

Orders had arrived in Norwich that all members of the nobility and gentry should arm and report for military duty. King Edward was engaged in suppressing dangerous insurrection in the north, stirred up, it was said, by the Earl of Warwick, once the strongest supporter of King Edward, who now had royal ambitions of his own. Whether Sir John should present himself for military service had reopened the wounds between father and son. The brief compromise between the two was at an end. When the King countermanded the orders to arm, all came home again, but not Sir John. His father forbade him to cross the threshold of the parental home, although neither was willing to tell me what had occurred between them this time. My suggestions to John that our new knight was suitably chastened and had become a worthy son went no way towards healing the breach. Thus we continued to be a household at war within itself.

'Well?' I asked.

'Mostly good,' he amended.

'Ah …! You might ask how I am faring. And your children, particularly your first-born.'

'And I will. But this is important.'

I would hear nothing until he had told me what had brought him back to Norfolk.

'We have done it at last. The foundation of the College of Priests at Caister, as Sir John Fastolf had wished. I have obtained a licence for it to be established.'

His voice was vibrant with this achievement. It had been a worry on his mind all these years. Our detractors – Yelverton and Worcester – had planned to wrest Caister from him, sell it and pocket the money, spending as little as they could – a mere hundred marks – on founding the college elsewhere. Even Thomas Howes, John's erstwhile ally, had gone over to the side of the enemy, while John had held tightly to Sir John Fastolf's wishes and to Caister.

If the college had not been founded at Caister, Fastolf had decreed that the whole castle should be torn down, every stone of it, to pay for a college elsewhere. John could not allow that to happen.

'What did it cost you?'

I knew that it would be heavy on the Paston purse.

'Three hundred marks, into the King's purse, but it is done.'

It was a momentous victory and should give John much satisfaction, although we both knew that this would not be the end of it. I drew him into the hall where the light could fall on him. What I saw worried me, his face almost gaunt, the lines heavily gouged, his skin pale beneath his summer bronze. Too many late nights, too many arguments, too many journeys to follow the King and gain his goodwill. Too little success to find us a patron to support our local interests. The will was questioned, John's integrity was questioned. He had dismounted from his horse as if he had ten years added to his age.

'What is it?' he asked, seeing my survey of his face and stance.

'You look weary to the bone.' For once I actually spoke the words.

'I *am* weary to the bone, but we will come through this. I have had good advice from a physician when in London.'

Which worried me even more. Why had he found a need to consult a physician? I was being kept further and further away from John's life. I did not like it. Nor did I like London physicians.

'Don't trust them. If you want physic, come to me. Your father did no good with medicaments from the London leeches and nor did my uncle.'

'Have done! I am well enough, Meg. I've come here for a little peace.'

He would resent more intrusion into his health so I asked: 'So that is the good news, about the college. And the bad?'

His sigh was deep as he bared his teeth in a grimace.

'I have played into their hands. My failure to attend the county court in Ipswich has turned to bite me. I was too busy following the King as far as Marlborough and such towns to the west. I swear I never stayed more than two nights in one place. King Edward is young enough to have all the energy in the world. I do not. My arse has no wish to make contact with a saddle again for at least a se'enight. Boils!' he added with a grimace.

I remembered his ill health when we were first wed, my fears that the fever that assailed him would prove fatal. I would dose him whether he wished it or not. But what was it that had brought him home at this juncture? Clearly something had.

'How can your absence from one county court be a danger?' I asked.

A slide of an eye. John could not look at me.

'John ...'

'I missed more than one session,' he admitted.

'How many?'

'I missed four sessions.'

'Four? Before the Blessed Virgin, John! Why did you not tell me? I would have got someone to represent us. What is Sir John doing in London? Could he not do it? Or either of your brothers. They could have been there. William would like nothing better than to argue the case with all his Court gloss and his Beaufort connections.'

John shrugged this aside. 'The Beauforts are not in favour and never will be with a Yorkist King. What would you have me do? It's my case to argue.' He grinned, suddenly unrepentant, all his youthful vigour returned. In that moment he looked remarkably like his recalcitrant son and heir. 'And they were four successive sessions.'

'Oh, John!'

'Well, I'll have to pay for it, even though I did get the college well established. I thought nothing would come of my absences other than a frown from the Justice but those who disparage my good name are out for my blood as usual. They've got a writ up against me and have declared me outlaw.'

'Outlaw!'

I had to take a breath. This was worse than I could have imagined.

'I am threatened with seizure of our goods,' he added, but did not seem repentant.

I looked round the hall where we stood at Hellesdon. At the carved coffers, a fine oak box chair, the tapestries that I had brought with me when I set up home here, including the prized birds and flowers from the Fastolf inheritance. I would not envisage the much-loved possessions in my chamber being picked over by those who came to confiscate them in the name of justice. It was like Gresham all over again. All I could do was pray that John would achieve a stay of confiscation. I had better pray immediately. I might not have a prie-dieu to pray at by next week.

Within the week of coming and going between local personages, and our property remaining safely behind our locked doors, John heaved himself into the saddle and headed back to London, accompanied by my assorted packages of potions to assure his good health.

'My case is transferred to the King's Bench,' he reminded me when I clung to his hand before he rode off. 'I swear I shall get more justice there than in Ipswich.'

'And my furniture and tapestries?'

'Safe for the moment.'

My bed might be safe from importunate hands, but John was not. By the first week of November I received word that my husband, with a writ against him from his adversaries, had once again been incarcerated in the Fleet.

In a moment of sheer weakness and frustration, I wept for my inability to change our fate. I rarely shed tears but on that day in the gloom of the buttery where no one would see, I wept. Until I was disturbed by Margery who was dragging a reluctant young Willem by the hand. If she noticed my emotions she said nothing, but Margery was always the quietest of all my children. Willem, five years old, was as watery-eyed as I but for quite different reasons.

'And what is wrong with you?' I asked, wiping away his tears and mine. When I gathered him into my arms, he burrowed his face against my waist and sniffed.

'Toothache!' Margery announced.

Here was a son whose problems I could solve.

'Come with me!'

By the time we had reached the stillroom, we had been joined by daughter Anne who had escaped her lessons to be part of the domestic drama. Willem struggled but we dosed him on a decoction of lavender in a little wine. Anne wrapped marjoram leaves in a piece of fine linen and Margery forced it between Willem's clenched teeth to fix it beside the offending tooth.

'Sit quietly for a time. The pain will soon pass,' I said.

Margery sat down on a stool and pulled him onto her knee. I patted his head and dropped a kiss on his brow, while I ordered Anne to come and stand before me. She looked pale and listless, which was not habitual for my youngest daughter. I would dose her too. I found a spoon and a phial of a tincture of common vervain.

'I do not have the toothache,' she protested.

'No, but you may have worms. Now drink.'

Which she did.

I surveyed them with a critical eye as Anne grimaced and Margery smiled encouragingly at her brother. My daughters were most efficient and compliant, both pretty girls with the gloss of youth. Time and enough that we were discovering husbands for them. Anne was ten and Margery sixteen. Once again it struck me that Margery was a woman full-grown and I would not have her neglected as Elizabeth had been until all her youth was dulled like an old tapestry. Even in the Fleet John would have some influence. I wrote:

*

To my most honourable husband,
  Margery is of an age to have a husband.
  Mistress Agnes has heard tell of a young man of eighteen years who is worth one hundred marks a year. He is the son of Sir John

333

Cley, chamberlain of the Duchess of York. I am sure that you would consider this an excellent match. Perhaps you could discover what can be done about this.

Young Willem has been crotchety with the toothache but is now much better.

I entreat Almighty God to protect you.

By your M PASTON

★

I sent more packages and physic to guard against fevers and bowel disorders, coughs and the flux, ulcers and vomiting. And since it was in my mind, to soothe a toothache. I told both William and Clement to re-employ the servant Master Spring to look after John. His health remained a concern. There was nothing I could do to remedy it.

★

'Have you read this, mistress?'

It was a letter from John. Richard Calle held it out for me. I presumed that it was estate business, since it had been given to him, but my bailiff, although he might be calm and solemn as he ever was, handled it as if it were poisonous, and I eyed the letter with some suspicion.

'No. Do I need to? Can you not deal with it?'

My temper was short. I was busy. After a sojourn of a matter of weeks in the Fleet, his case being upheld by the King's Bench, thus prompting his release, John had stayed in London, leaving the imminent business of the estates in my hands with the help of Richard Calle. John's latest demand had been that I send him one hundred pounds in gold and twenty in silver, as if I could magic them out of thin air. I really did not want to be in receipt of more such demands. Isolation and inability to take action always had a detrimental effect on John's temper which I knew would be as short as mine. Perhaps I should have sent dried leaves of the Greater Periwinkle for him to chew. It was efficacious for a surfeit of high spirit, and acted against nightmares. Would it not have calmed John in his incarceration?

Richard Calle was persistent.

'I think that you must, mistress.'

I took it and held it up to the light. I was prepared to let my eye run down a list of suggestions about grain and malt which my bailiff could quite well deal with on his own. What I saw made me read more slowly.

This was a letter from an angry man. This was a diatribe addressed to both me and Richard Calle. The House of Paston, it seemed, was not well run and needed better supervision. A long letter, it was full to the brim with disgruntlement. By the time that I was halfway through I was tempted to consign the whole to the kitchen fire. Much of this complaint, I noticed, was directed at me. I looked up, holding my bailiff's stare. It was impossible for me to excuse the venom that leached from the words to poison the air around us.

'Now what stirred this up?' I asked.

'I know not, mistress.'

'Do you suppose that he is unwell?'

'Whatever it is, we are clearly to blame for everything, mistress. What do we do?'

'I need to read through this again.'

Anger had begun to simmer, fast becoming a boiling pot. I had spent my life upholding John's authority, in supervising the running of the manors, in collecting revenues and placating tenants, and all I received was a diatribe on how inefficient I was. Before I could decide what to do, my husband was there on our doorstep.

'Have you read my letter?'

At least he waited until he had stepped inside before he began the complaint.

'I have. Master Calle and I have both read it.'

Sir John fortunately was not present or the emotions within our four walls would have been of vast proportions. Never had I seen my husband so self-righteous, so stiffly overbearing. And so wrong.

'Do you agree that my concerns have merit?'

'No, I do not.'

'Perhaps you did not read them carefully enough.'

I prayed for patience, unsuccessfully.

'Do you realise how pompous you sound? More like Justice Yelverton than the John Paston I know. I do not accept what you say. How can you know what is done in your name when you are not here to witness it?'

'There are too many excuses for your mismanagement. Do I now have to listen to more?' John was prepared to repeat every point he had made in the misbegotten letter. 'Nothing is done well. All is at fault, from the provisioning of our houses, the collecting of revenue, keeping the servants at work, selling and transporting Paston malt. Why is everyone always too busy to do a job well? You are in command here, Margaret. I do not wish to come home and discover more excuses.'

'Then perhaps you should have stayed in London. We have managed quite well without you. I will not listen to such calumny.'

Which stunned John into temporary silence.

The servants had become invisible, although I would swear that their ears were stretched wide. I wondered again what had stirred John to such poison. Was it his brief stay in the Fleet? If so, then I should have been compassionate, but I would not accept what was being said. What evidence could he possibly have that I was at fault?

I pulled him into the parlour.

'We will not scrub our soiled linen in public, John.' I shut the door gently behind him with all the control I could muster. 'I will make no excuses. I will deny the validity of your accusations. Show me one servant in this house that is lazy and discourteous.' I was remarkably calm. 'I will give you the documents dealing with the selling and transporting of malt. There is no problem. I have sent you the gold and silver when you demanded it. What more can I do? I swear that I have never been remiss in upholding your Paston name the length and breadth of Norfolk. Moreover the appointment of Richard Calle was your doing. He is an excellent bailiff. How can you accuse him of shoddy work on your behalf?'

Which he ignored, turning into a separate rant.

'Hay is being wasted, reeds and rushes not cut, the cutting of firewood inefficient ...'

'And who tells you all of this?'

'My source is accurate.'

'Who?'

'I demand that these issues be attended to immediately. I had expected better of you, Margaret. Do you deny it?'

'I do.'

'I have come to see for myself.'

I stood in front of him, a direct challenge.

'Ah! But will you stay beyond a se'enight to see the whole? Do you remain here to oversee these affairs that are being so neglected? Obviously Master Calle and I are incapable of carrying out your orders to your liking. Then you must do it yourself.'

'Master Calle will ride to London with money to pay my debts immediately. I will remain here.'

I stifled a sigh. I had hoped that John would have returned to London, taking his bad temper with him. He had not finished.

'As for your son …'

'Which one?'

'Do you have to ask? I have forbidden him to come home until he learns a more suitable demeanour. Presumptuous and indiscreet behaviour! A bad example to the household!' John strode up and down, tossing his accusations into the air. 'He tells everyone that he is frustrated at living at home, so now he will not. He is banned. He is an idle, cup-shotten, good-for-nothing, so I am told. He takes rather than gives, expecting me to pay for his extravagant lifestyle. All he does is eat and drink and sleep and ride out on his fine horse to make an impression on the local gentry. He will be granted no favour until he changes his ways. Hear me, Margaret. My son is banned from this house unless he is prepared to do some work. If I ever allow him to return.' He glared at me. 'And I don't want you welcoming him back here as soon as my back is turned.'

'Do you not think, John, that sometimes it would be good for our family if you could learn the art of making concessions?'

'I do not recall that you were willing to make concessions when Gresham was the issue, Margaret!'

'But this is our son, not a castle and a quantity of land.'

'I see no difference.'

There were no grounds for reconciliation here. Until John was in a mood to listen and compromise, I must retreat into wifely displeasure.

'Thank you for your instructions, John. I assure you that I will take them to heart and give them consideration. Have you anything to say that might please me?' I asked with no attempt to hide the sardonic tone.

'I doubt it. One more thing: guard your gates night and day from thieves that are out and about in large companies.'

Which convinced me that in that moment he was more concerned for his property and possessions than for me.

I had warned him about losing Sir John. I thought he was losing me, too. I resented being chastised for events beyond my control, or that did not even exist except in John's overactive mind. As for the sale of malt and the cutting of reeds and rushes, such matters had been dealt with by Richard Calle as carefully as they had ever been.

All I could do was make a plea for Sir John, but not yet, and not that I had any hopes that my irate husband would listen. I would continue to employ Sir John, although I might not tell John what I was doing. I needed all the help I could get to protect Hellesdon from the Duke of Suffolk and a company of more than three hundred armed men who were intent on taking possession. My eldest son might even learn the art of negotiation. If he succeeded he might earn his father's approbation.

I was not hopeful.

Temper continued to rumble between us. John and I spent a cool evening over supper when neither of us displayed an appetite, the divide between us continuing into the marital bed. The space was so wide that even if I had stretched out my hand, which I did not, I would not have been able to touch his shoulder. And he slept with his back to me. There would be no chance of a late child in our lives through this sad reuniting. I was not sorry when, delivering another list of orders to me, John decided that his time was better spent elsewhere than our home. My wifely kiss on his cheek was decidedly without warmth. As was his in return.

I did not even stay to watch him depart, my excuse being in my own mind that the rain was too heavy to linger, but then I wished that I had. It seemed a sorry comment on our marriage that I should send my husband off without God's blessing on him. In all the years of our married life, never had we been so strongly at odds. Nor was this rift between us of my making. I regretted that it was very much in the lap of my eldest son who had stirred up John's wrath. My heart was destined to be broken one way or another. Even worse, neither my husband nor my son would even think that I had a heart soft enough to break.

I remembered that once, many years before, when John and I had been at odds, I had written to him to express my contrition. I was now in no mood to be contrite. I had been unjustly accused by the one man whose opinion I valued most.

Chapter Eighteen

Anne Haute

Westminster: 26th day of May 1465

'Rejoice in the company of our newly crowned Queen Elizabeth.'

An announcement with trumpets and shawms. The Queen, flanked by bishops and the most powerful men of the realm, cleansed her now-royal fingers in a golden basin and wiped them on a fair cloth.

The banquet began.

Seated on a throne covered with cloth of gold, the Queen surveyed the ranks of her subjects in imperious fashion, while I took note of the splendour of the lady herself, with much envy. The Queen drew all my attention. Was she not wearing a royal-purple mantle with its ermine edge catching the light of hundreds of candles, the smudge of holy oil still gleaming on her brow? Her fair hair lay in a silken fall over her shoulders, covered by a translucent veil, as if she were the Holy Virgin herself. All those who served her at her meal had been ordered to show her utmost reverence. They knelt, even the most prestigious dukes and earls in the land, even the King's brother, some for the entire duration of the feast of three courses. My knees ached in sympathy with them as dish after endless dish of meats suffused with rich sauces was brought with a flourish from the kitchens to the blast of trumpets. The air was heavy with the scents of spices and extravagant cooking, even if the food was cold on its gold platters before it reached the Queen's table.

What of me, Anne Haute?

Now that I was full grown and more, at twenty-one years, I was generally acknowledged within my family, although with rancour from my sisters, as the most comely and talented of the five Haute daughters. I was also still unwed, despite being ambitious to wed a man of status. So far I had been disappointed, but on this day, the twenty-sixth day of May in the year 1465, any disappointments were set aside. I could never have imagined that I would be invited to attend the ceremony for the coronation of the Queen of England in the Palace of Westminster. Yet here I stood in the vastness of Westminster Hall, beneath the angels carved into the roof with their spread wings, in a little knot of Haute family to witness the event.

'Who would have ever believed it?' Meg, my youngest sister, whispered.

'I would not,' I replied. 'How could she be Queen of England? A widow. And a Lancastrian.'

Our King Edward, the fourth of that name, was the head of the House of York and, as many opined, had married the enemy.

'Did she use witchcraft?' Meg persisted.

There were tales abounding that she had.

'More like female allure in his direction and a glance from her acquisitive eyes,' I said. Our new Queen possessed a most direct stare beneath perfectly arched brows which doubtless owed everything to artifice. Nothing could be so perfect without. Mine would never arch so well even if I was blessed with her angelic fairness.

'But why would he marry her?'

I could think of no reply to this. It seemed the wrong time and place to discuss the more appropriate possibility of the Queen becoming the mistress of the King rather than his wife.

We curtsied and we bowed; we watched the Queen as she ate delicately, sparingly at that. We marvelled at her golden beauty, the artistically painted face. We assessed the value of the glint of gems at throat and finger. Was that not the purpose for our presence here? We were to admire and offer our unquestioning loyalty. We also shuffled and grimaced as the banquet became more and more prolonged with no seating arrangements for us, while accepting that this was the greatest possible honour for Elizabeth Woodville.

Now Queen Elizabeth.

Whereas I was merely Mistress Anne Haute, my father dead for two years and my mother also. Why would I and the rest of the Hautes be invited to so prestigious an occasion? Yet here I stood to witness the banquet after the crowning, considering what advantages it would bring for me. Would not doors be unlocked for me if I could but seize the key, as this new royal consort of England had done?

Feasting at an end, musicians played lustily, making conversation difficult, until a lute-player was summoned to kneel at the Queen's feet. The crowd hushed. The song-maker began with a ripple of notes from the lute.

★

White as the lily, more crimson than the rose,
Dazzling as a ruby from the East,
At your beauty past compare I always gaze ...

★

Such love, such earthly worship, such extravagance in its offering. Covetousness grew large within me, for I had no experience of such emotion, and greatly wished that I had. The Queen's subtly tinted face grew warm with colour as she cast down her eyes. Was this an offering from the King himself who had fallen in love with Elizabeth Woodville, if rumour spoke true, in a forest near her home at Grafton? King Edward was not present at this ceremony. This was his new wife's day.

★

With such delight, my heart's watch is close
To keep my service true to love's behest ...

★

The troubadour fell silent, presented with a gift of a gold chain cast over his head to lie gleamingly on his chest; the crowds of the high-born broke into gatherings for talk and comment and the reuniting of families. When my eldest brother, Sir William Haute, collected us together to bow once more and make our departure, I hesitated for just a moment and looked again across the superbly clad multitude to where Elizabeth Woodville was standing.

I was summoned, by a lifted finger from the Queen herself.

I approached, spreading my skirts into a deep curtsey, head bent. I had not expected to be so noticed.

'You are welcome here, Cousin Anne.'

'I am deeply privileged, my lady.'

I rose so that we were almost of a height since the Queen had descended from the dais to stand in the midst of her subjects. At close quarters I saw that there was a new glamour about her, even an aura of power, quite separate from the crown that rested on her temples, the holy oil on her brow.

'Once you would have named me Cousin Elizabeth,' she said. 'Once, when you were a little girl, you would have called me Bess and chided me for ignoring you for a whole day when we were in each other's company.'

'Once you were not Queen of England with a crown and sacred anointing, my lady.'

'How formal we are.' She took my hand in hers in acknowledgement of past intimacies.

'We must be so, my lady. Our circumstances have changed mightily.'

My family had received a stern lecture from Sir William on the suitability of any words exchanged with the Queen. The familiarities of the past must be forgotten.

She smiled at me, a friendly warmth in the curve of her lips and the shine in her eyes, and I recalled the cousin I knew well beneath the sumptuous regalia. I returned the smile. All nervousness I might have laid claim to, all my brother's dictates, had fled.

I was first cousin to the Queen of England.

It was my mother's birth that had brought me this connection and this invitation. She was Joan Woodville, daughter of

Richard Woodville of Grafton. Her brother was another Richard Woodville, now father of this newly crowned queen. Thus Elizabeth Woodville and I were cousins of the first degree. Yet although we were cousins, I knew that I must never presume on the relationship. My brother, Sir William, had made himself more than clear.

'We will accept any patronage that comes our way from the Queen. We will not beg for it.'

I thought that I might. The troubadour's words echoed in my mind.

★

White as the lily, more crimson than the rose,
Dazzling as a ruby from the East,

★

I had need of a husband who would pay me such fulsome compliments.

'I will invite you to my Court,' the Queen said. 'You may join my ladies-in-waiting. It will be an honour for the Haute family.'

She did not ask if I would wish to accept. Of course I would.

'I am gratified, my lady. It would please me to serve you. When will I come to you?'

I hoped that my brother was not listening. Or perhaps if the invitation was offered he too would see it as an excellent opportunity for me and for the Haute family.

'I will send for you,' the Queen assured me.

She turned to go, to give her attention to more worthy

courtiers, but I stopped her with a tentative hand on her sleeve. How daring I was. Oh, yes, I would beg for it; without it, I saw little hope.

'I would ask one indulgence of you, my lady.'

She smiled back over her shoulder. 'And what would that be, little cousin?'

I gestured towards the Woodville family who stood together, preening at what had been achieved in their name. Like me, Cousin Elizabeth was not without brothers and sisters.

'When you arrange marriages for your sisters, I beg you, do not forget your cousin Anne.'

I thought that she would agree. Instead a furrow was dug momentarily across her brow.

'Are there no plans made for you?'

'No, my lady.'

'Of course, you have four sisters. And your father is dead.'

'Indeed, my lady.'

'And your brother, Sir William?'

'He will do what he can.'

I sensed her reluctance as I prayed hard that she would use her queenly patronage to find me a husband.

'I will try, cousin. But my own sisters must take precedence. I have ambitions for them. I intend to see them all wed to the highest advantage.' I sensed a growing impatience now. 'I will try to remember your situation.'

My heart lurched, then sank to a new level of disappointment. It sank even further when she continued. 'When you come to join my ladies I think you will have to make your own choice of husband. You are a woman of wit and some small beauty.'

Some small beauty … Was I not as handsome as she? My

hair might lack the lustre of hers, my face was not as perfectly unblemished, my stature not as imposing, but I resented the slight. Cousin Elizabeth had become proud in her new status.

'Whom would you suggest?' I risked. 'You were brave enough to entice the King.'

Entrap, many would say. My aunt-by-marriage, Jacquetta, it was said, had lured the King to meet up with her daughter in the woods near their home at Grafton, and once there she had put a binding on him so that he must offer Elizabeth marriage. Whether it be true or not, I had no clear idea, but Cousin Elizabeth had wed far beyond anyone's expectations.

But, in her favour, Cousin Elizabeth had proved her fertility with her first husband, Sir John Grey, providing him with two sons to carry on the Grey name. Sir John Grey had died on the field of the second battle of St Albans, fighting for the Lancastrian side. Elizabeth's Lancastrian connections might be disparaged, as was her lack of virginity when taking her place in the royal bed, but her ability to bear sons was a valuable commodity when a King needed an heir.

I had only one advantage in entrapping a husband. I was of course a virgin.

Elizabeth frowned again, with some displeasure, as if she resented my suggestion that she had inveigled a King into marriage against his will, although she must have been as aware of the rumours as I. I expected her to walk on without reply. Instead she deigned to answer, albeit with a chill in her voice.

'Who would be a suitable husband for Mistress Anne Haute? Any young courtier with ambition, an income, and an eye to power. I will give you my blessing when you find such a man. Perhaps I will even give you a bridal gift.'

I promptly seized the opportunity to expand on my desires.

'I would like a man with a title.'

'Tell me the name of a woman who would not.'

'A man of good stature and fair features.'

Which made her laugh, the chill gone.

'You do not require much, cousin.' She surveyed the crowds that wove and changed the patterns of the Court. 'There is such a one.'

She picked out a gentleman, at random I thought, with a lift of her chin. A tall man with dark hair and arresting features, although I would not call him handsome. His nose was too long and his chin too determined to be described as comely, but he had a pleasing air of confidence about him and he had taken care with his festive clothing.

'Who is he?'

'I know not. How would I know all who have come here today, although I have seen him frequently in the company of my husband. He is one of the King's courtiers come to pay homage. He is handsome enough and young enough, and he has good taste in his clothing. He is not pressed down in poverty. Whether he has a title, I know not.'

'But is he wed?' I asked.

He stood with a man who, given the facial similarities, might be his brother. There was no woman accompanying him.

'It is for you to discover.' The Queen surveyed me, suddenly serious. 'Take care, Cousin Anne. My elevation to wife of the King will make you much sought after. You may not have a dower worth a moth in a flame, but your connection with the Court as my cousin will make you invaluable. Take care that a new husband values you for your own sake, and not merely for the doors you will open for him.'

I curtsied my thanks, thinking that doors worked two ways. I would indeed take care, yet a door that would benefit my husband would also bestow a new life on me.

I wondered if the unknown courtier would be acceptable to my brother William.

Would he be acceptable to me?

★

I would discover the name of the man pointed out to me. Not that anything would come of it, but with female curiosity I would like to know. The white cloth that had covered the table was being folded with careful reverence by the Queen's almoner and chaplain as Queen Elizabeth was escorted ceremonially from the Hall, the two sceptres of St Edward and of England carried before her. Avoiding my brother, I made my way towards another Woodville, Elizabeth's eldest brother, having to push through the crowd to his side for he was much sought after. I knew his reputation. An erudite man, a reader of books, but more important to me was the fact that he was an expert jouster as well as a lover of fine clothing. Any woman would be pleased to be seen at the side of the flamboyant Sir Anthony Woodville, now Lord Scales since his marriage to the Scales heiress. He was a born courtier. Suave, sophisticated, polished, elegantly garbed as ever in an eye-catching scarlet and black houppelande, he would do well for my task. He was not as fair as his sister, but handsome enough with a warm russet cast to his hair which was hidden beneath a beaver-fur hat, its low crown and upturned brim enhanced by a cabochon-cut sapphire.

'Well, Mistress Anne. Have you enjoyed your first visit to the Court?' He deigned to pay me some attention, and was not too condescending as he assessed me with light grey eyes. 'I see that you have enjoyed dressing for the coronation.'

I was impatient. 'How could I not enjoy it? And yes, I have always desired a gown of azure velvet and fur that is new to me.'

'Will you take my advice? You should wear green. The hue of a fine emerald would become you.'

'I do not favour green.' Why make so fatuous a remark when it was clearly of no importance? 'But I need your help, Anthony.'

He raised my hand to his lips. 'I will be honoured. Do you need more poetry than the poor stuff from the King's minstrels? I can provide it and extol the beauty of your dark eyes. Or I can play the knight errant with great skill and rescue you from this noisome rabble.'

'Nothing so difficult.' I laughed at his deliberate denigration of the high-born gathering. 'I need to know something.' I looked across the Great Hall, searching for the unknown courtier, finding him at last. He had joined a larger group. 'Who is he? The man with the violet-blue chaperon and the sable on his cuffs,' I asked ingenuously.

'Why?'

Anthony looked down at me, his brows raised.

'No reason. Your sister Elizabeth pointed him out to me but knew not his name.'

'Why would she do that? He is of no value to her. Or to you. His name is Paston.'

I was no wiser. 'It is not a name I know.'

'There is no reason why you should unless you are interested in the ongoing and frequently bitter land disputes in Norfolk. He is eldest son and heir of a Norfolk family of no great lineage.'

'Oh.' I experienced a little wash of disappointment. It did not sound promising after all.

'Some say his great-grandfather was naught but a peasant who earned his living by tilling his land. He has little claim to name or status. Is that all you wished to know?'

A peasant. This was not hopeful at all, but then Cousin Elizabeth had simply been mischief-making.

'Yes.'

He was not for me, however good the quality of his hose or his shoes, however imperious his nose. William would not approve, and neither would I. And yet.

'But if that is so, Cousin Anthony, why is he here at Elizabeth's coronation?'

Anthony grinned as he relented. 'Let me re-ignite your interest in this man, cousin. He is now Sir John Paston and has done well for himself. The King has seen fit to knight him for his family's services to the crown. He has good legal training, following in his father's footsteps, and will probably make a name for himself in Norfolk as well as at Court. The family are pushing a claim on Caister Castle which they gained through a dubious inheritance. They own considerable property in the eastern counties, although they have enough enemies to fill the royal barge from one end to the other. They spend their time fending off those opponents, with some success, it has to be said.'

'Are they rich?'

'Not enormously. Legal action through the courts is an expensive business.'

'You said his family were peasants. Yet he is a knight.'

'A recent achievement from the King. His father has been a prominent supporter of the Yorkists, even if he does not take to the battlefield. The son was knighted in his stead, at his request. They are moving up in the world.'

Suddenly Sir John Paston sounded more appealing. A man of talent and skill, and reputation.

'How do you know him so well?' I asked, turning my back on Sir John Paston. I had no wish to advertise my interest. 'Do you like him?'

'We have been at odds in the past,' Anthony admitted. 'I made a claim against Caister Castle myself, which put me in conflict with the Paston family, but I have since withdrawn that claim and we are amicable enough.' He shrugged as if it were of no importance to be at odds one week and in fairly amicable conversation the next. 'Paston comes to watch the jousts, and is learning to participate with some minor skill,' he continued. 'He has an interest in all Court events. I think that he is a clever man who sees where he can make the most of his ambitions. I swear he does not see himself as a lawyer, stepping into his father's shoes. He is a man of compelling character, I suppose that you could say.'

My interest was effectively caught.

'Have you fought with him in jousts?'

'I have. He is still a raw talent but does not lack for courage. Or swagger in the field.'

Better and better.

'Is he wed?'

'I know not. And I will not ask him. All I know is that he has an eye for an attractive woman, and that he and his father are often at daggers drawn over his extravagance and his unwillingness to set his nose to the grindstone of their legal commitments. Rumour says that ... But I will not tell you that. Of what importance will it be to you?'

'Has he a mistress then?'

'I'll not ask him that either!'

A rebellious son? It would be interesting to meet a rebellious son. My family were all superlatively obedient, and thus frequently dull.

'Do you wish me to introduce you?'

I suspected that he was laughing at me, but my decision was swift. 'Yes. You offered to be chivalric.'

Anthony shouldered his way through the crowd and I followed, ignoring brother William's sharply raised voice as I disappeared from his view.

'Sir John.'

'Sir Anthony.'

They met with a handclasp.

'Allow me to present my cousin, Mistress Haute.'

Sir John Paston looked surprised but his reaction was high in courtesy. The chaperon was doffed and swept in a flamboyant arc as he bowed.

'Sir John.'

I curtsied with calm aplomb.

'Mistress Haute. I think we have not previously met.' He looked as if he did not greatly care.

'No, sir. I live in Kent.'

'I have no estates in Kent, although my Aunt Poynings does.' And then to Anthony: 'Will you joust tomorrow, to celebrate this very tedious event?'

'Of course. Do you?'

'Yes. If I can find some man of means to invite me to join his retinue.'

Anthony laughed. 'I think I can find a place for you. How is the Caister dispute?'

'A thorn in my flesh,' Sir John responded shortly with a wry twist of his mouth. 'The Duke of Suffolk takes every opportunity to make an issue, either in the courts or with his retainers.'

'Does the King know?'

'Yes, but is reluctant to antagonise Suffolk. And my father fears being recommitted to the Fleet on some false pretext by his rivals who would like him out of the way for a week or two.'

'What about the Duke of Norfolk? Will he not come to your rescue?'

'He might. If he did not lust after Caister, too! The young Duke is keen to try his newly honed blade against us.' Sir John scowled. 'My brother, who is in his household, is whispering in his ducal ear. So far it has kept him quiet, but I would not wager a fortune on it lasting.'

I could think of nothing to add to this conversation, which soon drew to an end with more courteous leave-taking.

At last he addressed me again. 'Will you watch the tournament, Mistress Haute?'

I would promise nothing. 'It may be that I will.'

'It is not like you to be silent in company,' Anthony suggested.

'It is not like me to enjoy being ignored for a discussion of a possible joust and a contested will.'

I returned to an impatient William and we left the Hall. Sir John Paston was not for me. An unimportant figure, a cock crowing on his own little dunghill in Norfolk. Even Caister Castle was not truly his within the law. For sure there was no poetry in his soul. More like lists of acquisitions, payments and debts.

I must look elsewhere.

Perhaps I should follow the example set by my cousin the Queen and waylay some great magnate or enterprising knight on a road through the forest in Kent, looking romantically in distress. In my case, it would probably be a friend of my brother who would return me home with sharp words. Even if that was an impractical dream, I could do better than Sir John Paston.

I admitted a tinge of regret. I had admired his taste in hose and shoes. The jewel pinned in his chaperon had been noteworthy, a falcon enamelled in white with a ruby for its eye. Of some value, whatever the poverty of his legal dispute.

I would not give him the pleasure of my attendance at the tournament.

★

I persuaded a reluctant Meg to accompany me to the tournament. The Queen sat in her pavilion with the chosen ones from her household; Meg and I in seats found for us by a reluctant William who dispatched one of our retinue to accompany us for our protection if the event should become unstable as wine and ale was consumed. It was a colourful display with the banners proclaiming the livery of those who participated, although the heat and the dust and stench of hot horseflesh did not appeal. The horns blared, the combatants paraded and made their bows before the Queen. Sir Anthony fought with exuberant skill, admired by all, both noble and common, defeating all-comers with lance and sword. Sir John Paston was less impressive. His jousting animal fell lame at the first pass, thus forcing him to retire. How did he present himself in the sword combat? It was impossible to pick him out in the melee of knights. I did not think that Anthony would be quick to invite him to join his band of knights for a second time.

'Was he worth coming to watch?' Meg asked, bluntly, mopping perspiration from her face with a square of linen.

'Who?' My sister was becoming far too knowing.

'The knight you insisted on meeting yesterday.'

I considered my answer and did not dissemble. 'No. I do not think that he was.'

There was nothing more to say.

We left before the tournament came to its end.

★

Sir John Paston proved to be not my only disappointment. My cousin Elizabeth, now Queen of England, was a disappointment to me also. No husband of any description emerged from my new connection with the Court. Any man with a title, be he an aged peer or a young child with expectations, was snapped up to wed a Woodville, but not a Haute. There was no arranged marriage with a man of status or ambition for me. Cousin Elizabeth concentrated on providing for all her sisters. What an array of alliances she achieved into the most notable families of England. Elizabeth could be accused of family greed, while I had set my hopes too high.

Thus fortune was slow in stepping in the path of the two unwed Haute daughters. We were not even invited to Court, in spite of the Queen's assurances. I had such dreams, but they did not come to pass. I would willingly have fetched and carried for the Queen, stitched and danced and played the lute, although I was not adept at it.

The months passed, turning into years, while I remained unwed and unsought after, growing increasingly desperate

357

as I stayed at our home at Bishopsbourne in Kent. No troubadour penned and sang love songs to me. I had no wish to take the veil or become a spinster in the household of one of my brothers or sisters, but that seemed to be the most likely pattern for the rest of my life: caring for nephews and nieces and supervising the honesty of the servants. Life did not have the excitement that I hoped for on that day in Westminster Hall.

Envy rode me hard.

My path did not cross with that of Sir John Paston. He was nothing to me. We had been simply two ships, their courses convening, before they parted and sailed to vanish each into its own distance. When I occasionally gave him a passing thought, which I admitted to doing, I presumed he had wed elsewhere, to a Norfolk heiress with manors to add to his own. I hoped that he might find the time to write poetry to her.

Even his face had faded from my memory after two years.

I foresaw no change in my life and regretted it most deeply.

Chapter Nineteen

Margaret Mautby Paston

Fleet Prison: August 1465

John was once more an occupant of the Fleet Prison.

'Why does he not rent a permanent chamber there?' I asked of a nonplussed courier who brought me the warning, irritation warring with fear. Whatever he might say to the contrary, John was not as strong as he had been.

The accusation of being a churl had once again raised its head, as the despicable Wyndham had once accused me in the street in Norwich. Until the case could be investigated formally and thoroughly, King Edward had ordered that John be kept in custody. Which was exactly what his detractors wanted. I could no longer sit and hope for his good treatment. I sent Sir John to Hellesdon to prevent any bid to occupy it in my absence. Jonty would remain in Norwich with the younger children, and I took Margery with me. We headed to London with no sign of John's release on the horizon, due to a neat legal trick by Yelverton and his malicious friends, imputing Paston servile descent, giving them every chance to seize our land. How could a family that was once a parcel of bondsmen take ownership of a castle? If this were true then John had no right to own manors or exercise manorial lordship.

'Why travel all that way?' Jonty asked. He showed signs of being as argumentative and opinionated as his father, addressing me as if I were a difficult litigant in a court rather than his mother.

'He is in prison.'

'He has been in prison before.'

'It worries me.'

'My father has always worried you. I think it will not be for long.'

'What have you heard? Is he ill again?' I immediately thought the worst.

'No, mother. My father is as hale as he ever is, or he was when I last heard.' With a wry smile he hugged me in apology for his less than careful comment. 'All I meant was that they'll not have the evidence to keep him there long.'

I was not so sure. It would be good for them to keep John incarcerated and impotent while the lawsuits progressed.

'And what can you do when you get there?' he continued, echoing Mistress Agnes's derision when John first saw the inside of the Fleet.

'Probably nothing, but something urges me to go.'

He frowned, reading my anxieties. 'Do you truly fear for his health?'

'No more than usual.'

Jonty hitched a shoulder. 'Well, I can't stop you. When you see him, tell him, if you will, that a decision has to be made about the manor at Cotton. One of Suffolk's retainers is still holding it. What do I do about it? Stay clear, or take a force of our soldiers, drive him out, and take possession? I need to know. And if my father wants me to take action I need some money. It's an embarrassment to have Cotton in the hands of a man who has no right to it. He mocks us every time he collect the rents from our tenants.'

'I will tell him.'

Jonty gave me another hug, which made me suspect what he would ask next.

'And it would please me if you would send to me the two pairs of hose already made and awaiting me at the hosier's in Blackfriars Gate in Ludgate. I have not a whole pair to my name.'

I inspected the hose that he was wearing. 'They look perfectly serviceable. I am gratified that I will be of use to you in London,' I replied sharply. 'And it would please me if you had more on your mind than your hose, and could send your best wishes to your father.'

His face reddened a little but he was unperturbed. 'Of course. And I will keep all safe here.' He smiled at Margery, embracing her with an easy arm around her shoulders. 'Some advice for you, sister. Visit the cross at the north door of St Paul's and St Saviour's at Bermondsey. Pray there for a good husband. It always works, so they say.'

Margery blushed a fiery red. Her fair skin was prone to blushes and I dismissed it. I must talk to John again about negotiating a marriage for her since nothing had come of my previous nudging.

Thus with Jonty's errands and my daughter's company, I made the infrequent journey to London and demanded accommodation from William and the Beaufort bride who had still not produced a Paston heir. Perhaps I should have a discussion with her. I knew a nostrum or two to aid a lady who was finding it difficult to conceive.

★

My first impression of the Fleet was not good. The rank stench of it hit me, then the sight of sewage and refuse and various animal parts dumped in the moat that encircled it on the sides that the noxious River Fleet did not. Would not such a miasma spread disease? I was right to have come.

'God preserve us!' I held a kerchief to my nose, advising Margery to do the same.

Once admitted through the gate with all its locks and bolts, the walls held at bay the stench a little, and at least John had the coin to pay for some comforts and a private room here rather than having to face the squalor of sleeping with the destitute. I was met by Mistress Elizabeth Venour, Warden of the Fleet, who, by the quality of her clothing, made a good profit from the needs of her reluctant guests.

'How is he?' I asked without much of a greeting.

'Master Paston is in health, and well served by his servant Pamping.'

It was good news. I left Margery in her company, for I would not subject her to the inmates of the prison or the conditions, and I was shown to where John was incarcerated. It was no cell. My first impression on a rapid sweep of my eye was that he was comfortable enough. The door was closed behind me but there was no rattle of a key in the lock. Another quick survey showed me a bed, a table and chair, a stool and a fire that gave off some semblance of heat. It was a soft incarceration which was a blessing, although the mattress was nothing but a thin pad of straw and I could not swear for the absence of fleas. It pleased me that I had seen it for myself. William had ensured that enough money lined the gaolers' pockets, disgraceful as it might be to have to pay for such squalor.

And here was the occupant of the cell, working hard as if he had not a care in the world, when I had ridden to London in trepidation. I felt the breath of anger rise again.

'Margaret!'

There was astonishment in his face rather than pleasure.

'Good day, John.'

He dropped his pen on the table, pushed aside the pile of documents and rose from his stool as I stepped in. It was nine months since we had last set eyes on each other, and he was working, just as he did at home. His criticisms of me had stung on his last visit and they still did. It was difficult to feel generous towards him even as my heart threatened to soften.

'What are you doing here?'

'Visiting you, since you cannot come to me.'

'Who have you left in charge?' A heavy disapproval predictably descended.

'Sir John is at Hellesdon. Jonty is in Norwich with the younger ones. And Margery is here with me.'

'Here in the prison?' The frown grew deeper.

'She sits with Mistress Venour to pass the time of day. She is perfectly safe.'

'I'd rather you were in Norwich, where you can keep the manors under your jurisdiction.'

'The manors can exist without me for a week or two. Your sons are not incapable.'

'Not as capable as you. I don't trust their judgement.'

Oh John! Have you no joy in seeing me? Can you not dredge up one word of welcome? I let no emotion show in my expression.

'Your sons are quite capable of holding the reins in Norfolk. I come with requests.' I might as well get the business over first, and then see if there was anything more to say. My heart had fallen when I had been so hopeful, but he might even welcome me when he knew that his affairs were progressing. 'Jonty says I must remind you about the manor of Cotton. It needs your decision,' I said.

'And I'll make it.'

'He needs money.'

'I'll arrange to send him what he needs.'

'Sir John is well.' I hazarded a guess about the state of our son and heir. I had not seen him for some weeks. In John's mind he was still banned from home.

'Still wasting his time?'

Well, I might as well confess to taking Sir John back beneath one Paston roof or another.

'He is still working hard to keep the Paston name high in the King's mind. And, as I said, I have sent him to Hellesdon to make sure it is not invaded in our absence.'

'Then perhaps he can get me out of here?'

How unforgiving. And still unwelcoming.

'Is that all?' I still stood far distant from him beside the door. 'If you have nothing more to say I will collect Margery and go back to talk to William, who is at least good company.'

Which at last made him consider me, rather than legal

affairs. I watched as he took a breath, drawing his hands down over his cheeks.

'No. No, Meg. Of course not. It lightens my heart to see you, even if I had wished you had not come.'

He crossed the room, gripped my hands in a less than lover-like clasp, led me to where I could sit down on the crude stool, and kissed me. Which improved my temper a little, although John remained agitated.

'How do you go on?' I asked.

'I have no complaints. Except for my lack of freedom, or any indication of how long I'll be here.'

'Are you eating well? Are you sleeping? Does Pamping serve you as you would wish?'

John Pamping was one of our own household servants and to my mind completely trustworthy.

'I could have told you all that in a letter.'

He was not in good spirits, but then I should not have expected it. I had disturbed the routine he had created for himself. Even when I attempted to divert him, talking of family, of young Anne and Walter, and Willem's childhood ailments, he was distracted.

Eventually I must leave. Before I left John asked, 'Will you return tomorrow?'

'If you wish to see me.'

'Of course.' He began to write on a piece of rough paper torn from a sheet. 'But when you are back in Norwich I need you to send me this. Two ells of worsted for new doublets if I am to remain here during the cold of winter.'

'Anything else?'

'My brother William has a tippet of the finest worsted, almost like silk. It will be expensive but I would wish to look my best when I return to the courts.'

'Yes.'

'And a strip of the same material to enhance my collars.' He wrote again while I tried not to sigh.

'Why can't Pamping do it?'

'You have more authority. Don't forget, will you?'

'I will not forget.'

'And then there is a manor that I hear is being claimed from us by the widow of the Duke of Bedford. She has no right to it. Tell Jonty to look into it …'

I abandoned any further attempts at closeness.

★

I was making no good use of my time in London. Now that I had reassured myself that John was not at death's door, and indeed had more need of a clerk than a wife, I decided that I might as well go home. But, out of a perverse duty, and out of an affection for this difficult man I had lived with for more years than I could count, I visited once more, hoping for a warmer reception.

My hopes died an instant death. There was an anxiety about him, overlying a simmering fury, that had nothing to do with me or the Fleet.

'Margaret! I thought you would be on the road to Norwich.'

'I came to say farewell.'

'God's Blood! I think they will keep me here to the end of my days.'

He thumped his fist into the stone coping around the window, to the detriment of his fist, until I possessed myself of his hand to smooth the roughened knuckles.

'What is it?'

'It is a slur on me and all the Pastons.'

But he allowed me to pull him to his chair. All my resentments softening, I sat and looked at John across the much-scarred table; he sank to the stool, pushing aside an empty cup and a platter of crumbs, his gesture brusque as if he might have swept them onto the floor, except that I caught them before they reached the table edge.

'How can we put this right? We are vulnerable on so many sides.'

'We have always been vulnerable.' I could not see the problem that should bring him to such ire and dismay.

'But now our opponents are becoming more outspoken. They take vicious satisfaction in claiming that we are from a family of bondsmen. I cannot put it right.'

The old accusation of low birth. I let him speak, not interrupting.

'Not even your superior birth can rescue us, Meg.' His smile was little more than an aggrieved twitch of his lips, but at least it could be recognised as a smile. His knuckles had begun to bleed so I mopped at them with a kerchief. 'Our sons and grandsons will be burdened with it for ever. And my brothers, of course. No matter what we can do to aid the King with good service, there it is, a stain on our escutcheon, if we could actually lay claim to one. The voices of the nobility that surround King Edward are far louder than ours. And because we have no heraldic badge, we are blighted. My son is knighted, but what bearing does that have on the argument? We own one of the finest castles in the land, but that will be confiscated. We have worked hard to tug ourselves up into Norfolk society, but it stands to nothing beside the lack of a line of descent. Every time I bring a case to support our inheritance, there it is, facing us, like a fire-breathing dragon.'

He leaned to rest his chin on his hands after wrapping my kerchief around the abrasion.

'How long will I be kept here? I feel helpless.'

I closed my hand around one of his wrists. What could I do to reassure him, for indeed there was no reassurance? All he had said was a correct lawyerly summing up of the weapon that could be used against John for ever. That once in the past, the Pastons had been in the ranks of the unfree. And yet … I laced my fingers with his. Well, why not? I would swear that it was not the first time that it had been done by some enterprising peasant who wished for an ennoblement.

'We will make one,' I said.

'One what?'

'A line of descent.' Releasing him, I pulled a blank page of paper towards us, then a quill-pen which I sharpened and pushed into his hand. There was a pot of ink somewhere beneath the scrolls. 'We need a line of descent. So draw one. I am surprised you have not thought of it for yourself.'

'Is it legal?' His lawyer's mind spoke first through the disbelief at what I was proposing.

'As legal as Fastolf's will. And I won't ask you again about that.'

He laughed, a raw sound in that appallingly noisome place, for the first time since I had arrived.

'We will not be the first, I suppose.'

'Nor the last. Start writing.'

John wrote his name and mine, then those of our seven

children. His own brothers and sister were put in place. Justice William and his wife Agnes. And of course John's grandparents, Clement, the bondsman, and his wife Beatrice, a bondswoman; their serfdom must be hidden at all costs.

'What now?' I asked.

John had fully entered into the spirit of it. 'We make up some fruitful marriages with enterprising children before Clement and Beatrice were even born. You have the imagination, Meg. Help me here.'

It passed the hours most usefully. By the end of the day we had a truly remarkable Paston pedigree, of which no Paston, past or present, had ever been aware.

'How do we prove it?' John surveyed it, a final doubt lingering in the pursing of his lips.

'You are the lawyer. You write the documents. Or get a clerk to do so in an antique hand. Add some wax and seals. Then you present them in a court if you are ever questioned again about your lack of substance.'

'Those who despise me will question it for certain, as soon as I am released.'

'Then send a copy to the King. If King Edward and the courts can be persuaded, they can question all they like.'

It was a moment of unity for which I was most grateful. For that short time John's heart had been light, seeing beyond the weight that he had lived with for so long. Yes, I had been right to make the journey, if only for those few hours of intimacy in mind as well as in body, even if I was only staunching the blood from his hand. Since he had no other calls on his time during my visit, I made use of John Pamping to visit the hosier in Ludgate to purchase Jonty's hose. They were fine enough, as, on his return, I unwrapped them from their packet and laid them on the table, an inappropriate touch of self-indulgence in the bare room, to see why Jonty must order such items from London rather than in Norwich. One black pair and one russet.

'How much?' I asked.

'Eight shillings for the pair, mistress,' Pamping said.

'My son has expensive tastes.' John frowned over them, fingering the quality of the cloth.

'Your son is now the scion of a notable family and so can afford to wear fine hose.'

But John was no longer laughing. 'Who is paying for them?' he asked.

'You are. I will leave it for you to reimburse Master Pamping. It will show Jonty that you value his hard work for our family.'

He thought about this, then his mouth curved and his eyes shone with the light from the window.

'Very well. And I will do so because I value his mother more than every estate I own.'

We parted with a good understanding, as deep and loving as it had ever been.

'I expect that I will see you very soon,' I said.

'I pray that it will be so. And my thanks for coming here, Meg, even if I was in a sore temper. I have missed you inordinately.'

Our kisses of farewell, seated on John's uncomfortable bed, were warm and reassuring that this parting would not be for ever. His arms around me were strong with a comforting permanency. My heart was no longer sore.

They were indeed very fine hose.

★

Before returning to Norwich with a lighter heart than the one that had kept me company on the journey to London, a letter found me at my lodgings with William. The salutation was more than a surprise from a man who had been short-tempered, unwarrantedly critical, and with all the humour and tolerance of a snake for much of my visit. Here was the John I remembered from more carefree days in our early years together. Unexpected as it was, much as William had a curiosity to know the contents, I read it in private.

★

To mine own dear sovereign lady,
    I thank you for the great cheer that you brought to me in the
Fleet.

★

After which promising beginning it lapsed into business, unable to resist a scathing complaint about Jonty's request for money to help with the defence of Cotton. But then. I would never have believed it. A poem. It would not trouble the Court poets, I thought, but it was a joy to me. For after the usual legal business which John had put into atrocious rhyme, it fell into a personal ending for me.

★

And look you be merry and take no thought,
For this rhyme is cunningly wrought.
And wish you had been here still.

No more to you at this time
But God him save who made this rhyme.
Written on the Vigil of St Matthew by your true and trusty
husband, JP.

★

Never in all our marriage had I thought to receive such as this.

★

And wish you had been here still …

★

It was no love letter but it was the best I would get. After running my finger over those words, I folded it carefully and stowed it away. Who would have thought that my husband, lacking tender sentiment, would ever turn his mind and his pen to poetry, however dire the results? All day my heart sang, my mood so uplifted by the memory of that lovely gesture that I allowed Margery her visit to kneel at the cross at the door of St Paul's and St Saviour's at Bermondsey. She duly knelt and bowed her head. I knelt beside her, offered prayers for John and all my children, then stood back. She would make a fine wife for some rising citizen who would give her a good home. I mentally listed her attributes as my daughter. She was all Paston with her neat coif, her practical hands, her nimble footsteps; a tall young woman with an upright stance and a calm confidence beneath her quiet exterior.

'And did you pray for a good husband?' I asked as we mounted our horses and turned their heads to the east.

'Yes, mother.'

'We'll do what we can for you.'

'Yes, mother. I have no fears.'

She was more docile than I would have liked. But, since I could not remedy such a lack of spirit, I turned my thoughts away from my daughter to the mission I had to undertake for John. Returning to Norwich from London I journeyed first to our disputed manor of Cotton to see how the land lay. I expected to achieve nothing, but at least I could report that I had followed John's instructions, even if I was refused entry and turned away at the door by men in Suffolk livery bearing Suffolk weapons. If I was willing to send my sons to challenge the wilful occupation, should I not be prepared to face the Devil myself? For my own safety I ordered an escort and arranged for Jonty to meet me and bring a body of retainers.

Jonty had not arrived when I rode up in a heavy shower that drenched us all from head to foot. Plucking at my waterlogged skirts and the veil that clung wetly to my neck, I was determined to make my ownership of this manor clear to all, however disputed it might be. Even though the years had passed since my experiences at Gresham, and it might have been thought that I would have learned circumspection over the years, it still was not in my nature to retreat without showing resistance.

I rode up to within hailing distance of the door of my fortified manor house, kept a little distance, and waited, still mounted for a fast retreat if necessary. Would they fire at me from the gatehouse? Would they send out a repelling force? I could see no armed men on the walls. All I could do was wind up my courage and sit tight.

'Open up! This is Margaret Paston, rightful owner of this manor.'

My voice rang out. They could see who I was from the livery of my escort, even though the colours of the azure fleur-de-lys on white and gold were muted with the damp. No response. I urged my mount forward a few steps, my escort keeping restless pace.

'This is not wise, mistress,' my captain muttered in my ear.

'It may not be wise, but I am here.' I stared at my firmly closed manor-house door. 'Open up!'

I clenched my hands around the bridle and discovered that I was holding my breath as the gate in the protective wall was pushed back. Fear was hot beneath my heart as I braced for a rush of armed men. Instead, out walked one of our own tenants whose face I recognised even if I could not put a name to it. He bowed to me and stepped back. I could see no armed men of Suffolk's household behind him.

'Good day, Mistress Paston.'

Behind me I heard a commotion, the beat of hooves as I real-ised that Jonty had arrived at last, but I did not turn my head.

'Are you inviting me in?' I asked, unable to hide my surprise, my fear beginning to subside.

'I am, mistress.'

'Where is the man who flagrantly claims to be your new lord?'

'Away on the Duke of Suffolk's business, mistress.'

'Who is in charge here?'

'I am. Will you enter, mistress?'

Behind him had emerged more of my tenants. This I had not expected, but knew immediately that I must make this a formal occupation in the hearing of all those present.

'Do you relinquish ownership of this manor to me?'

'I do.'

'Then I accept.'

I dismounted, abandoned my mare and, in saturated shoes, squelched forward through the puddles, stepping across the threshold, touching the gatepost in ownership, and claiming Cotton once more as Paston property. John would have been proud of me. It had cost me nothing more than a little bravery. Now all we had to do was defend it when retribution would surely follow.

'You are late,' I accused Jonty as he rode up and dismounted beside me in the courtyard, the dozen liveried retainers following. My breathing was beginning to settle, my heart to resume its normal pace, but my wet garments clung nastily to my legs.

'I came as fast as I could.' There was no apology in Jonty's response. 'I have to congratulate you, mother. I could not have done better myself.'

'Thank you. If you had come sooner, it would have saved me a good dose of anxiety. I am too old for such excitements.'

'It did not seem so to me.'

He bent and kissed my cheek. I huffed a breath, but I was pleased, and returned the kiss. And then, barely dismounted, Jonty was preparing to leave again.

'Where are you going?'

'Since you seem to have this all well in hand, I'm off to negotiate with the Duke of Norfolk to enlist his support.' He saw my brows rise in disbelief and smiled in response, a conspiratorial gesture. 'The Duke in a surprising moment of casual magnanimity has promised to send reinforcements to aid us. I think he is enjoying usurping the power of the Duke of Suffolk hereabouts. You can hold the manor until I return in some strength. Be brave, Mistress Paston.'

I watched him go. John would be pleased. It was a morning's work well done.

But I would not write it in verse.

Norwich: October 1465

My pleasure over our reclaiming of Cotton lasted no more than two months. Any renewed confidence was undermined in vicious style.

The clamour was the resonance of marching feet from the direction of the market place. Grabbing a cloak and a sturdy manservant, I made my way there, the hubbub growing louder, until we could go no further without pushing through a crowd. Which I did, using my servant's bulk, until I reached the front.

The space where the market was held was full, a glittering armed force with banners proclaiming the power of the Duke of Suffolk. And there was the man himself, at the centre of it all, magnificently mounted on a polished bay stallion, backed by liveried retainers. His velvet chaperon, catching the sun, glowed rich purple like an autumn plum. His hands in gilded gauntlets gripped his gem-studded reins, as if his fingers were powerful enough to choke the life out of any man who dared to challenge him. The man was as self-regarding as his late-unlamented father had been.

'What is it?' I asked the man at my side, a substantial man from his clothing, one of the weaving fraternity. 'Are we at war? Is it an insurrection?'

He looked askance, his voice low-pitched. He clearly knew my name. 'The only war is against your family. You have some powerful adversaries hereabouts, Mistress Paston. This little venture is intended to cow the townsfolk into obedience when you come under attack. It might be best if you stay indoors for now. What friends you have after this show of force will not be keen on helping you. Go home, mistress.'

His concern unnerved me but I would not show it.

'I'll not go until I know what's happening.'

It did not take long. The Duke lifted an imperious hand to summon Mayor Toppes and bid him speak. The Mayor, clad in official robes for the occasion, immediately obeyed so that I knew where his loyalties lay, even if he and his wife had once broken bread in our house in Hellesdon. His voice carried over the crowd. One simple sentence.

'His Grace the Duke of Suffolk this day lays claim to the manor of Hellesdon.'

My heart gave a single hard thud against my ribs.

'I'll be struck deaf and dumb if he does!' I said in a surge of fury.

My neighbour nudged me into silence.

'The Paston family have stolen Hellesdon from its rightful owner, the Duke of Suffolk.' The Mayor inclined his head towards the Duke who nodded in sanctimonious piety. 'Now, citizens of Norwich, is the time to renounce any friendship you have with the Paston family. If you do not, if you send them aid, you will forfeit your freedom. I have given orders that my constables take you into custody.'

The Duke sat his animal without moving.

The obsequious Mayor, no longer a friend of ours, had not

finished. Once more he raised his voice. 'The Duke's troops will take possession of Hellesdon this very day, to put right a grave wrong.'

'I told you, mistress,' the weaver muttered. 'He's out for Paston blood.'

'More like Paston acres!'

Oh, it was well planned. Superbly planned so that there would be no quick retaliation. This attack on Hellesdon, a mere two miles away, had been chosen for this day when John still remained locked in the Fleet, Sir John was in London, and Jonty, whom I could have called on to resist an occupation of our manor, was attending the young Duke of Norfolk's formal investiture of his lands and titles. As everyone associated with the Court would know. As the Duke of Suffolk would know.

At that moment I could have happily wished the same fate on him as removed his father from this earth.

The Duke began to move off, troops falling in behind him, but the danger was not over for me. Some soldiers were left behind to intimidate and threaten and I was aware of a slide of eyes in my direction. I did not expect my neighbours to harm me but neither did I think that in the circumstances they would leap to my protection.

'Get you home, mistress.'

It was good advice.

I fled through the streets, suspecting hostile glances at every turn, from every window. What to do? Bar our door? I issued orders that we were at home to no one, then I sat and shivered, expecting a hammering of military fists to demand entry. The day waned towards an early dusk, and although I insisted that no candles be lit to make known our occupation, it was clear that the troops had dispersed. It did nothing to relieve my anxieties. They had gone to attack Hellesdon. By now they would have taken possession of it.

God preserve us against such men as the Duke of Suffolk.

There was no advantage in my informing John since the Fleet would prevent his response. Next morning I dictated instruction to be sent to Sir John, to abandon whatever kept him in London and to get himself to Norwich without delay. I did not mince my words.

★

As I approached Hellesdon, Sir John riding beside me, all I could think of was Gresham. That manor had mattered more to me than any other, being my very own. I remembered riding there with John at the end to see the despoliation. But this manor of Hellesdon mattered too. It had been a sign of our social advancement. What would I see? Would all be destroyed, or would there be some remnant to which we could lay claim? Now I had a grown son beside me, and a knight forsooth. I should not feel so helpless. I stole a glance at him, knowing full well that he would be more at home at Court than here where conflict and dispute threatened, but I could not impugn his courage.

I wished with all my heart that John was riding at my side. Sometimes I missed him outrageously.

'Are you sure you wish to do this?' Sir John asked. 'I can go ahead and see for myself, and send news back. There is no need to distress yourself.'

'There is every need. How can you ask it? It is for us to bear the burden without your father.'

'You don't have to be there.'

'Are you saying that I am too old to move beyond my doorstep?'

I was forty-three years old. At the thought I sat up straight in the saddle, lifting my chin as any Paston woman would.

'I would not dare!'

Manoeuvring his horse towards me, his hand closed over mine where they were wound around the bridle. I was reassured by the strength in him. By the Virgin, I was soon to discover that I needed that moment of comfort from my son.

My first impression was that there were many people in the streets of Hellesdon, and then that I knew their faces from Norwich, friend and foe alike. Some spoke to me in low voices as I rode towards the manor house, although many allowed their gaze to slide away from mine. There was a smattering of catcalls at Paston expense.

'Ignore them,' Sir John said.

I had every intention of ignoring them. But here was a Paston humiliation, and they had come to witness it. Yes, there was compassion, but many would pretend that they knew me not. The Duke of Suffolk had a long arm and a powerful punch. Some spoke of what had been done here at Hellesdon with shame. It made me feel no better, but at least it offset the jeers of the Suffolk allies.

Our tenants came out of their homes, full of distress, and I listened to them, as they gave me a terrible list of complaints.

'We are ransacked.'

'Our mattresses are taken away, mistress.'

'The pots from the kitchen have been taken. Or smashed against the doorframe. There was no need for it. What do I do now to make food for my children?'

'My iron gates are carried away by Suffolk's men, and the weather-vane from my roof.'

On and on they went, claims of petty retaliation against villagers who could not fight back. I could promise them no redress until I knew the drain on our own finances. I tried my best with words of encouragement, but I knew when we were beaten. Some of the houses had been robbed five or six times within the course of one day by separate bands of marauders, until there was no one item of value within the walls.

'Do we go straight to the manor?' Sir John asked when I pulled my mount to a standstill in the middle of the village street.

'I must speak to the parson first.'

I found him, clothed without vestments, standing in the chancel. The marauders had been here too. All was scourged of elements of holiness. No cross, no chalice and patten, no statues. The painted boards had been prised from the walls. The hangings were gone, the stained glass looted. No candlesticks or candles. Whether it be gold, silver or brass, or even wood, anything that could be carried had been hauled away. Light shone through the gaping holes above where the lead had been prised away from the roof timbers. The church was all but a sorry shell, robbed of its dignity as a House of God.

The high altar was stripped bare. 'I could not stop them, Mistress Paston,' the parson said, walking slowly towards us as if emerging from his worst nightmare. 'They put me outside while they did their worst. Everything of value taken.'

'You could not have stopped them.' It was all I could say as I gripped his hands in reassurance. There was no remedy for his grief or this desecrated church.

'What of the manor?' I asked.

381

'I fear that it may be even worse, mistress.'

I turned from the church and we covered the final yards towards the manor house on foot. As we rounded the final bend the manor came into view. I stopped walking. It was far worse than I could have imagined. It had been damaged beyond repair, the walls torn down. Anything that could not be carried away lay in a heap, hacked and burnt with malice. There were no walls standing, either wood or stone, to allow anyone to live there again.

'There is nothing we can do here,' I said. I felt as cold as the wind that billowed my cloak and dislodged my hood, as if it shared the malice of the destroyers of my property. At Gresham I had wept. Now I did not. My anger was stronger than my grief.

'We could ask the King to send some of his legal men to see this,' Sir John said, 'if we ever need witnesses.'

'Yes.' A few random flakes of snow drifted down. We had not expected such a change in weather so early in October. 'Before the snow. Otherwise the worst will be covered up.'

'It is all we can do,' my son agreed. 'Hellesdon lost to us. And Drayton. We can sue for restitution but the Duke of Suffolk is too powerful. I fear that Cotton will be next, in spite of all we did to reclaim it.'

It echoed my own thoughts.

Our only course of action was to retreat to Caister where at least we would be safe with a garrison to stand guard and protect our walls. It was a relief when the doors were closed and locked.

That night, after we had eaten a near-silent meal, I took out the inventory of all we had lost at Hellesdon. Two featherbeds, four mattresses, a collection of kitchenware. But then more personal items too. Clothing, a fine book that belonged to Sir John, an intricately carved comb of ivory that John had given to his daughter Margery on the occasion of a birthday. And so much more. All lost to us. It was a dispiriting exercise and gave me no relief.

'All we have to hold onto is this castle.' Sir John was as morose as I.

'And hold we will, but we need your father's release from prison if we are to get anywhere.'

Although what John could do, even in freedom, which he eventually regained in January of the New Year, I had no very clear idea. He returned to his rooms in the Inns of Court to take up his legal battles, as if there had been no hiatus, but Sir John Fastolf's legacy was slowly dripping away, vanishing like ice crystals under a fierce sun.

Chapter Twenty

Margaret Mautby Paston

The Inner Temple, London: May 1466

It was a bright morning towards the end of the month of May, a time of blossom and growth in garden and hedgerow, when the worsted weavers and leather dressers of Norwich were anticipating new deliveries of fleece and fine skin. Their yarn and leather, much in demand in Europe, would bring wealth to the town, but that was, for once, of no interest to me. It was a time of new life but I had been summoned to London. Within the hour I was on my way with little care for my appearance other than a serviceable gown, necessities strapped to a sumpter horse and two manservants as escort. The young children were abandoned to the care of Richard Calle. There was nothing I could do but count the miles that dragged, fearing what was happening at my destination. The days passed but I could travel no faster than any merchant. I was no royal courier with changes of horses. All I could do was offer up a constant litany of prayer as exhaustion drove me to put up at inns on the road.

Blessed Virgin, keep him from harm. Give me the grace to arrive in time.

I could not even recall the instructions I had left for Richard Calle. For once they did not seem to matter.

Once in London I made my way to the Inner Temple where John had his accommodation, where the deep foreboding that had kept me company became a black apprehension. I had come here with John when his father had died, so many years ago now. Then we had stood by Justice William's bed together with Mistress Agnes and the children. A solid rank of Pastons to witness the demise of the head of the family. Now I feared that this role was for me and I was alone.

'How is he?' I demanded of the physician who met me at the door.

'Weak, mistress.'

'Is it the pestilence?' I had heard of none. 'A fever?'

'Yes, mistress.'

John had been prone to fevers all his life; had I not dosed him and purged him, to some effect? Surely I could repeat the regime now.

The physician opened the door wider and gestured impatiently to me to enter, as if I would be afraid to do so. 'As you will see. It is an attack on his strength and his nerves.'

I walked in and stood by the bed.

'Leave us.'

'But mistress …'

'Leave us.'

I did not regret my lack of patience.

It was hot in the room where John lay on the bed covered with a light sheet, his breathing laboured. I touched his hand. It was clammy beneath my fingertips. There was no response. His eyes were closed, his lips lax. Even so I leaned and let my lips rest against his brow.

Then I pulled up a stool and sat, my hands folded in my lap. Outwardly I was quite calm, the physician would have no cause to dose me for a hysteric, but every inch of me was rigid with fear. Insects buzzed in the window. There was the intense aroma of some nostrum that the physician had been burning, probably to ease John's breathing. I could not recognise it: I would have burnt the leaves of Winter Savory. The bed-hangings were dusty and cobwebbed, I noticed. Whoever cleaned the rooms was not efficient.

The minutes passed slowly for I seemed incapable of any pattern of thought. Then the physician returned with a pottery beaker and a small jug. He poured dark liquid from one to the other.

'What are you dosing him with?' The Pastons had not fared well at the hands of London physicians, as I had warned John until he had snapped that he needed no more warning.

'The juice of the blackberry, in red wine,' the physician said. 'It will break the fever and hot distemper.'

It was better than nothing, and at least would do John no harm until I unpacked my own remedies. Together we lifted John and forced the liquid between his lips, although I feared that more dribbled onto the pillow than gave him any relief. I sought the leather satchel that I had brought with me and had dropped by the door.

'Try this.' I extracted a packet of leaves.

'Yes, mistress.'

I thought that he would not, unless I kept an eye on him.

'Boil the leaves in wine and allow them to cool. It is not to be drunk, but used to bathe his face and body. It will soothe and allow the body to heal. I will help you.'

It was henbane, poisonous if used in careless hands.

He left me alone. More minutes passed, or were they hours? When had John ever been so still, so distant from the world? I could not recall. I did not think that he had ever been so at ease, not even in our early days together. When he had first come to woo me, he had departed to deal with some tract of land, some unpaid rent. He had never been at ease. I was fitted into his life, to be picked up and viewed when he had the time.

Not fair, Margaret!

My conscience had a voice. Had we not worked together? Had he not relied on me? Had he not known that I could administer the affairs of the estates if he was engaged elsewhere? But I would have liked him at home when the children were young. I would just occasionally have enjoyed being important in his life. I would have liked the chance to grow together into old age, knowing that I would wake up on most mornings to find him in my bed beside me.

Here were wishes that I had had time and time again, but that was not John Paston. He was driven by ambitions, unable to hand over the burdens, even into the increasingly capable hands of his own sons. There was no movement from the bed. Was his breathing even harsher? I prayed, the beads of that simple rosary that John had bought for me when we were first wed sliding through my fingers.

Keep him from harm, Gracious Lady. Lay your hand of healing upon him.

'You should go and rest, mistress.'

The physician had returned to hover by the door.

'I'll not leave him. I have come this far to be with him. It took me six days. What point in going away again? I'll stay here until there is an outcome.'

I had turned to look at the physician in his black gown and linen coif tied beneath his chin, reading my own fears in his face. It was difficult to preserve any notion of hope when John's face was the colour of whey, his breathing as harsh as a woodcutter's saw. There was sweat on his upper lip, slippery as glass. I wiped it away.

The shadows gradually lengthened. I opened the window against much good advice, surprised by the singing of a blackbird in the damson tree beyond. How could there be such joy in the world? I leaned on the ledge to listen. Perhaps it soothed a little. I would guard John's life with all the strength I had, I would drag him back from the brink of this illness and make him strong again.

'Meg.' The barest whisper.

A quick step back to the bed. John's eyes were open and lucid and fixed on me. I stooped to kiss his cheek.

'You came.'

'Of course.'

'I told them not to send for you.'

'Of course you did. But I am here to make you well.'

God forgive me for such a little lie. Such a monstrous lie as I read death in his face. Grief almost overcame me.

'Where are the children?'

'At home with Richard Calle. Sir John and Jonty will come here. They know that you will wish to see them. They are good sons.'

'There is no need. I will soon be on my feet. There is much to do.'

'I know.'

'Has King Edward made any move to restore my rights as a free man?'

'I understand that he has it in mind. You are no bondsman, my dear love, as any man can tell on meeting with you. The King must see the sense of your declaration.'

Another lie.

'And Hellesdon?'

He had forgotten. Before I could lie again, his eyes closed and he sighed.

'I know you will look after it.'

'I will.' He had forgotten that Hellesdon was no longer ours to be looked after.

'And Caister.'

'Yes, and Caister.'

'Guard it with your life, Meg.'

'I will guard it with my life.'

John slid back into sleep. He had worn himself out. Three times he had suffered imprisonment in the Fleet, with all the long journeys between Norfolk and London, the constant struggle to secure every inch of land that he believed was his. He would not give way.

'And the main problem,' I informed him as he drifted into a world where I could not reach him, 'was that you turned your friends into opponents. All those who stood by you in Fastolf's household have come to see you as obstinate and intractable in that fight. Nor do they see you as honest. Not just Yelverton, but even William Worcester says you've become evil.

What sort of condemnation is that from a friend? I wish you had been gentler with him, but you were so taken up with the intrigues of lawyers and the enmity of great men. How could you allow every thought in your head to be dominated by a need to possess a manor here, or an acre there? You would claim that it was your duty to the Paston name, from the moment that you stepped into Justice William's shoes.' A ripple of anger swept through me, surprising me. 'What's more, John, it is difficult for me to argue against so strong a premise, in spite of all my remorse that it has driven you to this terrible destruction of your health.'

I was silent for a moment, then decided to say what was in my mind.

'I have to say, as I often did, you did not do enough to keep the loyalty of your sons. You should have done more, John. You should not have been so critical of them. They were young and desired to kick up their heels with the frivolity of life. Particularly your heir. You hounded them and turned their loyalty into fear. You thought they were lacking in respect. You were wrong. You should have lured them back into the fold with trust and responsibility. Not harsh criticism.'

I remembered those days after his release from his second sojourn in the Fleet, when he had seen himself under threat. Even I had come under attack.

'Where does tenacity become obstinacy? I know not. You made a rod for your own back. I am so sorry. You drove yourself to this. You were driven when we were first wed, you are no different now.'

I stood again to light a candle. On the coffer beside it there was the folded page of a letter. Without compunction I picked it up and opened it, recognising the well-formed words immediately. It was brief, but I could not have written better.

★

Have less to do with the demands of the world. This world is but a thoroughfare and full of woe, and when we depart from this place, we take nothing with us but our deeds, good or ill, that will be remembered after us. No man knows how soon God will call him and therefore it is good for every creature to be ready.

★

It was not a loving letter, but a concerned one. Mistress Agnes had had a care for her eldest son after all. The affair of Justice William's will had lingered long and bitterly yet she had held John in her thoughts. She had even written of her love. Tears pricked in my eyes that this woman of stone had finally melted.

'I love you, too.' I spoke into the room empty except for John's inert body. 'I always have. I always will.'

John's breathing, slow and difficult, brought me back to the bedside and I called for the physician.

'I fear the worst.'

'And I, mistress, but we will make him as comfortable as we can. It is no age for a robust man to depart from this life.'

Another draught, an infusion of rue and valerian in wine, was administered, which momentarily brought him back into my presence. Yet I might have smiled at his next words, uttered on a sigh.

'You were one of the best choices I ever made in my life.'

Such tender valediction had been beyond my expectations. But when I feared that I could not hold back the tears, he added:

'Fight for Caister, Meg. Make sure my son inherits it.'

'I will.' My tears had promptly dried. 'Sir John will inherit.'

'Keep the Paston lands together.'

'I will.'

'Don't allow my mother to divide our acres in her will. She will try.'

'I will not allow it.'

I was rewarded by a tightening of his fingers around mine. 'I know that you will do all in your power. You were always at my right hand.'

'And I will remain there.'

But I was aware of Death, hunched in the corner of the room.

At the end of the twenty-second day of May in the year 1446, John Paston died. His final words not of love or affection but about Caister and inheritance. I should have expected it, but it hurt.

I continued to sit, my hand covering his as it cooled in the darkening room. Then, after placing my hand where his heart had once beat so strongly, I found myself a room and lay in the dark on the bed, memories crowding in. John would not leave me again. He had left me for all time and would never return.

By the Virgin, John, I will miss you. How will I live without you?

★

Sir John, my son and now possessor of all our troublesome manors and the litigations attached to them, arrived early next morning, when any reconciliation was impossible. I did not ask where he had been or why he had not come sooner.

'You are too late,' I informed him.

'Did my father leave any message for me?' he asked.

'He was too weak in the last hours. He asked me to fight for Caister.' I swallowed hard against that final memory. 'I would have liked a more personal farewell rather than an instruction that he might have given to Master Calle.'

I had not intended to admit such selfish grief, but I did before I could stop myself. I thought that my son was on the point of agreeing: instead he drew me into his arms and I did not resist. It surprised me that my son was taller than I but he was twenty-four years and adult in thought and manner. He rested his chin on my head.

'Never question that he loved you. Never question his knowledge of your loyalty and your abilities. He asked you to safeguard the jewel in his life. He would not do that if he did not trust you completely. You can ask for no better acknowledgement of your life together.'

I would still have liked something to remember, that was not about an estate or a legal writ. I wept on my son's shoulder, but then dried my tears. John was gone and we must take up the burden of this inheritance.

'The task is yours now,' I said.

'And you will not be by my side?'

'Of course I will. Do you need to ask?'

And then I turned my thoughts to the practical once more. Did not the Pastons always do that?

★

John must be buried. The decisions were not difficult to make. This would be a splash of defiance in the sea of dispute and litigation, fraught with thieves and liars and ill-wishers, under the canopy of all the strains of the past years that had robbed John of his life.

I would make this funeral an event to be remembered by friends and enemies as they sat and talked, whether it be around their fireplace or in the tavern. John Paston would be recalled for more than the disputes over Caister Castle and the Paston estates. He would be praised as a citizen of Norfolk who had risen to be a man of influence and wealth, who had supped at the tables of the gentry and titled, whose sons held positions at the Royal Court or in ducal houses. Whose brother was wed into the Beaufort family. He was too young to die. He was too young to leave me. When had he last put his feet on a cushioned stool in his own Christmas-trimmed hall and done nothing but listen to the music of the minstrels or laugh at the antics of the mummers? Now he was at rest and I would make it a glorious departure. I discussed it with my sons, but the decisions were mine, as was the tallying of the cost. No expense would be spared.

'You must report to me that all is as I design,' I told Richard Calle.

And this was how it passed as John Paston returned from London to his home.

A priest and twelve poor men with torches walked all the way beside his coffin as it was carried from his lodging at the Inner Temple to the parish church of St Peter Hungate in Norwich where a funeral service was held. In all that long journey they did not falter.

I was already there in Norwich, gone on ahead, to see that the local luminaries were present, counting them off as I stood at the church door to receive them with Sir John at my side. This final journey would not go by without recognition from every citizen. The bell-ringers rang their changes with great energy. The thirty-nine boys in crisp surplices sang with good heart.

'Who do you see?' I asked Sir John, in case I had missed anyone.

He furrowed his brow. 'All you would expect, given your detailed commands. Would anyone dare not comply, on fear of a stint in purgatory? The four orders of friars are here, at the front. The warden and the nuns of Norman's Hospital are represented. And there is the Lady Prioress of Carrow. I can't count them but there is a massed rank of priests. How did you get so many?'

'I paid them. I need them to sing the Office of the Dead. Is it enough to have thirty-eight priests, do you suppose?'

'You could probably have done with half that number. How much did it cost?'

A typical Paston question. Like father, like son.

'It is best if you do not know.'

It was best that John would never know too.

Or about the sum I had paid out for the burial and funeral feast that would be held at Bromholm Priory, although my son would guess soon enough as a witness to the event. It had occupied the long days for me as John had travelled home. As a place of pilgrimage and home of a piece of the true cross incorporated into the Holy Rood, brought from Constantinople, the Priory was a fitting setting in which John should rest. Richard Calle and I had bent our minds to it when all I had wished to do was to shut myself away and grieve. This would be a funerary feast like no other, to be remembered by all who came to make their farewells to a man they either respected or despised. No one would ever say that the Pastons had skimped on the splendour of John Paston's interment. Even the burial of Sir John Fastolf would pale beside this show of ostentation.

'How many animals do we need to feed those who will come

to make their farewell?' I asked Richard. I wrote a list at his direction. Forcing myself to write the list would take my mind into calmer waters.

49 pigs 49 calves 10 cows

'Ten?' I asked, prepared to draw a line through it and rewrite five.

'Ten. It will not be good for our servants to explain that we have insufficient beef to serve to the mourners,' he replied, his habitual composure mien in no manner disturbed by this wretched task.

I continued again at his dictation, assessing every item as I did so, the full number of lambs and sheep to feed the crowd that would come to pay their respects.

'How do you know so precisely?' I asked.

'This is not the first funeral I have seen organised, mistress.'

Which was why he was so valuable to me.

'How many days will it take to prepare these?' I queried.

Master Calle wrinkled his nose in thought. 'We haven't much time, mistress. Two men for three days should do it, if you are willing to pay them.'

'Then arrange it.' I noted the employment of two men for three days and their reimbursement. 'And then there will be the hens and fish,' I said, continuing to add to my list. 'As well as eggs and milk and butter.' I completed the list with geese and bread. 'There! I can think of no more.'

He took the pen and the list from me, adding some detail at the bottom.

'What is that?'

'Eighteen barrels of beer, of the best quality. Fifteen gallons of red wine. I will arrange all, mistress.'

'I swear it will beggar me. What is that?' I pointed at another item he had added.

'The employment of a barber for five days. To ensure that the priests are well tonsured and seemly. Some of them have not seen a razor since the Easter festival.' I became aware of his staring at me, searching my face. 'I think that you should rest now, mistress.'

'Perhaps I should, but Mistress Agnes is sorrowful and in need of my company.'

She had of course come to stay with me to note the passing of her eldest son.

'Will you take my advice, mistress?'

'I think I am too weary to do anything other.'

'Send Walter and Willem to sit with her. I swear they will stop her from mourning for a little while. They cannot be downcast and quiet for long. Margery will help me with the organisation. She writes a fair hand. Anne can fetch and carry.'

'You have us all organised. Don't allow Margery and Anne to get under your feet.'

'I will not.'

I returned Richard Calle's bleak smile, full of understanding as it was, and went to lie on my bed. An empty bed. Which would be empty for the rest of my days.

Meanwhile Master Calle threw himself into it all, with James Gloys. Next morning he presented himself after the children and Mistress Agnes had broken their fast with the results of his efforts.

'We will need well-nigh one hundred servants to wait on our guests, mistress. And fourteen bell-ringers to sound the bells when the master arrives and during the Mass at the Priory.' He hesitated. 'It will be costly, mistress.'

I had recovered my determination after another night of sleeplessness. 'It will be essential, Master Calle.'

'The mourning-raiment that you ordered has arrived or been dispatched to the families who will wear it. Your own is here, too.'

'Thank you.'

He poured a cup of ale. 'Drink this. When did you last eat?'

'I don't recall.' I had eaten nothing that morning and could not remember yesterday.

'I will send a platter of bread and cheese. You need to keep up your strength.'

I was obedient, knowing that he had my best interests at heart. I ate and then went to assess the mourning clothing that the family would wear. Then all I had to do was await the torchbearers with John's body.

I saw him coming and watched as the flickering light drew closer, growing stronger with every yard. A weary procession but the bearers straightened their backs and stiffened their shoulders for the final yards to bring John home to Norwich. His body rested for the night at St Peter Hungate. The church on which we had spent Paston money to glorify God and the Pastons for all time, in black flint.

★

At Bromholm Priory we had prepared a hearse draped in fine grey linen, fringed with silk, lit with candles. The vast space of the nave was ablaze with more candles by the time the mourners had gathered in that first week of June. With the heat outside and the reek of tallow and the torches within, the atmosphere was almost too noxious to bear. I saw more than one wife, in the weight of her black garments and mourning veil, wilt against her husband. I wished I had a husband to lean against but pushed the thought away. I would lean on no one on this day.

I signalled to Master Calle, whispering as he approached.

'We have to let in more air. Or all will be faint.'

'The west door is already open,' he whispered back.

'Then windows.'

'They do not open, mistress.'

'Do we have a glazier?'

'I know not.'

'Then discover one and have some windows removed. I will not have John's interment remembered for the number of mourners who had to be carried out of the church through the effects of the heat.'

He looked shocked but turned to go.

'But carefully,' I added. 'We'll pay to have the windows removed and put back, but not to have them remade.'

Two panes were thus removed as we waited for the Prior in his new robe.

'What will it cost me for the glazier?' I asked when Master Calle returned to my side.

'Twenty pence, mistress.'

I nodded. The Prior was ready and the ceremony begun with just the faintest draught to ease the heat. John was laid to rest as it should be, the congregation sweltering in their black, the candles and torches still stifling. Nothing was allowed to spoil the reverence of the occasion, except for the addition of a small rabbit to the congregation, hopping along the edge of the chancel. I stiffened. How had that occurred? It was not appropriate for such a creature to be here. And then grief washed over me anew. I would never again order the cooking of rabbit in thick onion sauce.

The creature disappeared with a final hop, and I hid my tears behind my veil, concentrating on Anne and Walter and Willem, still so young, standing beside me. They grieved because they must, their father dead, but he had been a distant figure to them. A purveyor of gifts to mark days of birth and the New Year but more absent than present. They would feel little loss in their everyday lives, and I was sorry for it.

Afterwards I kept precise notes of expenses. And through all the preparations and the ceremonies sometimes I forgot that it was John who was to be interred. It was John who had left me and would not return to oversee what I was spending or send me instructions from London to curb any excess.

What did they say in Norfolk of the interment that I had created? That it was a final defiant display from me, the widow, to wipe away the stain of battle over the Fastolf inheritance, and the humiliating times John had spent in the Fleet. It was a worthy end.

Now I was left to continue alone, with two full-grown sons but still three young children, Anne, Walter and Willem, needful of my time and efforts. And there was Mistress Agnes standing before me in a spirit of interference.

'I have to inform you, Margaret, that eight pieces of the prior's pewter have gone missing,' she informed me with what might have been interpreted as trenchant pleasure that her son's burial had been so besmirched.

'Gone missing?' I asked. 'Or stolen?'

'Most likely the latter. They probably left in the sleeves of some of the mourners.'

I sighed and added to the accounting.

Twenty pence to replace eight pieces of the Prior's pewter.

And that I hoped was the final outgoing. I would pass it to Master Calle to oversee the payments. It had indeed beggared me. Two hundred and fifty pounds, more than a year's income from our estates.

All such a loss to me. But John was a greater one.

I wondered if Sir John would complain at the cost or feel it had been well spent?

I added the final expense:

Payment for two men that filled the grave.

All was at an end.

★

Then there was only one task for me to do. I travelled to Yarmouth to read for myself the document, sent to the bailiffs in that town. They displayed it for me, spread out on a table. I leaned over it with Richard Calle at my side, to interpret for me if the clerk's words defeated me. They did not. It was all as plain as a Lenten fast.

'Does it say what I think it says?' Just to make sure.

'It does indeed, mistress.'

Two months after John left this earth, and almost twelve months after his languishing in the Fleet on the charge of being the King's bondsman and so not a free man. When he was no longer with us to enjoy the victory. At last King Edward pro-nounced the charge false and restored dignity to the Paston name.

It was addressed to Sir John, *our trusty and well-beloved knight,* who would take up residence in Caister Castle. Mention was made of John's brothers William and Clement, too, as much beloved by the King. Formal wording, nothing but lawyer-speak, but it meant much to me and I would cherish it in my heart.

I laughed.

And then I wept that John had missed the ridiculous glory of it. I could no longer read the words for tears until Richard Calle handed me a square of linen and led me from the room.

Chapter Twenty-One

Margaret Mautby Paston

Mautby: June 1468

I missed him beyond reason.

Every draught to shiver the tapestries, every movement within the house, even if it was a rodent scrabbling behind the panelling, every distant footstep, seemed to herald his presence or arrival. When all was still, it was as if he stood at my shoulder with a critical eye, whatever task I had undertaken. John insisted on keeping me company in every room, in every Paston house.

I was lonely.

The chamber where I was now seated gave me great pleasure, surrounded as I was with some of the voluptuous hangings, stitched to enhance an arras, brought here from Caister so that I might live amongst the imaginative scenes. I had chosen the most appealing, rejecting the battle scenes and sieges. Keeping me company here at Mautby was a lively group of shepherds and their wives, as well as two handsome heroes, Jason with his

Argonauts and Lancelot with his hand held out to the beautiful Guinevere, luring her into adultery.

I had discovered a pile of documents. They were well ordered so they must have been seen by John before his death, but for some reason they had not been placed with the rest of the estate material. I turned them over. Nothing new here, mostly concerned with Drayton, Cotton and Hellesdon which were all lost to us anyway. Even my dramatic reclaiming of Cotton had regrettably been short-lived. Yelverton had lost no time in driving another successful claim to ownership through the courts, and then had promptly given it as a sycophantic gift to the Dowager Duchess of Suffolk.

Nothing to be done about it so no point in repining. I leafed through them quickly, thinking to pass them over to Richard Calle who would place them with the rest of the family documents until Sir John could look at them. When he found the time. I must have a sharp conversation with him to direct a wiser use of his energies. He continued to have none of his father's application. I despaired that he would ever willingly immolate his pleasures on the altar of Paston duty.

The documents were not particularly edifying. A compromise had at last been reached in the Court of Audience. We had lost all the estates and manors gained from Fastolf's will, since keeping a claim on them had become well-nigh impossible, but we had kept Caister Castle. The glittering gemstone in the inheritance was ours for all time. There were no interests ranged against it. Or at least none that had emerged in recent months.

I wished with all my heart that John had been alive to see it. Now our sons must enjoy the value of it.

Sir John Paston, undisputed master of Caister Castle. It had a fine ring to it, and I could be content.

At the bottom of the pile was a document of heavier weight than the rest. The parchment was of fine quality and it bore a royal seal. Opening it out, I read it. As I had read it in the bailiff's room in Yarmouth in the days after John's burial.

I had shed no tears for the rest of the losses, but this made me weep anew.

For a moment I was back in John's room in the Fleet Prison when we had sat together and John had written out a plan for the Paston past that would reflect on the Paston future. All trickery and sleight of hand but all entirely necessary. Another of his greatest achievements, of which he had had no knowledge.

Had my sons seen this royal communication? I did not think so.

When there was the noise of an arrival outside, and heavy feet in the hall, I wiped my tears on my sleeve and waited to see who had come, surprised when it was Sir John who entered, with Jonty close on his heels. It was not often I had the pleasure of seeing them together under my roof without there being some family difficulty. I rose to my feet and embraced one and then the other. There was a glow about them. They had certainly not brought ill-tidings to my door.

Yet I was always unsure after a lifetime of uncertainty.

In that one moment, as they filled the spaces in my chamber with the resonance of their voices, their sheer love of life, to my eyes they were as heroic and handsome as my tapestried heroes.

'Why are you here? Not that I am not delighted to see you. Do not spoil it by telling tell me of any new legal upheavals.'

Sir John lounged into a chair, Jonty perched on a settle by the window, the similarities between them very clear. They glanced at one another and laughed.

'Well, you will tell me in your own good time, of course.'

'I have an invitation,' announced Sir John.

He had come to boast to his mother. It was not the smooth, knightly image he would display at Court, of that I was certain.

'A valuable one, I presume.'

'I'll leave you to decide, mother. I am formally required to be part of the entourage, headed by the Earl of Warwick, to escort the Lady Margaret, King Edward's sister, to Bruges to marry Charles the Bold, Duke of Burgundy. It will be the grandest of occasions.'

A valuable invitation indeed.

'And how much will that cost us in wedding finery?' I asked. I would not show my satisfaction strongly. I had indeed become a mirror image of Mistress Agnes. Expenses were always on the very top of my list for creating anxiety.

'It will not come cheap,' Sir John agreed. 'There will be much jousting as well as the ceremonies, so my horse and armour will need refurbishment.' He grinned. 'I had a wager with a London merchant that this wedding would not take place for at least two years. I lost the bet, which was that he would take two pounds off the price of the horse I was buying from him. But I can't be too sorry. The horse is a fine one and I will surely need it if I am to joust against the Bastard of Burgundy and Lord Scales.'

I might be understanding of his high spirits, but I frowned in disapproval of such levity. Gambling, forsooth. John would have been damning of such wastage of money.

'Do you go, too?' I asked Jonty.

'I am to be part of the Norfolk retinue. The Duchess of Norfolk will be the most pre-eminent of the ladies-in-waiting for the new Duchess of Burgundy. So we will both be here to represent the Pastons.' He stood and walked towards me until he could take my hands in his. 'We thought you would be pleased with the news.'

'So I am. So would your father have been. You must tell me of it. I would enjoy a letter. So would Mistress Agnes.'

It would indeed be a grand occasion. How could I not be proud that my sons had been invited to be part of the official deputation? I regarded them as they fetched wine and drank, their confidence, their assurance. How had we come to this, that neither was wed nor even betrothed? They were both of an age. I should already have been in negotiation to find a suitable bride. With John's death and the legal closure it had been swept aside, but it would be remiss of me to postpone it longer. Both needed an heiress, bringing manors and a good dower with her, and both were old enough to have their own opinion over whom to choose.

'We must arrange a marriage for you, now that Caister is settled,' I said to Sir John. 'Have you made the acquaintance of any lady at Court whom we might approach?'

Sir John shrugged, a sly glance at his brother. 'My eye has settled on many. But none that I would consider for marriage.'

I would get no sense there. 'I have no wish to hear of your salacious affairs.'

'No, mother, I will not burden you with them, however delightful they are. I will tell you when I have found the lady who will become a Paston bride.'

I opened my mouth to broach a difficult issue with him but, catching a frown directed at me from Jonty, I closed it again. I had heard things not to my eldest son's honour but must accept that he would brook no criticism from his mother. I must accept that I could control Caister Castle, but not my son. Instead, to fill the little hiatus, I looked towards Jonty who was still standing at my side.

'I hear your name connected with a Mistress Boleyn.'

Jonty's handsome face with its straight nose and well-marked brows twisted in brief dissatisfaction, before settling again into good humour.

'Alice Boleyn,' he agreed. 'I had hopes of a match.'

'Why did you not tell me? Is it too much to ask that my son, seeking a wife, will inform me of it?'

'Because nothing came of it,' he replied as smoothly as the lawyer that he was. 'She is the youngest daughter of Sir Geoffrey Boleyn. Her widowed mother seemed not to oppose it. I met her at Court, but I was not encouraged in the end.' He did not seem too concerned. 'My birth is not good enough for a Boleyn, although why I cannot imagine. Sir Geoffrey was a hat merchant, knighted by King Henry and then became Lord Mayor of London. Is that better than being a Paston? I think not.' He shrugged much like his brother had done, like his father had been wont to do. 'There are plenty of other heiresses in the pond when I wish to cast in my fishing line. A Paston will not be held back by aristocratic superiority.'

He was so confident. I suddenly felt a portent of nothing holding Jonty back.

'Have you yet arranged a marriage for Margery?' he asked.

'Not yet.'

I would not tell them of my discomfort over Margery's apparent closeness with Richard Calle. Nothing inappropriate on her part, or on his, for that matter. Merely an occasional meeting of eyes, a bright colour in her face when he praised her ability to complete some domestic task with skilfull competence. I hoped that it was an infatuation on her part and that he would have the sense not to encourage her, but unless I sent her to stay with Mistress Agnes or with Eliza, their paths would cross a multitude of times during each day. He was old enough to know better, and indeed I had no intimation that he was encouraging her. He was a capable man, and I did not want to lose him. I pushed the thought aside. I expected that my anxieties over Margery would all come to nothing and that she would, in the fullness of time, marry well.

Directing my thoughts back to the present, I beckoned to Jonty. 'I think Sir Geoffrey Boleyn might be persuaded to see you in a different light, if you are determined on winning Mistress Boleyn as your wife. Come with me. Both of you.'

I led them to the pile of rent returns and manorial agreements that I had abandoned, handing them the recently unearthed document with the royal seal.

'I think that you should read this before you go to Bruges in the royal sister's train.'

Sir John showed his usual reluctance with a yawn of pure Court affectation, so much that I could slap him for lack of courtesy.

'Not more official documents.'

'You will enjoy this one. Your father and I worked hard to achieve it. I had forgotten about it. My only regret is that he did not live to see its fulfilment. But you will enjoy the fruits thereof.'

'Do I see a royal seal?' Jonty was opening it up.

Now Sir John was interested.

'Look for yourselves.'

Sir John moved to sit across from me at the table, Jonty leaning over his shoulder. King Edward in his wisdom, a handful of days after John's death, had sent out a proclamation, signed with the royal name. Sir John smiled with just a touch of old grievances. I knew that he would enjoy the opening statement, appertaining to the son and heir who was not always fortunate in having his father's blessing.

My eldest son read it aloud.

'Our trusty and well-beloved knight Sir John Paston …'

Such a regal commendation. We were cleared of all charges of being bondsmen. My husband John and his brothers were gentlemen descended in true line of worshipful blood since the Conquest. The King himself had issued a certificate to prove the line of pedigree that John and I had concocted together in the Fleet Prison.

'I did not know of this,' Sir John said, re-reading the King's proclamation, silently now and with care. 'We were never bondsmen, and we seem to have evidence and court rolls to prove it.'

'Your father was a careful man in keeping such evidence safe.'

★

The Paston family has long enjoyed appurtenances of lordship. They have held bondsmen of their own for many generations. They have licence to employ their own chaplain and hold divine service. They have endowed religious houses. They have enjoyed the privileges of homage, wardship, marriage and relief. They have married into the nobility. All lands with goods and chattels inherited from Sir John Fastolf are theirs to hold. Paston neighbours are advised to be friendly and neighbourly to Sir John in his right of ownership.

★

'It will be the first time ever for some of our neighbours,' Jonty remarked. 'So we have a certificate in the King's name, acknowledging our Paston forebear Wulstan de Paston.'

'We do.'

Every bit of it was false. Jonty began to laugh, his eye fixing on mine.

'A miracle. Is it true? I have never heard of Wulstan de Paston. And neither, I swear, had our father.'

'And why should it not be true?' I would admit to nothing, certainly not to my sons. John's imaginative attempts, with my help, in drawing our family pedigree had paid off after all. 'We have expunged the serf-like skeleton from the family coffers,' was all I said. 'We are not the first family to do so. Nor will we be the last. Why indeed should it not be true? We have the King's seal to proclaim it.'

'Does this recognition guarantee our ownership of Caister?' Jonty, always cynical, asked.

'So it would seem,' I said.

'I'll not believe it until I see a document stating the fact.'

Yet Jonty shouted for Master Calle to bring more wine. And when he did:

'Let us raise a toast to the Paston family.'

And so we did, Richard Calle invited to join us. The Pastons were descended in unbroken line from Wulstan de Paston, a close companion of the Conqueror, giving him much military support in the Norman invasion and so reaping the benefits in land and status, all drawn in an antique hand in an impressive document. Not a mention of bondsmen or serfdom anywhere.

'Truly a masterpiece,' Jonty declared, restored to good humour. 'I espy your hand here, mother, as well as my father's, but nothing more will be said of that. Let us drink again to the most superior Paston family.'

Which we did.

I wished with all my heart that John Paston, gentleman, had been there to drink with us. I drank the toast with fervour and looked ahead to the fortunes of my sons and daughters. And since I was feeling benign:

'Take some of the Fastolf wealth with you when you go to Bruges.' I took the leather pouch from a locked coffer on the table, opened the drawstring and spread the gems on the table before them. The valuable stones gleamed and glinted in the sunlight. 'You will need to make a good impression, after all, descended as you now can prove from Wulstan de Paston. But take care of them and bring them home safely.'

I watched their choice with interest. I knew which I expected them to take. Would they prove me right? And no, I was not disappointed. Sir John selected a large diamond set into the petals of an enamelled white rose, once pledged to Fastolf by the then Duke of York for a loan of six hundred marks. It would make a strong statement of loyalty to wear such a costly emblem on the brim of his hat. Jonty picked up a brooch in the shape of a falcon in gold and white enamel. They were both good items.

And then Sir John selected another.

'I will take this, too.'

'It is a brooch such as a lady might wear,' I observed.

It was a small object, made of gold delicately carved in the shape of a battlemented tower, the whole enhanced with a pointed diamond, a ruby and three pearls. It was an attractive adornment, suitable for a betrothal.

'So it is. And I might find a lady who would be gratified to wear it.'

I hoped that he would consider carefully before offering so important a gift, which might be interpreted as an offer of marriage in itself, but I made no reply. I hoped that he would not give it to the woman whose name I had heard linked with his.

★

The mood took me to Bromholm Priory, with a need to pay my respects to John.

My first reaction was one of displeasure, which built inappropriately to fury, as I stood before his grave. We had spent so much time and money giving John a funeral worthy of his position in Norfolk society, yet here there was still not one stone erected to mark his final resting place with any degree of dignity. There was still no name there, no record of the lineage of the man John had been. The cloth that lay over the grave was torn and unclean with clear signs of rot along the edges. I tried not to feel resentful against Sir John who had been given the task of creating a lasting memorial. He had had two years to make good our plans.

I should not have been surprised. Obligation did not bind him hard unless there was immediate benefit for him. Or unless it required him to dress in armour and take flamboyantly to his horse in a tournament.

I stood at the foot of the grave and bowed my head as any dutiful widow would do.

'My dearest John …'

Forgive me for this neglect, this lack of respect, I thought, but that was not why I was here.

'I am here to tell you that your sons and I continue your work to plant the Paston feet deep in Norfolk soil with all due honour. You will be more than pleased with this great victory. The King has put his royal seal on your ancestor Wulstan de Paston. Your family were never bondsmen.'

All was silent around me, but I could imagine John now listening intently. Images of him sprang into my mind in a colourful procession. John with a pen in his hand, his shoulders rounded as he pored over some close-written document. John, his eyes bright with victory when he declaimed the content of Sir John Fastolf's new will. John sitting morose and irritable in the Fleet Prison, eager for release, intent on bringing me and our sons to task for what he perceived as sins in the management of our manors. John in his moments of tenderness when he was happy that he had wed the Mautby heiress.

In that moment he was so close to me, standing across the grave, smiling at me. But I knew that he was not. I cleared my throat and continued with what I wanted to tell him.

'Your two sons, Sir John and Jonty, enjoy preference at Court and are invited to be part of the Lady Margaret's entourage when she weds the Duke of Burgundy. You should be proud of them. I apologise for Sir John's neglect of your tomb and will have it put right. He will make excuses but it will be done so that no man walking here will forget the work of John Paston, gentleman.'

What would he want to hear?

'We are treated with utmost respect in Norwich. Your mother Mistress Agnes continues in robust and argumentative

414

health. None of our children are wed, but I will not neglect this. Edmund's legal training is complete, but he needs an honourable and remunerative position with some great lord. Sir John must arrange it. Walter expresses a desire to become a soldier. Willem is still in schooling. I hope that Sir John can be persuaded to pay his fees. Richard Calle remains an exemplary bailiff.'

How often had I implied criticism of Sir John in my report? I tried to think of something praiseworthy but I could not.

'Your brothers William and Clement and sister Eliza prosper although Eliza is beset with inheritance problems for her son. It seems that Pastons are bedevilled with them.'

That was all. Had I no more to say?

'It was not always easy, but I regret nothing of our life together, John. I cannot regret that I was your heiress, to bring you good fortune.'

And then, because I could speak of it to no other, and Jonty had stopped me from airing it aloud, I blurted out the truth: 'Your heir has a mistress. She is called Constance Reynforth. They have a daughter together called Constance. I doubt he means to wed her. I do not know what to do. There is nothing I can do. I have not broached it with him. Perhaps I am a coward.'

The silence weighed heavily. I could imagine John scowling, but that was no help to me.

'What was it that the anchorite in Norwich said? Dame Julian? All shall be well, and all shall be well and all manner of thing shall be well. Something along those lines to lift the spirit in the bad times. I will hold to her belief, although what a nun would know about it, locked away from the world, I know not. She might be a holy person with an insight into God's will for us, but has she ever had to struggle with the Duke of Suffolk who will grab a parcel of land as soon as her back is turned? Even so, I believe that you can now rest without fear that this will be the pattern for the future and Caister is indisputably ours.'

I twitched the sad remnant of cloth into position. I really must do something about it.

'I will see that this is put right.'

What I did not say. That Dedham and Drayton were gone. Cotton a prize handed to the Dowager Duchess of Suffolk. Hellesdon destroyed. Caister under armed guard with our title not yet fully and legally secure. The matter of the Fastolf college, which John had fought for so assiduously, was still not yet set up as Fastolf would have wished. Could anything be reclaimed from Fastolf's will? Sir John was hopeful but I held out no prospect of it. What I did say, in the end:

'I loved you, John. I still love you. You have a place in my heart and will never be dislodged. Your loss overshadows me, and will do until the end of my days. I know that you loved me. I could not always compete with a legal claim in the courts, but I know that you loved me too.'

Chapter Twenty-Two

Anne Haute

Calais: early autumn 1468

We joined hands, man and woman in an alternate joining, to dance the carole, a simple dance, elegant when done well. A dance that everyone knew, beginning with a step with the left foot, the right following to strike gently against the left. No great skill was needed, merely some semblance of grace. Nor did we need the services of the minstrels. The music was begun by one of the dancing women who was known to be fine-voiced.

'You do not go the way I do, nor would you go that way.'

I did not know the words, which were repeated as we stepped, but the tune was well-known to me. Another singer, one of the gentlemen, picked up a different refrain.

'Love me, my sweet blonde, love me, and I shall not love anyone but you.'

The circle continued with a swish of damask and velvet against the painted tiles, the slide of soft leather. I knew that it would last as long as we had the mind for it, dancers leaving and joining as the mood took us.

'Reverse and sing!'

We changed direction in the dance, with much laughter as some were caught out in the simple step, then settled to the old rhythm as we sang the familiar chorus.

I was happier than I had been for some months in that autumn of the year 1468, four years after my cousin was crowned Queen of England, when I visited the English town and fortress of Calais. My family had a strong connection with Calais, and I was pleased to be invited to spread my clipped wings a little. My father had been, in his youth, one of the retinue of Sir John Stuard, the Captain of the Rysbanck Tower in Calais. It was while there that he had met and made an agreement with Richard Woodville, the then newly appointed lieutenant of Calais, that my father would enter into a marriage with his younger daughter Joan, my mother. The marriage, my father's second, happened in Calais.

We had lived there as a growing family until my father returned to England to become a member of parliament, and thus we had many acquaintances, enough to enjoy gatherings in the accommodations of the English garrison. There was dancing, the minstrels played well with verve and not a little skill, the hunting was good. There were masques and light-hearted mummery. To my pleasure my company was often sought and Meg was an easy chaperone when I could escape my brother Richard's eye.

A new voice took up a new refrain.

'If I have great joy in my heart, do not ask whence it comes! That I love with all my heart, you know full well.'

It was a man with a strong voice and a sense of timing, but a man I could not see until the sinuous line of dancers turned in on itself. And then I saw. It had been four years, and our acquaintance of the most inconsequential, and yet there was something about the figure and face that caught at a memory of Cousin Elizabeth's coronation. Those four years had added a gloss to his figure and character to his face. His dark hair, what I could see of it beneath the velvet cap with the sweeping feather, was cut short around his ears. He was as extravagant as I recalled, his doublet short, his hose smooth-fitting, exhibiting an excellent figure. His dark eyes flashed, only rivalled by his jewelled fingers.

Did he notice me? I did not think so. His whole attention was on the words he sang and the attractive woman whose hand he held on his left. But was I certain? Four years was a long time in which to nurture a brief memory.

'Who is that?' I asked my carole-partner on my right, nodding across. 'The man who is singing.'

He followed my gaze.

'That is Sir John Paston. He is proving to be a very popular visitor here.'

'So I see.' He was smiling down into his partner's eyes. I had not been mistaken.

'Do you know him?'

'We have met briefly, some years ago,' I admitted. 'He seemed a familiar face.'

'Young women tend not to forget him, it seems.' My partner, whose name I could not even recall, had a wry smile, as if he suffered no such attacks on his privacy. 'You will have seen him at Court if you visited your cousins there.'

'That will be it.' I concentrated once more on the steps as we turned and turned about, unsure of my interest after so long, but my informant wished to say more. I thought that he sneered a little.

'A Norfolk parvenu from a family with visions of

grandeur.' A denigration that I had heard before from Cousin Anthony. Clearly the Pastons were still looked down upon in numerous circles. 'But he is making a name for himself, if only in the courts when fighting off those who would steal his land from him.'

Again much as I had learned from Anthony Woodville. It seemed that Sir John Paston's reputation had received little polish over the four years. But now I knew that he could sing, and had sufficient income to buy red shoes with extravagant toes.

We reversed our circling once more, Sir John passing the singing to the lady on his left, my partner whispering for my edification.

'I believe that he came into his inheritance two years ago when his father died suddenly. Worn out with legal wrangling and visits to the Fleet Prison, so they say.'

I smiled at him.

'You know much of our singer, for a man whom you profess to despise.'

His hand gripped mine conspiratorially.

'I do not despise him, mistress, more than I despise any mushroom emerging from the dark of the Norfolk soil. His great-grandfather was a serf. His grandfather was a Justice who used his power to feather his family's nest. No estate was free of his sharp eyes. His father followed in his family's footsteps. Sir John is definitely in the same mould. He is the man who is making a claim, possibly fraudulent, for Caister Castle. It is well-known. It has been dubbed the War of Fastolf's Will. There has been a clash of arms already over some of the manors.'

So it was all true. 'Thank you.' I smiled, and turned the

conversation to the limitations of the present singer who could not hold a tune.

But not before my partner had said, 'He is still unwed, but if you were thinking of catching him in your toils, Mistress Haute, I fear that you will be disappointed.'

I allowed my brows to rise delicately.

'Toils, sir? I have none. I have no present designs for a husband, Sir John or any other man.'

'Does not every lady desire a husband? Sir John has no intention of being caught. He enjoys women's company, but without any chains attached. Unless she is a lady with a fortune in the family coffers for her dower, or a vast range of estates for him to inherit. It is understood that he keeps a mistress by whom he has a daughter.'

An opinion which might well quell any interest I might have. Did it pique my interest? An attractive man, a flirtatious man. What would my family think of such a match, with a man engaged in constant battle for his inheritance? I could imagine Richard's trenchant opinions on the matter and chided myself for even thinking of marriage when we had never exchanged a word beyond a greeting and a superficial invitation to watch a tournament.

That you even notice him is a level of your desperation to attract a husband.

It was the one thought that came into my mind and could not be dislodged. How much truth there was in such an observation I did not wish to consider. Dancing complete, I sought out my brother Richard who was in conversation with old acquaintances in the garrison, discussing with some fervour the present uneasy situation in England and the merits of one sword against another, that of King Edward or the Earl of Warwick.

'I need you, Richard.'

'To what purpose?'

'Introduce me to Sir John Paston.'

'Why?'

'He is an interesting man. I met him at Elizabeth's coronation, and we must do something at this interminable event.'

I had no more inclination than that, to pass a few hours with a man who was confident and comely, who could sing and who had a reputation.

'Come then, but take care to act with discretion. Meg had better come, too.'

'Safety in numbers?' I murmured.

'If you wish. I detect a gleam in your eye.'

'I need a gleam in my eye if I am to attract a husband.'

'I doubt this will be the man.'

Thus once again I was introduced.

'Sir John Paston. My sisters, Mistress Anne Haute and Mistress Margaret Haute.'

Did he remember me? He bowed. It was abundantly clear that he did not as his eye travelled over me, and Meg, too.

'I am gratified,' he said, hand courteously on heart.

'We have met before, sir,' I said with a dulcet smile.

There was not even a flicker of discomfiture. 'I am certain that we have not, mistress. How could I forget a lady of such style and elegance?'

He certainly had the wit to respond in flattering manner. Even if he was now uncertain, he covered it magnificently.

'Queen Elizabeth's coronation,' I announced, my smile becoming brighter.

'Then I can only give the crowds as my excuse for my

lamentable memory. I did not see you there amongst so many who were invited.'

No, he had no interest in me. Then or now. I could almost sense his gaze moving away, perhaps to the lady who had accompanied him in the carole and who could not sing. I gave Richard a tiny nudge with my elbow. The twist of my brother's lips became sly.

'We were there because of a family connection,' he explained ingenuously. 'Mistress Anne is cousin to Queen Elizabeth. As are we all in the Haute family.'

'Indeed?'

Did his eyes sharpen? I could swear that they did. Sir John bowed, took my hand lightly in his and kissed my fingers. He might be bred up from the soil of Norfolk but he had learned the manners of the courtier.

'I regret my lax recognition, Mistress Anne, and ask your pardon. Maybe you will allow me to remedy it. I believe they are starting another carole. Will you partner me?'

'I will be pleased to do so.'

My hand rested in his as we joined in the constantly moving chain of dancers. He did not sing. Nor did we converse, but I sensed his glance more than once fixed on my face. I thought that he would not forget me again. What would be the outcome? I had no idea. I did not yet know what I wanted. I had ambitions, but would this man allow me to fulfil them?

★

A tournament was fought by the knights and their entourages on the flat space reclaimed from the tidal marshes beyond the town walls and the double moat, at which I was a spectator. I would not normally have accompanied brother Richard, but on this occasion I had an incentive, despite the flies and midges that plagued us from the noisome morass on all sides.

Sir John Paston would fight.

'Don't expect so momentous an occasion as the tournament at Smithfield last year, Anne,' Richard warned.

'How could I? I was not invited to attend.' I felt a touch of petulance, and did nothing to disguise it. 'I did think that Cousin Elizabeth might have remembered me.'

'Cousin Elizabeth has more important affairs on her mind.'

Cousin Anthony had engaged in a formidable joust at Smithfield, so I had learned from family chatter. He and his entourage, clad in cloth of gold, their horses too, had fought with the illustrious Bastard of Burgundy in a memorable encounter over two days, until King Edward had stopped the contest in fear that the two would kill each other, so evenly matched were they. Cousin Anthony had worn a gold collar fastened around his thigh, a marvellous sight that had added glamour to the event. No, I had not been there although wished that I had.

'This will be a light-weight affair,' Richard said, 'but entertaining enough. You can always leave before the end. I doubt they will fight to the death. It is too hot to use so much energy.'

'Why are you not fighting?' I asked, all innocence.

'I am no jouster. Now, if you have come here to watch Paston, here he comes. Let us hope he is not unhorsed in the first event.'

And there he was, clapping a helm to his head, making a better display than he had at Westminster. His horse was a fine jousting animal, unlikely to become lame in the first pass, and his armour of good quality with an incised pattern to glitter as it caught the sun. Sir John Paston intended to catch the eye. He sat his mount with panache and launched himself into the mock battles with all the energy that Richard had denied. I did not expect any deaths but it gave a frisson to the encounter in which two teams pitted their skills. They began with lances, progressed with swords, then changed to the brutal force of axes.

I knew nothing of the niceties of the chivalric world of the tournament field. There was much battering and foul language as men were unhorsed or beaten to the ground. A rank stench of dust and sweat and horseflesh engulfed us. At the end there was much drinking of ale and rousing cheers from the victors, ribald jests from the defeated.

Did I learn anything of my quarry as I beat away the flying pests, pulling my veil over my face? He was much improved for the four years at Court. He fought with a flourish. He was not unhorsed. He was fair and generous to those he overcame. When he finally removed his helm again, his dark hair plastered to his skull, his face begrimed, he was still not uncomely to my eye.

'Was it worth an hour or two of your time?' Richard asked.

'Yes. I think it was.'

This time I stayed until the end. I was twenty-four years old and the time to catch a husband was fast running out.

★

'Mistress Haute. Perhaps you will walk with me on the wall-walk where it may be possible to pick up a breeze from the sea.'

Sir John Paston was much scrubbed and well presented since I had last seen him on the tournament field. The brim of his felt cap was adorned with an enamelled white rose, the large diamond at its centre flaring in the light.

'It will be my pleasure, Sir John.'

He sought me out and I was willing to be the subject of all such invitations from this ambitious lawyer. Those few scant weeks in Calais had awakened my senses to what was possible for the future if I could escape from Kent. Or, truth to tell, Sir John Paston urged my senses into life. Apart from frequenting the wall-walk on the pretext of discovering some movement of air, we conversed, we danced, we rode with the hunt. How much I discovered about him in those days, for he talked much of himself. He told me of his desire to take back the estates that he had lost in Norfolk. He told me of his delight in Caister Castle and his hatred for those who would make of him a pauper. He told me little of his family, all about his own ambitions. I was pleased to allow it. Encourage a man to talk and he will seek your companionship.

How much of his interest was centred in my cousinship to the Queen?

I was sufficiently sceptical to admit that it had a great bearing. If I had been simply Mistress Haute of some small manor that he had no knowledge of in Kent, with no dower of any note, his feet would not have found their way in my direction.

But he was not an unattractive companion.

'Are you so beset with problems?' I asked after a half hour of detailed Paston inheritance issues. I had become a marvellous listener.

'Can you win no support from the King in your dispute?' I asked as he paused for breath in his description of Caister Castle. 'Will none of the local magnates stand surety for you?'

Sir John leaned against a parapet, brooding over the inequalities in his situation. 'The King chooses his own interests first. He has his own battle to win against Warwick and Clarence. As for the local magnates, I suspect the Duke of Norfolk has his own desire to occupy Caister. The die is stacked against me, but I will have victory. I will not be unhorsed at the first pass!'

Again that wry cast to his features, not quite a smile but not a grimace. I began to glance around. This was poor stuff for a lady to hear.

'I need a sponsor at court,' he continued, still not noticing my growing boredom, 'who can guarantee the ear of King Edward. It is almost ten years since Fastolf's death and still we cannot call it our own, despite King Edward's recognition of our legal right to Caister. We thought it all settled, but every time my back is turned, a new claim is made against me, and the King vacillates.'

I stifled a yawn with an elegant turn of my wrist.

'I have hopes of being at Court in my cousin the Queen's household before winter sets in,' I announced, even though no such invitation had been offered, nor was there likely to be one. If the Queen had not remembered me in three years, what would remind her now?

Sir John focused on me, a keen glance of reassessment, just as I had intended. Perhaps at last he had realised my lack of attention. In that moment he switched effortlessly into a mood of levity and instant charm. He had indeed learned his courtly lessons well.

'Forgive me for neglecting you, Mistress Anne. You deserve a better companion than a man buried in a mire of land disputes. And will the Queen invite you?' he asked.

'I believe so. I expressed my wish to serve her.'

'If that were three years ago, I would not hold out hope.' His brutal cynicism hurt.

427

'She is my cousin.'

'And she is the Queen with much to occupy her in these troubled times. I think you must resign yourself to disappointment. Are we not a matched pair in this? I will never win the King's benign blessing on my inheritance; you will never grace the Royal Court.'

I would not accept it. 'When I take my place in the Queen's household, I will remind you of this conversation. I have very lively hopes that it will come to pass. Lord Scales will put in a good word for me.'

His glance slid to mine. 'Of course, Scales is your cousin too. Perhaps you are right in having high hopes. I am sure that Sir Anthony can be most persuasive. He is as eloquent with his tongue as he is lethal with a sword and lance on the tournament field.'

He made a flamboyant pass with an imaginary sword as if to cut down an opponent, then, smiling, he took my hand, tucking it within the crook of his arm to lead me along the walk, Paston inheritance pushed firmly onto a shelf, along with my Court ambitions. Our questioning progressed along more personal lines.

Did I have a betrothed? No, I did not. Did he? I was certain that he did not. Was there a lady preferred by his family perhaps? No, there was not. Were there family negotiations for my own marriage? None at all. We had reached the end of the wall-walk, where the steps led down into the courtyard.

'Why are you here in Calais, Sir John?' I asked before we could part. 'If Caister is so important to you, why leave it to your brother to shoulder the burden? What are you doing here?'

'We were both part of the entourage of the Lady Margaret, the King's sister, when she wed Duke Charles. My brother Jonty has travelled home but I decided to stay on here.'

'And why have you stayed here?' I could not resist asking.

'To make your acquaintance, of course, Mistress Anne.'

'But you did not know I was here when you made your choice. You did not even recognise me.'

'But now I do. I must have had a presentiment of how valuable – and pleasurable – remaining in Calais would be for me.'

Spoken in all seriousness. He had a tongue like the snake in the Garden of Eden, full of persuasion.

'Does your family not miss you, when you are away from home for so long? Would your mother not wish to see you?'

'My mother would miss the loss of one of her prize manors more than she would miss me. We do not all have close and affectionate families, although my mother has much goodwill towards me, which was lacking in my father.' He rapidly changed the subject. 'Will you walk with me tomorrow after Mass, Mistress Haute? When the sun has risen over the castle? I promise not to bore you to distraction with tales of Caister Castle. Instead I will sing praises to your beauty that rivals that of these glorious roses.'

Leaning, he plucked one and handed it to me with a little bow. How could I resist?

By now I would very much like to see Caister Castle for myself.

★

My brother Richard was sceptical. And highly critical as we prepared to attend Mass.

'What are you doing, Anne?'

'I am merely passing the time with a pleasant companion.'

'Paston has his mind set on preserving his inheritance, as you well know. Do not expect much from him, unless he thinks that you will come as a well-dowered wife.' He caught hold of my hand before I could escape his lecturing, so sharply that I dropped my missal. 'I hope you have not given him any grounds to believe so, Anne. Your dower will not keep him in expensive shoes.'

Richard picked the little book up for me, dusting the leather cover before handing it back.

'Who is to say that he sees me as a wife?'

'If not, why does he seek you out? I can give you one answer.'

I bestowed a gentle smile on him. 'He values my modesty, if that is what you implied by such an oblique comment.'

'That is not what I meant,' he responded crossly. 'If he needs a mistress there are plenty in the stews of Calais frequented by the soldiery. I have no doubt of your modesty, madam sister. I swear I should forbid you to meet with him.'

'Do not be foolish, Richard.'

'I am informed that he has a mistress in England.'

'Then he will have no interest in me.'

Our exchange was becoming a familiar clash of will.

'Should I be gratified? His interest in you is clearly because your cousin is Queen of England.'

'Do you then forbid me to keep company with him?' My stare was a challenge.

'I would if I thought you would be obedient. I would have to lock you up.'

'Which you would not do.'

'Or send you back to England.'

'We will be returning soon enough,' I said with a little jolt of dissatisfaction. 'Do not curtail my pleasure now.'

Briefly I read compassion in my brother's face for he knew well the life I led, but I would not acknowledge to him my regrets that there was no marriage settlement yet negotiated for me. It was not news to me that Sir John Paston kept a mistress. I was not without ability in summing up a man's interest. He might be distrustfully ambitious but he was handsome, he could be charming, he could be gifted in conversation when he set his mind to it. I woke each day in a keen anticipation that I would see him, and if he wished to walk in the garden with me, then I would be willing to do so.

I was destined to be disappointed.

Sir John Paston broke our arrangement even though, after Mass, I was waiting for him in the shadow of an espaliered pear tree. He appeared at the head of the flight of stone steps when his attention was caught. A servant approached and handed him what looked like a letter. Sir John thanked him with a coin, then spread out the sheet. I watched as he read it through, interested merely to observe him before our meeting. I thought that he read it through twice, his head bent, then looked ahead as if in deep thought.

Could he see me? I thought not. If he could, I was in that moment of no importance to him. The expression on his face was not one of pleasure at meeting with me. He tore the letter into small pieces and scattered them, then turned on his heel and disappeared from my view.

I did not attempt to discover them and piece them together, as another slighted woman might have done. I considered it but, when I sought for them, the pieces were long scattered into the shrubbery with a frisky breeze, or too small to give any clue, or I would have given in to temptation. I determined not to even notice that he had rejected a meeting that he had arranged with me.

I wondered what he would say when we met again.

I allowed a small brush of anger to spoil my morning, but I did not refuse the second invitation when it came with an apologetic posy of rosebuds that, it was to be admitted, were past their best blooming.

★

On the next clement morning we strolled in the castle garden, sister Meg keeping desultory company for form's sake. Sir John pointed out the views over the town, the planting of herbs, the late-flowering roses, but I was interested in none of them. Nor, I decided, was he. Neither of us made any reference to that broken engagement.

What had disturbed Sir John so greatly? This morning he was unfailingly cheerful and yet there was a tension about him that I could not readily interpret.

'Do you read?' he had asked at last as I considered another subject of brilliant conversation to attract his attention.

'Of course I read. Why?'

'Not every lady is instructed to do so. If I write to you, will you keep it secret? I would not wish for you to show it to your brother to read to you.'

'Certainly not. I will read it myself.'

From the breast of his tunic he plucked a folded page and handed it to me.

'What is it?'

'You must read it to discover. When you are alone.'

'Thank you, Sir John. I will go and do so immediately.'

With a curtsey, I left him, thinking that it would do him no harm to be abandoned so precipitously. I heard his laughter follow me. Back in my chamber with Meg looking over my shoulder I opened the folded sheet. It was a poem.

★

Laughing, flashing eyes whose print I bear
With pleasant memory within my heart,
Remembrance of you so delights my heart.
Unhappy love had killed my life here,
But you new strength to me do impart

★

I was impressed by the sentiment.

'Do you suppose he wrote it himself?' Meg asked.

'Of course not. He has borrowed it from some courtly troubadour.'

'At least he has gone to the trouble of discovering it for you.'

'Sir John Paston is a clever man. Don't tell Richard.'

I was highly pleased, even though he instructed me to burn it, and the rest that followed at regular intervals, thus truly keeping what was between us secret. I did not show them all to Meg, not believing in her discretion.

'Why do we need to keep it secret?' I asked, deciding with complete lack of modesty to ask him outright when we listened to minstrels in the gallery on a wet afternoon, enjoying cups of wine and platters of sweetmeats beneath the tapestries telling the tale of Paris and Helen and the siege of Troy. Helen had a winsome expression, Paris was merely lascivious. Did he send her secret offerings of poetry? I doubted it. 'Are you ashamed of wooing me with minstrel love songs? Or perhaps you are not wooing me at all?' Richard would have been ashamed of me. Meg was out of earshot. I had as little humility as Helen of Troy herself.

433

'Who could feel shame at keeping company with so lovely a lady?'

I noticed that he had not exactly answered my question. Was it or was it not a wooing? I had not burnt them. Did I not treasure them as a promise of what might ensue? Except that there seemed to be no promises, and certainly Sir John had made no attempt to discuss marriage settlements with Richard. I decided that it was much like our cook in Kent wrestling with a newly caught eel.

'Then, if there is no shame, why must I burn such evidence of your regard? Who will object if we find we have a liking for each other? If my family do not, then yours will surely not. My brother finds no fault in my walking with you or treading a measure of a round dance.'

How easy it was to forswear my brother's opinion.

'I have not yet told my family,' Sir John informed me after the slightest pause.

'Why not?' Although why should he? This was probably merely a pleasant interlude for him, of no importance whatsoever to his family.

'What is there to tell?'

Which put me firmly in my place. I had indeed behaved with unfortunate levity. 'Forgive me, I presumed too much.' I tilted my chin. 'I will accept no further poetry from you, Sir John.'

'Then to whom shall I send my poems, if you are unwilling? I swear that I cannot leave them unread. Would your sister enjoy them?'

I had no fears that he would carry out such a threat, but I had no intention of bowing before such blatant dissembling. I stood and turned my back on him, intending to leave him.

He exhaled slowly. 'Forgive me, Mistress Haute. That was

ignoble of me. Here is the situation. My father is dead these two years. My mother is of an interfering cast of mind. Better that she does not know anything of my private affairs.'

It was, I supposed, an apology of sorts.

'I accept your explanation of your mother.' I halted and turned back. 'What about your brother, the lawyer?'

'It is not his affair with whom I spend my time. We will keep it between ourselves, Mistress Haute, and your sister, if it pleases you. If I kiss your hand it is of no interest to any but ourselves.' And he did so. 'If I find you the most attractive lady here in Calais, who will argue with me?' He kept hold of my hand. 'I have men in high places, ready to attack me at the first opportunity, and I'll not advertise my personal preferences. What they don't know won't trouble them.'

'But why would it matter if they knew that we sought each other's company?'

There was again the faintest of hesitations before he replied.

'Because there are the magnates with interests in the counties of Norfolk and Suffolk who would do all they could to stop an alliance between us.'

'Why?'

'Because you are cousin to the Queen.'

There, now. He had said it at last. I let the silence develop a little. My cousinship was then a concern to him, one way or another. I turned to fully look at him.

'An alliance, you say? What is an alliance? Are you talking marriage, Sir John?'

This time it was Sir John Paston who kept the silence.

'Mayhap.'

'Are you wishful of being betrothed to me?'

He smiled at me, kissing my fingers again, then handing me my cup of wine, which gave him enough time to consider exactly what it was that he wanted. Meanwhile the thoughts raced through my own mind. Did I want this man? Did I want this marriage, this wooing? I was no surer of the answer than Sir John.

'I think it would be a marriage of advantage to you,' I suggested. I held his gaze.

'It would. I'll not deny it,' he admitted, cunningly waylaying a platter of candied figs. '*If* I was talking of marriage, Mistress Haute, would you accept?'

I bit gently into a fig, appreciating the soft centre with all its sweetness.

'If you ask me, Sir John, you will discover.'

'Then you must wait and see.'

I decided that he was clever in his seduction. He was careful, he had a stern self-control, he would not be carried away with passion. He would keep me waiting. Indeed I was not sure that he was moved by a passion, despite the emotion of his words. I could not deny that I enjoyed the experience.

'Would your brothers approve?' he asked.

'You must ask them, as any man who seeks a wife must do.'

I would give nothing away.

★

And then it was important that he return to his affairs in England.

'I go as soon as the tide turns,' was the first that I knew about it. He was restless, uneasy, standing in the Great Hall beside his possessions which had all been packed up and awaited transport. It was pure chance that I came across him or he would have gone without my knowledge. Would he have left me a message? I did not think so. Thus I was cool in my farewell, beautifully dismissive, hiding my dismay.

'I suppose that we will miss you, Sir John.'

'Yes.'

He did not seem to notice, so I decided to push the point.

'Was it the letter you received that draws you back to England so suddenly?'

'How did you know about that?'

Which brought his attention back to me.

'I have a keen ear and a sharp eye.'

He grimaced. 'It was a letter from my brother. I did not think it of vital importance so I did not respond, but things it seems have grown worse. He has sent me another letter, almost with the turn of the tide.'

'And this new letter is urgent enough that you must leave precipitately,' I said, still unwilling to unbend.

'It is desperate. The Duke of Norfolk seems to be holding off laying his hands on my castle, but his agents are travelling round my manors, warning my tenants to pay me no rents, threatening to lay hands on them if they do. It behoves me to go home and start recruiting men for my garrison again. I can no longer spend my time in jousting and dancing.' He glanced at me, as if dragging his thoughts back from distant Norfolk. 'Or in conversation with a beautiful lady. Much as I might like to do so.'

At least he had made some semblance of an apology, but nothing to persuade me that I would remain in his memory when he was assessing the value of archers and men at arms.

'We will return, too,' I said. 'We also have stayed here long enough and my brother has business at Ightham manor. He is much engaged in building works there. I swear the number of chambers has doubled while we have been here in Calais. He says that he must inspect them to ensure the building is of a good standard.'

'Will you go home to Kent?' he asked, rather too late for my pleasure.

'Indeed, no.'

He tilted his chin.

'You look inordinately pleased with yourself, Mistress Anne.'

'You are not the only one to receive letters, Sir John. I am invited to join the Queen's ladies.'

Indeed, I too had been the recipient of a long-looked-for letter while in Calais. I had read it, keeping it tucked in my sleeve so that I might re-read it at my leisure. It had taken all of three years for Cousin Elizabeth to remember me. Why had she done so at last? I had no idea, but I would not refuse it.

'When we return to England, will you still seek me out?' I asked.

'I will see you at Court, of that I am certain.'

'Ah, but will you still be interested in – what was it? – an alliance?'

Sir John Paston at last showed his teeth in a smile.

'I might be so. Unless you have been wooed by some great lord. Who knows what will lie in store for you?' He bowed formally. 'Farewell, Mistress Haute. I trust that you destroyed the poems that gave you so much pleasure.'

'Of course. Did you not wish me to do so?'

'I must, perforce.'

His servants were approaching with news of the tide and he turned away as if he could not wait to set sail, as soon as the winds would blow him to the English shore. I did not think that I could trust him. But then, could he trust me?

We had known each other a mere matter of weeks, a pleasant interlude and nothing more.

Did I climb to the wall-walk to watch his ship, sails hoisted, make a fast headway towards England with wind and tides behind it? I might have done so. Or I might not.

Chapter Twenty-Three

Anne Haute

Greenwich: winter 1468

We were established at Greenwich, a palace most favoured by cousin Elizabeth and one that had seen much rebuilding over the years to give a depth of magnificence unknown to me. The well-born ladies, with whom I would share my duties in my service for my cousin, made me welcome without much interest, whereas I was all curiosity. It was a new world to me of endless chambers, painted panels and vivid tapestries large enough to cover a whole wall. During those cold months of winter before the Queen retired into seclusion to prepare for the birth of her third royal child, I slid into my role with the Queen's ladies, a role that was not taxing for she was a tolerant mistress as long as we paid her all the homage due to her as Queen. I knelt before her as often as I knelt for Mass.

During all that time, I did not see Sir John Paston. Perhaps he had returned to Norfolk to oversee his estate affairs. I set myself to dispel despondency at his worthless flirtations. It was not difficult. There was much to do and there had been no substance in his promises. Had they even been promises? Only empty words to fill a moment of restlessness when life in Calais had become tedious. Once I re-read the poems, then consigned them to the flames as he had first asked. What use in hope when there was none?

I discovered a rhyme that was apposite for myself, sung by one of the Queen's minstrels.

★

The world has had enough of me
And I, likewise, enough of it.
Today I know of nothing fit
To make me take it seriously.

★

The ladies sighed in sympathy with the handsome singer. So did I, and wished for better times.

We celebrated the birth of the Christ Child and the New Year when Elizabeth gave slender gold rings to her ladies. King Edward set himself to rejoice with much jollity before the Queen would become enclosed in her private chamber, away from the world of men, to present him with the heir he so desperately needed.

And then Sir John Paston reappeared at Greenwich in the company of Cousin Anthony, Lord Scales, for the Epiphany celebration when there would be feasting and a tournament. There he was, just as I recalled. He strode into the audience chamber with its vaulted roof, brisk and confident, the swagger still evident, bringing with him an air of self-satisfaction, responding with a bow or a quick word to those who welcomed him. Against my better judgement, my attention was arrested and my heart lifted with a quick jolt, a leaf momentarily caught up in a gale, before falling inconsequentially back to the earth.

He bowed to the Queen, exchanged a suitably humble word with King Edward and made a quiet detour around the Dukes of Norfolk and Suffolk where the responses were cool. It was some half hour later before he found his way in my direction where I stood with the knot of the Queen's ladies, carefully ignoring him as seemed the best policy in the circumstances. All was formality since we were not alone, and I had no intention of giving cause for gossip.

'Mistress Haute.'

'Sir John.'

He bowed. I curtsied.

'It is good to make your acquaintance again,' he said.

'Indeed.' I was aware of ears on every side. 'I had quite given up any thought of it, of our paths ever re-crossing, Sir John.'

He was in no manner disturbed by my response.

'I have had much to demand my time in Norfolk.'

'I trust the affairs of Caister Castle continue to develop smoothly for you.'

The ladies drifted away, finding our conversation unedifying. As soon as we were alone:

'I should make my apologies, Mistress Anne.'

'Why would you find a need?' I would not let him off this particular hook. Here was a fine trout for me to play on the line. I was suddenly aware of an ambition to bring it to land.

'I have neglected you.'

'Yes. I would find it impossible not to agree with you.'

'But I have thought of you.'

'Between legal cases, I expect.'

'Indeed.'

I tilted my chin a little as I looked at him through my lashes.

'I had presumed that I had been forgotten.'

His smile was a knowing one.

'That would not be possible, mistress. As I think you are well aware.'

He was as assured as ever, with no sense of guilt. From his sable-edged over-sleeve he took a small leather-wrapped package. Clearly not a poem. Also proof that he had known I would be here, but then Anthony would have told him.

'This is for you.' He held it out. 'It is a symbol of my regard for you, Mistress Haute, and an admission of my neglect. I fear it is a trivial offering, not worthy of your beauty. Nor of the depth of my regard for you. One day I will do better.'

I unwrapped the package, unable to resist. Gloves. An easy gift to give between a man and a woman, signifying little. Had not my brothers given me gloves to mark New Year?

'They are beautiful, Sir John.' I would not be gauche in my acceptance. 'Is there not some other lady in the depths of Norfolk whose hands they would grace more finely than mine?'

'There is none other, Mistress Anne. I lack money for jewels, but I know that these will enhance your elegance.'

Was this an excuse or did he indeed lack money? He was as finely garbed as ever, aping the King himself in the short perfection of his velvet jerkin. There was a fine ruby, catching the light, on the forefinger of his right hand. I could not see the path we were taking with this exchange. Despite my intention to remain supremely impassive, at least on the surface, I was growing impatient.

'Are you so lacking, Sir John? Is not Caister Castle now yours, free from any legal dispute?' I asked. 'Or is the Duke of Norfolk still a threat to you?'

Of course I had made it my business to discover from Anthony, who proved infallibly useful.

'It is still in my possession, mistress, but my legal claim remains in question and there are constant demands on my purse. I do not even have enough ready coin to travel home. Thus I am here at Court during this festive season.'

'To beg the King for help?' I asked. 'Or to pursue your wooing of me, after some hiatus?'

He did not even need to pause to take a breath. 'Both, if you will allow the latter to be equally important to me.'

His face was serious; there was no flirtatiousness now. And yet ...

'If you seek to woo me for my money, Sir John, you will be majorly disappointed, for I have none, and no dowry sufficient to pay for the protection of Caister Castle. I am certain Lord Scales would have informed you of that one unquestionable fact if you had needed to know, which you would if you sought a wife.' How eloquent I was. 'I will be of no value to you in your quest to secure your inheritance.'

'I know nothing of your dower,' Sir John informed me.

If Sir John was honest in his attempts to woo me, he would be as interested in my dower, lowly as it was, as would any man. And surely a man in earnest would seek the support and permission of my brother. I knew that he had not.

'I value you for your own sake, Mistress Anne.' He bowed, an elegant little action.

I stroked the fine leather of the gloves, the gilded stitching, the leaves and feathers that had been embroidered around the cuffs. He still had not asked me if I would wed him. The hints, the mischievous meanderings of Calais, this trivial gift, were not enough for me.

'You once talked of an alliance, Sir John.'

'I recall it well. I did not think that you believed me.'

'You are astute, sir. I did not. Is this pair of gloves, then, a betrothal gift?' I asked.

If the Queen's ladies knew the direction of our exchange they would have returned like a flock of hens when grain was scattered, but if I was attempting to discomfit Sir John, once more I failed. My adversary was a man of devious qualities.

'I have not yet decided, Mistress Anne. Please accept them, for now, as a pretty Epiphany offering.'

'If you wish to wed me, you would have to ask my brother.'

'So I should.'

As enigmatic as ever. His attention was drawn away by another courtier. He bowed and left me with my gift that was, he said, all he could afford. What might be between myself and Sir John Paston was as complex and undecided as it ever had been. It seemed that we would circle in the continuous movement of the carole-dance for ever. Who to speak with but my cousin Elizabeth before her thoughts were taken up completely with the coming child?

'I seek your advice, my lady.'

Next morning the Queen was clothed in loose robes, her hair simply plaited beneath an unadorned veil, without pretension for a morning in her own household. There was no denying the gloss of power that she had acquired, although I could not fail to notice that she looked strained, even as she took care to enhance her appearance with artfully applied cosmetics from an array of small phials. She smiled and beckoned me close, taking her mirror from one of her ladies, waving her away, and handing it to me.

'I am weary and today I am just Elizabeth. Do you suppose I am carrying a son?' She rested her hand, as she often did, on the swell below her robes. 'The King is in desperate need of an heir to replace the rebel Clarence. I have carried two sons for my dead husband. Why should it be so difficult now?'

'We pray for your success,' I said. 'There are ways of determining what the child might be, so my married sisters say.'

'And you will tell me?' She looked askance.

I leaned closer. 'They say that you must take water from a spring. Then three drops of blood from your right side and drop it into the vessel. If the drops fall to the bottom the child is male. If they float on the top, it will be a female.'

'Does it work?'

'So they say.'

'Too much like witchcraft for me. I cannot be too careful. Besides, I will know soon enough now.' She sighed, took the mirror from me and placed it face down. 'What advice can I give you?'

'I seek a betrothal,' I said.

'As I know. To a particular man? I was not aware of an interest, but I have been distracted.'

'A man I met in Calais. A man who has sought my company. He has given me poetry and gloves. He is handsome and charming but ...'

But was he a man whom I could trust? Did I wish to be Dame Paston?

'… and a man I would wish to wed,' I continued. 'I think it to be in his mind that he would wed me. Yet one moment he seems to be about to make an offer of marriage, and the next he steps back as if I am the last woman he would want as his wife.'

'Does your brother not approve of him?'

'He has not yet asked my brother.'

'Would your brother disapprove if he were asked?'

'I think that he would.'

'Is the man so unsuitable?'

I could make a list of Sir John Paston's lack of attributes. And yet I replied:

'To me he might be very suitable.'

The Queen laughed. 'Who is this paragon of virtues, if only in your eyes?'

'Sir John Paston.'

Her brows rose a little. 'We have had dealings with the Paston family over the years. They are engaged in more lawsuits than jewels in my casket. A litigious family, and one beset with those who willingly seek their destruction.' She considered me, lifting the mirror again, holding it up so that I must look into it. 'What do you see?'

I looked, obedient to her directing. An oval face, fair of skin. A straight nose, lips that were ready to curl into a smile, a direct regard from eyes the colour of autumn. My hair was severely confined. I saw nothing of any true merit although no one would ever stigmatise me as uncomely. What should I say to this woman whose beauty shone in a shadowed room?

'Myself. Mistress Anne Haute, unwed and unsought after.'

'You do yourself an injustice, cousin. You know your own

worth. Here is something you should accept, Anne, when you look in my mirror. There are many in the country who will never give their allegiance to the King and his Woodville wife. Equally, there is a queue of nobility hoping for connections with the King, so many who look for an alliance through my Woodville children, through my own brothers and sisters. They are of use to us, and so the King and I have made those strong marriage alliances to tie the nobles to our Court. Are you certain that Sir John Paston does not see you merely as a road to travel to royal patronage? Did I not warn you when you came to my coronation? He would not be the first man. He might not look as high as my sisters, but he might cast more than a glance over a Queen's cousin.'

She smiled, reading the restlessness in my face, placing the mirror down so that neither of us might see our reflections.

'I think it is not an idea that is new to you.'

'No, it is not new.'

And yet I hoped that he had been genuine in his praise. I hoped he enjoyed my face and my conversation more than the fact that I could address the Queen as Cousin Elizabeth.

'He wished for a betrothal before he knew anything of my financial situation,' I said.

'But royal connection is worth far more than a purse of gold.'

'And he has never actually mentioned the word betrothal, except to deny it. Only an alliance. What would that mean?'

'It seems to me that Sir John needs to be pinned to the spot and his intentions demanded. Do you trust him? There are many lords with interests in Norfolk and Suffolk who do not.'

Because I knew that I could in this company, I spoke from the heart. 'Trust? I think he is cunning and wishes to draw me in before making any real commitment himself. It is like standing before a winter fire, when your face might be hot from the flames but your back is cold from the icy blast.'

'It does not sound to me to be a good base for a marriage.'

'And yet I think I will do very well with him. His ambitions will carry him far.' I frowned. 'He might be the best hope that I have to find a husband. He intrigues me.'

Elizabeth laughed, a light resonance that caught the attention of her women, but they kept their distance.

'Anne! You have fallen in love!'

'No.' I shook my head. 'I do not think it is love. I see too many of his faults. Sometimes I do not even like him very much.'

My mind slid over the questions and answers that had lived with me since my visit to Calais. Was it love? No. Not on either side. Attraction. Ambition. Nothing as selfless as love.

'Then what is it?'

'An answer to a prayer perhaps. The thought of being Dame Paston is not unattractive.'

'Love may follow.' And when I looked doubtful: 'I cannot deny it, can I? I know the power of love. So take him if you wish, whether you love him or no. Have your betrothal and your marriage with a Paston.'

I had the Queen's approval. Would she go further than that, to make my marriage even more acceptable? I could only ask, and since she was in a mellow mood, I did so.

'If he does seek me in marriage, and if I accept him, will you give him your support in Norfolk? Will the King? It would go far to easing his troubles.'

'But is that not what he wants you to ask? Is that not your value to him?'

I felt my face flush at this perennial inner dispute, for it could well be true.

'We will have a look at Paston troubles,' Elizabeth promised, touching my hand with the pads of her fingers in rare understanding. 'Make sure that your Paston suitor appreciates what you do for him.'

'I have no doubt that he will. The Fastolf inheritance dominates his whole world.'

I stood to leave her, curtseying low. She gripped my arm to keep me there, uncomfortable though it might be.

'One word of warning, cousin. If Sir John eventually promises marriage in unequivocal terms, be certain that it is more than a promise for the future, or you could be left waiting until old age catches up with you; or until he finds a better-dowered bride. Lure him, Cousin Anne. Entice him. Make yourself an object of interest that he must win, like a knight on a quest in the Court of King Arthur, and you the Holy Grail. Do not sell yourself cheaply.'

'And how do I entice him, my lady?'

'Refuse any valuable gifts. Do not be too readily available if he seeks for you. Bring him to heel like a good hound. On no account warm the sheets of his bed or yours, no matter how keen the desire. Get an oath from him that cannot be broken, and then a marriage. Beware if he becomes too importunate without such an oath. It may be that his legal problems need to be redressed, and he thinks that you can help. Get an oath of intention, cousin. Do you understand me?'

I did indeed.

'I think that it might be excellent strategy,' Cousin Elizabeth continued, 'if you accompany me when I retire for my confinement. If he wants you, your absence will spark his interest. If he does not and he forgets you, you have lost nothing and can emerge with dignity.'

★

I followed the path traced by the Queen. I was endlessly charming, smilingly flirtatious, but lacking in anything more definite than light-hearted companionship. It was not a difficult campaign, and I pursued it with enthusiasm. I was rarely to be found without the company of the Queen's ladies and would not, except with rare deliberation, be extracted from their chattering crowd. Furthermore I expressed my intention of going with the Queen into seclusion, to wait on her, until the birth and the churching. Our conversations were curtailed. There was no offer of marriage. I did not talk of Caister Castle, and neither did he.

'Mistress Haute.'

I had at last deigned to allow a moment's meeting, thinking it prudent or he might leave the Court for good. How formal he was. I was no longer Mistress Anne.

'If it would please you, Mistress Haute. Would you accept this?'

A brooch of gold in the shape of a crenellated fortress with a pointed diamond, a ruby and three pearls. A delightful little confection, and worth a considerable sum of money. Enough to entice any lady.

'It is beautiful,' I said, regarding it as it sat on my palm, twinkling bravely. 'Is this a jeweller's vision of Caister Castle?'

If it was, and he was prepared to give such a jewel to me … But was I reeling in this fine fish, or was he playing me at my own game?

'No. It is a fantasy,' he admitted. 'But it came to me from Sir John Fastolf. I treasure it, and it would please me if you wore it.'

'It is very grand.'

'There are more ostentatious jewels in the legacy. I chose this one for you.'

Had he indeed? If he had not been home during the festivities he must have had it in his personal keeping for some time, so I doubted he had chosen it specifically for me. I smiled. What had prompted him to make me such a gift? Even though my fingers itched to close over it and clasp it tight, I continued to hold it on my open palm, unaccepted between us.

'It is too costly for me, Sir John,' I said gently. 'I could not accept such a gift from a man who is unknown to my family. My brothers would not approve.'

I did not wait to see if he might be disappointed. When he did not take it, I pushed it back into his hand and stepped away as if I would return to my place beside the Queen, until he moved smoothly to stand before me.

'One question, then. Will you wed me, Mistress Haute?'

At last. An offer.

'I will consider it, Sir John.'

I granted him a smile as I returned to the Queen's side. I did not hurry in my making of any decision. It would not harm Sir John Paston to keep him waiting on my pleasure.

Would I accept?

The dilemma troubled my sleep.

Westminster: February 1469

A mere handful of months since we had exchanged conversation in Calais, Sir John Paston and I stood together in a most festive of crowds at Westminster. The Court gleamed and sparkled for this most auspicious occasion, the final event which Queen Elizabeth would attend, before withdrawing to her private accommodations, cushioned from the world by tapestried walls, heavy curtains and closed windows. The King was ebullient with high spirits.

I saw Sir John Paston in the crowd, resplendent in blue with hanging sleeves bordered in embroidered flowers, but made no move towards him. Let him come to me, when he had finished a conversation with a cluster of ladies of the court which was giving birth to much frivolous laughter. I waited. I would not approach, however dilatory he might be. The choice must be his if he wished to win my hand. I applied myself to a conversation with the Queen, my back turned to him. Watching him was too wearing on my patience.

Until there he was, at my side, asking the Queen's permission to talk with me. I stepped aside with him, smiling but giving him no encouragement. I was done with encouragement.

'Will you withdraw with the Queen, Mistress Haute?' Sir John asked.

'That is my plan, Sir John. The Queen needs me.'

'Then we may not meet again for some months,' he said.

'No. I will not be at Court.'

'I will regret your absence.'

'I am certain that you will survive it, Sir John.'

Suddenly there was an urgency about him. 'Have you perhaps come to a decision at last?'

'I have, Sir John.'

'Will you wed me?'

His eyes on mine were searching and I knew that I must wait no longer. I could not continue to play the butterfly or I would lose him.

'If I do, sir, do you offer the gift of the little fortress brooch again?'

It appeared in his hand as if by magic. 'Do I pin it on?'

He made to do so, in the embroidered panel that edged the low neckline of my gown, but hesitated at the last. 'Well, Mistress Haute? Do we seal an agreement in gold and jewels?'

'We do, Sir John.'

Were we not both as self-centred as each other? And yet I felt the heat of victory, that what I had wanted had been achieved. Remembering the royal advice, I suddenly stopped the pinning with my hand on his, eyes downcast in a parody of shy agreement.

'I will agree to an alliance between Haute and Paston, but I would like proof of your regard, Sir John.'

'What more proof, than the beat of my heart? And the gift of diamonds and rubies?'

He still held the jewels in his hand.

'I would most like an exchange of vows. Of our intentions for the future.'

His smile was a little twisted. Would he do it or would he find an excuse?

'You have a legal turn of mind, mistress. I cannot fault you in it. If that is what you desire, to assure you of my honesty, then I will gratify you.'

'Where and when?' I had visions of a moment of privacy with perhaps one of the Queen's ladies as witness.

'Here and now,' he replied promptly.

Which took me aback. Why was it that Sir John had the ability to do so?

'Here?'

A crowd of courtiers. A mass of Woodvilles. The conversation around us had risen to a cacophony of noise as wine was drunk and news exchanged.

'We have enough witnesses, mistress.'

'Are we to shout our vows above the chatter?'

'Only if you wish to.'

I shook my head. 'I would rather it were more private.'

'It will be private between the two of us. But this is where we will exchange the simplest form of words, so that you can doubt me no longer.'

And there it was. We made our private commitment in one of the most sumptuous audience chambers at Westminster, surrounded by courtiers who had no interest in what we did. They did not even hear the words we spoke, but would serve as a multitude of witnesses if we should ever need them. But then, why should we need them? The words of intent were spoken quite clearly between us.

Sir John held my hands lightly in his, the brooch clasped between us.

'Here in this chamber at Westminster in the sight of the King and Queen, if not in their cognisance, I take you for my future wife.'

I copied him.

'Here, in the presence of all the Court, I take you as my future husband.'

That was it. No priest. No family. My brothers would howl at what I had done. And yet I was aware of the heavy word 'future' still hanging there, still not a true assurance.

'Is this a betrothal or a marriage?' I asked, uncertain, even though I knew that this was a legal binding.

'It is both. A statement of our commitment now, and what will be when we discover a priest. You are my betrothed wife in the eyes of God and man. It cannot be put aside, except by God.'

There was no one to congratulate us, no bride gifts, but I would assuredly be Dame Paston.

'Do you take me to your home?' I asked, curious as to what we would do next. 'Do I meet your mother, your family? As you must meet mine.'

'Not yet.' His hands fell away from mine. 'I cannot always be with you. My affairs are too pressing. Remain with the Queen in seclusion and I will come to you when I can. Remember that my heart will always be with you. You are mine, Anne Haute, as I am yours.'

At last he pinned the brooch to my bodice.

I had what I had sought. I had no doubts of his commitment to me as his wife. His farewell salute to my fingers was warm, just the hint of a controlled passion. And I now had a boon to ask of the Queen before the doors closed against her and she withdrew from the world.

★

Secluded from the world with the Queen's confinement, no man was allowed to enter unless he was the Queen's physician. Even the King must wait without, sending in gifts and notes of love. Thus I did not see my betrothed husband or learn of the

456

consequences of our oath. It occupied my thoughts but not to the exclusion of all else. To keep the Queen calm and entertained was not always an easy task, and I had no skill with the lute or singing. We stitched and gossiped and played fox-and-geese while we waited for the heir to make an appearance.

When on one occasion I was released to carry a message for the physician, Sir John Paston was waiting for me at the end of the corridor, leaning against the wall, looking inordinately pleased with himself as he surveyed the fine view over the Thames with the ever-changing pattern of craft going about their own affairs. When he greeted me with kisses to each cheek and then to my lips, I admitted to a joyful surprise and returned his greeting.

'Do I presume that you knew I would be here? Or have you been waiting here in hope for endless days?'

'A gold coin to a physician can have excellent results.' So he had asked for me. 'And here you are. You have my heartfelt thanks, Anne.'

He lifted one hand to his lips, then the other.

'And why is that?'

'King Edward has sent a letter to the Duke of Norfolk, ordering him to put all matters concerning my estates into abeyance until the King himself has considered the matter of the Fastolf inheritance.'

'And will the Duke obey?' I enquired.

'I doubt he will reject a direct order from the King.'

'I know nothing of it,' I said, eyes ingenuously wide.

Which was true enough; I had not known the detail of what might occur. As she had promised, Cousin Elizabeth had taken steps to ease the problems faced by my betrothed.

'What's more, dearest Anne, the Queen has shown interest

in me, and considerable acumen in appreciating the power of women in a household.'

'Indeed?'

'She has written personally to the Duchesses of Suffolk and Norfolk, encouraging them to exert some influence over their menfolk. They should advise their lords to give weight to the King's advice. The Dowager Duchess of Suffolk has offered her gracious goodwill for our marriage and promised not to interfere in Paston dealings. She has agreed to acquire a diplomatic illness if necessary to keep out of events dealing with the Fastolf inheritance. How can the Duchess have been persuaded to step back from her previous hostilities? It beggars belief.' Elizabeth had done far more than she had promised. Sir John was regarding me. 'Did you have anything to do with the Queen's intervention?'

'Not I.' He must value me for my own sake. And yet it would be good that he should know that I had worked on his behalf. 'We merely had a conversation about your plight,' I explained.

He kissed my fingers once more in farewell.

'I see that I have a betrothed worth her weight in gold.'

A betrothed. The word lingered with me as his figure disappeared into the shadows and his feet clattered as he leapt down the stairs in typical exuberance. Betrothed. It seemed that I might yet need a priest to make all well and transform it into a marriage.

Since there was more that I could do for my espoused husband, I set myself to visit my cousin Anthony. After my message for the physician was delivered, I sought him through the rooms where courtiers were most likely to linger and converse. I tried the stables where his horses were kept, the tilt yard, the chambers where courtiers gathered to talk. As a last resort, although I should have made it a first one, I opened the door into the King's library.

There he was, turning the pages of a leather-bound tome. He looked up as I entered, not entirely pleased at being disturbed, then smiled at me.

'Now what will you want with me, cousin?' He closed the book, and I sat opposite him, leaning across the spread of the table. 'I hear you have affianced yourself to Sir John Paston, against my advice, if I recall.'

'I have. And I am here to ask your intervention on his behalf in Norfolk.'

'How could I not guess that you were here on his account. Can he not ask for himself?' He opened the book again at the page where he had kept his finger to mark his progress. 'Why should I bestir myself on his behalf?'

I placed my hand flat over the open page to make him look up.

'Because he is your jousting friend. And because of your most advantageous marriage to Lady Scales, it may well be in your interest to dip a toe, or even a whole foot, into those troubled Norfolk waters.'

Pushing my hand away, once more he closed the book. He rested his chin on his steepled hands, his interest caught.

'You may be well advised to offer Sir John your protection, cousin,' I continued. 'He has need of a sponsor when so many magnates are involved in those counties to snatch up whatever they can get.'

'But why would I bestir myself to sponsor a family of so little merit? Except that he is a good companion to have in a tournament. His swordplay has become worthy of merit.'

'Never mind his swordplay. Who is to know what merit he will achieve with your patronage? Your marriage to the Scales heiress has given you vast estates in Norfolk. Will the Duke of

Norfolk threaten them? It might be good policy to exert your authority there at the expense of the Duke. What better way than by proclaiming yourself protector of the Pastons? The Duke should end his harassment of the tenants of Caister now that your nearest and dearest kinswoman contemplates a marriage with the castle's rightful owner. You will be successful with the King behind you. It will make Norfolk think twice before threatening any of your estates. And Sir John's.'

Anthony considered this, frowning slightly.

'I thought the King had already warned the Duke off.'

'He has, but I suspect the Duke will do as he pleases if the King is preoccupied elsewhere with insurrection in the north. Now you, my very dear Anthony, are a power to be reckoned with.'

'And you are a clever woman, Anne.'

'I think that I might have need to be, if I am to be a Paston wife. I want a castle to my name. Will you do it?'

'I will think about it.' Once more he opened the book, signalling the exchange of views to be almost at an end. 'Will you take this advice? Make sure that he rewards you well.'

★

The world turned. On the twentieth day of March, in the year 1469, the Queen gave birth to her third child. It was not the son and heir she most desired; instead a girl who was named Cecily for her paternal grandmother. Cousin Anthony was as good as his word, if not better, since he had promised so little, becoming sponsor to Sir John, warning off the Duke of Norfolk from forcing Paston tenants at Caister to pay their rents to him.

460

When the Queen had been churched and celebrations were held for her return to Court, after the solemnity of the candles and the Mass we danced the familiar carole-dance, as we had in Calais, joining hands, man and woman in an alternate joining. A step with the left foot, the right following to strike gently against the left, the music carried by one of the dancers rather than the minstrels. It was for me as if time stood still.

'*You do not go the way I do, nor would you go that way.*'

Sir John Paston held my hand and sang:

'*If I have great joy in my heart, do not ask whence it comes! That I love with all my heart, you know full well. Love me, my sweet blonde, love me, and I shall not love anyone but you.*'

I knew that the dance would last as long as we had the mind for it, as long as the mood took us. Would our marriage be the same?

Sir John's hand tightened around mine, so that I was conscious of it as we wove our sinuous way with elegant assurance. It would be like our marriage. A strong connection. A unity. We would proclaim our vows before a priest and live as man and wife. It pleased me; perhaps I did love him after all. I would love him all the more when I had become his wife in the eyes of the world. The crenellations that I still liked to think of as those of Caister Castle with their diamond, ruby and three pearls made a fine show on the dense sable fur at my neck.

When we reversed our steps, I turned my head to smile at Sir John.

Sir John smiled back at me.

'When will we be truly wed? And the whole world know of it?' I asked as another voice took up the refrain.

'When I am certain that Caister is mine for all time. I doubt it will be long now. For now, let us celebrate our betrothal and all the promise of our future together.'

And yet suddenly, in that moment of Sir John's achievements, a deep bell of foreboding tolled beneath my heart, as if to announce a death. Our true marriage seemed as far away as ever.

Chapter Twenty-Four

Elizabeth Paston Poynings

Southwark: late summer 1469

'I wish you were ten years older.'

An opinion I announced to my son Edward when we celebrated the tenth year of his birth and I gave him Robert's sword, and the gloves I had sewn for Robert before he rode off to battle. Gloves he had never worn. They had been returned with some of his belongings in the saddlebags of the grey Grisone, now long dead. The gloves that I had so carefully stitched, and with such hope and prayer. They had never been used as far as I could see. There was no wear on the fingers, no blood to recall that dreadful day at St Albans. I had packed the gloves away for this moment so that the stitchery was still fine, the gilding perfect.

'I soon will be,' Edward said, having a child's imperfect sense of time. The gloves dwarfed his small hands as he pulled them on.

'So you will.'

And I had second thoughts. I was delighted that he was only ten years old. I prayed silently that Edward would never have to wear these gloves in battle, or use the sword with its newly sharpened blade. With animosity rife between the Earl of Warwick and King Edward, only a fool would deny the imminence of more battles, more bloodshed. How could I wish that on my little son?

I kissed his brow until he squirmed away with a laugh and departed carrying his treasure. He was growing tall, a fine boy, all Poynings with his broad brow and sharp cheekbones, except that his hair was darker like mine.

The years following Sir Robert's death were not good for any of us with the Paston name. Our inheritance of Caister Castle continued to be a matter for perennial debate, legal retaliation, and force of arms, the manors inherited from Sir John Fastolf under as much danger as were mine. Was it my brother's time in Fleet Prison, or was it the constant demand on him to protect all he had achieved that had brought him to an unexpected death?

Margaret remained a rock in the Paston households when John died.

I mourned, but thought Margaret fortunate in that, unlike my situation, she had full-grown and capable sons to aid her in the ongoing battle. Sir John might have acquired the reputation as a dilettante, frittering away his time as a courtier, but Jonty was a son to be relied on, with a sword or a pen. John's brothers William and Clement would stand beside Margaret, whatever happened.

They did not stand beside me.

'Do I have a Paston family?' Edward once asked.

'You have a grandmother. You have Paston uncles and cousins. You have a Paston aunt who is a very formidable woman.'

'What does that mean?'

'That she likes to get her own way.'

Edward thought about this.

'Will I ever meet them?'

I made an excuse. I did not know.

'I would like to meet my Paston cousins,' he remarked with all the wistfulness of an only son.

I thought that he was destined to be disappointed.

As for my Poynings family, Edward might thrive, but his inheritance did not.

John Dane and I sat across from each other, as we so often did, regarding documents of ownership and access to rents and produce. On the top was Robert's will with its seal and signature, leaving all to Edward but in my care. All legally binding. There was no question of the right of ownership here. But, suddenly in this time of renewed war and upheaval, with the King himself under threat from the forces of the Earl of Warwick, legal right stood for nothing unless I had a powerful protector.

Which I did not.

I felt exhausted and knew not where to turn.

The death of the Earl of Northumberland at the Battle of Towton had not brought me any security. How many times had John Dane fought our own battles of possession in the courts? John Dane had a list of the court conflicts beneath his hand. We were beleaguered and would seem to be so for ever.

First Eleanor, now widow, who after Towton and the death of her husband promptly sent her people to occupy a handful of the Poynings manors. She did not even do me the courtesy to visit me first. Not that I could blame her. Still, she had destroyed any compassion I might have had towards her widowhood. She was as avaricious as she had ever been.

Then Sir Robert Fiennes, sniffing out a Poynings weakness,

took possession of the remaining Kentish manors, causing great destruction and damage to our tenants, stealing all the revenues and profits, thus depriving me of my legal rights.

That was not all. The Earl of Kent began to nibble at the edges, quick to seize an advantage, without any right to do so, shortly followed by the Earl of Essex.

I felt like a beetle under the eye of a flock of malevolent crows and there was no one to stop them. A widow with a young son and no ear at Court was fair game when the King was too taken up with his own inheritance to come to her aid. Now my stalwart John Dane had been accused of a felony by Fiennes, a despicably false charge, but he risked imprisonment.

'I am so sorry,' I said, 'that your work for me should have brought you to this.' I allowed myself an intimacy and touched his hand with mine. It seemed to be that the litigation had greyed his hair over the years.

'I will be the sorrier.' He could be nothing but mournful. 'I am too old for this. I have no desire to have to fight my way out of the Fleet.'

'There is nothing I can do to help you. I have no influence.'

He paused, then looked at me from under his heavy brows.

'You could look for a wealthy and influential husband with a foothold at Court to take the burden from you, fight for the inheritance, and get me off Fiennes's hook.'

It was not a suggestion I had expected. Nor one that I believed possible.

'Have you the name of such a man?'

'No.'

He almost smiled.

So did I.

'I doubt I would be successful in running one to ground,' I admitted. 'You would not believe the difficulty I had in getting the first one. Who would willingly take on such a troublesome parcel of land?'

Another pause.

'Then ask your family.'

'I swore that I would never ask them again. Not one of them had willingly come to my aid in securing my inheritance.' I had thought about this often, and had never regretted my impetuosity in stepping back from my family.

'But you have two brothers who are not unknown in the legal world. You have two nephews with legal knowledge. And as I see it, Sir John Paston has a strong reputation at Court.'

'Except that the Court is in disarray.'

'I have no better suggestion. Perhaps you should reconsider, mistress.'

I was reluctant, but what alternative did I have? It would be despicable of me to allow my man of business to suffer incarceration due to nothing but malice.

'Then I suppose I must approach them, if only to save your skin, John Dane.'

Who knew whose voice would be loudest at Court? The Earl of Warwick and the royal brother Duke of Clarence had defied the King, Clarence wedding Warwick's daughter, creating a powerful alliance. After Warwick's victory over royal forces at Edgecote, Edward had fallen into Neville hands and was now a prisoner in Warwick's castle at Middleham far to the north. Who was King now? Edward might still have the crown but Warwick pulled the strings and had the old King Henry in his care. There were even rumours that Henry would once more wear the crown.

What hope was there for me to gain royal support, even though Sir Robert had fought and died for the Yorkist cause?

Despite my doubts, I wrote to my nephew Sir John, directing it to the Inns of Court although I had heard that he might still be in Calais. He might be more interested in Court intrigues but we were of the same blood.

★

I need you to intervene with the King on my behalf. I need help now even more than when I had needed a husband. Can you not beg for royal mercy for me before my son is stripped of all his inheritance? My legal man is accused of felony and is threatened with imprisonment. Do you wish your aunt to be similarly accused?

I would be grateful if at least one Paston could come to my aid.

★

I waited for an answer. I think that I was without hope. If Sir John was indeed still in Calais then no reply would be forthcoming. Perhaps I should have written to Jonty instead. When my son reached the age to inherit in his own name I feared that he would be landless and I would have failed in my duty as Robert's executor.

I felt that I had failed all my life.

Chapter Twenty-Five

Margaret Mautby Paston

Norwich: August 1469

It was early morning, but not before the cock started its crowing in the garth and the summer sun was well up with some heat, causing a prickle of perspiration along my hairline as I sat in my chamber before embarking on the tasks of the day. I was tempted to remove my coif but that would not be seemly in a woman of my years. Lethargy tended to take hold these mornings so that I must drive myself to action.

I had no presentiment of any untoward event to stir up the dust in the Paston household. Did I not have enough to concern me in our present dire shortage of money? Sir John's optimism in the influence of Lord Scales and the Queen had been ill-founded and had died a precipitate death. Despite the promises of King Edward and Scales to curb the ambitions of the Duke of Norfolk and his associates, the Duke's shadow continued to dominate our every move, and a persistent fear of retribution still persuaded our tenants to refuse to pay their rents into our coffers. The result was that my household accounts were barely afloat. As for our servants, their pay was severely in arrears. Even Richard Calle had not been paid what was due to him for the whole of the last year. His loyalty was a thing of wonder in the circumstances.

I walked slowly to stare out of the window, mildly cursing the vociferous cockerel with a threat to consign it to the pot, noting that the begrimed glass needed attention. I wrote my name on one of the panes, then scrubbed it out with my thumb, impatient of my frivolity. Perhaps I would go to Mautby for a few weeks. I missed the house with its spacious rooms, the even stairs and painted tiles in the hall. I would like to see that my swans were in good health. Could I not oversee the collection of rents equally well from Mautby as I could here in Norwich? I would not go to Caister. I did not relish Caister with its eternal draughts that made my ageing bones creak. One of my shoulders ached despite the warm weather. I massaged it with my hand to little avail. Perhaps I should leave more of the harrying of our tenants in the hands of Richard Calle.

'Mistress Paston!'

As if summoned by my thought, Master Calle stood at the door to my chamber. When I gave him my attention I saw that his eyes were alive with emotion, his face lined with some new anxiety.

'What has Sir John done now?'

'It's not Sir John, mistress. It's worse than that.'

'How could it be? Sir John is invariably the harbinger of bad news.' But perhaps there was a death in the family. Mistress Agnes, now permanently resident in London with William, was surviving to an impressive old age yet I had had no warning of any untoward infirmity. There was always the pestilence, of course, to snatch up both weak and strong; there were no new outbreaks to my knowledge. A quick stab of fear touched my mind.

'Is there sickness? Is it Walter or Willem?'

'No, no, mistress ...'

'Then just tell me before I expire from a terrible anticipation,' I said, losing patience.

Master Calle beckoned in the messenger who stood in the doorway behind him and now fell to his knees at my feet in a cloud of dust, the aroma of horse and sweat strong. His first words of apology were delivered in a breathless gasp. Which was all the warning I had on that day.

It was not the pestilence. It was war that had arrived, fully formed, fully armed, on our own threshold. With Richard Calle's help I lifted the man up, recognising him as Thomas Stumps, an old soldier lacking a number of fingers from both hands. He was not built for fast riding, nor was he handy on a horse, which immediately awoke my fears even if Richard Calle's announcement had not. Thomas Stumps was part of the garrison at Caister Castle. Jonty, also living at Caister to keep a high Paston profile there, had not had the time to write down his warning before dispatching this unlikely courier. At least Thomas Stumps had been able to wind his reins around his wrists before kicking his horse into a fast gallop.

My breath caught at the implication. I presumed Jonty had needed every able-bodied man he could muster at his side.

'Is it bad?' I demanded.

Thomas puffed out his breath. 'Worse than you could imagine, mistress. We're under attack.'

How many times had I received bad news during my life as a Paston wife? How many times had some dread finger pointed itself at me and the safety of my family? And now this, when I had thought late rents were my worst trouble.

Many would have said that I should have expected it, the country being in a state of flux with no man to wear the crown. Old King Henry was incarcerated in the Tower of London, incapable of ruling even if he had been invited to resume his crown, if rumours were not false. King Edward, our Yorkist hope, was inconceivably in the hands of the Nevilles after the Yorkist defeat in the Battle of Edgecote Field earlier in the year, now kept prisoner far to the north in Middleham castle by the Earl of Warwick who had yet to decide what to do with him. There was a claim on the crown from the royal brother, the Duke of Clarence.

All was in turmoil. No King. No law and order. No hand to curb the greedy nobility.

The great magnates were free to do as they wished in their own localities, mustering their personal bands of soldiers and using them as they saw fit. There was no recourse to the law for us lesser folk when military power ruled supreme. The Pastons could never raise sufficient forces to stand alone and claim victory in a local clash of arms.

'It's the Duke, mistress. The Duke of Norfolk.'

Of course it was, in spite of all we had done to build good relations between Jonty and the Norfolk household. All for nothing. My heart sank.

'In the name of God, Thomas! Tell me what he's done.'

And there it was, spelt out for me. The Duke of Norfolk had sent a force of three thousand men to appear before our castle at Caister, weapons bristling; an array of guns and culverin and archers. There they had set themselves down with many ribald gestures for a long siege.

'And he – the Duke, that is – he says he'll take it, and we can't stop him,' Thomas added at the end.

A siege: our castle was under siege. I discovered that I was gripping hard to the edge of the table, my nails digging into the grain. The sweat along my hairline had dried with the onset of fear. Here was disaster.

I knew why the Duke had dared to do this thing. Jonty's advantageous connection with the Duke of Norfolk had already died a painful death over the contentious issue of Caister Castle. When Sir John refused to hand Caister over to him, on the false grounds that the Duke had legally bought it from the despicable Yelverton, the Duke had simply acted, wasting no time in peaceful negotiations. Yet I looked at the flushed face of Thomas Stumps, still unable to grasp the enormity of it, when I had believed that all had been settled by King Edward's decision in our favour.

But King Edward was no longer at liberty to enforce his decision or to come to our aid.

'Three thousand men,' I repeated, realising in horror that if I had been ensconced in Mautby they would have marched past my door, probably sweeping me up in the same operation if the Duke was feeling vindictive. Even if he had not I would have been well aware of what was afoot.

'Aye, mistress.'

'How many men does my son have, to defend the castle?'

I thought that I knew the answer.

'Twenty-seven, mistress.'

'Blessed Virgin!'

Seeing dismay printed on my face, Thomas Stumps tried to reassure with a futile promise. Could not all women be soothed by kind platitudes?

'No need to fret, mistress. You may be sure that Young Master Jonty will never hand the castle over.'

'Ha!' Twenty-seven men against three thousand? 'Do you take me for a fool, man?' But when he took a step back and flushed an even deeper red in discomfort, I patted his disfigured hand. It was not his fault that he had been sent to deliver this appalling news. 'Is my son supplied for a siege?' I questioned him. I doubted it. They would not have been warned. 'How can they survive such an attack?'

Thomas Stumps's spurious confidence had fast waned in the face of my denial. 'No, mistress. We didn't expect it. It's a chancy business. I see no hope.'

Well, there it was, written large.

'Will you return?'

'If I can get in, mistress. It may be that I cannot, but I'll try the postern gate. Do you have a message for Master Jonty?'

My mind began to work again, breaking free of the panic, my thoughts now running into the usual pattern of plan and discard. The lethargy was a thing of the past. Lack of money would just have to wait, although how we would pay for a siege I could not envisage. I felt strong and resolute in what was demanded of me.

I must write to Sir John immediately. He must drag his mind from his Woodville-connected bride and come home. I could not deal with this alone. Had I not warned him that he should settle his affairs first before leaping into marriage, however prestigious the connection?

Leaving my messenger to recover his breath and his dignity, I directed Richard Calle to go ahead of me and prepare to write a fair hand of my instructions. I could never make more than a poor fist of it, even after all these years. And I? I must remain as stalwart and assured as I always had been. I would continue the struggle to safeguard every acre of Paston property. John would never regret his marriage to the Mautby heiress.

I was sidetracked by a shadow as the sun hid behind a cloud, casting the staircase into sombre hue, a deeper shadow emerging from the newel post where the stairs met the upper landing. For a moment it was as if John himself stood there, waiting for me, to give me some order or complain about the disinterest of his heir in some new acquisition. Or even to give me a quick embrace in passing, promising to take the Caister problem under his own wing.

'Oh, John,' I murmured. 'I am so sorry.'

What I would not give for his presence, his confidence, his blistering tenacity which could be so uncomfortable to live with, his driven nature to let nothing rest to protect his inheritance. It was not my fault but still I felt the need to speak my regrets.

There was silence, except for the dull echo of Master Calle's booted feet below me on the stair and some comment he made to Thomas Stumps. I shook my head, turning to follow them. This was nothing but a false image caused by light and shade, an old trick that, after three years, no longer disturbed me.

We had a siege on our hands. If we lost Caister Castle, all John's efforts to keep it, all the strains on his life and his health that had brought him to an early death, all would be for naught. I would never forgive myself if I let it go. On a practical note, I must be sure to hide Fastolf's jewels that I still kept safe, despite our penury.

But first I must see the disaster for myself.

★

It was difficult to find a vantage point on higher ground at a comfortable distance from Caister, but not impossible. Taking with

475

me a small escort for my protection, I sat my mare, looking across to where the distant keep was shrouded in mist, until a strong ray of sunshine, breaking through, illuminated the whole: the strong walls, the barbican, the glint of the moat, the Paston banner flying bravely over all. What I could also see was the surrounding force. Camped around the castle on three sides I could make out tents and pavilions, lines of horses, the ant-like scurry of soldiers. And there were the banners proclaiming Norfolk's interest.

'I don't suppose the Duke himself will be here,' I said. I scanned the troops, then turned to Thomas Stumps who sat at my side, low in the saddle as if weighed down by foreboding. 'How many men did you say, Tom?'

'Three thousand, mistress.'

'Well, I'm not counting every man at this distance, but I doubt it. Three hundred more like.' Enough to threaten us. There was no way in or out. 'You'll not get in through any postern gate, Tom, so resign yourself to staying with me.'

'One less to fight against the enemy,' he muttered.

A distant explosion of gunpowder made me stiffen, but it was not aimed at us. The puff of smoke was evident from a cannon fired by the attackers.

'Do you suppose it hit the castle wall?' I asked.

'I know not, mistress. But there's a reply. I expect the Duke will be sending reinforcements soon enough.' Master Stumps was particularly lugubrious.

Another shot, another cloud of smoke; a different noise, a different gun.

My heart fell. It might be only three hundred men but it was clear to me that victory for Jonty, incarcerated within, would prove to be impossible without a miracle. Miracles were hard to come by. For some reason my thoughts resurrected the fatal night that Sir John Fastolf died and left us this prize. The night that John extolled the merits of the royal game, a contest to seize power and seek advancement, to look higher than we ever had before. We had tried. We had done all that we could. Now failure was staring us in the face. We had lost the contest unless my sons could find some means of recovery.

I turned my mare towards home, then halted again, looking back. The mist had blown in from the coast to obliterate the view, as if it would pre-empt our loss of the castle.

'How can we possibly resist this?' I asked into the silence, as once I would have asked John. 'How can we possibly repulse three hundred men when all we have is twenty-six at best?'

There was no reply, only a little breeze springing up to whip my veil into knots.

I had no idea what the answer would be.

And afterwards …

All is to be revealed in the second Paston novel which will pursue the family as they continue their search for stability and social aggrandisement as well as keeping hostile hands off Caister Castle.

Margaret Paston holds onto the reins in spite of siege and legal dispute, but also is forced to face domestic tensions. **Margery**, Margaret's daughter, casts all into scandal when she absconds with the family bailiff and, against all opposition, marries him. **Anne**, another daughter, is unhappily married, paying the price of Margery's wilfulness. And then there is **Margery Brews**, providing Jonty Paston with just the wife he has so far failed to find, a true love story. Meanwhile **Elizabeth** continues to fight to preserve her young son's inheritance, taking a most momentous step to strengthen her position. **Anne Haute** ultimately must accept the truth behind Sir John Paston's desire for marriage.

And through this tale, Sir John Paston and Jonty continue their pursuit of power and influence through the courts and even onto the battlefield.

What a gift the Paston Letters have been to us.

Why write a novel about the Paston family?

What appealed to me about the Pastons? The Paston men are interesting characters, but it was the Paston women of the famous letter-writing Norfolk family who intrigued me most. What a remarkable group of women they were, highlighted through their letters, engaging the full range of emotions. It would please me to allow their voices to be heard from distant Norfolk, loud and clear. And what better way to discover the remarkable Paston men than through the eyes of the women in their lives.

Margaret: the keystone, the matriarch, keeping a tight rein on husband, sons and servants, through siege, battle, legal dispute and the essential provision of household necessities. A woman of substance with important connections and a will of iron, who did not willingly hand over the reins until the day of her death.

Elizabeth: Margaret's sister-in-law, a regrettable pawn in the marriage stakes, whose search for a husband was marked with cruelty and grief, until chance took a hand and dealt her much-deserved happiness.

Anne Haute: cousin of Queen Elizabeth (Elizabeth Woodville), who saw the value of becoming a Paston bride, enthralled by the ambitious and charismatic Sir John Paston. But could she entrap his interest and win his hand in marriage?

This became for me a tale of dramatic social climbing. Of female household management, of driving ambition, of love affairs gone heartbreakingly wrong, and marriages that became perfectly right. Then there was the permanent battle over landownership, to keep for the Pastons the inheritance from Sir John Fastolf, particularly the jewel in the Paston crown, Caister Castle.

In the background, the Wars of the Roses moved on apace, where the Pastons must decide which side to support for their best interests, Lancaster or York.

How could I resist writing about them, a perfect example of a family on the rise?

In the footsteps of the Pastons

To follow in Paston footsteps will entail a visit to Norwich and Norfolk, and the use of a car since the manors are well spread.

Norwich: where the Paston family had a home in Elm Hill from 1413 and where John and Margaret paid for the rebuilding of St Peter Hungate Church in 1458, then financed the hammer-beam roofs in St Andrew's and Blackfriars' Halls.

Caister Castle: a 'must visit' place, built by Sir John Fastolf following a European pattern. It became Paston property when Fastolf left it to John Paston, Margaret's husband, in his will, together with all the other Fastolf manors and estates.

Bacton: where the Paston estate included now-ruined Bromholm Priory. This is where John Paston, husband of Margaret, was buried.

Dereham: inherited from Sir John Fastolf and promptly lost.

Gresham: the castle that was owned by the Paston family, part of Margaret's dowry. Sadly lost to them.

Hellesdon: where the Duke of Suffolk laid siege to a manor house owned by the Paston family, pillaging the village, the church and the manor house.

Paston: where the family began its rise from peasantry to aristocracy within just three generations. Clement Paston owned a small amount of land but saved enough money for his son to train as lawyer and become a judge. The family went on to acquire land across Norfolk.

Mautby: where Margaret Paston was born and where she was buried in the church. The manor of Mautby was part of Margaret's own family inheritance.

Oxnead: a Paston manor where Agnes Paston spent much of her life.

Acknowledgements

My thanks to my editor, Finn Cotton, who saw the possibilities of the Paston family from the beginning and encouraged me to write about them. I appreciate his dedication, expertise and professionalism, and his enthusiasm for my characters. Also my thanks to the whole team at HQ Stories who have produced such a splendid cover and launched *The Royal Game* into the world.

My thanks to my agent Jane Judd who is always the first to read my completed manuscript. I am grateful for her balanced judgement, and her appreciation of my historical heroines. Thank you, Jane, for enjoying medieval history as much as I do.

For all things technical and for the creation and care of my website I must thank Helen Bowden and her team of IT experts at Orphans Press. I am constantly in their debt.

ONE PLACE. MANY STORIES

Bold, Innovative and
empowering publishing.

FOLLOW US ON:

@HQStories